A Fair Wind Home

RUTH MOORE

A Fair Wind Home

William Morrow
and Company
New York

To
Frances Phillips

This is the story of three men: Nathan Ellis, of Massachusetts, Francis Carnavon, of Cork, and Maynard Cantril, a shipbuilder of Somerset in the Province of Maine. The time of the story is the seventeen-hundreds before the Revolution, between any periods of war there may be. Wars are for historians, and this is not a work of history. In fact, an historian might find that liberties have been taken and that little attempt has been made to reproduce accessories of the period. Those who wish battles and massacres may imagine them as taking place when and where they did; but there were times when people worked and built, and this is the story of three men of peace who lived in one of those piping times.

"New Somerset" was a precolonial name for the Northeast Province, and for the name Somerset, I have picked the brains of history; but this is all. The people, the names, the geography, the town of Somerset up the Crookshank River are fiction, and I doubt if there are, or ever were, any such swamps as "The Flowage" within ten miles of Boston.

A Fair Wind Home

The Lord only knew what Edward Ellis had been up to or where he had been for three years, but he had certainly brought home some fine presents. For his mother and the girls, he had rolls of dress silk in three colors, blue, yellow and pink. For Nathan, his brother, he had a gun, not new, but better than new because it had been used and limbered up by someone who liked guns. Its ramrod was of some kind of tough, oiled wood, black like ebony; its powderhorn was of ivory, carved round with a line of little running men. It was a beautiful gun. Edward didn't say what he had brought for his father. He hadn't known Pa had died while he had been away.

Away where? Nathan wondered. At first Edward did not say. He arrived home in the middle of a rainy April night and no one had so much as heard him come.

Ma and the girls, Betsey and Caroline, were asleep upstairs, Nathan in the room off the kitchen. Usually he slept lightly, for now with Pa gone all the responsibility was on him. Horses' hoofs on the cobblestones automatically waked him; he would hear them clop off the turnpike into the inn yard and know he would have to get up to tend to some late traveler. But the night Ed got home Nathan didn't hear a sound.

At four in the morning, when he got up to build the fires, he saw that someone had come in, piled all the logs there were into the hearth and was sleeping on a settle dragged in front of a tremendous heap of coals.

The spring morning was rainy and cold. A nasty, gray light filtered through the windowpanes, and Nathan's first thought was that now he'd have to go out to the shed in the wet and bring more wood before he could get his fires going.

Fellow had his gall—come in like that, burn up all the firewood. Well, he'd soon find out a thing or two. Nathan strode around the settle.

He stumbled over a pair of filthy sea boots flung down in front of the embers. Beside them lay a horrible heap of clothes which stank of mud flats, vessel-bilge—it was hard to say. Nathan's jaw dropped with outrage when he saw the coverlet the fellow was sleeping under. It was the yellow quilt from his mother's bed in the room off the parlor, unused since Pa's death. Ma hadn't felt like sleeping in there alone. She'd cleaned the room, washed all the things—Nathan recalled what a job she'd had with this heavy quilt, getting it dried and aired in all the rainy weather. Now this tramp had it wrapped around his stinking self; he must have gone into that room and—

Nathan reached out to haul off the cover and give the man a shaking up. His hand stopped in midair.

There was a dirty, blood-stained bandage around the fellow's head. A matted mess of hair and whiskers covered his face and neck. That was all Nathan could see showing, but something said, This isn't a tramp, this is Ed, and his hand dropped gently down to the rounded-up shoulder under the coverlet.

The sleeper jerked. He stared up out of a pair of glazed eyes. "I was cold. I went into Pa's room. He wasn't there." He rolled over, shoved his awful face out of sight and slept again.

Nathan felt numb and shaking. All this time they'd thought Ed must be dead. No word from him, no way even to let him know Pa was gone. Now, when he'd come back, the first place he'd made a beeline for was Pa's room, and Pa not there. The tears backed up, hot and stinging, behind Nathan's eyelids. Before he could stop himself, he put both arms around Edward, laid his cheek against the flat back. Just by the feel he would have known it was Ed. He and Ed had warmed themselves together in bed on too many cold winter nights for Nate to mistake the long, tough body, hard and limber at the same time. But thin now. Thin down to the bones.

The yellow quilt had the faint fragrance that was on all Ma's things, but right through it you could smell vessel-bilge, or whatever it was, foul and ammoniac, on Ed. The wound under the rag on his head had bled and dried. Blood was matted in his hair, on his whiskers. There were dark purple, almost black shadows under his eyes, and the little piece of his cheek showing was greenish-tan.

He looked to be bad hurt, got to be cleaned up and tended to right away. There'd have to be hot water and soft rags, and stuff. Better get Ma.

Still—no. Filth like this wasn't any job for the womenfolks.

Nathan got up. He stuck an iron tub under the pump, pumped it half full of water. Then he hauled it over to the hearth and shoved it into the middle of the pile of hot embers.

As he straightened up he saw that Ed was awake, watching him. He guessed Ed was grinning—there was a gleam of teeth through the whiskers—but in that mat, it was hard to say. Nate felt his own face split apart in a stiff, foolish grin that he didn't seem able to control.

Ed said, "You old devil. Grown up to be the size of a man, anyway."

His voice was hoarse and shaky like an old man's, and for a moment Nathan couldn't say anything, only stand there with the grin on his face that wasn't really a grin. Then he managed, in a kind of choke, "Ed, my God, what's happened to you?"

Ed grunted something—it sounded like "Fell in the brook"—but he went right on, not explaining. "Where's the folks, Nate?"

"Ma's upstairs. She sleeps there now." Nate stopped, waiting for his voice to steady.

Ed looked up at his face. "I guessed something was wrong when I didn't find them in the bedroom last night," he said.

Nate nodded. As far back as he could remember Ma and Pa had always slept in the downstairs bedroom.

"When was it?"

"December. There was a kind of lung fever around. We all had it; but Pa . . . he couldn't seem to throw it off. It happened quick. We all thought he was better, he was sitting up in bed writing a letter to you, in case you . . . and then Ma looked and he was gone."

Ed lay still, looking at nothing, and Nathan thought, I've had all this time to get used to it, but it must be hitting Ed hard. Must have been the last thing he expected. Pa wasn't old, only in his forties. He ought to have had years yet.

Funny Ed didn't wake someone up last night. If I'd got home after all that time with no news and found that bedroom empty, I couldn't

3

have waited to know. But he was done up, that must've been it. And right now he hadn't ought to talk, he ought to be tended to.

Nate thrust a tentative finger into the tub of water, but it was barely warm. He could heat some water in a basin though, and dress the wound on Ed's head.

Lord, he thought, while he filled the basin and thrust it on to the hot coals, I'm running around like a hen.

"Come on," he said. "Let's start scraping you out from under that mess."

Ed said, "Where's the letter?"

"Letter? Oh, Pa's letter, you mean. Ma's got it put away."

"You read it? Know what it says?"

"No. Pa sealed it. None of us read it."

"Ma has," Ed said. "Unless she's changed some."

"Oh, no, Ed, she wouldn't," Nate said, jolted.

Of course, Ed had been fighting mad at Ma the night he ran away, but three years was a long time to hang on to it.

"Unless," Nate went on, "she might've thought you weren't coming back. Lord, you old cuss, we thought you were dead."

He grinned down at his brother with affection.

Ed didn't grin back. He lay looking at the fire.

"I sent word home," he said. "Didn't you get it?"

"No. I wish we had. That last afternoon, Pa . . . he kind of kept saying—"

"He leave any will? Besides the letter?"

Cut off short, Nathan gazed down at him. After three years Ed was going to take some getting used to, he guessed.

He said briefly, "No."

Ed drew in his breath slowly. "That's that, then. I know what he wanted done. Of course, I'm the eldest son."

"Well, gee, yes. Sure."

Nate thought of all the staggering months since his father's death, when they'd barely brushed by trying to salvage something, trying to keep the inn open. They had all worked like dogs; but you had to face it, Ma and he didn't have Pa's knack of innkeeping. They could make people comfortable; laugh and talk with them and make them feel at home the way Pa had, they couldn't do. A good many old customers didn't come any more, and new ones seldom came twice.

Ed was saying, "I'll have to have the inn, and—"

4

Nate almost laughed with relief. All Ed was saying was that now he was home, he'd do his share.

"Have it and welcome. Lord, Ed, you ought to know—if there's anything in God's world I hate it's running an inn. This water's hot. Come on, le's fix up that head of yours."

"Wait," Ed said. He put up his hand, fended Nate off. "This has gone awhile, it'll go awhile longer. What I meant, I'll want the rest, too. The wharf and the warehouse. You'll have to kind of get it out of your head I'm going to innkeep while you roll around Pa's office in Boston."

"Oh, my Lord, Ed. I keep forgetting—"

He could pass over the queer look in Ed's eyes, the tone of his voice. Ed was worn out, sick. He'd straighten around as soon as he felt better. What Nate started to say was, "I keep forgetting how much you don't know." There was so much to tell him.

"Uncle Charley's dead, too," he said. "He and Pa lost the business in Boston."

Ed stiffened. "Lost it?"

"Yeah. We were lucky to be able to keep the inn."

"What happened?"

"They got arrested. The King's customs officers confiscated the warehouse; Uncle Charley never really got over it. He died two years ago. Carnavon Brothers own the business now."

"The hell they do! Why, Grandfather Ellis built that warehouse. It's mine. What kind of funny business were they trying to pull, they got in trouble with the customs officers?"

Nate stared at him curiously. He sure was changed.

"They were only carrying on business the way our folks always did," he said. "Only the British keep a man-o'-war in Boston Harbor now. Pa bought a cargo from Holland, that's all, and unloaded it." He looked down at Ed's uncomprehending face. "You must know about the trouble in Boston," he said. "Unless you've been out of the world altogether. The colonies can't trade with any country but England, one law after another. A tax here and a tax there, till an honest trader couldn't keep up with them. Pa hardly made expenses the last year he had the business."

He stumbled and stopped, not wanting to come right out and say that Pa never had really got back on his feet after he'd had to pay out so much to old Newman to square up Ed's fracas, the fracas which had ended in Ed's running away.

"I'll have it all back, don't worry," Ed said. "You can make money if you handle things right. I expect I know a trick or two that Pa and Uncle Charley didn't."

Nate said carefully, "I guess you'd need a pile to buy that warehouse back."

Three years ago when Pa had pleaded with Ed to go into the business with him, Ed had declared furiously that he wouldn't be caught dead doing it. Three years ago he'd thought Pa made the world and set it going. Now he seemed to think he was the only one.

There was a coolness about him, too, a you-go-to-hell manner he'd never had before. You'd naturally expect him to be different at twenty-two than he'd been at nineteen. But Nate felt a kind of homesick ache—they'd been like a right and a left hand, he and Ed, for all Ed was three years older.

"I wouldn't worry my head, if I was you," Ed was saying.

"Well, I *have* worried my head. I thought maybe I could buy it back, got a job working for Moses Brown over in the shipyard. I'm a pretty good shipwright now, believe it?"

"Sure, you always took after Pa with tools."

Blast him, you could see he wasn't interested in you and your doings. He appeared to be a hundred miles away.

Nate shrugged and grinned. "I found it would take a lifetime, the rate I was earning money. And then I had to quit anyway and help Ma with the inn. Damn an inn, Ed, I hate the cussed thing. I'm glad you're home, you old buffle head. You can take over."

"I aim to."

Nate hauled the tub of water off the fire. "Come on now, get into this and soak. You look like an old deer hide left out all winter. Come on, unless you want Ma and the girls around. They'll be stirring pretty soon."

Ed put his feet down off the settle. He rocked dizzily for a moment, then freed his arms and pressed both palms to the sides of his head. He was naked under the coverlet, and Nate let out a gasp. He had never in his life seen anyone so filthy.

"Good God!" he said. "How'd you get like that?"

"I've spoilt Ma's quilt," Ed said, "which I'll hear about."

"Oh, shoot, Ed. It'll wash. So'll you. Come on, get in the tub."

6

Ed squatted shakily in the tub, his knees drawn up under his chin, while Nate scrubbed him with soft soap and clean rags from the linen chest. His body, emerging clean from under the layers of grime, was skin over bone, welted all over with old and fresh bruises. Nate saw quickly that one tub of water wasn't going to be enough, and he filled another one to set on the fire. It wouldn't be hot, but the chill would be off the water by the time he was through with the first one. "Here," he said gruffly. "Let's get that string out of your way."

The string was a leather lanyard tied around Ed's neck with something—an iron key, it was—dangling, the leather getting wet. But Ed shook his head. "Leave it." He clutched the key and Nate didn't argue. He couldn't trust his voice anyway. He felt sick to his stomach and outraged at the shape Ed was in, and the sweat was running down all over him.

The wet lanyard would be uncomfortable under a nightshirt, but it could be slipped off after Ed went to sleep and put somewhere safe for him.

With set teeth Nate soaked off the soggy, bloody rag around his brother's head—it was the sleeve of an old shirt—Ed swearing a blue streak because it hurt like blazes. Nate had to cut through a lot of hair and whiskers, leaving a stubble; Ed could shave when he was rested some. There wasn't anything in the matted mess a man would want to keep, or anything that could ever be washed clean. The wound was a knife slash across the forehead. It had bled a lot, the way head wounds do, and it would probably leave considerable of a scar.

He said, "This has got to be sewed up. It's wide open."

Ed grunted, his face screwed up with pain. "Well, do it, will you?"

"Lord, Ed!" Nathan all but retched at the thought. "I'll run down and get the doc after I get you to bed."

"I don't want the doc. Look, it's no trick to sew up a cut. I've seen it done a hundred times 'board ship, done it myself. Skin's no tougher than sailcloth, and you've sewed plenty of that."

Nate dropped the washrag and had to grope for it in the gray water under Ed's skinny flank.

"A cut like that, Ed! It needs the doctor and a good cleaning out. I couldn't—"

Ed grinned at him, the old, impudent, merry grin that he had once known so well and hadn't seen for so long. He grabbed Nate's hand with the wet rag in it and squeezed, so that gobbets of dingy suds ran out of it and down his thigh.

"God, I'm glad to see you, Nate."

"Ayeh," Nate grunted. "Shut your mouth before I get it full of soap."

"I'm in a scrape," Ed said. "Or I may be, I don't know. But I can't handle anything till I've had some rest and sleep. I don't want the doc or anyone else outside the house to know I'm here, not till I can stand on my feet again. Let the cut go if you can't stitch it."

"What is it, Ed? What happened to you?"

"I been in the 'tween-decks of a vessel for three months. In irons. We got away two-three nights ago in the ship's boat, another fellow and I. The skipper may try to catch up with me, I don't know. He was pretty put out."

"Put out," Nate said slowly, staring at the dark welts on his brother's body. "I kind of wish he would catch up with you. I'd like to get my hands on him. I feel kind of put out myself."

Ed sagged a little in the tub. "No," he said, "I don't guess you'd care to get anywheres near him."

"I'd take a chance. Where's the other fellow? He in as hard shape as you are?"

There was a short silence. "What other fellow?" Ed shook his head as if to clear it. "Look, I'm pretty tired. Mixed up. I can tell you after I've slept some."

"Sure. I ought to know better. Come on. You're clean enough to sleep, I guess. The rest of it we can hoe off later."

Nate put one of his father's warm woolen nightshirts on Ed. He had to set his jaw while he dug it out of the big blue chest where Ma had packed away Pa's things. He wished the inside of his stomach would stop fluttering. Maybe Ed wouldn't want to sleep in the shirt, knowing whose it was, but there wasn't anything else. He himself liked to sleep under bare poles and didn't own a nightshirt.

Ed, however, snuggled gratefully into the warmth of the nightshirt. He stood swaying a little, his eyes closed. He didn't say a word when Nate picked up his lath-thin body and carried him into his own bedroom off the kitchen.

"I'd hate to try to live on what they fed you in that 'tween-decks," Nate said, carefully keeping the tremor out of his voice.

8

Ed lay back against the pillow. "So you would," he said without opening his eyes.

Nathan looked at him a moment, grimly, before he went out into the kitchen to fetch the things he had to have. He brought back soup from the stockpot, warmed over the embers, and made Ed drink it. Then he held the wincing head while he swabbed out the cut with brandy. The stitching job was workmanlike—he and Pa had made too many boat sails for it not to be—but when it was done the tears were running down his face, and on Ed's temples were the angry red prints of his fingers. He bandaged the closed wound with clean linen.

Ed said faintly, "You're green as a frog."

"I'd hate to tell you what color you are. Go to sleep now."

"All right. There's a couple things. I swiped Ev Piper's wagon to haul my stuff up from the shore. It's in the wagon shed. Take it back to him, tell him some lie, like you found it on the road, some kids must have borrowed it. Don't say anything about me."

"Sure. I'll tend to it."

"And then go down . . . Cowrie Cove. Hide . . . boat. Tell Ma be sure. . . no one. . . knows. . . I'm home."

His voice trailed off and Nate saw he had fallen dead asleep.

Nate stood still, looking down at his brother's face. Under the scraggle of whiskers the lines of it were sharp, the chin jutting out, the cheeks sunken. Three years could make an almighty difference in a face. Ed's cheeks, when he went away, had been pink, his chin covered with a kind of downy bloom. The lank hair had been crisp black curls. Only Ed's eyelashes had stayed the same. Below the closed, purplish lids they lay long and curling, soft as a girl's.

Nate's fists clenched into two hard balls. Where had Ed been and who had done this to him? Somewhere, and not only last night or yesterday, he had taken some terrible beatings. And he looked as if he'd been starved for weeks.

He was in trouble again, too, just as he'd been when he left home three years ago. Only worse. At least it looked to be, though, Lord knows, the trouble with Newman had been bad enough.

How bad it had really been depended on whose story you believed —Ed's or old Squire Newman's and his daughter Mary's. Nate for his part had always believed Ed's. Pa had, too. But Ma—well, Ma had always been pretty hard on Ed. It was after the quarrel with her that night Ed had run away.

9

He said he hadn't done anything to Mary Newman outside of courting her. They had been sitting in the old squire's kitchen, not even near each other, when the old man had walked in with a club.

He had been a huge, powerful old man, but Ed at nineteen was pretty wiry, too. The fight ended with the room wrecked and old Newman's leg broken. He swore at the inquiry later that Ed had kicked him. Mary sided with her father.

Ed said chances were he hadn't kicked Newman; he'd been taught to fight with his fists, he didn't believe using his feet would have occurred to him. He did remember Newman's taking a kick at him and slamming a leg against the woodbox, which might have been the way he broke it. Ed didn't recall very clearly. He was fighting for his life, he said; it was hard to say just what he'd done.

Before anything was decided either for or against him, Ed ran away. Perhaps it was a good thing he had, seeing everyone in town was against him, telling around what a crazy temper he had, always getting himself in trouble. Well, that was true in a way, but not all true. Ed's temper was quick but not crazy, and if he was in hot water a lot, it was partly because people were all ready to blame him—say, a bunch of kids broke a window, Ed was the one who got caught.

In the watery mirror above the bed Nate caught sight of his own sober face, and thought suddenly that he himself looked now about the way Ed had looked at the time he ran away. He had the same black curls and pink cheeks, tanned from the sun on salt water, the same tough, six-foot, wiry body. Well, he was nineteen now and Ed twenty-two.

Old Newman was dead now, his daughter married to Roger Witlow and migrated west. Pa had paid the damages; Ed could have come home any time he wanted to if he'd only known.

One of the wet, V-shaped strands of hair above Ed's head bandage, drying in the warm air of the bedroom, stirred a little and then stood up in a tight, crisp curl. Nate felt the hot, hard lump come back into his throat. He put out a finger to touch the curl, then turned and went softly out, closing the bedroom door on the wreck of his brother.

Lizabeth Ellis was standing in front of her bureau combing her hair when Nate opened the door to her bedroom. She was a small, nicely made woman with a fine figure; the hair she was combing into a tight bun was as black and curly as Nate's own. She did not look her forty-two years, except for a certain tautness about her mouth, which had drawn into disciplined lines too many times to have kept much of its youthful freshness. Nate admired her looks and her neatness—for all she had few pretty clothes now that the inn was on the rocks, her old brown woolen dresses were trim, their white collars crackling with cleanness; unless you knew where to look, you couldn't see the mended places. He admired, too, her hands, small and long-fingered, though it was an admiration tempered with respect. As a youngster growing up he had felt the sting of those fingers too many times not to know, even now, that there were times when he did well to stay outside her arm's length.

Lizabeth had brought up four children, her own two sons and two adopted girls, Betsey and Caroline Carey. She had definite ideas about the relationship between grownups and children. Young ones had to be taught what was right and what was wrong; they were the ones who must learn. They were not people but children. And since to Lizabeth black was black and white was white, without shadings, and the four children vastly different in temperament from each other, her household, particularly after her husband's death, was in a constant state of war.

Joel Ellis had been a good man and a kind one, serious-minded and, to her, dull. He knew how to make companions of his children. They adored him. But he did not know how to make a companion of his wife. To him a woman was a woman, a different breed from himself, whose sole functions were in the household and in bed; he performed the sexual act first as a duty, second for his own enjoyment and release. It would have shocked the good Joel ever to have dreamed that the woman might enjoy or be released; a good woman could not be so sinful. Lizabeth had loved him for himself because he was kind and good. If intercourse with him was at first slightly disgusting and later a bore, she endured it, and she put down her feelings firmly, well knowing a woman's duty to her husband.

She had spent nearly half a lifetime taking it for granted that the menfolks had all the fun. Their hunting, their fishing, their planned projects out-of-doors were things in which a woman had no part, or if she did she was unwomanly. That she could have planned as well, performed as well, any of their enterprises, she did not even consider. She turned her strength and her clear, logical intelligence inward to the lesser slavery, which was not enough; so that in time the damned-up energy burst out in niggling and naggling, and the house which she ran so well became neither a refuge for a tired man, nor a place of comfort for children.

The thing was a closed circle now and could have been foretold on Joel Ellis's wedding night.

The war between Lizabeth and her children was a controlled one, for she stood for no nonsense. Edward was the only one who had ever really stood up to her. His rebellion seethed and overflowed all through his childhood. She put it firmly down and was thunderstruck when he ran away and grief-stricken, for unknown to any, even herself, she loved Edward best. He was the brightest of them all; she was convinced he would make a fine, brilliant man. If he were all temper, fire-hot and blazing, then he must learn to control himself. She was puzzled when he did not. The more she corrected him, the worse his temper seemed to be.

With Nate her war was of a different tempo. She never expected to have much trouble with Nate. In some ways his temper was harder to stand than Edward's; it burned undercover for a long time and after it burst out, if it burst out at all, still lasted. As a child Edward made a terrible towse over a spanking, screaming and throwing things; once he even bit her. But Nate would go off by himself and be quiet for hours; he remembered a spanking for a long time.

As for the girls, Betsey and Caroline, she had never found them much trouble. Betsey was twenty now, Caroline sixteen. They had come first as bound girls, but no one remembered now that they weren't members of the family.

Joel Ellis had gone up to Boston to see if he could find a husky maidservant in a shipload of transports from England; he found one, but he also found two forlorn and tear-stained waifs whose parents had died on the long voyage over. No one seemed to want Betsey and Caroline Carey. Joel brought them home.

Lizabeth was taken aback, but the plight of the two dreary little girls touched her heart. She took them in and made them her own. Long ago she had forgotten that they were adopted. She gave them the same discipline she gave her sons, the same training she had received herself. Little girls grew up to be women and good wives; the little Careys were properly trained.

They were a great help about the inn now. At least Caroline was. Betsey was, too, if Lizabeth walked right behind her. She was inclined to be lazy and to scamp her work; at times there was a cold sullenness about her which Lizabeth couldn't abide. Privately she thought Betsey was something of a lump, pretty but not clever, but Lizabeth prided herself that she never made a difference, on the surface, between Betsey, her two sons and Caroline.

Caroline was a girl after her own heart, biddable and good. She learned quickly and worked fast; she was, at sixteen, an excellent cook and thrifty housewife. Caroline had never been an instant's trouble. If she were a little too thin, not so pretty as Betsey, and if in her small, pointed face there showed at times a kind of woods' wildness, Lizabeth thought little of it.

It occurred to her sometimes that Caroline had spells of looking, in the face, like a fox cub she had once seen out walking in the woods in wintertime. The woods were deep with snow, and Lizabeth had seen only the fox's small face peering out at her from a snowy hole under the roots of a great pine. The little thing hadn't looked either friendly or unfriendly, only remote, untouchable somehow, apart in a world of secret woods and snow.

Lizabeth laughed at herself for the fancy. She had been taught to think of a fox as a sly, coldhearted thing. Caroline was as nice a straightforward youngster as you'd want to see anywhere, and Lizabeth thought the world of her.

As for the rest of Lizabeth she was neither stupid nor unkind by intention, and she was implacable only in one thing: right was right and wrong was wrong. She herself was judge and jury and woe betide a sinner!

Nate, coming into her bedroom to tell her about Ed, found the words stuck in his throat. He said finally, "Ma," and sat down weakly on the edge of her bed.

"Nate!" Lizabeth said. "Get off the bed. You smell like a— What on earth's the matter?"

"Ed's come home, Ma."

For a moment she stood absolutely still, her eyes searching his face. Then she said, "Thank God."

The last one of the bone pins she'd been using to pin up her hair

13

was in her hand. She glanced down at it as if she had never seen it before or had any idea what to do with it. Then she took it in both hands, broke it in two and dropped the pieces onto the floor.

The sharp little *snick* sound the pin made breaking somehow shocked Nate. If she had sat down and cried, it wouldn't have showed more what she was feeling. But bone pins like that were hard come by. They had to be carved by hand. Pa himself had carved this set for Ma. Didn't seem as though she ought to break one on purpose, seeing there'd never be any more. Been better if she'd cried, like womenfolks were supposed to.

But Lizabeth never cried, not even when Pa died. The most Nate had ever seen, her face had crumpled once, like a handkerchief, and then the next moment she had herself in hand.

Lizabeth took pride in keeping herself in hand. She leaned down now, picked up the pieces of the pin and tossed them into her trash basket.

"Is he all right?" she asked quietly. "Where is he?"

"Asleep down in my room," Nate said. His voice, he was relieved to find, didn't shake now. "He got home in the night. He's hurt—got a cut on the head—and he's awful thin. I—"

Better not tell her Ed had been beaten up and starved, spare her as much as he could. He finished, "I think maybe he's all right, Ma."

Lizabeth glanced at him. She shrugged a little, walked quickly past him out the door and down the stairs.

She recognized very well that spare-the-womenfolks look. She had known it for a long time, first in his father and now in Nate, and while she understood and was at times touched by their consideration for her, she was also impatient. Nine times out of ten when disaster struck, sickness or accident, the womenfolks were the ones who had to cope with it. They had to know eventually, why not be told at once so that sensible plans could be made for what certainly had to be done? But it was useless to expect the simple truth about disaster. You could only prepare for the worst.

Nate followed her slowly down the hall. Now what did I do? he thought, recognizing the impatience. I told her as careful as I could.

In the hall behind him Caroline came out of her room, headed for the kitchen. She stopped when she saw him and stared.

"You skedaddle!" he ordered fiercely.

"What ails *you?*" she asked amiably. "Wrong side of the bed?"

14

"Go on down and start breakfast," he ordered. "Make yourself useful for once."

"I was just passing by you. Don't be such a turnip."

"Ed's home," he burst out. "He's sick."

He was unprepared for the effect on Caroline. Her mouth opened, at first he thought, with astonishment; then she said, "Oh, no," as if it were the last thing she'd wanted to happen. She turned around, went back into her room and closed the door.

For heaven's sake, he thought, of course she and Ed always fought like cats and dogs, but—didn't seem like she was very glad he was home after three years. Maybe it's because I said he's sick. Sure, that's it. He called through the door, "You and Bet go down and start breakfast, Caroline. The rest of us is pretty busy."

He went on down the stairs and across the kitchen, hesitating outside the closed door of his own room. Everything was dead quiet in there. Ma would be standing looking down at Ed, seeing how awful he looked. Nate wished he could have saved her that, but there hadn't been any way. As the silence lengthened he felt the sweat break out on his forehead in a sheen of tiny drops. He wiped it away with the palm of his hand.

Lizabeth came out, closing the door softly behind her. She was white in the face, and she sat down quickly on a kitchen chair as if her knees had buckled.

"Nate, what happened to him?"

"I don't know, Ma. Something aboard a vessel—he was too tired to talk much."

"That stink," Lizabeth said. She looked at the mess on the hearth of slopped, filthy water, the horrible clothes. "He's been in the Flowage. If any of that rotten mud got into his cuts— What did you do, clean him up yourself? Why on earth didn't you call me?"

With a start Nate realized that of course that's what the stink was, the stagnant mud and marsh-gas smell you ran into down by Cowrie Cove, where the system of slow streams called the Flowage drained miles of back-country swamps down into salt water. Funny he hadn't thought of that, he'd smelled it times enough. Must've been he was so stirred up over seeing Ed.

"He said he landed in a boat down that way," Nate said. "I bet he fell down coming up through the swamp."

"He ought to have had a doctor last night," Lizabeth said sharply.

15

"I know it. He wouldn't. He says he's—he may be in some kind of trouble."

"Oh, Lord. What trouble?"

"I don't know that either. He said just let him rest. He'll handle it when he's back on his feet. He doesn't want anyone outside the house to know he's home."

"Well, that's just on account of that old fracas with Newman. You told him that had all blown over, didn't you?"

"No, it isn't, Ma. It's something else, he said so. He said be sure, Ma. He'll explain when he wakes up."

Lizabeth was silent. "I wish I had some way of knowing what this is all about," she said at last, half to herself. "What's the matter with his head?"

"It's cut. I dressed it—"

"Bad?"

"Kind of deep."

"It's crazy not to have the doctor for him. You sure you got it clean? That Flowage mud is rank poison."

"Yes, I am. I washed it out and doused it with brandy." He thought he'd better not say it had had to be sewed up. She'd find that out soon enough.

He said, "Look, Ma, I better go. Ed borrowed Ev Piper's wagon to haul stuff up from the shore on. I've got to take it back before Ev finds it's gone."

For a moment he thought she hadn't heard him. She was sitting thinking.

"Well," she said. "Sleep's the best thing now, I guess. We'll see what he's like when he wakes up. If he needs the doctor, he's going to have one, trouble or no trouble. Go ahead, wherever it is you want to go, but lug those tubs out first and clean up that mess."

"But gosh, Ma, we'll have Ev Piper up here yowling after his wagon! The girls can—"

"Womenfolks that can't stand it to hear bad news aren't likely to bear up any better under two heavy tubs of water," she said dryly. She slapped her hands impatiently against her lap. "If you aren't just like your father— Go on, clean up that hearth, and then run along out of my sight and let me think."

Nate set his teeth. He lugged the two tubs out of the kitchen, slopping a good deal of water on the way, dumped them out in the backyard, turned them bottom up to dry.

Of course he was like Pa and proud of it. You could see how she might be wrought up over Ed, but that didn't excuse her criticizing Pa like that.

Now that he'd lugged out the tubs, the girls could mop up the slops. He'd be damned if he was going back in there. To hell with breakfast, too. He guessed he could manage without it.

Nate crossed the yard to the wagon shed. The night's rain had turned to drizzle and a cold fog off the ocean had come in over the land. Ordinarily from the back door of the inn, which stood on a rise overlooking the harbor, you could see across water and on for miles to the horizon. Now the fog lay so heavy that the peak of the barn, a hundred feet or so away, was out of sight in it. He could feel the wetness, thick and raspy in his throat.

If old Piper had come hunting his wagon, he wouldn't have had any trouble finding it. The door of the wagon shed was open; in the muddy yard a wabbly line of deep-cut wheel tracks and footprints led straight to it. The shore road was deep in mud this time of year; without a doubt those tracks were in plain sight all the way to Piper's. The wagon was just inside the shed door.

It was a two-wheeled affair, a shallow box fastened to a light ex, which the old man used to haul salt fish to his drying flakes. Under the weight of a big sea chest and a jammed-full canvas bag, the wheels looked to be kind of sprung.

Nate whistled as he heaved at the chest.

Now what could be in that? It was like lead.

No wonder Ed was done up, the shape he was in, hauling that load from Cowrie Cove all uphill and the road mud and sand.

With a good deal of puffing and grunting Nate hauled the chest off the wagon and into a corner of the shed. He stood for a moment looking speculatively at it, his curiosity getting the better of him. Wouldn't hurt to peek into it—nosey, maybe, but Ed wouldn't care.

It was a plain, ordinary, beat-up old ditty chest, made out of punkin pine, bigger than most chests of its kind, lashed round with tarred rope. Then as he started to undo the rope he saw the lock—a big, wrought-iron padlock, three inches square.

Nate straightened up, feeling foolish and as if he had been served right. That must be the key to it, that one Ed carried on the lanyard round his neck. Didn't want anyone snooping into his things.

After a second's thought Nate moved some empty barrels to stand in front of the chest and sea bag. After all, Ed wanted his homecoming kept secret for a while; no sense leaving his stuff uncovered for anyone who wandered in to find. The girls—not that Caroline would do any snooping, but Betsey was plain nosey.

About as nosey as I started out to be, he told himself sheepishly. But then, I know I wouldn't've fooled with anything, just looked. With girls you never could tell, they might get excited, let something slip out outside the house.

He rolled the wagon outside the shed. Its wheels were sprung, all right, loose and wabbly on the ex. He and Ed would have to make that up to Piper somehow, even if they were going to say kids must have borrowed the wagon. The right thing to do, of course, would be to take it back and say, "Look, Piper, Ed and I had to borrow your wagon and we accidentally broke it. We'll build you another one or pay you. Whatever you say."

That's what I'd do, if it was up to me.

But it wasn't up to him. Not until Ed woke up and did some explaining. In the meantime the wagon had to be returned.

He trampled out the tracks leading to the door and across the yard. Then he went back inside the shed and picked up his gun from where it stood behind the door. Piper, or anyone else who might see him wandering along the shore at this time of day, wouldn't think it was funny at all if he had his gun. Most anybody might take it into his head to go down around the swamps in the morning to see if he could get a shot at something. If anybody saw him with Ed's boat, why, it could be just a boat gone adrift from somewhere that he'd had the luck to find while he was hunting.

Nate picked up the wagon tongue and set off down the shore road, the aged vehicle wabbling and creaking behind him. The road led between two lines of scrubby bushes that marked its rambling track down the side of the sandy hill. Fog drops lay heavily on the young green leaves and rasped heavily against his throat. The fog was a pea-souper. A sluggish southerly breeze was puffing it in off the ocean. On either side of him he could see only thirty feet or so of bushes and boulder-mottled sand. Off back of him, in the town which lay sprawled out mostly on the crest of the hill, he could hear early-morning sounds. A dog barked somewhere. He heard a door open and a baby crying, then the door slammed cutting off short the sound of the baby. Someone down on the shore road had built a cooking fire, which he could smell. Probably Piper, since the wind was from that way. Maybe if Piper and his wife, Jenny, weren't too sore about the wagon, they'd offer him some breakfast.

Ahead of him Ed's wavering tracks, followed by the deep-cut track of the wagon, went from side to side of the narrow muddy road. Looking at the footprints, Nate thought, He must have had an awful time.

Why didn't he just leave his stuff down there and let me go get it?

Well, he hadn't wanted anyone to know he'd come home. Not many people went to Cowrie Cove, but some did, hunting. He couldn't have wanted to take any chances. What kind of trouble was he in? And where's he been all this time—why hasn't he come home? Maybe he sent word, maybe he didn't. Look what it would've meant to Pa. Ed, Ed, was all Pa'd thought of, all he'd talked about on the afternoon he died.

Thinking back to that stricken afternoon when the bottom seemed to be falling out of the world, Nate felt a sudden sharp anger. It was just like Ed to have gone off somewhere and not bothered to send home word. Have an exciting and adventurous time, come home when he was ready, with a chest packed full of stuff.

If that's what it was, it'd do me good to beat the tar out of him, the crazy fool.

But at the sight of a wallowed place in the road where Ed must have fallen down and struggled to get back on his feet again, Nate's anger died away.

Who but Ed, weak and cut up, barely able to walk, would have fought that heavy wagon up the hill? Anybody else would have dropped everything and come on home himself. In a pinch Nate couldn't think of anyone he'd rather have alongside him than Ed. Crazy, irresponsible, but stubborn. And there wasn't anything wrong with his courage.

And now, after thinking for so long that you'd never have Ed alongside of you again, it was wonderful to know that on a common, ordinary night, rainy and cold, when you'd gone to bed as usual, feeling things hang over heavy—the inn no good now with Pa gone; the family slipping down into a kind of day-to-day miserableness; feeling himself the last man of the long line of Ellises, a man of nineteen with the responsibility of three womenfolk—it was wonderful to know that on this ordinary night when nothing good could have been expected to happen, Ed had come home.

Let Ed get back on his feet, he'd know what to do about the inn. Let him take over, he wanted to. Lord, Ed would be himself as soon as he felt better. All that business of seeming to be so anxious—and mean—over Pa's will, likely that was nothing but a touch of fever, the effect of a cut on the head.

God knows, he's welcome to that blasted inn and everything that goes with it.

And I'll go back to building ships with Moses Brown. I'll go north, maybe, and find Maynard Cantril's place and work with him, as soon as I learn all I can from Mo.

He remembered the day Maynard Cantril had come into Mo's yard in his compact, clean-lined little vessel.

"That's a ship!" Mo had said, jerking his thumb. "I couldn't build one like her if I went to the devil, and neither could any other man except Maynard Cantril. You want to learn shipbuilding, you hunt him up and work for him. He knows more about it than any man living."

"Where's he come from?" Nate asked.

"Him and his father and nine brothers sailed north off the map long time ago," Mo said. "Took along a sawmill, parts for anyway, settled up a river. They got three-four them vessels, come down every so often, trading hides and lumber. They're all wild men, my God, I d'no what kind of a rig they run up there, old man's crazy, boys married up with a lot of Injuns. But they build ships; I'd swap my liver for a crack at the model of one of them Cantril vessels!"

Nate took a good look at the dark, silent, bearded man, Maynard Cantril and at his neat vessel, the *Mary C.* He'd know them both if he saw them again. Maybe sometime when the *Mary C.* sailed out of Boston Harbor, Nathan Ellis would be aboard of her, going north off the map. Now that Ed was home and he was free.

Nate took a deep breath, driving the heavy, fog-laden air into the bottom of his lungs. It felt like the first deep breath he'd been able to take since last December.

20

Ed's home, his mind said. Whatever trouble he's in we'll get him out of it.

Ed's home.

He'd like to stand up on the top of this hill looking down into the cold fog that lay over the water, gray with mizzling rain and comfortless as a slab in the graveyard, and fill his lungs again and yell, "Ed's home!" So loud that everything alive down there could hear it—the gulls and gannets out on the harbor, the mink and foxes and rabbits in the rocks and caves.

So loud that everything dead could hear it, he thought soberly, the exultation ebbing out of him. So that Pa, wherever he was, could hear it and know that Ed was all right and safe home at last.

At the foot of the hill by the shore, Piper's ramshackle buildings dripped dismally in the rain. There were three of them, a low dwelling house and two fish sheds built close to the edge of the land. In fact, the house, supported by ancient piles, was partway out over the water. It would have been hard to tell, unless you knew beforehand, which of the buildings was the dwelling house. They all looked alike, put together out of odds and ends of lumber which Piper had salvaged, roofed with shakes so old that their edges were stitched with moss.

Ev Piper lived there with his wife, Jenny. They were old people, nobody knew how old, but Nate's father had said that as far back as he could remember the Pipers had looked just the same.

"Piper's pickled so many fish," he said once, "that years ago he probably run of an idea to pickle himself and Jenny, and that's why they ain't changed any within the time of man."

The Pipers were known to be light-fingered in the matter of small things like oars and an occasional ham from somebody's smokehouse, but you could always whittle out a pair of oars if you had to, or get Piper himself to make you a set for little or nothing, and what was a ham or so? Everybody had hams to spare, and most people liked Piper. Cross him though, and he could be a mean cuss, even if you were his friend. Nate wasn't at all sure how Piper was going to act in this matter of the wagon. He was a man whom kids tormented anyway, and he was likely to start cussing first and listen to explanations afterward.

Nate left the wagon by the first shed, stepping around the corner to the kitchen door. Piper and Jenny weren't around, but they couldn't be far away, because somebody not too long ago had tended to the crackling fire on the hearth. Jenny's big yellow tomcat sat in front of it licking himself dry; he must've just been let in, for the fur on his back was stuck together in wet, hackly peaks.

Nate called, "Hey, Piper!" but there was no answer. From somewhere in the house came a scuttling sound, as if a mouse had taken a short run up between the studs of the wall.

Oh, well, he could explain about the wagon later.

He listened again. There was no sound but the faint lapping of the flood tide up under the pile foundation of Piper's kitchen.

Funny for a man to build his living house out on this wharf, instead of his fish shed, which would have been handier. But Piper said he liked to hear the water come up under the house at night. Helped him to sleep, he said.

And it would be a good sound to go to sleep by, Nate thought, hearing the low, peaceful splash and gurgle of the tide. You snug in bed, knowing the winter sea so close and you safe from it; in summer, the quiet sound, almost under the pillow. Maybe Piper wasn't so funny.

Like to have me a cove like this, Nate thought. Build a wharf with a house on it, live out over the water. He grinned a little, picturing himself hermited up like that. Still, it wouldn't be bad. Step right out of the house into your boat; you wouldn't have Ma in your hair all the time, or that blasted inn. . . .

The scurrying sound came again, sounded as if it might be someone in the bedroom.

"Jenny?" Nate said.

There was no answer.

"What's the matter with you?" Nate said to the cat. "You too busy to go see about that mouse?"

The cat stopped licking and favored him with a green, baleful stare.

"Oh, all right," Nate said, grinning.

He turned and went out, closing the door carefully behind him.

Cats beat all, darn things were next to human. Couldn't tell him Jenny's tom hadn't understood what he'd said and had said back, "Mind your own damn business."

22

As he went past the bedroom window he caught a movement out of the corner of his eye, and turning, he saw Jenny's old, narrow, brown face dodge back out of sight behind the rain-streaked glass.

"Oh, hey, Jenny, there you are," he called. "Piper around?"

She could have heard him clearly through the ramshackly wall, but she didn't come back to the window.

That's funny.

"Look," he said loudly. "Tell Piper I found his wagon up the road a piece. Looked like some kids must've borrowed it. I brought it down."

The window remained blank, reflecting the brown twigs and nubbin-like leaves of Piper's crab apple tree.

Nate went off along the shore path, a nag of worry nudging at his mind. It wasn't as if he and the Pipers weren't friends. He went there off and on; it was fun to talk fishing with Ev. Not friends the way they and Pa had been; the Pipers had both thought the world of Pa. Of course they were kind of odd, but if Jenny hid away from Nate now, there must be a reason for it. Had they seen Ed borrow the wagon? No, it couldn't be that. Because if Piper had seen anyone near his house at night, he'd have come boiling out all over him. He wouldn't stand for any kind of prowling on his premises after dark, on account of the way the kids plagued him.

Well, what was it, then?

There was no doubt as to where the wagon had gone, he thought morosely, following the deep-cut track in the sand. Looked as though more than one man had come along with it, too.

He leaned down, studying the tracks closely. Two different boot heels, intermingled and overlaid, so he couldn't tell much; seemed to be quite a few of one set though, and only one track of the other. Well, let's see.

Ed had come up to Piper's from Cowrie Cove and swiped the wagon, taken it back along the shore road. There were the light tracks of it, unloaded, under the deep tracks made when Ed had hauled it back with his chest and sea bag. Three sets of tracks alike—Ed's. That made sense. The other set overlay Ed's, so far as he could tell.

Piper, he thought suddenly. That's where Piper is, down here tracking his wagon. What if the old puffer finds Ed's boat?

He started at a run down the road, hardly more than a path now as it sloped into the wet marshy bottom, beginning the long string of salt marshes known as the Flowage.

He saw Piper before Piper saw him, coming warily up the rocky slope carrying his gun. Nate waited until he was close, then called out, "Hi, Piper."

Piper straightened with a jerk. He jumped sideways out of the path, stared around wildly and brought up with his old rusty gun aimed straight at Nate's chest.

"Hey," Nate said, astonished. "What's the matter with *you?* It's only me."

"I see who 'tis."

Piper lowered the gun, but he did not point it away from Nate, and he stood, his eyes narrow and beady under the thatch of overhanging, bushy brows.

"Well, take your gun off me then," Nate said impatiently. "I could be onto you twice before you got her primed anyway. What ails you? You act scared to death."

"I ain't scairt."

"Well, if you ain't, you act pretty cussed queer. You and Jenny both. She hid out on me. What have I got, horns?"

"You can have horns and a tail for all of me." Piper began edging around Nate on the path, while Nate stared at him in amazement.

"No call to be sore at me about the wagon, Piper. I found it up on the shore road, hauled it home as a favor to you, that's all. It's up by your shed. I took it some kids swiped it on you."

"Kind of big kids, wasn't they?" Piper said, indicating the tracks.

"Blest if I know. I only found it. Thought while I was down here I'd go on to the cove, see if I could get a crack at a duck."

Piper was past him on the path now; he continued to edge away, putting space between them. "No ducks down there," he said. "I just been. No use you to go. Go on, git home."

"Oh, for Godsake!" Nate burst out. He figured he'd had about all he could stand. "I d'no what ails you, you old coot. But I know this, your blasted wagon can rot before I haul it home again for you."

He was just as mad, he realized wryly, as if he'd told Piper a true story and Piper had disbelieved him. Damn fool, not to have remembered the size of those footprints!

He turned his back on Piper and marched off down the path to the cove. As he was passing out of sight around the first turn, he heard Piper call out something.

"What you want?" Nate said, not turning around.

24

"Don't want nothing to do with it," Ev was hollering. "All I come down for was to track my wagon. And you can stay away from my house, you and your whole tribe."

He turned and made off at a hobbling trot.

Nate glanced around, stood looking after him. His nag of worry grew into a man-sized lump.

Ev had heard or seen something down here. He knew that Nate was somehow connected with it. Maybe he saw Ed last night. In the dark Ed and I'd look alike—but no, Ed had all those whiskers.

Whatever Piper had seen, it had scared him. Or something.

The path split three ways here around a big boulder. The main branch went straight on around the shore, the left one led into an old wood road that ended a mile or so farther on. The third was a wet, slippery track down a sand slide into Cowrie Cove. Nate took it a little too fast and almost went headlong into the water. He saved himself by grabbing at a tuft of grass, which tore out but which checked his slide.

He landed with a thump on his hands and knees at the sandy margin of the cove, plowing up to his wrists in a little pocket of blue clay. He got up swearing under his breath, scraping the sticky stuff off his hands. Only one clay-hole here, and he had to land in it. Lucky he'd had the sense to drop his gun. At least he hadn't stuck the muzzle of that into the clay.

Cowrie Cove was a tiny pocket of a place, brimful now on the high water, so that it had barely two feet of sandy shore. Facing southeast between Cowrie Island and the sea, it was nearly landlocked, with rocks on the south and west sides. To the northwest a high bank dropped down into the Flowage, which led away for miles into the back country—marshes which were first salt, then brackish, then fresh water as they swept farther away from the sea. The inlet past Cowrie Island was wide and shallow with a trick channel, plenty of water at all times of tide. Only you had to know where the channel was.

Well, Ed knew the channel well enough. Pa had taught it to him and Nate both. Nate and Ed and Pa had fished and shot ducks and trapped mink and muskrat all over this part of the coast and up the marshes. They knew—none better—the two or three safe paths through the marshes, too.

As for the cove itself, it was unusually deep; the scour of tide around the sharp curve of the Island kept it free of sand and mud brought down by Salt Marsh Brook, and a frigate could have floated there, if her skipper had known how to make the channel in. It was a fine place to land when you wanted to keep your landing secret, as Ed had; though, Nate told himself, not many would want to run that channel at night. The boat must be along here somewhere.

But there was no boat, nor any sign of one.

Through the fog he could just make out the dark circle of the tiny cove. The shores were bare, except for some odds and ends of drift-wood. He walked all the way around it, as far as the inlet and back, to make sure and then stood staring, puzzled, out across the calm water, lightly freckled with rain.

Maybe Ed, tired and worn out as he had been, had forgotten to fasten the boat and she had gone adrift. But wait. Part of the filth on Ed—God knew what else there was, but part of it, certainly—had been Flowage mud. So Ed must have been overboard up the marsh somewhere. That meant he must have come in here early enough so he could take his boat up Salt Marsh Brook.

Sure enough, what a fool not to think of it first off. Ed had a load he couldn't have hauled up the steep bank of the cove. He would have gone up the brook and landed on the swamp side.

Nate stared at the mouth of the brook. It was bouldery between rocky shores, and on the ebb tide the current made a rapids which was almost a waterfall. He had always liked to watch the tide change at Salt Marsh Brook. First the water lay still as a lake, the inlet of the brook looking like part of the cove. Then it would start almost imper-ceptibly to move. Eddies smooth as silk and lazy as snakes in the sun would begin swirling, slow at first, then faster, growing into whirl-pools, until suddenly the whole surface broke and the pent-up water of the salt flood tide with the fresh water of the Flowage behind it, would come churning down in bubbles and foam. It was something to see, the tide-change at Salt Marsh Brook.

Nate walked along the margin of the cove and climbed the rocks at the brook-mouth. Beyond the natural dam of the rocks the land sloped quickly to the reed-matted banks of the stream. He could see the pool, glassy and motionless, stretching out of sight in the fog. It was full of salt tide now, tide must be nearly high, not enough current running in to stir the water.

He went along through reeds, stepping from mat to mat of soggy grass roots, feeling the mud squelch and give under his boots. Here it was fairly solid underfoot; it was only farther up the Flowage that you went in over your knees or over your head, however lucky you were that day.

Here were the footprints, the ones he had come to think of as Ed's. There were three of them in a line, and then they stopped ten feet from the margin of the brook, as if whoever made them had been snatched up into the air.

For a moment Nate thought, I'm crazy. Then, as he bent down and looked more closely, he saw what had happened.

Somebody had taken a flat plank or something, and laid it down over the footprints. They had tramped back and forth on it until most of the tracks were mashed out. There was the plank, a big, old, worm-eaten two-by-eight, floating out there in the water. You could see the mud and fresh boot tracks on it.

Fresh boot tracks, he thought, staring with a crease of concentration between his eyes. It rained all night. If Ed was the one who'd tried to hide his tracks, you wouldn't be able to see traces on that plank now. If you looked close, you could even make out nail prints in the boot heels trampled into the fresh mud. Nails? Ev Piper! Those were Piper's tracks on the plank. That's what he was doing down here, not half an hour ago. Why?

And knowing Ev Piper, the way he was, always on the lookout for windfalls, Nate could guess pretty well what he'd been doing. He'd followed his wagon tracks down here and found Ed's boat. And seeing an empty boat, no owner in sight, in a place where no boat should be, Piper had made hay while the sun shone. He had shoved the boat out of sight somewhere along the brook, figuring the owner'd think it had gone adrift when the tide turned. Sometime later he'd sail it over to the docks in Boston and sell it.

That was why he didn't want me to come down here this morning. He knew I'd find traces and get to wondering. The old coot!

Funny he hadn't done a better job of covering up though.

Because there in the mud at the brook-edge was a flat, smashed-over place, with a deep groove in it where a boat's keel had lain.

Maybe he thought the rain'd do it for him, the lazy old son. Only I came along too soon.

Sure, that explained why Piper acted so queer. Wasn't scared, hadn't seen anything at all last night. Just wanted this boat. Relief swept over Nate. He hadn't realized how worried he'd been. Because if

Piper and Jenny knew anything about Ed's getting home, in a matter of minutes the whole town would know.

Where would I hide a boat down here? he thought. There aren't too many places. He didn't take her up into the swamp, because he'd have to come back the path along the brook and there aren't any tracks.

What I'd do at this time of tide, I'd take her out into the cove and slide her into that place behind the ledges.

He whirled and set off at a run the way he had come. He scaled the rocks, his boot heels grating, and half-slid, half-fell down the steep bank of the cove, leaving grooves in the soggy sand.

He remembered as he ran, the time he and Ed had discovered the narrow, sliplike niche behind the ledges on the south side of the cove. Nobody would have thought offhand, that you could put in a boat in there. They had both been surprised at the ease with which Pa's old skiff had slid in over the shallows and come to rest in the tiny, locked-away pool. True, they'd got caught aground, for they'd gone in on the first of the ebb, and while they'd been fooling around, the water left the shallows before they'd noticed it. They'd had to leave the boat there till the next high tide, and Pa had been madder than a hornet.

That was what Piper probably had in mind—put a boat in there on the high tide, she was safe; nobody could get her out till the next flood, unless he wanted to carry her on his back, or unless someone came there walking on Piper's heels.

Maybe I'll be in time, if she's there. I know the tide hasn't changed yet.

He was so sure he would see the boat that he was not even surprised when he stepped up on the ledge and looked down, and there she was.

She was a ship's launch, sixteen feet or so long, sturdily built, with a spritsail and a mast which had been unstepped and laid flat along the thwarts. She had oars and tholepins, a set of canvas-covered lockers. For'rad she was decked-over with a sheet of tarred canvas, slit and ragged in a dozen places.

Quite a haul for Piper, he thought grimly, jumping down into her.

In a great hustle he shoved the boat out of the pocket behind the ledges and across the shallows. She moved surprisingly easily for a boat of her size, didn't draw so much water as you'd think. Lord, what he and Ed couldn't do with a boat like this! What a hunk of luck he'd remembered to look in this place for her!

28

He knew what he was going to do with her, take her in through the mouth of the brook and hide her up in the swamp; he knew a thousand places Piper didn't, trust Pa for that. The water was still plenty deep; as he paddled into the brook he found there was still even a little current running in. Once over the tricky bottom where the rapids would be when the tide turned, he could sail her. With this little puff of southeast breeze coming fairly constantly through the fog, he could get up into the swamp in no time.

Out in the middle of the brook he put down the oar and laid hold of the mast which, with the spritsail lashed to it, was thrust partly up under the canvas deck. It was caught on something, or seemed to be. It had been shoved in there all anyhow, without any attempt made to furl the sail or stow it. Hauling on it didn't free it; he ducked down under the deck to see what was holding it.

He couldn't see much in the half-darkness. There was a funny smell in there, partly the smell that had been on Ed, but something else, too, sickly and queer, that made the hair stir on the back of his neck. He reached into the forepeak, freed the sail from the flukes of a small grapnel anchor which were holding it caught, and backed hastily out from under the canvas. For some reason he felt scared and a little sick to his stomach. And then, as he pulled the mast out, the sail uncrumpled from around it; he saw that on the sail was a great, soaked-in, brown stain.

That must've been where Ed got his head cut, he thought, gulping, at the same time wondering how anyone could bleed that much and still stay alive.

Maybe it's paint, he thought, staring at the dark cavern under the canvas deck.

But it wasn't paint.

After a moment he forced himself to crawl under the deck again. But there was nothing there, only the anchor for'ad, with a hundred fathoms or so of frayed rode spliced to it, and the queer, sweetish smell.

For a moment Nate wished he could set the sail, point the boat's nose out of the cove and let her go adrift, that he'd never laid eyes on her, let Piper keep her. If only he'd just decided to row, not pulled out the sail at all.

He pulled himself together. Ed would be able to explain. What was the sense getting goose flesh all over, getting the horrors over something you didn't know the full story of yet? The job now was to get the boat hidden up the marsh, and then go home and hear what Ed had to tell.

Working fast, Nate stepped the mast and shook out the sail. A puff of wind snapped the canvas, not loudly, but he ducked as if it had been a pistol shot.

What's the matter with me? I'm crazy. What's there to be scared of?

But, he thought, grabbing at the sheet and making it fast, I *am* scared. And I'm worried out of my life.

He settled himself in the stern to steer. The boat slid away up the waterway. She was a good boat, a ghost of a boat. Ordinarily he would have had the time of his life sailing her. But as he went up the brook he couldn't help glancing fearfully from side to side, though he knew there was no one, nothing there to see what he could see, if he merely lifted his eyes to the taut sail.

Salt Marsh Brook, a few hundred yards from its mouth, split into three or four smaller streams, which in turn divided. You had to know which was the deep one, keep to the channels. He didn't worry; it was tricky sailing, but he knew the marsh. Tall reeds, growing taller as he got deeper into them, grew on either side of the waterways, cattails and a tall, dry, flat rustling blade which he didn't know the name of. The wind made a lonesome sound rattling across them. In the summer they were all brown and green; now they were pale tan and white, with little pale sheaves coming out of the mud at their roots where this year's reeds would be.

He took the boat a quarter of a mile into the swamp, as far as he dared in the shoaling water, and left her hidden in a bed of reeds. Nobody, not even Piper, would come in here at this time of year. The marsh was too treacherous when the water was up. Even hunters and trappers seldom came this far up. Still—he cut armfuls of cattails and laid them over and around the boat's stern, until, ten feet away, she looked like a covered mudbank. Then, as he was about to go, he took the sail, which he had carefully rolled up around the mast, and dropped it beside the boat into the water. It would rot, of course, if he didn't get back here right away. But who cared? Who'd ever want to use the horrible thing anyway? He and Ed could make a new sail sometime. Maybe.

Still, if anybody wanted to use the boat in a hurry—no sail— He lashed the foot of the mast to a thwart to keep it from drifting away.

30

Then, picking his way carefully on a roundabout path he knew, he made his way back out of the marsh.

It wasn't easy going. At this time of year the swamp was high, water coming down from the back country with the spring thaws, up from the sea with the tide. He went in up to his waist, had to stop to pour icy mud out of his boots.

He came out at last in the alders on the south side of the brook. Pa could've shown Ev Piper a little something about covering tracks, he thought, regarding the unmarked muddy tufts behind him with a grim sense of accomplishment.

He was cold, wet and hungry; he felt as if someone had hit him in the stomach with the flat side of a board. Better get home. Talk to Ed, get some answers to the questions that roiled around in his head like muddy water. Piper maybe had hidden the boat, not to steal it, but because he had been Pa's good friend.

Nate stopped on the brook-bank, breathing hoarsely. Have to wait a minute, get his breath.

The tide had changed, the current downstream beginning to speed up. The water was a clear, brownish-green here, fresh water mixed with all the salt that had flowed up into the marsh and was now going back again to the sea. Nate could see the bottom two feet or so below him, brown mud with little tan threads of weeds, all tailing away downstream. Strings of rockweed, grass tufts, pieces of reed, chunks of driftwood had stopped turning aimlessly in the pool and were heading at a fair clip toward the mouth of the brook.

And here came a black, lumpy object, something water-soaked and heavy, like a log, moving slowly past, bumping a little on the bottom, coming to rest, so that the current tugged at it and made little whirlpools. It turned as it rested; the pull of the water unfolded what seemed to be dark, thick sticks from its bulgy center, and Nate saw that what was in the brook was the body of a man.

He stood looking down at it, a sharp, rotten taste in his mouth, his belly crimping inward on itself with a cold quivering. For now that he had made out the body, he could see the man's face—young, no more than a boy's, with open, surprised blue eyes and a thin, pointed chin. There was a button gone from the ragged, trailing coat.

For a moment, while he stood paralyzed, Nate could have reached down through the water and touched the man. He could have caught hold and drawn the wet, dead body up on to the bank. And for a moment he meant to. It seemed the least you could do for a stranger. But as he stood, caught in horror and a sick and shaken pity, the worrying water pulled the body free, and it was too late. He saw the face, clam-white, go glimmering and sliding out of sight. A moment later the whole body surfaced, hurried all anyhow into the rapids at the mouth of the brook where the broken water churned into the green depths of the cove. One hand came up, as if in a kind of helpless protest. Then the thing was a long, dark log in the water and, as quickly, was gone.

Edward slept for fourteen hours straight. Then he woke up, dazedly drank a bowlful of broth and went to sleep again. He didn't stir when Nate gathered him up and carried him upstairs to the back bedroom over the kitchen—because if he wanted his homecoming kept dark, he couldn't stay in Nate's room, with people coming and going through the downstairs part of the inn. Nate finally convinced his mother; she agreed not to call a doctor until Ed came to enough to explain what his trouble was. She did not agree, however, until she had taken the bandage off Ed's unconscious head and had examined his wound, which seemed to be healing cleanly.

"Hmph," Lizabeth commented. "You didn't tell me it had been sewed. You just said you cleaned it out."

"So he did," Ed said, unexpectedly. "The skunk, he like to killed me, sloshing raw brandy into my eye."

His voice was weak and high in his throat, hardly more than a whisper. He caught Nate's eye and grinned, then turned his head and went to sleep again.

Lizabeth stood looking down at him soberly. She was worn out; Nate knew she hadn't been to bed the night before, because he himself had been up and down all night. He hadn't been able to sleep. He'd kept thinking, what if Ed got uncovered and caught cold, the shape he's in. So he'd go padding up the stairs in his bare feet, and inside the door of Ed's room he would see the glimmer of Ma's candle and she beside the bed. The last time he went up, toward morning, Ed was stirring around and muttering. He stepped anxiously inside the door, but Lizabeth, bending over Ed, looked up and motioned him sharply to go away.

"It's all right," she said. "Just a nightmare. Go back to bed, Nate."

So he went back downstairs with an added worry spinning around inside his head—if Ed was talking in his sleep, what was he saying? What would Ma hear?

He got back into bed and closed his eyes. The same picture came again, *flash* in the darkness behind his lids, a glimmering white, underwater face, with open, surprised blue eyes. The way it looked, Ed and this other boy had been in the boat together. Because where would a strange sailor have come from, if not in the boat with Ed? And Ed had certainly been in a fight. Nate's thoughts would go full circle, and *flash* the face would come again.

Nate couldn't remember a night when he hadn't been able to sleep. Even when Pa died, after everything was over, he'd fallen exhaustedly into bed and gone blessedly unconscious until morning.

Ed would be able to explain as soon as he woke up, but it didn't look as if there'd ever be a time when Ma wasn't right beside him. She made the girls tend the inn while she sat in Ed's room, her knitting or sewing on her lap. Half the time she didn't knit or sew; she just sat still, watching Ed while he slept. If anyone went in, he or Betsey, she just jerked her head at them to go away. Caroline didn't go up; she was falling all over herself keeping things going in the kitchen. But Betsey hung around; it was natural, he supposed, Betsey'd always been partial to Ed. As children, when they'd divided up for games and stuff, it had always been Nate and Caroline, Ed and Betsey.

On the third morning after Ed's arrival home, he woke up and began to mend. He still looked like the ghost of himself, but his bruises were fading; his hair curled up cockily over the white bandage which somehow had got tipped rakishly over one eye. He ate a ravenous breakfast, and Lizabeth, after she had him fed and tidied for the day, called Nate to come in and see him.

But it seemed to Nate now, sitting in Ed's room, with the clean, thin April sunlight pouring through the east window, that there'd never be a time when he'd be alone with Ed so he could talk to him. In a minute, he knew, Lizabeth would pick up her things and start for the kitchen, but before she went she'd think of seventeen thousand chores for him to do, make sure that he went and did them. And it seemed to him that if he couldn't get a chance to talk to Ed alone, the worry swollen out inside him would burst and bleed like a wound.

Sure enough, his mother picked up Ed's tray and started, saying as she went, "Come on, Nate. You've seen Ed. I know you'd like to sit around here, but there's those flounders to dress and the girls have got to have wood lugged in."

She paused, and you could see her counting up what else there was to do, but Ed said, "Oh, let the old barrelhead stay with me, Ma."

"You're in no shape to do much talking. You ought to rest and sleep."

"Rest and sleep! I feel fine. Look, Nate, go on down to the shed and haul my chest up here. I've got presents in it for everybody."

"Lug that thing upstairs on my back?"

"Why not? If I can handle it sick, you ought to be able to well. Or is all that beef nothing but a mess of fat?"

Nate grinned at him. This was the old Ed, the Ed he knew. There couldn't be anything too wrong with him. "You get back on your feet I'll show *you* fat," Nate said. "But that chest'd be a devil to handle on the stairs, one man alone. Why don't you give me the key, let me take some of the lead out first?"

It was as if a curtain pulled across Ed's face, leaving behind it the face of a stranger—not a pleasant stranger.

Nate stared with a dropping jaw at the slitted eyes, the mouth drawn down, pinched and ugly.

"No, you don't!" Ed said harshly. "You'll keep your damned nose out."

"Why, good Lord, Ed, I only—"

"I knew when I came home that the whole tribe of you'd be up to your ears in my business. Well, you listen. Unless I'm mistaken, I'm the boss here. Pa told me once he meant for me to have the inn."

"For heaven's sake, Ed," Lizabeth said. "We all know he did. That letter he wrote you is his will. What of it?"

Nate shot a quick glance at her. She was standing there quietly, watching Ed. You couldn't tell from her expression what she was thinking.

"Nothing of it," Ed said. "Only it means I've got the say around here. Don't it?"

"I can't say I'd thought about it," Lizabeth said crisply. "But it's nothing to get stirred up over. Why don't you rest now, think about it when you feel better. Nobody's going to bother your things."

34

Ed's eyes, opaque and unwinking, stared at her out of his white face, thin and bony as a monkey's on the pillow.

"Seems to me," he said, "seems to me if a man's father leaves a deathbed letter, it ought to be read, not kept out of sight. Unless you've got some reason."

"Since you got home, you've been awake less than an hour," she pointed out. "And I don't know's I've thought of much else, except how sick you are. The letter's in my box. I'll get it."

She went out of the room quietly, but two red spots burned on her cheeks and her slim shoulders were stiff.

Nate gazed outraged at his brother. "What the hell's that kind of talk?" he demanded. "Sick or no sick? What's happened to you?"

"Can you lug that chest upstairs? Or not?"

"Oh, for Godsake! Sure, if I had to."

"Well, go do it, will ya?"

"I don't know," Nate said, "whether I will or not."

Lizabeth came back, and something about the way she carried the letter in her hand, her fingers, the big blob of wax Pa had sealed it with made him see suddenly the bedroom downstairs, winter sunlight coming through the window, his father's big shoulders propped with pillows, the long bony legs stretched under the coverlets on the bed. He heard again the painful, slow scratch of the quill, punctuated by long pauses; remembered his mother's melting the wax and Pa's sealing the paper, the wax sputtering and smelling as it dripped down into the candle flame. That letter was the last word any of them would ever have from Pa.

But Ed ripped it open, running his eyes quickly over the writing. Nate could see the swift, darting little movements of his eyeballs. When he finished Ed shoved the letter under his pillow.

"Ed," Nate said. "That's a letter from Pa. The least you could do—"

"Says what I thought it would say. Everything he left belongs to me."

"By God, his tools don't!" Nate burst out. The great blob of grief and worry inside his chest seemed suddenly to let go in a gust of anger. "He gave his tools to me."

Lizabeth spun on him. "Hush!" she said.

But Ed's good humor came back as quickly as it had gone. The queer look left his face. "Tools?" he said. "Sure, have them all. What

35

would I do with tools? Only don't make any mistake about who's giving them to you. Lug that chest upstairs for me, like a good feller."

"If you can, Nate, I think you'd better," Lizabeth said. "But I think you ought to rest some more, Ed, or you'll be—" she paused a second, then went on "—sicker than you are."

"Sick? Me? Never felt better. Go on, get it, Nate. Let me dole out my presents. I've been to Africa, Ma, and the West Indies and England. I even saw the town in Essex where the Ellises came from. There's still some of Pa's folks there, they gave me a fine time. Wait'll you see what I got for you. Silk—from China, I guess it came, but I bought it in Algiers. And get the girls in, Nate, I got stuff for them, too."

The stranger was gone, but in Nate the sense of grief and outrage did not change so quickly.

"Oh, shoot!" Ed said. "Don't be sore. I got a new gun for you I want you to see."

"Go on, Nate, please," his mother said.

He went blindly out, stumbling a little over the threshold. In the downstairs hall Caroline, crossing from the kitchen, glanced at him once and stood in the doorway without speaking. When he came back from the wagon shed, bent double from the weight of the chest on his back, she was still there.

"Ma wants you and Betsey up in Ed's room," Nate said. He was panting, and the words came in gasps.

Caroline put her head through the kitchen door. "Hey, Bet! Come on in here."

"Oh, stop your racket," Nate said wearily.

Half the time that holler was the way Caroline addressed Betsey. He guessed maybe she had to, to get any results. Usually you had to put up a mark to see Betsey move.

This time, though, she came through the door on the lope, all agog. She was sure interested in that chest, too. She said, her eyes sparkling, "What's that? Ed's things?"

"Muckle on," Caroline said. "Help us carry it upstairs." She watched sardonically while Betsey thrust eager hands under a corner of the chest. "Don't yank *too* hard. You'll have the lid off before Ed's ready to dole out."

"I don't see *you* holding back," Betsey said. "He's probably got a present for you, too."

36

They appeared to know all about what had gone on upstairs.

Oh, well, Nate thought, tiredly. Bet was probably stashed away in the hall, listening. It wouldn't be the first time Betsey had listened at doors and then gone and glabbed everything she'd heard. She must've told Caroline Ed had presents. One thing Nate knew, it wasn't Caroline who'd done the listening. She wasn't that kind. She might nose into your business, but it was only inquisitive-kid nosiness, aboveboard, not behind your back.

Ed was sitting up in bed, bright-eyed and perky. From the lanyard around his neck, he produced his key. You would have thought, to see him, that he was fifteen years old at his own birthday party.

"If you folks ever saw anything to beat what I've got here, I'll eat it," he announced. "Shove the chest a little closer, Nate. I can't reach it."

He had some trouble opening the lid, but, Nate told himself, he'd be damned if he'd offer to help.

Whoever had packed the chest had done it in a hurry, things thrown in helter-skelter. On top were six slender rolls done up in an oily fabric. "China silk," Ed said proudly. "Two dresses apiece for each of you."

He ripped the covers off, tearing the fabric, unrolling rustling sheets of color that shimmered like water on the clean, faded coverlet.

"Blue, yellow, pink," he announced. "The blue's for you, Ma, it's your color."

"I never saw anything so lovely," Lizabeth said quietly. "Thank you, Ed."

She was sitting in the rocker by the window, her hands folded in her lap. Her face had a kind of still watchfulness about it, if it had any expression at all; there was no way to tell what was in her mind. But Caroline! Good Lord, Nate thought. A few years ago, when Caroline got that white look, you could tell she was on the verge of throwing up. Betsey must've blurted the works in the kitchen—how Ed had talked to Ma, how he'd acted about Pa's letter. And then, of course, she and Ed never had got along too well anyway.

Only Betsey was the kind of audience Ed ought to have for this business of his presents. Only Betsey hung over him, lips parted, eyes ashine. Betsey, all agog.

We mustn't act like this, Nate's stunned mind told him. Three years he's been gone, we all ought to feel the way Bet does, any present he's

37

brought is a treasure to keep. It's only old Ed, bragging, wanting us all to know what a hell of a fellow he is. Old Ed. . . .

But the man who lay in the bed with the sunlight from the window across his bony yellow hands was still a stranger.

He can't even let people unwrap their own presents, he's got to do it himself, show each one off. Nate thought, watching the darting, clawlike fingers, Like mice in a straw pile. My God, I can't stand this.

There were many lovely things in the chest. Ivory boxes, little jade elephants and figurines, a sword with a thickly jeweled handle, all tumbled together with rings and ornaments. Ed held up a necklace of heavy greenish metal.

"This don't look like much," he said, jingling its links together. "But clean it up, you'll find it's gold."

"Oh, it can't be, Ed!" Betsey said. "It'd be worth a fortune."

"It's gold, all right. I know, because I took it off a—" He stopped. "Well, never mind where I got it. It's gold. You clean it up, stick the links inside some sliced-open potatoes, Betsey. Whichever one of you girls steps around the liveliest, waiting on me, I'll make a present of it."

The coverlet was weighted down with all the things. Ed's face slowly took on a flush, high on his cheekbones, as his hands continually darted here and there, ripping wrappings, feeling, laying out things.

He kept the gun for Nate until the last, as a climax, pulling out the bulky parcel tied with leather straps, wedged crosswise to fit in the chest.

"I had to take the stock off to get it in here," he said. "Parts are all here, wrapped up. Greased, too. Things rust so 'board ship. Package of little screws here somewhere."

His hands rummaged the chest, still by no means empty. Something bulky was wedged into the bottom of it, a round object covered with tarred canvas. Ed, pawing around, shifted a corner of the canvas, and Nate caught sight of what seemed to be the bottom of a big, up-ended copper kettle.

He wondered, What on earth's he got a cook-pot for? But Ed yanked the canvas quickly back in place.

"Here," he said. "Here's the screws. You ever see a gun like that in your life?"

Nate hadn't. It was the most beautiful gun he had ever seen any-

38

where. Ed unwrapped each piece and handed it over—ramrod, powderhorn, everything.

"There. That's all." He reached out, banged-to the lid of the chest and turned the key. "I want this chest left right here by my bed. The first claw I catch fooling with it gets whacked off. That understood?"

There was a small silence, during which the members of Ed's family looked at him. Nobody could think of anything to say.

"Well, I must say, you don't any of you seem overcome," Ed said. "Here I bust my back lugging you home a lot of nice stuff from around the world and look at the faces on you!"

Lizabeth began talking, cheerfully and naturally—a little too much, perhaps, a little too easily.

"I won't know myself when I get my new blue dress made. It's been so long since I had a new one, too. The things are all lovely, Ed; if we don't make a great towse now, it's because you ought to rest. Let's move all that off the bed, girls, let him lie down."

"Gee, yes." Nate managed to find his tongue. "My gun—sure never saw such a good one. I guess I was kind of overcome, not to say thank you."

It was feeble. It was the best he could do.

Caroline said nothing. Of them all, only Betsey gurgled and cooed, standing beside Ed, touching first this thing, then that.

Ed's hands slowly became still.

"Wait, Ma. Cad, come here and get your dress."

He was the only one who had ever called Caroline "Cad." She had always hated it. Once the nickname would have meant a fine bicker between her and Ed, now she only stood looking at him, her eyes big and black.

"What's the matter? Don't silk suit you?"

"It's the way you act!" Caroline burst out. "What ails you? As if we— Who'd nose into your things anyway?"

"Come and get your dress, Cad," Ed said softly.

She spun on her heel and ran.

Ed screamed after her. "You come back here and get your dress, or I'll heave it at your head, you stubborn little bitch!"

The hoarse voice, breathy and wheezing, cut off short. Lizabeth had leaned over and slapped him on the mouth.

It wasn't a hard blow, merely a brisk one, for his illness stayed her hand, but Ed's flush heightened; his eyes began to glitter.

"All right, Ma. I knew when I came home you and I'd meet head on, sooner or later. It's all the same to me, but I didn't think it'd be quite this soon."

Lizabeth's own eyes had begun to shoot sparks. "I'll allow you plenty of leeway while you're sick," she said. "I already have. But we'll certainly meet head on if you swear at the girls in the house."

"Look, Ma. I'm more than ten years old. I'm a man grown. I've been all over the world. This is *my* house. You better remember it."

"Oh, hush. You haven't given me any chance to forget it. Have the house, what of it? Nobody's stopping you. Now for heaven's sake, lie down and rest!"

"I told you, I've rested all I want to. Besides, I want to nail it down that no one goes glabbing around outside the house that I'm home. You might as well hear it, what'll happen if Jake Ringgold catches up with me."

Jake Ringgold? Nate thought. The name rang a bell somewhere, he'd heard it, but for the life of him he couldn't think where. Oh, yes. One day over at the shipyard, when he was working for Moses Brown. There'd been a fellow bragging a lot about how lucky he was, and Mo had said, jerking his head and grinning, "Thinks he's Jake Ringgold." But that didn't mean anything.

"Catches up with you?" Lizabeth said.

She had been moving around the room, carrying the stuff from Ed's bed to the dresser, but she stopped in her tracks. "If anyone comes here making trouble, he'll soon find out that decent people are entitled to the protection of the law."

"Oh, God, Ma, the law!"

"Betsey," Lizabeth said. "You hop downstairs and start dinner. We're way behind. Put your silk in your room and hustle. I'll be down soon."

She eyed Betsey as the girl, still agog, still hanging over Ed, picked up her two rolls of cloth and started for the door reluctantly.

"That means downstairs, Betsey, not just out there in the hall."

Her voice was gentle, and it was this queer and unusual gentleness in her that pulled Nate momentarily out of his own misery. Ma—she must be feeling awful. If he himself felt this way, how must it be for her?

40

Ed said under his breath, "Still riding Betsey, aren't you? We'll change all that."

"Say what you've got to, Ed, and then go to sleep. It's not good for you to—"

"I heard you. I'm all right. Be up in a day or so." He leaned back against his pillow and closed his eyes.

He was still so long they thought he had gone to sleep. Lizabeth went quietly on with her tidying. She straightened the bedclothes with care not to wake him, motioned to Nate to go out of the room. And then Ed began to talk. The story came out of him as if it had been dammed up a long time.

"The night I pulled out of here, three years ago, I went into Boston. I met this fellow there, this Fig Frazer. We shipped together on a lumber vessel for England. Been together ever since. We got to be able seamen at the same time. Went to France. The Mediterranean. All over. Fig Frazer. Shipmates with me. And that's rich, if you only knew it."

He stopped, opening his eyes, looking past them through the window where the wide stretch of ocean sparkled, blue and cool under the April sun.

"Where was I? The Mediterranean. North Africa. Some pirates overhauled us and burned our ship."

"Pirates?" Lizabeth said. She sounded as if she had never heard the word, and it did have in the clean, quiet bedroom a remote and ugly sound.

"Oh, yes. Pirates. Mean and stinking, you wouldn't believe. There are such things. We ran into some and they burned our ship. Fig and I got away. We shipped for the West Indies. That was two ye— That was two months ago. I was on the way home, didn't care much how I got here. Ringgold's ship, the *Nancy*, only she isn't the *Nancy* now, the little bastard changed her name to the *Turkey Feather* for his trip to Boston; this *Turkey Feather* was loading molasses at Port Royal."

"Molasses? At Port Royal?" Nate asked.

"Why not? Ringgold was figuring on pulling a trick that'd make his luck talked about all over the Caribbean."

Ringgold's Luck. That was what he'd heard Mo Brown mention.

"We heard she was a tough ship, but it was a way to get home. It was tough. Ringgold was—he was—well, never mind. His first mate, Windle, was worse than he was, knocking everybody around. The first night out, Windle hit me. I got an awful clip and it made me mad. Fig and I sailed into him, knocked him out cold. Must've been quite a time since anyone'd knocked out Jack Windle.

"I don't know why Ringgold didn't pitch us overboard. We thought he was going to. But he stuck us in irons and left us there. I guess we'd have ended up down in the 'tween-decks, no air, no food or water. But this other sailor, this Manny, we knew, he started sneaking us water and stuff to eat, and when he could he'd unlock the irons and let us out on deck. We'd crawl into the ship's launch, stay there till morning. The watch, some of them, knew about it. Nobody cared. Most of them hated Windle's guts anyway. We did that for three months."

"Three months? On the West Indies run with molasses?" Nate asked, surprised.

The stranger said politely, "If it took Ringgold three months to sail to Boston, put it that he had things to do on the way."

His tone said, "If you don't believe it, I don't care a damn, it's nothing to do with me.

"We were getting nearer home all the time, that's all we could think about. Laying in the ship's boat at night, we got the idea of making off with her in the dark, when we got near enough to the coast. So we began to get ready, little by little, sneaked our stuff out of the forecastle, stowed it in the launch. Manny and Fig helped me lug up my chest. I'd be damned if I was going to leave all that stuff behind, when I'd sweat for it all over the world."

A look of righteous indignation came into his face, the look of a man contemplating the loss of his just deserts.

"A few days ago, I guess—I've lost track—Manny told us we were off the coast here. It was foggy and dark, quiet on deck. Ringgold and the mate had some kind of a row earlier in the night, then they'd made it up over a bottle, so Ringgold was dead drunk and Windle, Manny said, not much better. We wanted to go down and stick a knife in him, but Fig was afraid he'd yell and wake up some of the boys."

He rolled his head on the pillow and looked at his mother. "Make a towse where there's reason to, Ma," he said. "Not over such a thing as a little cussing."

Lizabeth didn't say anything. She had sat down in the chair by the bedside, and her hands lay relaxed in her lap. But she had about her a bright, frozen look like the glare on ice.

42

Ed stared at her.

"Well," he said. "I guess it's all in how you look at it. The three of us swung out the ship's launch, but the davys squawked like hell. Someone woke up and called Windle, and he came roaring out on deck. I got this cut. Manny got shot and I think Fig hurt Windle, I don't know. My eyes ran full of blood and I passed out cold. When I came to we were in the launch, away from the ship. Fig was all right, didn't get a scratch. But Manny was dead."

A sweat of relief broke out on Nate's forehead. The body in the water—Manny. He was aboard the launch, they must've put him up under the canvas deck, then overboard in the cove. It had been Manny's blood on the sail.

But through the relief the doubts began at once to pound around in his head again. That cut on Ed's head, it had been a fresh cut, looked like. How could he have got it aboard the ship? A few days ago, he said. Well, he was mixed up; he might have it wrong about the time.

But then Ed said, "At least Fig said he was dead. We had to leave him behind aboard the ship."

"Ed," Nate said. He couldn't have stopped himself, even if he'd thought in time. "How old is Fig? What does he look like?"

There was a silence. Ed said heavily, "Fig's a young kid. Nineteen or so."

"Blue eyes?"

"What the hell?" Ed sat bolt upright. "What are you talking about? Yeah, sure, he had blue eyes, but how would *you* know?"

Under the appalled gaze Nate felt his tired, confused mind start to flop around like a fish on a line.

"Oh, Fig Bowden," he said, thinking, My God, he'll never swallow this. "Kid I used to know over at the yard. He ran away to sea. I was wondering if it might be him. Funny name, Fig—"

Aware that he was floundering he came to a stop, but Ed was going on, lying back against the pillow.

"No, couldn't be. Fig's name's Frazer. His folks live down Marblehead way. That's where he is, gone to see his folks."

Lizabeth got up, picked up his tray from the stand, hung the clean towel she'd used that morning on him over her arm. Her face was greenish-white, but her hands were steady. She said, "I guess you better really try to sleep now, Ed."

"Sleep comes so easy, doesn't it? I've got to get back on my feet.

43

Ringgold's in Boston Harbor now. He might run across someone who knew Pa."

"Yes," she said. "Most anybody on the waterfront could tell him where Joel Ellis lived."

She spoke in a tone cool and thin, as if she were without comprehension of the whole matter, only put out by it. Both of her sons had heard this tone many times in their lives, and Ed said angrily, "Look, Ma, this is something you can't straighten out just by giving all the kids a licking. Will you listen, just once? You can see, can't you, why I don't want Ringgold to catch up with me?"

"You mean this man, this Ringgold who abused you so, will come chasing after you? Why would he do that? Unless you've got something that belongs to him?"

"I had wages coming—"

On the defensive, brought straight down from being the man-grown who had been all over the world to the youngster of fifteen or so, Ed started to justify. Then he realized and stopped short. "Let it alone, Ma. It's my business. I'll handle it. Only will you, for Godsake, not talk it around that I've got home?"

"No," she said. "We won't talk it around."

She looked down at him for a moment, then turned slowly away from the bed. As the towel on her arm swung past his face, Ed reached out and grabbed it. He scrubbed it over his cheeks, pressed it hard against his mouth and nose.

Lizabeth stopped and waited until he put it down.

"God," Ed said. "A clean towel. Dried outdoors on a line. Been a long time since I smelled a clean towel."

"Nathan," she said. "You come downstairs with me. I want those fish dressed."

Nate followed his mother downstairs. Even if there'd been time, he couldn't talk to Ed now. No need to. The question pounding in his head had been answered. The sailor, Manny, had been left behind on the ship; nobody went away in a boat. Of the tracks leading up out of the swamp, there had been Ed's, Piper's, Nate's own. No one else's. Fig Frazer hadn't gone to see his folks in Marblehead, or anywhere. It was his body in the water.

But it must've been self-defense, Nate told himself desperately. Ed. Old Ed. If only I could get *to* him, in past that ugliness, he could explain it. I know he could.

44

Lizabeth was standing by the sink drainboard. She had set Ed's tray down, but her hands were still on it, the knuckles white against the red, roughened skin.

The girls must be working in the taproom, he could hear the trenchers rattling in there. He waited a minute, but Lizabeth didn't say anything or turn around.

"He's pretty sick, Ma. No telling how much of that he dreamed up."

Lizabeth let go the tray. The shock rocked the dishes on it and a pewter pitcher full of milk fell over. She didn't seem to notice.

"It might not be as bad as it sounds, Ma."

She spun around. "Don't try to save my feelings now, Nate, I can't stand it. It's a time to try to think straight, not blither around sparing the womenfolks. Ed didn't dream up being half-starved and beaten. Nor that boy's being murdered, he didn't dream that up either."

Nate started to turn cold before he thought, She means Manny.

"He talked and mumbled in his sleep," she said, "both nights. Pieced together it's *worse* than it sounds, and we've got to face it."

Nate felt his tiredness grow outward and expand like a creeping sickness in his joints. He looked around for a chair and sat down. Sunlight, clear and thin, on the bare, scrubbed floor highlighted the worn-down places, so that knots in the wood stood out like brown and polished growths. It fell bright across his mother's flattened-out shoes, touched the hem of her threadbare skirt.

He had been asleep that night he didn't know how long, when he woke up with a start. His mother was standing by his bed with a lantern in her hand. Through the window past her shoulder, he could see the half-moon bright against a whitish sky, low in the west, so he judged it was near morning.

She said, "Nate, get up and dress. I want you to help me."

"What is it, Ma? Is Ed—"

"No. He's sound asleep. Hustle now. I need you."

He fumbled on his clothes, shivering in the cold light, almost too sleepy to wonder, but he came wide awake as she talked to him.

"We're going into Ed's room and carry out that chest. I've unlocked it, but I can't budge what's in it without making a racket. So we'll have to carry it down to my room."

"But, Ma—"

"Don't argue, Nate. I know what I'm doing. I've thought it out, and I've prayed for guidance."

"What if he wakes up?"

"If he does, that's too bad. But the way he sleeps, he won't wake up, unless you tumble all over yourself. I've got to see what's in that chest, if it's something I've got to do anything about. If it turns out not to be, we'll put it back where we found it and nobody the wiser. Leave your shoes off."

"It's too heavy for you—"

"I can heft one end of it. Stop talking, Nate. There isn't time."

Dazed and apprehensive, he followed her up the stairs.

Lord, it's Ed's own business; she can't nose into it like this. If he finds out, he'll split open—

But something pushed at him to make no more protest. He told himself it was no use to argue with Ma when she got like this, but part of his willingness to go with her was curiosity over what Ed had in the chest. He put that part firmly down into the back of his mind.

Ed was sound asleep, his face half-buried in the pillow. Nate could see part of the leather lanyard around his neck, but the key was tucked inside his nightshirt. How she'd got it out and back without waking him no one could say. Put it down that Ma could do what she set out to do. Though maybe it was that exhausted sleep of Ed's —in the morning light, gray on his gray face, he looked like a dead man.

Nate lifted his end of the chest; it was heavy still, but not too heavy now that so much stuff had been taken out of it. He wondered about his mother, but she walked backwards ahead of him, straight as a poker, as if she were carrying nothing at all. He followed her, feeling as if he were walking on eggshells, praying they wouldn't bump the jamb as they went out through the door. They went down the hall past Betsey's room, past Caroline's, into Lizabeth's. She set her burden down, came back past him and quietly closed the door.

As she lifted the lid of the chest, Nate couldn't help the surge of curiosity that made him lean past her shoulder. He wouldn't have opened it, he told himself, but now that she was doing it . . .

The big greenish copper kettle was wedged down bottom-up

46

against the sides of the chest; whatever it was covering was bulky and filled it heavily. Lizabeth couldn't stir it; Nate had to reach in and haul it right side up by main strength.

Four stiff canvas sacks had been jammed into it so tightly that they did not fall out even when he held the kettle bottom-up and shook it.

Lizabeth felt of one of the sacks and pulled her hand away. She sat back on her heels, looking at the sacks as if they were snakes. Her face, in the subdued light, was grim, and at the sight of her Nate felt the sweat start out along the back of his neck.

He said, "What is it, Ma?" and when she didn't answer, he leaned down, fumbling at the leather thong which held one of the sacks closed. He expected her to stop him, but for once Lizabeth didn't have anything to say.

The thong had been tied up with granny knots—in a hurry, must've been. The leather was slippery with damp. He felt his fingernails give as he tugged.

The bag was full of gold pieces.

He glanced at his mother, but she still didn't move. She stayed huddled there on her knees, and presently Nate, unable to help it, thrust a hand into the sack. The money felt cold, damp, a little slimy; at the feel of it in his fist and the sound of it, a chill shot down his spine.

"You get your hand out of that bag," Lizabeth said tautly.

She got to her feet, shoving herself up stiff by the flat of her hands braced against the floor.

Nate looked at her without really seeing her. His hand, as if by some will of its own, stayed in the sack, buried in the smooth, round, cool feel of the coins.

Look at it, it's money. More than a man could make if he worked a lifetime. Everything's here, the things you think about. The boat you want, the good living, the getting ahead. It's all here, what you work and plan for. Ed's brought home a fortune.

"Nate! Take your hand away!"

He lifted his fist, opened it. One coin stuck to his wet palm, dropped coldly, softly chinking down into the sack.

"It's not yours," Lizabeth said. "Nor mine. Get away from it."

He said, "I know. It's Ed's."

She stood staring down at the sacks, and at the look on her face he moved a little back from her.

47

"No. It's not Ed's, He stole it."

"Oh, no, Ma—"

"The night they tried to jump ship, those three boys, they emptied out Ringgold's lockers," Lizabeth said. "I know, Nate. Ed's lived through it for two nights in his sleep."

"But Ma, he's sick, feverish. No knowing what—" he began and stopped.

That wasn't right. There was a knowing what.

"I didn't want to believe it either. How could I believe it? Of Ed? But I've been all night thinking, piecing things together." She met his appalled eyes steadily. "He stole it."

Her hands went down to the sacks. One by one she lifted them out of the kettle, laid them on the floor.

"And I've thought what to do. Help me, Nate, don't sit there. Put the kettle in the way it was, and then let's take this chest back before Ed wakes up."

He needed no prodding for that. He thought suddenly, What would happen if Ed woke up and found the chest gone, and he came alive, in a fever, to help her. But when they set the chest down again noiselessly by Ed's bed, Ed still slept, bone-limp, exhausted, his face ground against the pillow.

She made no attempt to get the key again and relock the chest. He thought distractedly, Lord, she'd better, but he didn't dare make a sound in the quiet room, only followed her out of it as she beckoned him along the hall.

Back in her own room, she went straight to her closet. Fumbling around among the boxes and chests stored in the end of it, she came up with something bulky—Pa's old canvas carryall, Nate saw, peering anxiously and curiously past her shoulder. She lugged it across the room, set it down, began to stuff the bags of gold into it.

"Ma, what are you—what are you going to do with it?" he asked her, and Lizabeth closed the bag, buckling its leather straps with firm little jerks, before she answered.

"Well, it's pretty simple," she said, "what to do with it. Ed stole that man's money. It's got to go back where it came from."

"But you can't—how could you find him?"

"His name's Ringgold. His ship's the *Turkey Feather*. And he's in Boston Harbor right now. You go down and harness Dolly while I change my dress."

48

For a moment he stared at her unbelieving. Then he realized that this was Ma and she'd do exactly what she said she'd do.

He thought of the months of penury, the hard sledding, the very dress she was going to change into, her good one, threadbare and old. A sudden fierce emotion swept over him—frustration, anger at Ma, he didn't try to think what it was—sparked off by the idea of all that money going out of the house.

"You can't, Ma. You're not going to!"

"Your pa and I worked for twenty years," Lizabeth said in the tone cool and thin that he knew. "Hard and honest as we could and we did well. We saved ten gold pieces like that."

"You don't know for sure that Ed stole it. We've got to wake him up, make him tell us the rights of it."

Distractedly he laid urgent hands on her arm.

Lizabeth shook him off.

"Do as I tell you. Go harness Dolly."

"I won't! Not till we think. Not till we know!"

Her hand moved in an arc and cracked him once hard across the cheekbone, hauled back to let him have another one. Nate backed precipitately out of its way.

"Goings-on and killing," she said. "If we're to believe Ed, at least one man's been murdered over this business, whatever it is. I don't know what kind of people he's been with, but that Ringgold is after him, and I guess we don't need to be told what for. You listen to me, Nate; it was messes like this, people starving and murdering each other, it was what your folks came to this country to get away from. I've heard your grampa tell, seemed to him in a new, clean country a man could start out decent. He fought all his life to keep so, and your pa and me, we fought, too. To bring you boys up to know what a new country meant, and decent, law-abiding people."

Nate stood looking from her to the carryall and back to her again. The whack he had got stung. He put up his hand and rubbed it.

"That was a good thing they had," she said. "And something that's never happened before within the time of man. A chance to leave the old and the dirty and the handled and start out over again, with all your time in front, and what you made of it was up to you. Many's the time I've heard your grampa say that if you slacked up the least little bit, in come the hellions and the hoodlums. Well, I won't stand for it. I don't know what's happened to Ed. I don't know how any boy's

49

folks could figure it out, that the boy . . . the boy they raised clean and decent could ever do . . . could ever do a thing—"

She stopped, and for a second her face seemed to crumple; then, as quickly, she had hold of herself again.

"You can hear it right out of my mouth, I righteous and holy won't stand for it if one of the hellions and hoodlums is my own son."

"You don't know for sure—"

"What can I think, the story he's told and now—" she jerked her hand at the carryall "—now finding this. You go harness Dolly. I'm going to take this money into Boston and hunt up that Ringgold and give it back to him. If he isn't there and I can't find him, I'm going to turn it over to the town magistrate. Then if Ed's got honest title to it, he can go claim it. If he hasn't, I don't care what happens to it. Not knowing, I won't have the stink of it in my house. Your grandfather took his stand against the hellions and hoodlums," said Lizabeth. "And so do I."

She turned her back on him.

"You take that carryall down and put it in the wagon. And then you harness Dolly."

Down in the wagon shed Nate set the carryall on the floor. He stood looking somberly down at it, rubbing at the pink, stinging welt on his cheek. It had been a long time since Ma had hit him like this.

The Lord knew what the right thing was now, but the way Ma was going at it wasn't the way to handle it. No matter how bad things looked, Nate knew he couldn't stand here and believe that Ed had thieved and murdered for four sacks of money. There was an explanation somewhere.

Maybe Fig Frazer had been hurt in the fight on the ship and had died of it; maybe he was the one who'd tried to kill Ed, and Ed had defended himself. You couldn't know, not till Ed said. The thing to do was wait till he did.

If only Pa were here! Times before, Ma had got the bit in her teeth and started out over hell and high water to do what *she* thought was right, Pa'd been able to hold her in a little. One of the times was when Ed ran away, three years ago. Ma had got on just such a tear as this about old Newman's girl. She'd had exactly that same look on her face, saying to Pa, "If he's done what they say he's done, he ought to go to jail. I wouldn't lift a finger to stop it."

You could see she'd been ripped right in two, but she was going to do what she thought was right.

And Pa had said reasonably, a little tired, the way Pa was, "Wait till we know for sure, Lizabeth, that it's in Ed to act that way. Wait till we know the rights of the matter."

But she had jumped right in, made up her mind, and when once she'd made up her mind, you couldn't move her. With the best intentions in the world, with all that goodness in her, she wouldn't give a damned inch.

All that talk about hoodlums and hellions—that was all right as far as it went. Nate didn't know as he cared any more for them than she did. But the thing was, they were there. So long as they were, you had to shove over and make room, handle them the best you could. It was foolish to think you could put them out of the world, keep them, even, out of the place where you were.

So far as he could see, there was a good deal of both in anyone he ever saw. Who was to say who the hoodlums and hellions were? A man walked on a narrow plank; let certain things happen to him, he might fall off the best he could do. Or he might let himself get shoved off, or he might think he was doing right, when it was the blackest kind of a mistake. Pa always said so.

Ma couldn't know. A woman, taken care of inside a house all her life, she didn't meet up with things. So Ma was able to walk along her plank straight ahead no matter what kind of holes yawned on either side of her, because she'd never in her life looked right or left or down. Right was right, wrong was wrong. Pretty simple.

Nate thought now that if she'd been reasonable about the Newman business, instead of tearing Ed apart, Ed would have stayed home. They'd all have been together, maybe Pa'd have been alive. Because more than half of what ailed Pa was thinking Ed was dead. He'd written that letter to him, but it was only trying to convince himself. None of them ever thought they'd see Ed again.

If it hadn't been for Ma, the whole trouble never'd have happened. Any way you look at it, she's the one responsible.

In his fury at his mother, he went right on, thinking out the things that maybe had been half-thought out before, but had been pushed back underneath because they scared him. Take Ed, the only way he could function was by being approved of. He had to know, Ed did, that everyone thought he was the hell of a fellow. Take anyone

51

like that, start harping he was no good, headed for the dogs, the only thing to straighten him out was a spell in jail—what would you think would happen? And now Ma'd taken up again, right where she left off three years ago.

Nate looked down again at the carryall full of money, and suddenly, in spite of himself, he found he was feeling sick. What would it be worth to you if you knew you'd left someone staring up through two feet of water, with blind, surprised blue eyes? If it was stolen, if somebody had been killed for it, would you want any of it?

Yes, he thought, you would. It wasn't the money's fault, you'd want it. No matter what. It was all you could do right now to keep from clawing that carryall open with both hands and jamming your pockets full.

It was right there that a man could fall to hell-and-gone off the narrow plank he walked on, reason himself right around in a circle.

Reason or no reason, somebody had to do something quick. Ed was a man; he was the only one who had a right to say what to do with his stuff.

After all—

Nate's eyes narrowed. His glance, moving wildly about the shed, fell on a keg of old iron scraps stowed away on a shelf—Pa's old ketch-all keg where he'd always chucked iron he said was too good to throw away, iron was too hard come by.

Working fast, Nate opened the carryall, hauled out the bags of money. He untied the first one, emptied it into the hogshead in the corner. The gold pieces landed with a clank to wake the dead; he froze, listening. Seemed as if Ma, even upstairs in her room, must be able to hear that, but there was no sign she had. He filled the bag with scrap iron, tied it up again, shoved it back in the carryall. He had the second one untied, ready to dump—the leather thong that closed it was knotted a dozen times—when he heard his mother close the kitchen door.

There wasn't time after all. Couldn't dump it, she'd hear the racket. He'd done what he could. Hastily he grabbed a couple of handfuls of gold pieces, crammed them into his pocket. They made a bulge, but his jacket covered it. Feverishly he tied up the bag, thrust all the bags back into the carryall. He had the last buckle fastened and was in Dolly's stall when she hove in sight past the wagon-shed door.

52

She was dressed in her best black gown, her bonnet strings tied neatly under her chin. Her mouth was set tight, and she gave him a look because he was only just leading Dolly out of her stall.

"What's the matter the horse isn't harnessed?"

Nate grinned nervously. It wasn't much more than a grimace, a jerking of his face muscles.

"Dolly didn't want to," he said. "Wouldn't get on her feet."

His mother always said he wasn't any good with horses, and Dolly was known for her trick of lying like a boulder if she didn't see the logic of leaving her warm stall to be harnessed to the wagon. She was old, darned near as stubborn as Ma herself.

When, a few minutes later, the horse harnessed and waiting, he looked into the shed, Lizabeth was standing silently beside the carry-all. He wondered, feeling cold, if she'd noticed anything. He saw he'd forgotten to shove the nail keg back on the shelf.

She hadn't. She said, "This is too heavy for me to lift, Nathan," and without a word he picked up the carryall and carried it out to the wagon.

Lizabeth got in herself and picked up the reins.

"I'll be back when you see me," she said. "If I'm late I may stay the night with Cousin Annamaria Bussey. I guess I can trust you to handle Ed and tend the place."

She picked up the reins, clucked to Dolly. The wagon moved out of the yard. The last he saw of her was her slim, straight, stubborn back, stiff as a stick above the low seat, as she turned the horse into the turnpike and set out on the way to Boston.

Single-minded as a mole. She gets set on what she thinks is right, then she goes stone blind. How does she think I can possibly "handle" Ed if he finds out before she gets back?

Well, he'd saved a quarter of Ed's treasure, that might help some. He'd have to hide it though, where Ma wouldn't find it, until he got a chance to tell Ed. What lay in the bottom of the hogshead drew him back into the shed as surely as if it had had him tied to a rope.

The nail keg, he thought. I can bury it somewhere.

She might miss the keg, but he'd have to take a chance on that.

He dumped Pa's old treasure-trove of iron out on the shed floor, picked up the hogshead and emptied it into the keg.

It lay in a diminished heap on the floor, Pa's treasure. Nate set the hogshead down. Lord, what there'd been in that keg! There was

53

the busted hinge off the springhouse door; Ed had broken that, slamming the door in a rage, when he was twelve years old. Nate remembered the row that had caused. Pa had picked up the pieces, merely, and fixed the hinge. Here were some other things. The old iron bolts from the wood sled they'd taken apart, fixed good as new; a rusty spike, left over from the time he and Pa'd put the new sill under the barn.

Why, he thought, soberly fingering the hard, knobbly, rust-caked pieces, turning them over, there was a whole memorial to a man's life here; most any one of these old scraps called up a picture of Pa, the kind of man he was. A man who worked hard, a skillful, practical man whose tools were sharp and taken care of, their handles velvety with use; a man who put things away and knew where they were, could go get them when he needed them.

He could see Pa's hands, turning over this old iron, looking for the piece he wanted. Rusty, not good for anything, the shape it was in, but he'd take it out to the forge and work on it, heating, hammering, tempering, until it was a hinge or a door latch or a fish hook. Anywhere on the place were the tracks of Pa.

The chairs he'd made for the parlor out of ash and oak—he hadn't been able to get hold of the kind of seasoned wood he needed and Ma'd wanted the chairs, so he took chunks out of the woodpile, rough-hewed them, turned rounds and legs on his hand lathe, planing, polishing, oiling, growling all the time about how hard it was to make chairs, the angles were all different. But there the chairs were, six captain's chairs, built to last a hundred years.

The chests he'd made, mortise and tenon fitting like silk; close your eyes and run your fingers over, you couldn't tell where the wood was joined.

He learnt me a lot, I can go on from there. I wish there'd been some way of handing along all the things he knew how to do.

Yet all his life, working hard and saving, he leaves Ma ten gold pieces; while Ed, at twenty-two, comes home with a fortune.

From the disloyalty which seemed logically to follow, he backed away, horrified.

No, by God, I wouldn't rather be Ed.

A picture came into his mind of his father's serene head, bent down, his eyes quiet and merry, his big, blunt-fingered hand on the surface of a smooth-planed board. "There," he'd say. "Made a beginning. Now we can eat our lunch and go home." When it wasn't a beginning at all but an ending, the work, for all Nate could see, perfect.

Whatever else he could do, Ed couldn't plane a board. If he touched a tool, he broke the tool. And he was lying upstairs now, looking like a little, gray old man, with whatever he'd done to get that fortune on his mind.

It was too heavy to hold long, too heavy to carry. No matter which was worth the most now he had to hide them both, Pa's treasure and Ed's.

In the end he gathered up the pieces of scrap iron and dropped them, one by one, into the keg on top of Ed's money. He stood the keg back on the shelf exactly as it had been, the only changes being, he thought as he stood back, that some of Pa's iron is on the way to Boston and some of the dust is scraped around on the shelf. Carefully he got a handful of fine sawdust kittens from under the workbench and blew them from his palm over the scraped places around the keg. Now no one, even looking closely, could tell the keg had been touched.

He washed up at the pump, letting the water run cold and stinging over his hands. Now he had to go up and see Ed, sit there sweating, hoping to God Ed wouldn't notice anything. Ed would want to know where Ma was. He'd know something pretty unusual was in the wind if anyone told him she'd gone in to Boston. The possibilities began to spin in his head. He wished feverishly to be out of it all.

They've got me stopped, he thought. Ma and Ed. The way they are. Between them, what do I amount to?

Give up the job at the yard, come home and help run the inn. God, I hate an inn! Chores, chores, chores, dress the flounder, take up the hot water, wait on the taproom. While your tools rusted and your hands got stiff and your heart did, too, with longing to get tools in your hands again. And now handle Ed. . . .

The helpless resentment in him suddenly gave way to rage.

I'm sick of it and through with it. Let them handle it between themselves. Let them grind on each other, not on me. I'm not responsible for it. I've got to be my own man, tell myself what to do.

Well, then, I'll go, he told himself, glaring at the pump handle as if it were the one thing responsible for all his troubles. As soon as Ed's better. When Ma gets back.

Something down inside him said, Go now. Pick up and go before the row, while Ma's away. You'll never go while she's here to stop you.

Go where? And how? To sea the way Ed did? It would be easy enough, just go in to Boston. But he thought of the ships he'd seen, the smallness of them, the way men were all tumbled in together in a forecastle, the way the mates slammed them around; and he knew that never, so long as he could stand on his two feet, would he go to sea.

There were lands to the north, unsettled still, where a man could go and pick out his own place. There was Maynard Cantril's ship-yard somewhere to the north. He could go and work for Cantril till he decided what to do.

It might be lonesome for a while. But a picture floated before his mind of small, solitary beaches, dreaming in the sun, silent woods, sun-spangled stretches of water. No people with their complications to burst in tangling up your life and your privacy, pressing their concerns, their wishes, their problems on you, until your own life seemed to dwindle, until you had no life at all you could call your own.

Somebody was coming down the stairs—Caroline, he could tell from the step. Nobody else walked with that quick, decisive little sound.

He turned away from the pump, the lonely beaches and the solitude retreating somewhere down into the back of his mind. He couldn't go anywhere till Ma got back. Not leave the girls with the respon-sibilities.

Caroline came in carrying an empty tray, empty, that is, except for some stuff that had been spilled on it. She took it over and plunked it down in the sink, and he realized with a start that she was madder than a hornet. Her eyes were snapping, her cheeks pink with anger; she looked rumpled up, not neat as a pin the way the girls always were and better be, or Ma'd have had the hide off them.

"Well, it sure seems to be a time for flying off the handle around here," he commented. "What ails you now?"

"Ed," she said tersely. "He was bawling for his breakfast, so I took him up some. Well, it's all over him now."

"What'd you do, throw it at him?" Nate was shocked because, he realized suddenly, there was something in the idea that appealed to him.

56

"Yes, I did," Caroline said. "I let him have the whole trayful, right in the face."

"Good Lord, why? He's sick."

"Look at my dress."

He saw now that her dress was torn as well as rumpled, the collar hanging partly free around her neck.

"He was getting back at me for yesterday," Caroline said. "I guess it must've been, I don't know. When I went in, he said, 'Where's Ma?' and I said I didn't know, I hadn't seen her this morning, and when I went by the bed he made a grab for me and tore my dress. So I let go the tray and it went all over him."

"What'd you go near him for? You know you always fought with him cats and dogs. Why didn't you let Betsey?"

"*You* get Betsey out of bed," she said. "Go on. Try it."

For all she spoke with a certain amount of venom, her voice was shaky, and she was looking more and more woebegone. "Where *is* Ma?"

"Gone in to Boston. Good thing, too, she'd probably take a stick to you."

"No, I don't think she would," Caroline said. "He told me to get out of the house and stay out. What's she gone to Boston for?"

"Told you to get out of the house? Oh, shoot, Caroline! He's just sore. He'll say anything when he's sore."

Caroline looked at him. "All right. He's just sore."

Nate glanced away uncomfortably. "I know," he said.

"You *don't* know. We don't any of us know," she said. She stopped, then went on with seeming irrelevance, "Betsey's an awful goop."

"Always was, wasn't she?" He grinned at her. "Take it easy, Caro—"

The yell from upstairs stopped him short. It was more a screech than a yell, the pounding and banging that went along with it half-drowning it out.

"Oh, Lord," he said, starting for the hall. "Don't come up, Caroline."

"Not likely," she said. "Nate—Nate, be careful."

Ed was sitting straight up in bed when Nate came through the door. The lid of the chest was closed, but Ed had the key in one hand, and the noise he'd been making, Nate judged, was by pounding the lid up and down. At least there wasn't anything else nearby he could have made such a racket with.

He started to say, "What is it, Ed?"

Ed cut him off. "Where's Ma? What's she doing? Where is she?" His voice was hoarse and gasping, the bright patches on his cheeks burned red.

Nate said, choking a little, "She's gone in to Boston."

"What for?"

"Lord, Ed, I tried to stop her."

"What's she up to? Tell me!"

"She took the money," Nate said. "She said she was going in to Boston and give it back to Ringgold."

He thought Ed was going to faint. His jaw slackened, his eyes bulged. The patches on his cheeks faded to a sickly gray.

But he didn't faint. He said in a voice that was almost a whisper, "By God. I might have known. And you let her go. You didn't stop her."

"Yeah, sure, I tried to—"

"Oh, Jesus, what good are you, you blasted dish-faced fool? I thought you'd grown up to the size of a man, maybe you could be one, if you had to. You tried to! You're bigger than she is, why didn't you knock her down?"

Nate said, "Knock . . . Ma . . . down?" looking at his brother, not believing the change in him, the bloodshot eyes, the mouth thinned and drawn back over the teeth, spitting rage and curses.

It's fever, he tried to tell himself, fever and being so mad and God knows I can't blame him.

But it was more than fever. It was Ed himself, he was like this now, and the sickening surety grew.

"You're all in it together, by God! You none of you could ever stand it if I had any luck, and I guess you ain't changed any. Go on, get out! She's got to be stopped. Go after her and stop her!"

"Ed," Nate said, in a kind of grief-stricken horror, holding out his hands. "Listen, let me tell you—"

But Ed wasn't hearing anything. His voice rose to a howl. "Fig Frazer, by God, that's who you need! He'd tear the face off you and wring it out like a rag! A good dose of him, and would I like to see it! I'd even wish he was here—" He stopped, opening his eyes wide, staring at Nate; and Nate, not knowing why he said it, only trying desperately to think of something that would stop the screaming, said, "Where is he—down Marblehead? I could fetch him here, if you think he could help."

The rage seemed to go out of Ed. He said softly, "You're a pretty wise little feller, ain't you?"

He was suddenly cool and quiet, or so Nate thought, unprepared for the quick movement of Ed's hand. It shot out to the earthen water jug on the bedside stand, gripped and let go. The jug smashed against the doorjamb, an inch from his head. A piece of it stung his cheek making a small cut. The water drenched him.

He thought dazedly, He meant to hit me, and then, All right, That's all, and he turned and went out of the room closing the door.

Sitting stern-faced and stiff on the low wagon seat, the sheepskin laprobe tucked over her knees, Lizabeth drove the ten miles in to Boston.

The wind had backed around into the northwest during the night, and it was a fine day.

But not for long, she told herself. With the wind backing around the wrong way, it'll storm tonight. I'll do well to make it home before it rains.

She wouldn't, she knew, because the road was deep in mud, the pull almost too much for the old mare. She'd be lucky if she even got in to Boston before afternoon. Then it would take time to hunt up this Ringgold; say he was there in Boston at all. She might as well be resigned to spending the night with Cousin Annamaria Bussey, not that she relished it. She and Cousin Annamaria had grown up together. They didn't see eye to eye.

But if I go there, the least she can do is take me in.

It was a fine day now, with the wind drying up the mud. Towering masses of cumulus cloud, white and gray and cream, hustled across the blue as if they were going somewhere with a purpose. Everywhere in the watery land the brooks were high, making a fine bustling noise. The sun shone on the little pale new leaves.

In spite of the turmoil in her mind she couldn't help thinking, What a drying day!

If only she could have stayed home to get out the washing. It was a big washing, with all Ed's dirty clothes; no knowing now how long they'd have to set around, stinking up the shed. Because the weather was sure to turn bad tonight, she could feel it.

In April, you had to grab the washdays.

What she wouldn't give right now to be home in her kitchen, with the washboiler heating up on the coals, the tubs out in the middle of the floor; herself, the prime mover, and the girls' shirttails out straight as they ran to do her bidding!

The habit of her house was strong in Lizabeth, layer upon layer of habit, encrusted through her lifetime. Her house was all she had. She had made of it a fortress against boredom, an outlet for boundless energy, because, she had early learned, it was no use expecting anything else.

In the beginning she had been deeply interested in the Boston business, in a way that Joel and his brother Charles weren't; they were both happier pottering around with wood-working tools, more at home with jack planes than with ledgers. Unobtrusively she followed the business, listening to Charles and Joel talk. It seemed to her they were singularly stupid in their handling of it, but she had long ago given up making suggestions. A problem would seem to her as clear as a bell—no problem at all, if you did thus and so; Joel and Charles would talk it over, evening after evening, worrying at it like a couple of old dogs with no teeth. Their discussions might last a week or a month; in the end they would do the wrong thing and lose money. But if Lizabeth made a suggestion, they only turned bland, unhearing countenances to her— "Yes, yes," waiting for her to stop so they could go on talking.

When they had got into what seemed to them irrevocable trouble, she had seen what might have been a way out of it and she had suggested that way; one evening, after the warehouse was lost, she had heard Charles make the same suggestion, wondering why they hadn't thought of it, why they hadn't tried it.

So Lizabeth turned back to her household. At least there her opinion counted. She had seldom left the house anyway, except occasionally to make this very drive with Joel to the warehouse in Boston. That was where she was going now. She had never met Frank or Michael Carnavon who owned the warehouse now, though Joel had. But if a ship captain named Ringgold had unloaded a cargo recently, it was Carnavon Brothers' business to know where. They could tell her where to find him if he were still in Boston, and she could return his money to him and, thankfully, go home.

The habit of home was more than half physical; her hands on Dolly's reins seemed to be wanting to go through the actual motions of chores she'd be doing, if only she were there.

Menfolks! They never grew up. They remained little boys forever. Tantrums, scrapes, troubles. And who of them, except grampa, Joel's father, had any sense at all of right and wrong?

That was Ed's trouble, always had been.

The girls she could boss, and Joel and Nate, too—not Joel, now, she thought. It was hard to remember sometimes that Joel was gone. Mind and body, she had never been able to reach him, but around the house she could boss him. Ed, she had never been able to boss.

It broke her heart to see him brought down, his whole fresh boy-hood laid in ruins. He had been a handsome, healthy baby and a lively boy, keeping them all on the go. With Ed, if it wasn't one thing, it was another. She thought of the days when he was little enough so she could put him right down across her knee and pound some sense into him. Not that she had ever licked him when he didn't deserve it. Ed had never had a licking in his life that he didn't deserve, and never was there anybody a licking did more good to. Why, the life would go right out of him, even the curl would go out of his hair. For a couple of days you wouldn't have been able to find a better-behaved boy. Then the devil would start to work on him again and they'd all be right back where they started.

He ought to have a good one right now, she told herself grimly.

It was all she could think of to do, at first, because all her life with her children, her mind automatically had put the two things together: Bad child—licking. It had always worked. If it wouldn't work now it was only because you couldn't take the grown man, who was, after all, only Ed, and put him right down across your knee. You could, however, see that justice was done, wrongs put right. Ed's punishment would be not to have this mess of money, wrongfully come by. Unless she was mistaken that would be worse than any licking.

She felt better now that she had made up her mind what to do and was doing it. All night, sitting beside Ed, trying to piece together his story and the mumbled nightmares, she had fought off a sense of terrible shock and outrage. That Ed should be mixed up in any such wicked business! Ed, her own son!

He had been in a sea fight, seemingly, had seen men killed, had perhaps killed someone. The vague mutterings coming from the bed through the long, candle-flickering hours of the night had chilled her blood. The thin face on the pillow had seemed the very face of evil, nothing to do with her and hers, as if the devil had sent a changeling.

But in the morning she remembered that when Ed was little the least bit of fever would send him off into the wildest fancies, nothing real or true. Nothing you'd be fool enough to believe.

There was in Lizabeth's mind a busy, little mechanism which started to work on reality the moment it was presented to her, giving it wings and motion, so that presently it flew around to another quarter. She could not believe, however bad Ed's story sounded, that a decent boy, raised right, could go wrong. No claw could ever stretch up out of the swamps where lived the monsters, the hellions and the hoodlums, and actually touch a good, law-abiding family. Not possibly. Evil was a thing you watched out for and prevented, not something which merely happened.

And so she told herself firmly, Ed was half out of his mind with sickness. What he mumbled about in his sleep likely never happened at all.

She had made up her mind, to her own satisfaction, what *had* happened. Ed had always been easily influenced; he had fallen in with bad companions. This Frazer boy he told about, had influenced him to make off with Captain Ringgold's money.

Of course they had made off with it, no boy of twenty-two ever came by that much money honestly. To be honestly owned money had to come in hard and slow, a drib and a drab at a time. If after many years you had ten gold pieces earned and saved, that was honest. More than that in a shorter time wasn't, and that was all there was to it.

Actually, she had no sense of reality whatever about what was in the leather bags in the hold-all. She had never seen that much money before with her own eyes; therefore, she could not believe in its existence, certainly not in connection with her and hers. The reality for her was the sense of terrible outrage over the fact that here was Ed, a disobedient, runaway boy, up to now a child to be corrected and controlled, in possession not of punishment for his wicked doings but of a great reward.

That was not what she believed in. Ed must have his licking; the money must be returned. Once it was back where it belonged there would be an end to the whole affair.

It was likely that this Ringgold was a hard man, but she meant to give him back his money along with a piece of her mind for the way he'd treated Ed. And then she meant to report to the authorities the death of the sailor, Manny.

It did not occur to her that it might be prudent to reverse the procedure, report to the authorities first. She told herself she was not going to miss the sight of that wicked man's face when she walked in with his money and his tongue-lashing, and the threat of law and order to give him something to think about. Besides, if he had his money back, he couldn't retaliate with any threats to have Ed arrested.

She had things all straightened out in her mind now, never considering that one step in her logical thinking, if wrong, might throw out all the other steps. It was as simple as doing a washing. Dirty clothes to washboiler and tubs, to clothesline and sun and air. All clean.

She made better time in to Boston than she had hoped for. The northwest wind, as the day wore on, dried up some of the mud, so that old Dolly could clop along. It was hard, when Lizabeth passed Cousin Annamaria Bussey's cottage on the highroad, not to stop and make Cousin Annamaria feed her. She hadn't had a mouthful of dinner, of course, and it would be almost worth a delay to witness Cousin Annamaria's consternation. Cousin Annamaria was tighter than the bark on a tree. She fed well herself, but if her relatives went there and she knew they were coming, they'd get cornmeal mush or the like of that, and very little of it. Besides, she was a rotten housekeeper. If Lizabeth went in there now, what a mess she would find! It would be something to see Cousin Annamaria scurry around. Not that Lizabeth relished putting her to shame, but she did like to see justice done.

Well, she could call in on the way back from the waterfront. Supper would do just as well as dinner. And if the weather turned bad she'd stay all night.

She went down the scrubby, uncovered hills of Boston, bleak in the afternoon light, for the sky was clouded over now and the north-west wind was cold. It was certainly a shabby approach to a town, this one she was coming in on, with the crooked paths running every which way and the smell of horse and cattle dung sharp under Dolly's hoofs. Dolly was shambling a little now; she was tired. But she could rest at the warehouse, and they were getting down close to the water-front now. Lizabeth could tell from the smell of mud flats, saltwater and hides, mostly hides. She knew that smell of old, from having ridden in here with Joel. There were warehouses along this street stored full of hides waiting for shipment. It was because of that smell—that, and other things; the waterfront was no place for a woman—that she had never come with him unless she could help it. But he had always liked to have her drive with him, and sometimes she'd gone. She had never been here alone before.

There were four ships in the Harbor and a great many smaller boats, most of them fishing sloops and one or two trading scows. There was no way to tell which of the ships was the *Turkey Feather*. The big one, over there at anchor, she knew was the British man-o'-war. The other three were trading vessels, all more or less alike.

She clucked to Dolly who walked now with her head hanging down between her fetlocks, and the old horse sighed almost like a human being.

"All right, Dolly," Lizabeth said. "Not much farther."

She stopped the wagon in front of Carnavon Brothers' warehouse and spoke to a man sitting on the step there.

"Good day, Job. Can you tell me where I can find a Captain Ring-gold?"

"A *who?*" the man said, staring at her.

He was a very old man, dirty, with a growth of scrubby beard stained with tobacco and spit. From where she sat in the wagon, she could see above the neck of his jumper a great black ring of grime. Lizabeth knew him. He was Job Crawford, who used to work for Joel, and Joel would never have put up with filth like that either. Apparently these Carnavon Brothers were kind of slack.

"Captain Ringgold," she said distinctly. "Captain Jake Ringgold. Where can I find him?"

Old Job's mouth opened, revealing the fact that he had two teeth, one upper and one lower, in front. His gums were pink. He said, "N-kek, kek, kek, kek."

"It's nothing to laugh at," Lizabeth said sharply.

Apparently he didn't recognize her. He went on cackling, wagging his head up and down.

"Can you answer a civil question, or can't you?" she went on.

The old man went on wagging his head.

"She's crazy, Francis," he remarked to someone just inside the open door behind him. "You hear who she wants to see?"

"I heard." Whoever was inside didn't come out but spoke through the doorway. "You go about a thousand miles south to the Spanish Sea, you'll likely find Ringgold. Begod, if you're unlucky, he'll find you first. What will you do with him when you find him, ma'am?"

The voice was very male, deep bass and full of amusement, the exact kind of thing which all her life had never failed to raise Lizabeth's hackles. Men laughing at women.

"My business is private," she said. "With Captain Ringgold."

The voice said, "Won't I do? My name's Carnavon."

The tone carried a leer of sorts, at least she translated it that way, and she set her teeth. She was aware, too, that behind her a group of loafers was gathering around the wagon.

She said, "If nobody here has the manners to answer a simple question, I'll move on."

She clucked to Dolly and switched the reins, but the old horse was too tired. She merely stood with her head hanging.

There was a movement inside the warehouse, and the owner of the voice stood in the door. He was a man tremendously tall and wide, dressed in workman's gear which was too tight for him, so that his thighs bulged the straining fabric and his belly billowed out over the top of the belt. The grin was on his face as well as in his voice, and he said, "I say again, won't Francis Carnavon do?"

Lizabeth's glance raked him, a glance which stated plainly that he would do neither for her nor for any other woman, and after a moment of it Carnavon's grin faded and a dull color crept up into his face.

Faith, he had only been doing a chore in the storage cellars to help out old Mike. He knew he was sweaty and streak-ed, and the clothes he had on not his own but borrowed for the job from one of the boys. But she'd no call to look at him as if he were the dirt under her feet.

He said shortly, "And what is it you want to know, ma'am?"

"Which of those vessels is Captain Ringgold's, please."

"Not Jake Ringgold, surely?" Carnavon said. "Not here in Boston Harbor. To see a lady." He bowed. "Not likely."

"I see." Lizabeth jerked at the reins. "You might have said you don't know in the first place, not wasted my time."

Dolly, jerked awake this time, stirred and rumbled, prepared to move on. But Carnavon stepped down from the warehouse step and laid his big hands on the wagon wheel. Dolly felt the brake of his strength; she gave up without a protest.

"I know what vessels are here in the Harbor. What's all this non-sense about Ringgold?"

At the sound of the name in Carnavon's booming voice, a murmur went up from the loafers, who, gathering out of nowhere, were now around the wagon in a tight ring. Lizabeth heard the name being passed from mouth to mouth.

"I've not been the one to talk nonsense here," she said. She didn't know as she cared for his standing so close, and her upper lip twitched. "I happen to know Ringgold's here in Boston, and I want to see him. That's all."

"Oh, you do, do you?" Carnavon began to grin again. "Somebody's lied to you, ma'am. Is it likely Jake Ringgold'd stick his neck in here with the lobster-backs there like a set rattrap? It's a slice off their backsides they'd give to lay their hands on the bugger."

"Watch your tongue!" Lizabeth sharply. "And take your hands away from my wagon wheel. What *are* those ships out there?"

"That one," Carnavon said, pointing, "is the British warship, as all folk of Boston know. Next to her is Josiah Winlick's *Bessie and Mary,* loaded with lumber for England. Next is the *West Wind,* owned by me and me brother Mike and sailed by our cousin, Corkran Teague. And the other one—"

He came to a full stop, his eyes speculatively on the outermost lying vessel.

"She's a stranger, surely, but—Job, what did yon man, unloaded here last night, what did he say his name was?"

The old man, listening agog on the warehouse step, said, "Morrison. Captain Morrison. His ship's the *Turkey Feather.*"

"From the West Indies," Lizabeth said. "With molasses."

"That's right," Carnavon said, eyeing her.

66

"Then I don't doubt but I can do business with her captain, whatever he calls himself."

"Well, he's not Jake Ringgold, ma'am. Good Lord above, that's crazy!"

"I want someone to row me out there," Lizabeth said. "Unless he's ashore here now."

Old Job said, "No, he's aboard; they're sailing with the tide in an hour or so now."

Francis Carnavon's grin spread, showing a mouthful of strong, white teeth. He shrugged his shoulders, lifted one shaggy eyebrow at the loafers.

"I'll row you out there, ma'am, if you really want to go," he said.

"All right. Where's your boat?"

She could see he hadn't thought she was serious, the way he drew back and hauled in his horns.

"If you're able to row a boat that far," she said, running her eyes over his stout figure.

Carnavon turned red, and a roar went up from the loafers. Old Job cackled his brief "N-kek, kek, kek." He said, "One on you, Frawncis. Haw."

Carnavon said, "My boat's at the foot of the steps."

He jerked his head at the alley which led down by the side of the warehouse.

"I'll have to find someone to watch my horse."

"I'll watch the horse," old Job said.

He was cackling to himself at a great rate, and the loafers were finding it all a great joke on Frank Carnavon. Everyone knew how he hated work, and the *Turkey Feather* was a long way out in the Harbor.

"It would be an act of mercy if you could find a little feed for her," Lizabeth said. She eyed the old mare with compunction. Dolly looked poorly, and that was a fact.

Job said, "I'll find her some grain, ma'am."

Lizabeth put down the reins and climbed out of the wagon.

"This bag's too heavy for me to carry," she said, looking at Carnavon.

"Eh?" Frank stared curiously at the hold-all. "Is it your belongings you'll be taking aboard the *Turkey Feather*, ma'am?"

"No. Just bring it, please, and show me the way to go."

67

Carnavon reached for the bag and hauled on its handles. Then, finding it heavier than he expected, he hoisted it out and dropped it on the ground. It landed with a chilly, clanking sound.

"Begod!" he said, astonished. "What is it, then? Morrison's trip of ballast?"

"I'll thank you to be careful," Lizabeth said. "Both with your hands and your tongue. If you can't carry the bag, say so. I don't doubt for what I'm willing to pay, I can find someone else who can."

Carnavon said hastily, "Oh, no, now, I'll carry it."

He was, by now, more interested and amused than ever. He said, "You go down the steps there," pointing, and he swung the hold-all, almost without effort, on to his shoulder. He found himself annoyed that she paid no attention whatever to this feat of strength.

What a woman! To skin a man so with the eye of her alone, he thought, impressed by the slim, forthright back moving ahead of him down the warehouse alley.

From the look of her she was about to skin Morrison, and serve the overbearing little tadpole right.

Could be she's his wife, she has that righteous-judgment look about her, God bless her pretty bottom.

It would be worth the row out there, just for the sight of Morrison's face when he laid eyes on this nice, holy, madder than a hornet little woman coming aboard his ship.

Frank hadn't liked the fellow anyway, doing business with him last night, helping him get rid of his cargo. Standoffish and touchy kind of fellow, with noble black mustaches. No bigger than a woodcock. Seemed odd for a man the size of a fourteen-year-old boy to be in command of a vessel. Somewhere Frank had heard that Ringgold, the West Indies pirate, was a small man. Not many who had encountered him on the high seas had lived to tell what he looked like, according to reports, but there was a sailor who had seen him in Port Royal.

But, Lord, Ringgold wouldn't have the gall to put in here at Boston. The British would have him strung up before a man could spit on a cockroach. This Morrison was all right, barring his nasty manners.

Wasn't a lot of change to be got out of him because he wouldn't load cargo, just wanted supplies. Canvas, ship's stores and gunpowder.

Gunpowder, Frank thought suddenly, feeling a little chilled. Well, if Morrison were Ringgold, Carnavon Brothers had supplied plenty of death for honest men on the high seas. Barrels and barrels of death.

And it was another queer thing altogether, a man to want to take his ship all the way back to the West Indies in ballast, when there was plenty of cargo to be had, money to be made.

Frank had thought the fellow a fool at the time. But that wasn't Carnavon Brothers' business. Let him be a fool; he'd paid for his supplies and canvas in good West Indies molasses, which was worth its weight in gold, or would be when it was made into rum and shipped back to the West Indies where it came from. All in all they'd done a profitable bit of business with Morrison, though not as much as they would have done if he'd been willing to take a cargo. And with Mike and him it had been a kind of challenge to get a cargo unloaded right under the noses of the British, who'd seen some of it and stuck their damned tax stamps on, but not all of it, begod, not by a damn sight!

Well, this would pay Morrison off for his manners, taking this woman out there, God help him. Francis Carnavon wouldn't have missed it for a ball.

He went down to the small skiff lying at the foot of the landing steps and climbed into her. Dropping the hold-all between his knees, he sat down on the rowing thwart with a great groan of relief. The bow of the skiff sank under his weight until it had a bare three inches of freeboard, for the boat was built for sailing not rowing, and the rowing thwart was too far forward for a proper trim. Also he had had the skiff out on the Bay earlier in the day. She had shipped some water which he had not yet had time to bail out. This bilge now ran down into the bow and backed up there, so that his big stern, overflowing the thwart, was only an inch or so above getting a soaking.

"I hope there's nothing in your bag besides old iron that'll be the worse for a wetting, ma'am," he said, looking up at her blandly. He planned to provoke her still more because the edge of her tongue tickled him. He was surprised at her reply.

"No, there is not," she said. "But the hold-all I cherish because it belonged to my husband, who is dead."

"Stiffen me, ma'am, I'm sorry." Uncomfortably he lifted the bag out of the water, and bestowed it on the seat beside him.

"And you'll bail out that skiff before I get in there," she went on.

"Why don't you keep her clean? She's a swab's boat. She's disgusting. I won't set foot in her till that water's out and she's dry."

Carnavon stared. He pulled out his pipe and got it going while she stood, tight-lipped, on the step, not moving a muscle.

He said, "You'd better get a hustle on. Morrison's sailing with the tide."

But then he chuckled, picked up his bailing scoop and bailed the boat dry. He was half tempted to step the mast and sail out to Morrison's ship; with this wind blowing, he could give the woman a proper wetting, soak some of the airs out of her.

A swab's boat, indeed! He'd have her know this was the fastest sailing skiff on the Harbor, built from one of Maynard Cantril's designs, dirty only because he'd been using her and hadn't taken the time to clean her out yet. ——

But he hadn't the heart, he found, to set the sail. For all her wicked tongue, speaking to Francis Carnavon as if he were one of his own workmen, she was a nice little woman; the wind blew hard and she'd be cruelly cold if she got a wetting.

Lizabeth got in, fastidiously stepping on the slippery floor boards and settling herself in the stern. Frank shoved the boat away from the landing and unshipped his oars.

"At your age," she said briskly, "your wife should've knocked that sloppiness out of you years ago."

Frank paused in the business of turning the skiff around so that he could shove her, stern-first, with the oars. That way he himself would get wet behind without doubt, and the woman might take a few slops in her lap; it would be nothing to the flying spray should he set the sail.

"I have no wife," he said politely. "I have not the good fortune."

She said, "I'm not surprised to hear it."

"Why?" Frank asked, astonished to find his feelings hurt. " 'Tis not bad-looking I am. I've some money."

"You might not be bad-looking if you got rid of some fat," she said. "But it's impossible to say."

"Fat, begod! It's muscle," he said, cut to the quick.

What he had said was true, as many people had found out to their loss. It had always been his cross that his looks were somewhat deceptive.

70

"Well, if you're all muscle, as you say, you'd better use some of it to row," she said. "I haven't got all day."

"And I have no trouble finding a woman when I want one," he said stiffly. "Begod!"

"That'll do. I don't care to hear such talk."

"Then do not begin it. 'Tis a soul of vinegar you have. I'd as soon try to talk to a needle."

"Please row, my man." She was revenged, she saw, for his laughing at her in the beginning. She couldn't help a final thrust. "Some women, I don't doubt, will put up with a good deal for the sake of a little money."

"Begod!" Frank said again. He dug his oars deep, sending the skiff shooting. He was astonished to find that he was angry, and she had done it without even raising her voice.

They made a curious picture as they crossed the Harbor on that squally and overcast afternoon, and many people marked them—the big man with the pipe in his mouth, sitting low in the skiff's bow, so low, indeed, that it seemed almost as if he were skating across the water on his bottom; the woman perched high above him in the tip-tilted stern, as neat and compact as a tern on a channel buoy. Some British tars, loafing on the deck of the warship, noted with delighted guffaws that the cross-chop slapping in over the bow had got the fat man's tail wet, and two boys, fishing, mentioned to each other that for some reason, Frank Carnavon was rowing a woman out to the West Indies vessel, the *Turkey Feather*.

It wasn't like Frank, they said; ordinarily, with a fine fresh wind like that, he'd be sailing gunnel-under in a cloud of spray.

Those who happened to be casually watching, observed that the woman hailed the *Turkey Feather*, or seemed to, that there was a bustle on deck, a rope ladder was thrown down and the woman went aboard. Then Frank Carnavon went partway up the ladder, handing up something black and bulky like a bag, and the ladder, with Frank still on it, was abruptly hoisted and dumped in over the ship's rail.

"Whoever done that," one of the boys, fishing, remarked to the other, "was a mighty man."

Shortly after, a great activity was seen to be taking place aboard the *Turkey Feather*. Her sails were broken out, her cable slipped, and she stood away down the Harbor under a great spread of canvas,

71

with Carnavon's small skiff, made fast under her quarter, towing alongside like a sucking pig hung to its mother.

Lieutenant Niles, of the British man-o'-war, had not been interested in this departure, until he observed the slipping of the West Indies skipper's cable, though out of boredom he had been watching it through his glass.

"That's an odd thing," he said to the officer on duty. "Lower the gig. I'm going ashore."

He supposed none of these stiff-necked colonials would give him much information, but it could certainly be found out on shore who had owned that skiff and perhaps something about the fracas which, through his glass, he had observed taking place on the deck of the *Turkey Feather*.

For once he had no trouble at all getting all the information he needed. Frank Carnavon was known and liked along the waterfront. The crowd of loafers had watched his progress across the Harbor with glee; his brother Michael had also been looking from the office window upstairs in the warehouse, where he was going over a manifest with Corkran Teague, the skipper of his and Frank's vessel, the *West Wind,* and with Maynard Cantril, the shipbuilder from the north, who was just in with a cargo of lumber and furs.

For two hours Mike and Corkran had been listening, fascinated, to Cantril, hearing him talk about the chance there was for trade and development in the north, about the sawmill set up and working at Somerset up the Crookshank River, and the shipyard going to rack and ruin because of the lack of honest workmen to build the ships.

"It could be bought," Cantril was saying. "My brothers'd sell it. Ain't no good to them with Pa gone. I'd want to keep my share, account of I want the shipyard."

"Begod, I'm tempted," Mike said. "I'd move off the face of the earth in me drawers alone, paddling a shingle, to get rid of the British with their tax here and their tax there. Boston's no place for business, now."

"You won't find any taxes in Somerset," Maynard Cantril said in his big, easy voice. "Unless you make some yourself."

"When'll you be down again?" Mike asked. "Begod, I could know my plans in a month or so. 'Tis short notice, Cantril, to make up my mind all of a heap. It'll take me a month alone to persuade my wife."

"No hurry," Cantril said. "Some of us'll be down again before the summer's out. What's your brother up to?" he went on, looking curiously past Mike to the window. "That's no way to handle a good sailing skiff."

He stiffened with outrage, and Mike leaned out past him to see what was causing it.

"Look at that dog of a Frank, Corkran," he said gloomily. "At it again. Carnavon's would be well off today, Mr. Cantril, if me brother Frank'd pay the mind to business that he does to any oddity that comes along."

Carnavon's, of course, was very well off, but might as well, Mike thought, establish a proper business relationship, just in case, with Cantril.

Cantril, however, wasn't listening. He was watching Frank's awkward progress down the Harbor and spluttering with rage.

"I built that boat, I s'posed the son of a bitch knew how to sail her." His voice choked off. "Look—look—"

Corkran Teague grinned behind his hand. He didn't know Maynard Cantril well, nobody knew the old man well, but Corkran did know that to mistreat a boat was worse to Cantril than to mistreat a human. He judged it was time to throw a little water on the coals, seeing Carnavon's wanted the Cantril business.

"It's the lady, Mr. Cantril," he said. "Frank doesn't want to get her wet. You should see him alone in a gale though; he sails that little boat like a cloud through the sky."

"Well, goddam a woman," Maynard Cantril said.

He picked up his hat, jammed it down to the bridge of his nose and departed. He muttered, "Hell of a way to treat a boat," as he stumped through the door.

"Now blast that spalpeen of a Frank!" Mike said irritably. "It's taken me two years to get half a word out of old Cantril."

Corkran grinned again.

"Frank'll fix it," he said. "He's sociable, that one. It's the belly on him, Michael. Had he one like yours now—"

Mike was thin and tense, where Frank was big and easy. Oddly enough, the two brothers looked alike, except Frank was the elder by five years, forty to Mike's thirty-five.

"Belly and brains," Mike snorted. "Though, begod, sometimes I think his belly's where he carries them."

73

"Haw," Corkran said. "Nothing the matter with Frank's brains, when he wants to use them. What could've set that fool woman off, thinking this Morrison was Jake Ringgold?"

"Somebody told her a mess of lies."

"She couldn't know who Ringgold is, coming down here and asking after him as if he were a man like any other. Who is Morrison, anyway, Mike?"

"A West Indies man, he said. Seemed aboveboard, except all he would load was stores. No cargo, and that's an odd thing, surely."

"No cargo," Corkran said thoughtfully. "Would you take an empty ship back to the West Indies, now, Michael?"

"No, begod, I would not."

"Ship's stores, h'm? Any gunpowder?"

Mike eyed him.

"What are you thinking, Cork? A man who'd hang higher than Haman if they caught him, would he stick his nose into Boston Harbor, now? For all the British have the brains of pea-hens, they shoot straight."

"From all I've heard of Ringgold," Corkran said. "He's the laddie who might try just such a trick. Did he or did he not load powder?"

"He loaded an uncommon lot of powder," Mike said. "Shot, too. For his trade, he said, in the Indies. Don't be a fool, Cork. We do ourselves, in case we might run into Jake Ringgold on the high seas. Do we not? What are you thinking?"

"Be a pretty mess for us if it turned out to be Ringgold, and he loaded to the gunnels with Carnavon Brothers' powder," Corkran said.

He took down Mike's spyglass, extended it and focused on the Harbor.

"Frank's getting his arse wet," he said, grinning.

"Serve the idle lubber right."

"Well, you know," Cork said, "there's a thing or two. If I was to see that rig come up over the horizon, I'd break out the muskets."

"The devil you would," Mike breathed. He reached for the spyglass. "There's many a West Indiesman looks like that, as you well know."

He focused the glass just in time to see Frank hoisted, all anyhow, in over the rail of the *Turkey Feather*, and he stiffened where he sat, the eyepiece glued to his eye. "Jesus and Joseph, Cork!"

He couldn't tell for sure, but it looked to him as if about six sailors at once jumped on Frank and flattened him out on the deck.

"Get us out there, Cork! If it ain't Ringgold, it's some kind of a murdering puffer. He's killing poor old Frank!"

Mike went down the warehouse stairs in two jumps. He appeared on the landing steps, going like a battering ram through the gang of cackling loafers who had watched Frank's progress across the Harbor without knowing in the least what was happening now.

Corkran stopped long enough to take another look through the glass. He saw two sailors holding the struggling woman by the arms and a cluster of six or seven others around something which lay prostrate on the *Turkey Feather's* deck. He couldn't locate Frank anywhere, so he judged it must be Frank. There was plenty of activity on deck, too. The ship, in a hell of a hurry, was making ready to sail.

He reflected a moment on what must have happened.

The woman, of course, had wanted to see Ringgold. She had gone out there and asked for him.

If 'tis Ringgold, it must've been a shock to him. Cork couldn't resist a grim, inward smile, at the thought of the look on the so-called Morrison's face. Lying within spitting distance of the British guns, sure as could be that not a soul in the world knew who he was, and here was this decent body in a hat and a bodice, come off aboard with her satchel, asking polite as you please for Captain Jake Ringgold.

Cork went down the stairs, following Mike. Being a practical man, more so than either of his cousins, he stopped long enough in the warehouse to send every available hand, including old Job, off through the town to round up the crew of the *West Wind.*

Dolly, left unhitched, lifted up her hanging nose and sniffed. She didn't like what she smelled, a nasty stink of hides, and so she turned the empty wagon around and lifted one shambling foot after the other on the road home.

Maybe there'll be a few of the boys who won't be drunk as coots, Corkran thought. But seeing the *West Wind* was loaded and ready to sail, he didn't doubt the crew would be having a few last drinks at the taverns nearby.

Even if they weren't, the *West Wind,* loaded to her marks with what the British, dog rot 'em, thought was barrel staves and heads, wouldn't be able to keep that thing, *Turkey Feather,* in sight an hour. And if they did overhaul her, what could be done? Ringgold's ship, the report was, carried cannon.

But when we catch him, we can give the bastard a scrap, he told himself. It'll give the boys time to sober up anyway.

Corkran, his mind full of plans, went down the landing steps after Mike.

Mike was standing there, waving his arms and yelling.

"God stiffen him, the murdering devil's running off with Frank, Cork! Look at that!"

Across the water the rigging of the *Turkey Feather* was swarming with men. A new suit of sails—Carnavon Brothers' best canvas—was beginning to bloom on her yards. The sails caught the afternoon light, gleaming bright as gulls' wings. Something splashed off the bow, and the vessel began at once to move with the brisk northwest wind.

"Slipped his cable," Cork said tersely. "It's Ringgold, Mike, or I'll eat my own foot. Raw."

Mike stopped yelling. The tears started to run down his face. "Ah, jasus, what'll we do? What'll he do to Frank? What *can* we do, Cork, for the love of God?"

"I've got the boys coming," Cork said. "Set on it, Mike, we'll take out as soon as there's enough hands here. Looks to me as if the Britisher's got his wind up about something. Here comes his gig ashore!"

Mike began again to jump up and down.

"Do something, ye fat gobbler!" he bawled at the gig. "Don't set there in the stern of that dinky, growing barnacles on your arse! That ship's Ringgold, the West Indies pirate, and he's running to hell off with me brother Frank!"

The gig wasn't near enough for the British officer to hear anything, though he heard plenty when he did come within earshot, and he didn't linger.

Late that afternoon three ships lined out before the northwest gale, the New England coast a purple mist fading out at sundown. The

76

Turkey Feather slid south like a black ghost, silent as a hawk on the wing. Behind her, under a terrific spread of canvas, her gun-ports stripped and ready, the guns manned by grim-faced marines, came the Britisher, closing up the distance fast. And far in the rear, heavy with her cargo, the *West Wind* wallowed like a sturdy tub, her muskets broken out, most of her crew with their heads in and out of buckets of salt water, and Mike Carnavon perched in her maintop, cursing the world and crying like a baby.

Jake Ringgold was, in the true sense of the word, one of those whom Lizabeth called a hoodlum. He was not the great pirate and freebooter of the Spanish Sea which he thought himself. He could not even navigate a vessel; Windle, his mate, sailed his ship for him. Ringgold was merely a bloody little thief and murderer, who, for six years, had had so much luck that he now considered himself immortal.

Luck had lifted him out of the forecastle, where he had been kicked around all his life and had changed him from ordinary seaman into Ringgold the Pirate. Without his luck and his own belief in it, he would have been a common, small man of no courage, with the ability to grow large glossy mustaches and a paranoid lust for killing. But never once during a career of piracy on the high seas had a plan of his gone wrong. Ships of the British Navy, sent out after him, arrived in the place where he had been to find him gone; they did not catch up with him. "Ringgold's Luck" was now a byword among the coast brotherhoods: men believed in him as he did in himself, that he was untouchable, that he could do anything. And having become a legend, he was more dangerous than if he had been a man of more than ordinary courage and ability.

His luck, which on this windy April evening was running out, had begun to turn without his knowing it, on the foggy night when two young sailors whom it had been his whim to abuse had jumped ship with his personal hoard of gold pieces. He had been in a terrible rage, merely; he did not at the time consider it a bad sign. Windle had gone after the sailors and had killed them. At least he said he had. He had not brought back the gold pieces, nor the ship's boat. One of the sailors, Windle said, had dropped the leather bags overboard as he was dying; the boat had been too holed with shot to be worth bringing back to the ship.

It had not occurred to Jake to doubt Windle, or to suspect what actually had happened—that the sailors had got away in the fog and Windle hadn't dared to tell him. His mind was too full of the fact that his gold was gone. He was, in fact, in such a taking over this that the whole ship's company walked softly and in fear of their lives, and Windle was no exception. There were others aboard who knew how to navigate, he was well aware; his prestige was nicked because he had not brought back the gold. And what was the strength of a mortal man against the supernatural powers of a legend?

Windle was over a barrel. It was foolhardy to put into Boston now, with two men ashore knowing who Morrison really was, knowing that the trading vessel, *Turkey Feather,* was that murderess, the *Nancy.* Ringgold had no necessity to come to Boston for stores and powder; the same could be got with less trouble in Tortuga, or for nothing from the first ship he happened to waylay and board. But he had taken a notion to add to his legend. It would be talked about for years to come: How Jake Ringgold had taken a load of molasses into Boston, had bought stores like a respectable ship's captain, and had come out again under the stupid guns of a British man-o'-war. That was the stuff to feed the troops. He spent a good deal of time relishing it inside the pin which did duty for his head, and he couldn't wait to get back to the Indies to see what people would say. Meantime, Jack Windle was caught like a fish in the net of his own lie because he couldn't, on any account, tell Ringgold why the ship must not put into Boston.

He had not only the ship's peril to think about, he had four sailors to shut the mouths of, the four who were in the pursuit boat with him and who knew as well as he did that Ed Ellis and Fig Frazer had got away. Two of them were cronies of his whom he felt he could trust. To silence the other two was simple. Windle was a great knocker of heads—that was *his* legend. In an hour or so after his return from the pursuit, he managed to lay out the two sailors stiff and stow them in the 'tween-decks. It was expert head-knocking. Long years of experience had taught him. Neither of the sailors would come to while the ship was in Boston Harbor, if ever. Once safely out of Boston, he felt he could handle any contingency.

The first day there, while the ship unloaded molasses, he lay in his cabin and shook and sweated, telling everyone he had a dose of fever. The second day, when nothing happened, he came on deck, feeling better. After all, Ellis and Frazer, with all that money, would have to lie low; they weren't going to tell around Boston, of all places, that they were two of Ringgold's men. He cursed himself for not having realized that at first. He felt better still when he found that the two sailors in the 'tween-decks had died during the night. On the third day, standing on deck, with the *Turkey Feather* loaded and ready to sail with the tide, Jack Windle was himself again.

Ringgold's Luck, he told himself, pacing up and down, sometimes varying the words with a thing he had never before permitted himself to say aloud, Windle's Luck.

Therefore, the crack of doom could have had no greater effect on him than Lizabeth's voice, breaking his pleasant reverie, asking politely for Captain Ringgold. He had been so preoccupied, he hadn't noticed the skiff come alongside. For a moment he stood frozen in his tracks. Then he heard Jake say, a sound somewhere between froth and sputter, "Get them aboard here, quick."

The woman came up the ladder neatly and quickly under her own power. The man, handing up the canvas satchel, was too slow, to Ringgold's way of thinking. He flapped his hands with a kind of bird-wing beat, and six sailors hauled up the ladder, man, satchel and all, and dumped them on the deck.

Frank Carnavon was a prudent man who thought fast in emergencies. He preferred to outthink adversaries when he could, because he was a man of peace and did not care for fights—at least, not with six sailors at once. Feeling their hold on him when they dumped him over the rail, he couldn't doubt their intentions; so he relaxed and fell forward, letting his head hit the deck with a hollow, punky thud. He lay with eyes seemingly closed as if he had been knocked out. Peering through his heavy lashes at the faces around him, he thought, "Acushla machree, I don't like the look of this."

He heard Lizabeth say indignantly, "You great clumsy lunks, you've hurt him," and then in a voice of anger and shock, "Get away from me, you dirty scut!"

And then she choked off with a glubbing sound as if a hand had been clapped over her mouth.

He saw Morrison a few feet away and heard him say, "It's Carnavon.

Hustle them both below out of sight. Jack, get canvas on her and out of here fast. Slip the cable—"

And then Frank was yanked and pushed and rolled down a companionway, kicked in the stern when he stuck there. By the time he was dumped down wherever it was they dropped him, he was bumped and bruised; a thin trickle of blood was running down his cheek from a cut alongside his eye.

Begod, he said to himself, somebody'll sweat for this! But, jasus, it may be me.

He kept himself limp and his eyes closed, except for the imperceptible slit through his lashes. He could see Morrison sitting on a table—the captain's cabin, this looked like—and Lizabeth standing back-to in front of him. Her back looked as stiff as a board. You could tell, just from the sight of it, how mad she was.

Good for the little whippet! Frank thought. She should be scared out of her life, and begod, she ain't, she's mad.

Lizabeth gave herself a shake, settling her rumpled clothes. She said, "You nasty little polecat, where's Captain Ringgold?"

Morrison said, "I'm Captain Ringgold."

You could see the bastard lap his chops, waiting for her to wilt down and be scared to death at the tidings.

"Then I'll finish my business with you," she said icily. "And you'll be good enough to set me ashore with Mr. Carnavon. If you and your gang of hoodlums haven't killed him."

It hauled Ringgold up a little. He didn't care for it, not one bit, that she hadn't gone right down on her knees at the sound of his name.

"We ain't killed him—yet," he said.

He waited on that, too, to see how she was going to take it.

"It's not your fault if you haven't," she said. "And I promise you, you'll hear from your actions, if it's the last thing I do."

"Just what do you think you can do to Jake Ringgold?"

"I can swear out a complaint before the law. And I will."

That tickled him. He put back his head and laughed.

Lizabeth said, "I don't know who you are, mister, to think you can laugh at the law. It's caught up with bigger men than you are."

"You don't know who I am, huh?"

Enjoying himself, cat and mouse.

"Look here, mister, it's like my gra'mother said once, when someone told her not to be scared of the butter, she said she wouldn't be scared of it if there was twice as much. I don't know you from a hole in the ground and I don't want to. My boy Ed came home with some property of yours, that's all. I don't doubt it would've been justice to let him keep some of it, seeing he was half-dead from the way you treated him. But it wasn't his, so I've brought it back. It's in my hold-all, wherever that is. I'll thank you to take it out, so I can have my hold-all back, and then set me and Mr. Carnavon ashore."

Ringgold's face, above the big, glossy mustaches, burned red as a beet.

He sputtered. "You'll find out who I am."

Lizabeth snorted. She said, "I'll wait till I do. But I'd hate to see anyone have to hang by the neck until I'm scared of you."

Frank caught back a howl of laughter just in time, for Ringgold turned a greenish color, the look on his face enough to kill a man.

Lizabeth didn't even notice. She was looking around for her hold-all, and seeing it held by two sailors behind her, she stepped back and gave one of them a smart push. "Put it up there on the table, let the little blowhard see his money."

Ringgold froze. "Money? What money?"

"The money my boy Ed brought home. Belongs to you, doesn't it?"

"Ed? Who's Ed?"

"Ed Ellis, my boy. He was on your vessel."

The little man darted away from his table. He yanked and fumbled at the satchel, and the sailors holding it lugged it over to the table, open-mouthed. Then they got back away from Ringgold, as if the touch of him were hot.

He hauled out a knife and began slashing at the hold-all.

"Don't you dare to cut my husband's satchel!" Lizabeth said.

She reached across the table and took the knife out of his hand.

The sailors grabbed her and twisted the knife away. She let one of them have a prod in the stomach with her elbow.

"Here," she said. "Stop that."

She shook off the other sailor, leaned over and unbuckled the straps.

"It opens by unlatching. If you were a decent man, ever saw such a civilized thing as a hold-all, you'd know it. There. There's your money. Now I'll thank you to set me and Mr. Carnavon ashore!"

There'll be no setting of us ashore now, begod, Frank thought.

81

He could feel the motion of the vessel; under his cheek pressed to the floor of the cabin, he could hear the rush of water past her keel.

Ringgold looked at the four canvas bags. He took the knife from the sailor who held it, slit the thong that bound one of the bags shut, scrabbled around in it with his hand. A look of deep satisfaction came over his face. From his small hand, full of gold, the pieces cascaded richly back into the bag.

Begod, 'twas gold she had in that ruddy bag! Frank Carnavon thought.

In his amazement he almost opened his eyes, but managed not to, just in time.

He'd thought it was rocks or old iron from the weight of it and had even considered the idea that the woman might be a little crazy, though he'd doubted that. But now the pieces of the puzzle fell into place, and in spite of his plight, Frank felt his stomach heave and roil with the held-in laughter.

Why, the sweetheart, he thought. Crammed and jammed with gold to bring back to a pirate because it didn't belong to her! Pray God I live to laugh at this in me own good time and in peace.

He doubted if he would, but if, in ten minutes or so, he and she were both dead and fed to the fish, 'twas worth having lived to see a woman, muddled though she was, as honest as an angel.

Ringgold closed the money bag. His eyes slitted and began to gleam with rage. "Jack Windle said this was lost. Jonas, go git me one of the boys went after Ed Ellis in the boat that night."

The sailor named Jonas said, "Them boys is dead, Cap. The two that wasn't Windle's boys is in the 'tween-decks now, waitin' till we git outside far enough to bury 'em."

Ringgold said softly, "So that's how it is. The bugger lied to me. Ellis and Frazer got away. *Didn't they?*"

The shout was a sound halfway between a screech and a squall, and the young sailor began to stutter with terror.

"I d-don't know, Cap. I g-guest they must of."

"Lied to *me*, by God!"

He strode up and down the cabin, stumbling once over Frank's feet, which he kicked at solidly, and Frank thought, There's one I won't forget, friend.

Suddenly Ringgold grinned at the sailors, his lips stretched over his teeth like a dog's when the dog is about to bite something he considers unpleasant.

"Go git me Windle," he said. "Jump him and them two boys of his and bring 'em down here. It ain't their fault the whole kaboodle of us ain't hung by the neck in Boston this minute."

The sailors looked at each other as if they couldn't believe their ears and then, as it dawned on them that Ringgold meant what he said, with unholy joy. Not one of them but carried somewhere on him the marks of Windle.

Ringgold strutted and stuck out his chest. You could see he liked to have people think well of him.

"Tell him while you're seizing him up that Ringgold's Luck kept him from being hung," he said. "But it's Windle's luck that's going to cut out his guts and feed them to the sharks while he looks on. Go on, git him down here!"

The sailors departed through the cabin door on the run.

Humming a little, Ringgold picked up the bags of money, hefting each one. He seemed to notice no difference between three of them and the one stuffed with Pa Ellis' old bolts and screws. He turned around, opened a big locker behind him, stowed the bags in the locker.

When he turned the first time, Frank started to gather himself together, waiting for the right minute. Ringgold was a small man, but he had pistols in his belt, and he needed to be back-to a trifle longer than he was, for a man the size of Frank to get across the cabin.

Ringgold closed the locker door, still humming. Then something seemed to occur to him. He whirled around staring at Lizabeth. "Why'd you bring it back? A trap? A trick? You didn't have to."

She was white in the face, so white that her eyes looked black. She said, biting off the words, "The Ellises don't use what doesn't belong to them."

That did it. At the stupefied look on Ringgold's face, Frank Carnavon burst into a great bawl of laughter.

Ringgold spun around, fumbling for the pistols in his belt, but Frank made his dive before he could yank one free. No one looking at Frank Carnavon could know he was fast when there was need to be.

He got hold of Ringgold by the ankles, feeling the small bones like bird's legs under his hands. He grunted, "Stand away, ma'am. This is going to do all three of us good."

The back of Ringgold's head hit the deck. Frank let go the ankles. He got one hand on the little man's belt and the other in the fine, ruffled front of his shirt, lifted him and whacked him down as if he were whacking the table top with a paddle. Ringgold's arms flew up, his legs pedaled; he twitched once or twice and lay still.

Frank hauled the pistols out of his belt, shoved them into his own waistband. He said, "Open that locker door, if you please, ma'am. I'm sorry for you to have to see such a sight."

He stuffed Ringgold into the locker, locked the door and thrust the key into his pocket. "They'll be a while finding the divvel, unless he comes to and hollers, which I doubt. Them boys'll think twice before forcing the captain's locker."

He made sure the pistols were loaded and primed and looked around for more arms, but there weren't any, except Ringgold's knife.

"You take the knife, ma'am," he said, opening the cabin door quietly and standing back of it to listen. Up on deck an unholy battle was going on. Windle, he thought.

Lizabeth said, "I'm sure I don't want the nasty thing."

"Take it. You may need it."

He cocked an ear, listening to the thwackings and thumpings on the deck above, then turned and grinned at her.

"Take it anyway, ma'am. It'll make a nice keepsake."

He advanced his head slowly around the door, and seeing no one, beckoned to her. "Come on. Them sailors'll be back. Come on," he whispered urgently, when she did not move. "Have you grown to the deck, then?"

He saw she was white as a sheet, trying to force herself to pick up the knife.

"Hell's bells," he said, grinning at her, unaware that his own face was a terrible sight, blood-streaked and sweating. "'Tis the brave lass enough you've been. Leave it there. I've got the pistols."

She picked it up then, and came over to him.

"Well, go on," she said, seeing him hesitate outside the cabin door. "Wherever it is you think you're going."

"Begod, I don't know," he said. "But keep behind me back. Through me is a long way for a bullet."

They went cautiously up the companionway, the same one down which Frank had tumbled a little while before. It took him a minute

84

to get up enough courage to stick his head out of the hatch and take a look along the deck.

The fight was going on forward of the mainmast. It looked like a good one—as if the whole ship's company were in on it, too busy to notice anything else. Frank fervently hoped so.

The ship was bowling along under full canvas before the wind. God alone knew where they'd got to by this time. There must be a man at the wheel, unless they'd lashed it. He doubted if they'd done that in this gale.

He pulled himself up out of the hatchway, turned around to help the woman, but she was right behind him. He led the way, bent over and running on his tiptoes along the deck, ducked behind the after house. At least they were out of sight of the fight now. No one could see them here.

He thought, Well, what next? Begod, I wisht I was out of this.

He glanced along the deck. On the section of it that he could see, the sounds of the fight seemed to be dying down. No doubt by now they had Windle. In a minute they'd be trooping below with him. No telling how many would stay on deck. And then the ones who went wouldn't stay long, when they found Ringgold missing, himself and the woman not there. There'd be a witch hunt up and down the ship, and God help all.

Lizabeth gave him a little poke with one finger in the small of his back. "There's the ladder we came aboard by, Mr. Carnavon."

Frank spun around. The rope ladder was still hanging on the rail, part of it in a mess on the deck, where none of those swabs had taken time to stow it neatly away.

God's mercy, he thought, would they have taken time, either, to cut me skiff loose?

He had better go and see.

But at the thought of moving out of the shelter of the house, he felt a shrinking, jelly-like sensation the whole length of his back, as if, all by itself, it expected at any moment to feel a knife or a bullet into it.

Lizabeth poked him again and he all but leaped into the air, before he realized. She was saying, "That man at the wheel, he sees us."

The man at the wheel, above and a little aft of them, had plenty to do. He couldn't leave his post with the ship cracking along the way she was, but he could holler. As Frank stared up at him he put his head back, his mouth wide open, and yelled for somebody to come.

Frank pointed the pistol at him. He yelled, "Shut up your noise, you scut of God, or I'll blow it back into the craw of ye."

The man didn't hear, or if he did, he didn't scare. He went on hollering at the top of his lungs.

Frank thought, If I shoot him, the ship'll broach to, likely take the masts out of her, dump us all in the drink, maybe a good thing, too.

But he couldn't shoot. His sweating finger wouldn't tighten on the trigger. He was a good shot with a pistol, firing at a target. He had never fired at a man.

He thought, It's a scandal to the jaybirds to find out that rather than shoot a defenseless man, I'd take a chance on being shot at me-self. Sure, I didn't know that before, the milksop I am.

He lowered the pistol, ducked down, got himself over to the rail. The skiff was down there, towing back on her stern, all but bouncing clear of the water, but she was there. He could see no reason why she wasn't towing bottom up—no doubt keeping that for us, when the weight of us goes into her, he thought.

He shoved the pistol into his belt. The rope ladder, clawed all any-how over the rail, was in a tangled mess, but he scooped it up and tossed it down. The tangle didn't reach all the way to the skiff, but it was a ladder.

He said, "Tch," looking at it, and then, "Come on, ma'am. Climb down there quick," aware that the cold jelly of his back and buttocks was shaking worse than ever, that the two pistols shoved into his waist-band had tightened it beyond the power of man's flesh to endure.

Lizabeth stood frozen at the rail, looking down at the whipping ladder, the little skiff yawing wildly at the end of the fiddlestring-taut painter. She said, "I can't. You'll have to go first," and closed her eyes.

"Oh, jasus," Frank said prayerfully. "Don't let her give out on me now." He put an arm around her rigid shoulders. " 'Tis a lion you've been already, to be scared at a bit of a ship's ladder," he said. "Go, then, or they'll be on us like tigers."

But she only stood stiff as a stick, Ringgold's knife point upright in her fist as if she were carrying a lighted candle.

Frank pried the knife out of her clenched fingers and stuck that in his waistband along with the pistols, but he felt his wind going and hauled it out again.

86

It won't do, climbing down there, it will gut me like a codfish. But I will need it quickly to cut the skiff free.

The way the skiff was towing, any weight in her might fling her bottom-up at once. Whoever went down first would have to move quickly and skillfully, cut the painter, balance the wildly bouncing little craft. The woman was lighter, but there she stood in some kind of a trance. And if he went without her, there'd be no time to wait for her to come down the ladder, because God knew what Frank Carnavon's weight would do.

"Go, lass, lie flat in the boat, for when I come, it will be a chimney falling."

He heard a chorus of yells, the pounding of feet on the deck behind them.

"Go, then," he shouted.

And when she still did not move, he thrust the knife between his teeth, picked her up and dropped her over the rail. He heard her cry out once and the splash when she hit the water, missing the skiff entirely. Then he went over the rail himself and down the ladder. He thought, God help all!

He felt the skiff lurch as he dropped and start to capsize, but he knew of old the trim of his little boat. He flung himself from side to side, balancing his weight against hers, waited a split-second until she yawed away from the *Turkey Feather's* humming black-tarred planks, and slashed the painter.

The skiff slatted sideways, her bow careening wildly, beginning to go under as she lost way.

He thought, It's all over now with Frank Carnavon, but he hurled himself back into the stern, just in case. For a moment he clung to the rudder post, waiting to swamp. The skiff, half-full of water, plunged logily, shipping more water, but she floated.

The *Turkey Feather's* sails were a bright pile of snow against the dark sky, going away.

Begod, I'm living. But God help the poor woman.

He reared up and stared anxiously at the crested water, he couldn't see her anywhere. There was little he could do anyway, until he got the water out of the boat.

Working like a madman, he rooted his water keg out of the locker —praise God, 'twas only half-full and would float—and slung it securely to the end of his long anchor rode. He dropped it overboard for a sea anchor, let it trail out behind. Then he broke out his bailing scoop, bailing furiously, throwing a great cloud of water down the wind. The skiff shipped some as he bailed. He found he could keep ahead of it, and she shipped less as she lightened.

He thought mournfully, A good, sweet woman, honest as the day. A ball of needles to live with, drive a man out of his mind, it could be; but look at the way she moved earth and hell to take the bloody little murderer's money back to him—a queer thing, surely, but who in this world of selfishness has honesty that shines like the sun in spring?

Dear God, what could I have done, but what I did? I could not leave her to be rent into tatters by them fiends.

He had thought he might cut loose the skiff at once and pick her up, as God knew, she never could have picked him up, had he been the one to go in the ocean. For how could a man of his size have climbed up out of the water into that dancing little banshee of a skiff, say she did not upset it, and it with its gunnels awash in a gale of wind? Francis Carnavon, with no time to think at all, had done the best he could with what he had at hand. But the fact that he was living and she was gone was a worrying thing, surely, and conscience put up its ugly head.

God forgive me, if I have drowned such a woman! She was a decent, brave body, and God rest her soul.

And then, looking astern, he saw her, head out of water, lifting on the crest of a wave. She was keeping afloat by a kind of choppy little dog paddle, trying to swim downwind to the skiff.

A great burst of relief and joy went through him. Even in his hurry to get to her, he was amazed at his own feelings, seeing her alive.

"Keep going, me darling," he bawled, as he got out the oars, pulling furiously against the wind and the dead weight of his sea anchor. "Don't wear yourself out entirely. Paddle to keep afloat, and let the wind blow you to me!"

He couldn't pull ahead much against the wind, but he could stop the drift of the skiff away from her.

She came feebly and desperately, her bonnet still on, tied as neatly by its strings under her chin as if she were sitting in her parlor.

"Begod," Frank said earnestly, as her hands clutched the gunnel. "I couldn't think of anyone, met here, that I'd be gladder to see. Don't try climbing over the side, you'll have us over. Let yourself along to

88

the stern, easy-like, if you can. I'll make out, somehow, to haul you in."

He couldn't have told afterward how he got her in over the stern, for her hands were slipping and she was done. She lay in the bottom of the boat with her eyes closed, not moving. He saw by the blue look of her face and hands that something would have to be done for her, or she would die of the cold and soaking.

"God forgive me, ma'am," he told her unhearing ears. "But what has to be done must be done quickly."

Francis Carnavon took off all her clothes and wrung the sea water out of them with his powerful hands. Then he put them all back on her again, with the exception of her stays, which he could not manage. The sight of them, shrunken stiff, stained with sea water, gave him a cold grue. He flung them overboard, where they rose to the top of a tall, curling comber, flapped once as if they had wings like a hen and vanished.

Good riddance to them, he thought distastefully. What prison bars for sweet and lovely flesh to wear!

He unrolled his sail from the mast, unstepped and slung along the thwarts and wrapped her snugly in the canvas. It was damp enough, but it would keep out the cold wind. That was the best he could do. He might have pulled her about some, rubbed her limbs to start the blood moving, but he was at the end of his own strength, sweating even while his teeth rattled with the chill, and that was bad.

He took off his own clothes and wrung them out, and then drier and perhaps a little warmer in their dampness, crept in himself, beside her, under the sail.

Faith, I hope she's unconscious, he told himself uneasily. For if she is not, she will never look me in the face again, and that would be a pity. She would know, too, that I am not the clumsy great lunk she thought me, that I have had some experience in these matters. But never, he silently assured the mound of canvas beside him, never under such circumstances of necessity.

The skiff rode the water like a duck, God bless Maynard Cantril, and the wind increased. In a little while he would have to add the mast and spreet, possibly a set of oars to the sea anchor. But meanwhile, he must rest.

The mound beside him stirred. Lizabeth said in a stupefied voice,

89

"My stays are gone," raising up and looking around in a daze, not even seeing him.

Frank stuck up his head like a turtle.

"Ma'am," he said, "they are gone indeed. If a large fish ate them off while you were in the sea, 'twas only with the respect and reverence due, and only with the aid of God it was, that I myself kept you from the ravening maw of him. 'Tis our lives we have escaped with, at least so far. I'm thinking a pair of stays is a small price to pay."

Far away to the west his eye caught the white prick of sails against the twilight, and he let out a roar of joy.

" 'Tis all the good saints on our side, me darling," he shouted. "For here comes the British ship, and she'll pick us out of here in an hour's time."

But it was not the British ship which picked them out of the increasingly angry waters. The man-o'-war swept grimly by, running like a hound, so close they could hear the shrill cry of wind in her cordage, see the open ports with the ugly, naked mouths of her guns. For all Frank's shouting and waving, she did not pause a second's time. The sight and sounds of her thundered away, diminishing down the horizon to the east, roiled and tumbled with the clouds of coming storm.

To give the British commander due credit, he knew that the *West Wind* was not so far behind him that she would no doubt see and rescue the castaways before dark; otherwise he would have stopped and rescued them himself, for Lieutenant Niles was a more humane man than his unpleasant job often permitted him to be. But Frank was an Irishman; besides he did not know about the *West Wind*.

Silently he fixed the additional weight to the sea anchor, crawled, grim-faced, back underneath the canvas.

"A nasty sight, that," he said. "Men more for killing other men than for saving helpless castaways. God stiffen all such! 'Tis true the British are all for duty, and it's Ringgold the Pirate they're after. But if they turn up in Boston to say they have not blown him and his ship to hell, I will slowly wring their red necks, one by one. Though small good that will do us now, whether or no."

The *West Wind*, wallowing along on the edge of dark, spotted them and picked them up, half-frozen. Then she went about for the long night's tacking back to Boston.

It was nearly a week before the man-o'-war returned carrying the battered remnants of Ringgold's crew, Jake Ringgold himself recovering from a broken head, and the news that the *Turkey Feather*, with Windle and all else, was at the bottom of the ocean.

Well, Nate thought. Now I'm going.

For half an hour he had stood in the sheltered spot on the east side of the house, where the jut of the L broke the cold northwest wind. It was warm there in the sun and quiet, but the fury inside him did not go away. Instead, it seemed to chill and harden like a rock. Ed had meant to kill him; with a little more strength in his arm, a little better aim, he would have. In spite of the sunshine, Nate had to set his jaw to keep his teeth from chattering; he could not get warm.

Times past he and Ed had squabbled plenty and he had got mad; not like this. He had never felt anything like this ice-cold anger, coiled up in a knot and settled down to stay. And yet in spite of it, perhaps because of it, he felt curiously free.

This business, whatever it was, this trouble, it wasn't his doing. It was Ed's doing; let him straighten it out. Ma and Ed, neither of them believes I'm good for much. Maybe I'm not. But from now on I'm going to have business of my own. It's time to start thinking and planning for it.

He strode around the corner of the house and into the kitchen. Caroline was doing something at the hearth; there was a fine smell of cooking.

"I'm going on a trip," Nate said gruffly. "I want a bag of stuff to eat."

Caroline dropped her spoon. She whirled around from the kettle she was stirring. "Oh, Nate, no! Where you going?"

Ordinarily there would have been a friendly bicker which would have ended in her putting down whatever she was doing and coming to help him, but now Nate strode silently past her into the larder. He found he was still too stirred up to talk without being mean; he didn't know as he wanted to leave Caroline thinking of him as ugly as he felt right now.

The canvas meal sack was about a quarter full he saw, peering into it, and he took that. In on top of the meal he dropped three loaves from Lizabeth's last baking of bread, a ham she had hanging from the rafters.

What else?

He could live on fish and game once he got started. For that he'd need salt, but the salt was in a bin. He began looking around for a bag or a pouch to carry some in, found a small sack of beans which he emptied in on top of the collection in his meal bag. He was aware that Caroline was watching him, open-mouthed, from the door, but he did not look at her. He filled the bean sack with salt, tied the mouth of it securely with string.

His eye, roving around the storeroom shelves, fell on a package carefully labeled *Seeds*. Ma was a great seed saver, there'd be a little of everything tied up in there. He picked the package off the shelf, dropped it into his bag.

Caroline said, "*Seeds*, Nate?"

Suddenly her thin, pointed little face began to twist up.

"Seeds? Oh, no, Nate! You can't go away and stay."

Oh, Lord, if she was going to cry that was the last straw! The one thing that could shake his resolution was for Caroline to cry.

Only she doesn't know it, he thought. I better get out of here, too, before she does.

She said shakily, "Oh, not to stay, Nate! Not now. Not with every-thing so— No, you can't!"

He said, "Maybe you think I can't," and shouldered the knobbly, bulging sack. He went past her and out to his room, setting down the sack beside the door.

A change of clothes. His heavy winter jacket. His gun and the things that went with it—ramrod, powder flask, flints.

Standing there in the corner beside his old gun was the fine new one Ed had brought home for him.

Damn him, I won't take anything to remind me of him.

But in spite of himself his hands went out to the gun. His own gun was old; where he was going above all else he'd need a good gun.

It wasn't the gun's fault. Why cut off your nose to spite your face? He took the gun.

Picking up his load, he went out of the kitchen and along past the wagon shed to Pa's old workshop.

Here, at least, he knew where everything was. The good tools with their polished handles, the blades sharp, burnished.

92

The ax. The saw. The adz. The crowbar. The jackplane. The auger. The hammer.

What else?

Nails.

He looked with dismay at the size of the load he'd never be able to carry. But what earthly good were a lot of tools to build with and no nails? He added a keg of assorted nails and spikes to the pile.

All right, he'd take the hand wagon. No doubt Ed would put that down as a theft, seeing he owned everything here now, except the tools. Unless the wagon itself were a tool—oh, hell, what a mess you could get into, just *thinking* about a thing like dividing up somebody's property. How could you ever consider any of this stuff as anybody's but Pa's?

Somebody could haul the damn wagon home from the shore after he was through with it. If Ed wanted to call him a thief, he could, with justice, too, and not for just borrowing a wagon. Nate knew suddenly what he must have had in the back of his mind all the time. That boat hidden up the swamp, after all, was salvage. Ed had stolen it, left it on the shore for anyone to find. Piper had found it; Nate had found it. Whose was it? Loose on the shore, not even tied?

Whosoever it is I'm going away in it, he thought. Thief or no thief.

He got the small, two-wheeled wagon from the shed and backed it up to the shop door. He could ask Piper to haul it home from the cove someday when he had time. Turn about's fair play.

Nate was finishing the lashings on his load when Caroline came down from the house. She was carrying a big, unwieldy bundle wrapped in a big tarpaulin of heavy, oiled canvas. At least the lower half of her was Caroline, that was all he could see below the bundle.

"What d'you think you've got there?" he hailed her ungraciously. Be mean to her, get her mad. Then maybe she wouldn't cry again.

"Blankets," she said. Her eyes were red, but she was quite composed otherwise. "You forgot 'em."

She dropped the bundle beside the wagon.

He said, "Thanks," sheepishly, for he'd forgotten all about blankets.

She stood by watching, while he added the bundle to his toppling load.

"Well," he said. "I guess that's all. Good-by, Caroline."

"Oh, Nate. Where you going?"

93

He said, "I don't know," realizing bleakly that he didn't. "Somewhere north, I guess. I won't know till I see the place."

"Will you send me back word?"

It was thinking too far ahead. He couldn't see that far. He couldn't see much beyond the wagon, the road to Cowrie Cove and the boat hidden under a mess of withered cattails up the swamp. Leaving home was a bleak business after all. It wasn't too late to stay. For a moment, looking at her, he wavered.

"No!" she burst out. "You mustn't stay! It's time for you to go. Between them they'll scrabble you to pieces, Nate!"

He stared at her, open-mouthed. He might have known she'd have that much sense, he told himself.

Two tears formed in the corners of her eyes and ran down her cheeks. "Nate, your mother's good. I don't know where I'd be if she hadn't taken me in. I'll be grateful to her till I—and I ought to be. But being grateful—she's so busy, she doesn't stop to think how people *feel*. Oh, Nate, take me with you! Please take me with you."

Lord, this was a complication he hadn't looked for!

"Don't be crazy," he said shortly. "I can't. You know I can't. Look, it's hard enough without you."

She put up her hand as if she suddenly realized about the tears and dashed them quickly away.

"I know," she said in her normal voice, a little sharp, clear, as if she were biting off the words. "I'm sorry. I'll walk along with you a ways, help pull the wagon."

"No need to. It's all downhill."

"You're going to the shore, then. You've got a boat, haven't you?"

"Oh, shut up," he said angrily.

If only—if *only* she'd go into the house and let him be gone, not stand there with the wet patches on her forlorn cheeks making him feel like a brute. "Go in the house," he said. "It's none of your business."

"Why, it is, too!" she said, outraged.

"Now go and tell everyone I went away in a boat!"

"I don't know why you think I would."

He picked up the wagon tongue, started out of the yard. The wheels started a sing-song creaking against the axle. It had been all winter since the wagon had been used.

I meant to grease it when I put it away. Pa told me to.

94

Caroline followed along beside the wagon. She hadn't any wrap. Her hands were blue with cold.

Nate stopped.

"Caroline!" he said wrathfully. "Go back. You'll get your death of cold."

"You haven't got half the things you need for a long trip," she said, sniffling. "Hens grease and molasses—"

"Hens grease and molasses, for Godsake!" he exploded. "Go on in the house and take some yourself. You've got a snotty nose right now! Go on, Caroline! Git! Or I'll give you a licking, I swear I will!"

She began to cry in earnest, a kind of mournful, little-girl howling, which only increased his rage. He dropped the wagon tongue and made a grab for her.

Caroline turned and ran. She shouted back between sobs, "Little boy going camping! Look at all that mess!"

The kitchen door slammed behind her.

Nate thought, Thank the Lord.

All the same, he had never felt so mean and low in his life. That wasn't any way to say good-by when you were going away to be gone a long time, maybe never coming back. And he and Caroline had always been close. He stopped, thinking maybe he'd go back, say good-by decent. But no. It was over. Let it alone. No knowing what might hold him up if he went back there now.

He went on down the hill, followed by the squawking of the wagon, past the squat lines of hardhack beside the road, the alders rattling in the wind.

Good sailing wind, he thought. Northwest. But if it gets worse, as it probably will, I'll have to hole up somewhere till she blows herself out.

He passed Ev Piper's place, the curtainless windows making it look bleak and deserted the way it always did, except for Jenny's peaked brown face peering out past the forest of plants she kept on the window sill.

Piper came round the corner of the shed, his pipe in his mouth, letting off clouds of smoke. He stood, his hands on his hips, looking at Nate for a moment. Then he said, "You're going off in that boat, ain't you?"

"Yes, I am," Nate said, giving him back the stare. "It got anything to do with you?"

"No. Can't say's it has."

"All right, then. I could ask you and Jenny to keep your mouths shut about it, but I don't s'pose it'd do any good."

"Yaas," Piper said. "It'd do some good. We won't say nothing, Jenny and me."

Whatever hostility Piper had felt three—was it three?—days ago was gone. The look in his eyes was friendly, a little humorous, the way it had always been. The way it had used to be with Pa.

"Thanks, then," Nate said. "I'd appreciate it, Piper."

"I never meant nothing that other morning," Piper said. "I was all tore out over what went on down there to the Flowage, that was all. Besides," he grinned, "I kind of had a notion of gitting that boat for me and Jenny. Looked like 'twas left there adrift. Warn't tied, nor nothing. Next tide would've took it out."

"Piper, what did you see down there? What happened?"

Ev puffed on his pipe. "I d'no, Nate. Warn't good."

"No," Nate said. "I guess it wasn't."

Their eyes met for a moment, then both of them looked away.

"You look like your pa," Piper said. "The spitt'n image. I liked Joel Ellis."

Nate said miserably, "So did I."

"Yaas," Piper said. "Well, you go and keep a-going, Nate. I don't know nobody better able to handle things than your ma, if 't turns out there's a thing to handle. Jenny and me, we won't say nothing. I don't doubt everything'll blow over. But you go, make your own place where you find a likely one. Your own pa couldn't give you no better advice."

He stuck out a bony hand. Nate shook it.

"Good-by, Piper."

"G'by," Piper said. "You got wind and tide. You can make knots before dark. Watch the wind in the channel though. It's going to blow hard, bime-by."

At least, he thought, grunting up the slope, sweating with the weight of the heavy wagon, after he'd fought with everyone, Ed and Ma and Caroline, he was leaving one friend behind him. Two, because whoever Piper liked Jenny did, too. It was pleasant to feel that someone, even if it were only Ev Piper, was backing him up, thought he was doing the right thing. For half that ailed him, that made him feel so ugly and mean, was the continual nagging thought that it was

96

a tough thing to do, to leave Ma alone now with only the girls to help her and Ed turning out to be—whatever it was Ed had turned out to be.

A murderer, if you wanted to come right out and say what you couldn't help believing.

He almost turned around right there and went home, but at the thought of hauling the heavy wagon up the steep hill from Piper's, his will failed him.

Maybe that's all it takes, he thought, with a wry face. The thing that sets Nathan Ellis out on his travels is he's too damned lazy to haul a wagon up a hill!

The tide had been up over the marks on the bank of the Flowage. The lonely place was as deserted as it had always been, the water bright with sun, rippled by the wind. There was no record at all of what had happened there, except now in the minds of a few people.

He left the wagon on the bank and started at once into the swamp. The water was higher than it had been three days ago. All the rainwater, collected in the lowlands, had gathered now, the muddy, sluggish courses above the tussocks roiling down to pour out through the brook-mouth into the salt water.

It'll make bringing the boat out easier, he thought, panting and struggling through the mud and reeds. And the northwest wind would be fair. He ought to come down in jig-time. Say he didn't freeze to death before he could get into dry clothes. It was a good thing he had a change of clothes along.

He found the boat exactly as he had left her, except the cattail screen had blown or floated away so that her stern showed plain for any passer-by to see.

He scrambled aboard the boat. She had caught some rainwater. Or maybe she leaked some, water was up over the floor boards. No, it was rainwater, there wasn't any mud seepage in her. The water had washed away the smell for'rad under the canvas.

But, he told himself through rattling teeth, the first thing I do, I'll scrub and paint her up there and get a wooden deck put over, take the place of that canvas.

The canvas spray-hood was rotten anyway, no good for a long trip.

He found the boat's bailer, scooped out enough water to lighten her. The rest of it could act as ballast. Have to see about ballast, he thought, say she doesn't trim just right.

The bailing had warmed him up a little, but when he fished the mast and sail up out of the water he had to cut the sail lashings, for the knots were swollen tight and his fingers too numb to untie them.

He stepped the mast. The dripping sail unrolled with a jerk, slatting in the wind, showering him with water. The canvas was soaked to a uniform mud-tan. You could see faintly where the bloodstain had been —maybe it would show up more, maybe it wouldn't, when the canvas was dry. But another first thing, he'd get a new sail.

He shoved and paddled a little with an oar until the boat swung around and the wind caught the sail. He grabbed for the sheet, hauled it taut, felt her begin to move and heel. Her bow in the water started to make a little, puddling song.

He thought, If only I wasn't so cold.

The wind blew right through his wet clothes; his feet were lumps of lead. He had even stopped chattering now, felt as if his whole body had turned numb.

With the northwest wind behind him he was only ten minutes or so coming out of the swamp. A couple of times he had to slack off the sheet and let the boat lose way; she was tearing along so fast that he couldn't round the winding turns in the waterways. As he came around the last of them into the pool at the mouth of the brook, his heart jumped into his mouth. Two people, a man and a woman, were standing on the bank of the Flowage. They had built a big bonfire out of driftwood, and they were standing close to it back-to him. If he could have stopped he would have, and he cursed himself for not having glanced that way before he came around the last turn of the brook, because he would have seen the smoke.

But what have I got to be scared of? The worst anyone can do is hold me up for a little while.

And his whole, icy, shivering body yearned toward that fire.

The man turned around and lifted a hand to him, and Nate saw that it was Piper. The woman was Caroline. She had on her heavy coat and mittens, the wool thingamajig she'd knitted last winter, a kind of bonnet, tied around her head.

Piper came down and fended the bow of the boat, hauled it up on the bank for him to land.

"Git over by the fire," he said. "She took the dry duds out of your sack, she's got 'em out warming there for you."

Nate was so cold he forgot to be mad with Caroline for chasing him down here.

He said to her, "Turn around back-to," but his chin was jerking now with chill so the words made only a glubbering sound.

She turned around though, without saying anything, and Nate stripped off his wet, stinking, muddy clothes, feeling against his skin the beautiful, the glorious, the heartbreaking warmth of the fire. He put on his dry outfit, so hot that the wool and the wooden buttons smelled of scorching. They even had a bucket of hot drink on the coals at the edge of the fire; Nate reached for it and got a big swig down before he realized what it was.

"Jeezus!" he said, spitting and sputtering. "Catnip tea! What a trick to play on a man, Piper!"

Caroline turned around. "Don't blame Piper," she said primly. "It was me. Catnip tea's for a feverish cold. You drink every bit of that."

"Bthah!" he gagged.

But the hot, bitter-herby drink went down into his stomach, spreading and melting his lining of ice, and presently he took another big swallow.

"Well," he owned up, "I guess I needed it at that. And, by golly, whoever thought of that fire I'd like to thank!"

"*She* did," Piper said, jerking his head at Caroline. "She come by my house with a whole mess of junk, made me come along with her, help carry it. When she saw you'd gone up the swamp afoot, she made me build the fire. Looks to me like you was going to have company on your trip, Nate."

He stopped, giggled a little, glancing from one to the other of them. "Ain't a bad idea."

Nate said, stupefied, "Don't be a damn fool, Piper."

But he saw now the pile of things he hadn't noticed before. Pots, pans. Stuff from the kitchen. A spider. The mortar and pestle. Some little boxes with lids. A canvas carrying-bag stuffed with clothes. Women's things.

"Caroline," he spluttered. "You pick up that trash and hyper for home!"

"No," Caroline said. "I won't."

Her eyes were still red, but she had stopped crying. Her chin was set, square and stubborn, which was quite a trick for a chin as pointed as hers was. He knew that look of old, it meant a fight.

"If I don't go with you, I won't go back there."

"Dammit, you will too! It's likely I'd take you, aboard that wet boat, out on the water no knowing how long. You'd die, get sick and scared to death. You git for home!"

"No," she said. "I haven't got any home to git for, Nate. Ed's turned me out of it. He was downstairs when I went in there. He said to go and not come back or he'd—he'd—"

She stopped. Her eyes grew big and black; the firmly set chin wabbled a little.

Nate stood looking at her.

"Don't be so foolish," he said. "Betsey's there. Ma'll be back soon. She won't put up with Ed's acting like—"

"B-Betsey likes him. She helped him."

"Betsey's your own sister!"

"She wants me to get out," Caroline said distantly.

"I don't believe it."

"Well, I won't go back there, Nate. I'm scared of him."

Piper said suddenly, "I'd take her if I was you, Nate. She won't slow you down much."

"For Godsake, Piper, you know I can't!"

"Why? You're damn lucky she wants to go. You keep on, in a minute she ain't going to want to."

"Well, I darn well hope she won't!"

Ev Piper hawked and spit with a fine sizzle into the fire.

"You young fellers," he said, "make me laugh. Either you never had a woman, or you don't know what 'tis to be without one. Where you're going they ain't none. Why, you goddam fool!" he howled suddenly. "You don't know nothing! Going off, big as life, to make a place in the wilderness, and you ain't got neither one of the two things makes a man's life worth living. You don't even know what they are!"

Nate had turned red as a beet. He burst out, "Shut up, Piper! Mind your own business!"

But Piper was good and going, he paid no attention.

"If 'twas me headed into the woods, you know what I'd think of first? A good window sash, maybe two, with slats over the glass, lashed down in the bottom of the boat under the floor boards so nothing could damage 'em. And the next thing I'd load in, by God, 'd be a woman."

100

"I'm about sick of the noses stuck into my business, Piper. Why don't you go home?"

"What's so nice as a nice woman? Why, I wouldn't be a huckleberry in a bear's arse without Jenny. And where'd you be right now, if Car'line hadn't thought to come down here, build you a fire and a hot drink?"

"Well, I've thanked her for it."

"You ain't got the sense to see what it'd be like all your life—fire and a hot drink when you need one. All right, you poor, simple damn fool. The time'll come," Ev said.

Caroline said quietly, "Nate, I don't have to go with you. But you'll have to take me somewhere, maybe Dulverton, where I can find a place to stay."

"Ma'll look out for you, Caroline."

Caroline gave a little, sucking gasp. She got up stiffly from the bag she had been sitting on, started down the bank toward the boat.

Piper jumped after her. "Hey, wait a minute," he said. He caught up with her just before she got to the mud, lifted her off her feet and carried her to the boat, his boots sucking in up to the ankles as he staggered under her weight.

"There," he said triumphantly, putting her down on a thwart. "No sense starting out a trip with your feet wet. Set down there, so's we can stow the load in around ye."

He came back to the fire, thrust his wrinkled face with the aged, bloodshot eyes to within a few inches of Nate's.

"Nate, if you wasn't born with any sense, listen to some. Maybe you don't want her with you, but find her a place to stay before you go. The rest of 'em up there, they can look out for themselves, but a little, nice kid like that, she can't. Ain't likely."

"Ma—"

"That brother of yours," Piper said, "I follered him back here the night I heard him steal my wagon. I stayed clost enough to him till I made sure who 'twas, too. I see him pick a fight with the young feller he was with, stick a knife in him. Come on, I'll help ya stow your load aboard. You want to git going before you lose the tide."

Nate stood, feeling sick, while Piper began to untie the rope lashings on the wagon. He hadn't needed to be told what Ed was, he'd known it. But with Piper's coming out and saying, nailing the thing down, he realized that at last he believed it, and it hit him like a ton of brick.

Ed, he thought. My God, Ed!

He could feel his own heartbeat and a queer, heavy grind of pain in his chest as if something were wrenching itself out.

No, he couldn't leave Caroline there. He couldn't take her with him; it would be a burden like the Old Man of the Sea's, for she would be a cord binding him to the home he never wanted to see again. But he could stop in Boston, Dulverton maybe, find her a place to stay. He'd meant to stop somewhere anyway, where there was a good shipyard and work on the boat—get her decked-over, check the calking, make sure her timbers were sound. It wouldn't take long to find a place for Caroline.

He said numbly, "All right then," and laid hold with Piper to stow the dunnage aboard the boat.

They made a comfortable seat for Caroline among the things, so that the ragged canvas spray-hood behind her would give her some shelter. Piper put a blanket over her shoulders and wrapped that around with the oiled canvas tarpaulin.

"Ride snug as a mouse in a shoe," he said, winking at her. "Get a little salt water down your neck, maybe. Got to expect that."

She nodded silently. She hadn't said a word since she'd been put aboard the boat; she sat in a kind of frozen silence, not helping either, so that Nate was able to take out some of his feelings on her.

"Catch hold, can't you?" he said irritably, handing her a kettle.

She took the kettle, set it down stiffly between her feet.

"You'd be a big help," he said. "Anchor it under something. We get into a rough water, it'll slam around all over the boat."

She picked up the kettle as if it were too heavy to lift and looked around helplessly for a place to put it in. The indecision was so unlike her usual quick efficiency that for a moment he glimpsed dimly what she must be feeling, but the idea only made him madder than ever, seeing he himself was responsible for it. Swearing under his breath, he picked the kettle out of her hand, chucked it under the sacks up in the forepeak.

Piper set his shoulder to the bow, pushed the boat lustily off into the pool. He picked up a stick and began methodically scraping the mud off his boots.

"Jenny, she'll skin me, I bring that stink into the house," he observed amiably. "G'by," he called as the boat swung into the current. "Now, don't forget them window sashes, Nate."

Nate sculled the boat down the mouth of the brook. She scraped some on the boulders, being heavily loaded, and it came to him as he worried her down into the cove against the still slightly running flood tide, that he wasn't going to worry about ballast. Not for a while anyway. In the cove he trimmed the sheet, settled himself in the stern to steer. The wind would be fair except in the bights down the channel, not much current to buck; for the last leg, which was the trickiest, he'd have both wind and tide with him.

The boat was a dandy. Before the wind anyway, she'd go like a scared cat now she was ballasted right. Against the wind she might need a dite more heft on her keel; he'd have to see.

He'd have a chance to find out this afternoon all right, if he headed into Boston Harbor. Wind and tide would both be dead ahead of him, the ebb running strong by then, the wind stronger, too, probably. It was just right now, but the way the clouds looked, puffed-up and crumply, there'd be a lot more of it soon.

Might be a gale, last three days. Likely would be. Be hard to make Boston before dark. Better sail right on past, not try to beat up the Harbor. Dulverton was just as good as Boston anyway, for what he'd need; and while he waited there for the weather to settle down, he could rig the boat for a long trip, tend to finding a place for Caroline.

She was sitting there all muffled and hunched up, not saying a word. She wasn't even looking at him. She had turned around back-to on the thwart, was watching the water out ahead, past the mast and sail.

On the way at last, his head full of plans, the boat sailing sweetly under his hand, Nate realized he felt better.

He said, "You warm enough?"

She nodded her head, but she didn't turn around.

Mad, he thought. Well, all right. She ought to know she can't go. She ought to have realized it from the beginning.

He had his hands full steering the boat. The narrow banks of Cowrie Channel went flashing past, the tide up over the mud banks, lapping into the pale-tan stands of last year's reeds. It was harder on the turns than he'd thought it would be, for in the bights out by Cowrie Island the channel doubled back on itself; this meant coming up into the wind, slacking off the sheet, shoving the heavy boat with an oar. In the narrow channel there was no chance to tack. The tide was beginning to help, the ebb running lightly down, but he was sweating and out of breath when around the curve of the last bight he saw the bright blue of the open ocean, running white-capped to the horizon.

"Going to be rough out there," he said to Caroline, and when she didn't answer or turn her head, he thought grimly, She'll soon find out how far she wants to go with me.

The boat came boiling out of the mouth of the channel into the green, crested rollers. Nate let her run before the wind to get the feel of her in open water; then he headed northerly following the coastline. She slatted some, taking it on the port bow; the spray began to fly. But she was all right.

Go to England in her if I wanted to, he thought with elation, feeling her settle down and dig in.

A big dollop of spray smoked in over the bow, slapped across Caroline's hunched-up body and took him fair in the face. It ran down across his mouth, and Nate licked it off his lips, tasting the salt.

It seemed to wash, cold and clean, across the blackness that had settled in his mind for so long. How long? Three-four days? Yesterday he couldn't remember a time when he hadn't had that icy, sick, hollow feeling. It would be a long time before he lost it all. But the clean spray made him feel better; he braced his feet, leaned hard on the tiller, turned his face to the hard, stinging drops. In a little while he'd be cramped, soaked and shivering again, but that was part of it, too.

The water hissed alongside; the spray flew. The boat lurched and pounded, hustling away like a scared crow into the north.

By dusk it was not possible to sail up Boston Harbor. It was not possible to sail anywhere. A small tear in the canvas of the sail kept working bigger; the wind had picked up to half a gale. Nate kept inshore to take advantage of the lee of the land. When he saw the long, low cape ahead of him, he knew he'd be foolish to try to weather it. There was lee on the south side of it, but on the north the wind would be slamming full on to its low shore.

He kept his eye out for a sheltered place and finally saw what he wanted—a wing of shore that made out into a cove. He put the boat into the cove, ran her as far as she'd go up on to the shore. He ran the anchor up the beach, made it secure and then went back to the boat.

Caroline hadn't moved. She was still tucked up under the tarpaulin. She still didn't look at him.

Well, she was here, wasn't she; he'd brought her along against his better judgment, hadn't left her back there. She might as well quit sulking.

He said, "Don't move or try to help me out or anything, but unless you want to sleep cold and wet tonight, I've got to dig out the ax."

"I saw where Piper put it," she said. "Under the second thwart there."

He peered in at her face, expecting to see it green with seasickness, thinking it was maybe that that ailed her, but the cheek that he could see seemed to be pink enough.

He went along the shore looking for driftwood sticks he could sharpen into stakes to drive into the sand. When he came back with the stakes over his shoulder, he saw she had come out from under the tarpaulin and was out of sight somewhere.

He drove the stakes with sharp, powerful thwacks of the ax; then he unshipped the mast and set up a low lean-to out of the sail. He was finishing his lashings when he saw Caroline coming back along the shore with an armful of firewood.

He said gruffly, "Thought you'd gone off to be seasick somewhere."

She said, "No."

She dumped the wood down by the lean-to and, turning, set off the way she had come.

He spread the canvas tarp on the floor of the tent. It was damp, but it might keep out some of the chill of the sand. One thing, it had kept the blankets dry. Later, if it turned out to be too damp, he could haul it out by the fire.

The canvas shelter made a lee for starting the fire; his flint, snapping under the light and powdery wad of dry marsh grass, caught spark at once. He fed the fire carefully with bits of wood until it was burning brightly. Then he went down to the boat for the meal sack he'd taken that morning from his mother's pantry. Some broiled ham and bread were going to taste darned good.

While he was rooting around in the boat he heard Caroline dump down another load of wood. When he came back up the beach with the sack, she was sitting in the shelter, spreading her fingers to the warmth of the fire.

"Sick!" she said. "I never had so much fun in my life."

So that's the way the wind blows, he thought wrathfully. Going to make out she likes being slatted around in a boat in rough weather. Well, I won't take her with me, and she might as well know it.

"Bring up the water jug and that little kettle out of the boat, Nate," she said. "I've got a bag of tea."

"You'll have to do your own waiting on."

He hunkered by the fire, untying the meal sack. The bread was smashed up some, and it and the ham were powdered over with meal, not that it hurt anything.

"Oh, shoot, Nate," Caroline said. "We'll need some more wood. Why don't you fetch it before it gets too dark to see? I can fix supper. I'd like to have the spider to fry some of that ham in, and you'll have to let me have your knife to slice it. But if you don't want to bother, or if you don't want any tea, I can make do with what's here."

Well, she was right, of course. They did need more wood, and some hot tea'd be just the thing to wash supper down. Might as well let her boil some. But she needn't think she was going to make herself indispensable.

He went down to the boat, got the things, dumped them on the sand by the fire and walked away down the beach with the ax.

She called after him, "There's a big pile of driftwood just around the point."

He made three or four trips carrying huge armloads, more aware each time of the glorious smells of frying ham and hot bubbling tea near the fire. Caroline seemed to be doing all right, but the wind baffled around the fire. It was hard to cook over; she was weeping from the smoke and had a big smear of smut on one cheek where she'd wiped away the tears. On his second trip he stopped long enough to drive another stake and rig a rope from it to the corner stake of the shelter, so he could hang the tarpaulin on it. The heat would dry the tarp, the tarp would shelter the fire.

Not that he was going to make anything easier. But might as well dry out the tarp.

When he came back the last time and stowed the ax under a corner of the shelter where it would be handy in the morning, Caroline had a slab of hot bread ready for him, with a thick slice of ham fried the way he liked it with the fat left on. The tea was bubbling in the kettle.

"We forgot mugs and sweetening," she said. "But it'll be hot, and we can drink out of the kettle soon's it's cool enough not to burn our tongues."

She sat on the warm sand by the fire, eating her own supper. Under the coating of smut her cheeks were pink, her eyes, in the firelight, dark and bright. She didn't look sulky or miserable now, and she couldn't have been seasick to speak of, because she was putting away darned near as much food as he was.

The food made him feel better. It was a long time since anything he'd eaten had tasted good to him. But this did. The ham and bread went right down and nestled, and the hot tea laced on top of it just right.

After supper Caroline scrubbed the cooking things with sand and sea water, left them bottom-up on a clean board by the fire. She took off her shoes, which were soaked he saw; she must've got wet feet from the water slopping around the boat's floor boards. She stood the shoes by the fire to dry.

"One thing," she said into the blankness of his silence, "one thing about a nor'wester, it dries things out. We haven't got damp, foggy weather to contend with."

She took the tarpaulin and the blankets and crept into the shelter. Back-to, he could hear her rustling around in there; he caught himself wondering with keen curiosity and interest, if she were going to undress, and the discovery that he was curious and interested made him mad all over again.

What the hell did she think? He had to sleep in there, too, didn't he? He had half a mind to take a blanket and go down under the spray-hood on the boat. But the thought of the cold and damp down there away from the warm fire, changed his mind at once.

Not by a damn sight, he thought.

He fixed the fire for the night, took off his own wet boots, stood them beside her shoes. Then he crawled into the lean-to. In the fire's flickering light he saw her rolled up to the eyes in one of the blankets, over to one side, out of his way. He couldn't see her clothes anywhere, except her coat folded under her head for a pillow, so he guessed she must have kept them on. She had left two blankets for him he saw, taken only one for herself.

He grunted impatiently, tossed the second blanket over her, rolled himself up in the other. In a moment or so he found he'd never been so cold in his life. His clothes had dried on the outside in the wind and heat of the fire, but next his skin they clung damp and chilly; he had to clamp his teeth together to keep them from rattling. At last he crawled out of the lean-to, undressed by the fire and hung his clothes on the rope. Then swearing under his breath, he rolled up in the blanket again.

Caroline's voice said out of the dimness in the tent, "It'll be nice to have dry clothes to crawl into in the morning. Tomorrow, before we start, you better bring your other ones up and let me wash and dry 'em. Then, at least, you can start out with all your things dry."

He started to make a short answer, then his conscience smote him. "How about you?" he asked gruffly. "You dry and warm?"

"Warm as toast," she said. "I was under that canvas so I only got my feet wet. But I'm awful tired, Nate."

He realized suddenly that he was, too. He could feel his bones as if they didn't have a thing but skin over them. He started to say so; then, thinking she might hope he was giving in if he were too civil, he said, "Nobody'll get rested if you talk all night."

Silence fell inside the lean-to. The fire burned brightly, with a comforting sound. The wind, increasing, baffled it around, blew away most of the heat, but inside the lean-to it was just right for sleeping.

He could thank Pa, he thought drowsily, for the knowledge of how to build a lean-to and a fire in wind and cold, so that one of them would shelter the other. Sand made as good a bed as you'd want, provided you wiggled a hole in it for your hip bone.

He wondered if Caroline would know enough to do that. He decided not to tell her. The more uncomfortable she was, the quicker she'd decide she didn't want to go north with him. Save him deciding for her.

The wind was really beginning to make something of itself. From far away, over all the thousands of miles of wild land to the west, the great gusts bore down; he could hear one coming for a long time before it hit the shelter, snapping his lashings taut, making thunder in the canvas. With a howl and a rushing it would be gone, out over the water; there would be a lull when he could hear the hiss and boil of the ocean, the slap of water against the boat secured down in the cove. The tent ropes would go loose, the canvas slacken with little flopping sounds. Then, far off, the growing whistle and shriek as another gust came tearing out of the black sky.

In one such lull he heard Caroline's soft and pleasant breathing and realized with annoyance that she had gone to sleep before he had.

In the morning the wind had not gone down. Nate, getting up in the gusty dawn, fixed the fire and got his breakfast in a scud of flying sand and ashes. The sun was coming up clear, but already in the west were forming the big, crumpled clouds of northwest weather. The ocean was flattened down, white to the horizon. There'd be no leaving today.

Well, he thought, give me a chance to clean up the boat. Sort out the stuff. See what I've got to do with and stow it secure.

His mind full of plans, he went down to the boat, hauled her up on the sand as far as he could, began methodically to unload her cargo, lugging everything but the boat's equipment up to the sand near the fire. He didn't call Caroline. She was worn out; let her sleep.

He was all stirred up about her anyway, thankful for a chance to be alone and think it out, furious at her for fastening the responsibility of herself on him, when what he wanted now was to get away from responsibility; yet, at the same time, he couldn't help remembering she was Caroline. They'd always thought a lot of each other, taken each other's sides against Ed and Betsey, even against Ma when there was need of it. When she was little he'd routed her, the big-eyed, poky-fingered, nosey kid that she was, out of his business a good many times. He'd be a fool if he didn't know how much she thought of him; of course she was all tore out at the idea of his going away.

But now he wanted to go free without having to be reminded of home, and there she was. Every time he looked at her, he could see standing behind her a picture of Ma. Ma had brought her up, trained her, as a girl ought to be trained, to look after a man. He couldn't make a move without running head-on into Ma coming out in Caroline. Wear this, dry out that, don't get wet, eat so-and-so.

Well, that was all right; Nate could see how it wouldn't come amiss in a man's home. Around a camp, outdoors, it was out of place. A camp was where you knew best how to take care of yourself; he recalled how he and Pa had reveled in freedom on their hunting trips up the marshes, how wonderful the camp had always been. A man undressed where he liked, made water in peace and freedom, had only himself to think about.

Besides, in emergencies, when you had to think fast, what could you do if, always, the first thing you had to do was make sure the women were all right?

Dammit, the idea of leaving her behind among strangers made him feel stinking mean, but that was the way it would have to be. He'd have to say that when he got settled up north, found a place, house built and all, maybe he'd come back and see her. But she couldn't go with him.

By the time Caroline got up, sheepish over having slept so late, Nate had hardened his heart, had his arguments all ready. He was going to use any trick he could think of to get rid of her, being sure, of course, before he went that she was settled somewhere with decent people, looked after and comfortable.

Caroline got herself some breakfast, using the coals of his breakfast fire. She looked rested, but otherwise, he observed with disapproval, she was a mess. Her hair, which he'd never seen anything but neat, was matted and frowzly; she must have forgotten to bring a comb. Her hands and face were streaky with smut from the fire, which sea water alone didn't seem to take off.

He said, "You ought to see yourself. You look like an old burdock," and went down the shore to the boat, not waiting for her reply.

He spent the morning happily, cleaning out the boat. He ripped off the ragged spray-hood, sloshed the forepeak out with sea water, throwing it in and bailing it out by the bucketful. He took up floor boards and scrubbed them clean, laid them up on the sand for the wind to dry. Then he went inch by inch over the boat's planking and timbers, outside and in. She was in good shape. No leaks that he could find. But her calking was old—replace that, once he got her to a boatyard.

He was aware of Caroline moving briskly around the camp. After a while she came down the beach with an armful of his clothes, the ones he'd got so muddy in the swamp yesterday. She did the washing, sozzling everything up and down in salt water to get the mud off. Then she wrung the clothes out, lugged them back by the fire. He could see them flapping in the wind on the rope he'd fixed last night for the tarpaulin.

That'll be nice, he thought absently. Have dry duds when I need 'em.

After that he got so absorbed fixing up the boat that he forgot all about her until noon, when she called to him.

"Want to eat now, Nate?"

"Sure."

He was good and hungry. Ham and bread and tea might get monotonous after a while, but they hadn't yet. He ate a lot of both.

If we're stuck here much longer, he thought, washing down the last of the food with a mouthful of tea, I'll have to take the gun and go inland, see if I can knock over some birds or a rabbit.

Wonder what the land's like here, back from the shore?

Might as well take a look and see.

He began looking over the pile of stuff for his gun. Lord, she must have worked every minute since she got his washing done, sorting things out. She'd done a good job, too. You wouldn't ask for a handier camp. But he didn't see the gun, she better not have dumped that down anywhere, got sand in it.

"Where's the gun?"

"Inside the tent," she said briefly.

Thank the Lord she'd had the sense. The gun and its equipment were lying on the tarp, neatly covered by a fold of the canvas. He picked it up, his eyes going over it critically. No sand. Clean as a whistle. And then he jumped as if he'd seen a snake.

On the tarp, beside where the gun had lain, was a little heap of gold coins.

The gold he'd shoved in his pocket when he'd tried to save some of Ed's treasure for him. The money he'd meant to give to Ed. It had gone right out of his head. He'd walked off with it like a common thief. Of course Caroline had found it when she'd washed his clothes.

And he'd not only walked off with this pocketful. He'd been so mad and stirred up that he hadn't made Ed listen, as he'd meant to, while Nate told what he'd done with the rest of the money. He'd hidden it and gone off, planning never to go home again, and there the gold sat on the shelf in the wagon shed under the remnants of Pa's old scrap iron. Nobody but him, Nate, knew a thing about it.

He'd have to go back after all. He'd have to go back and tell Ed.

Miserably he hunkered down on the tarp, with the gun laid beside him, staring at the money. With all the things he'd thought of, tools, fishhooks and lines, grub, canvas, to take on his journey, he hadn't thought of money. He hadn't even considered he'd need any. So far as the repairs on the boat were concerned, what he'd planned to do was to stop at a Dulverton boatyard and get a job for a few days till he'd earned enough to pay for what had to be done to the boat. It wouldn't take long. He was handy around a boatyard. The supplies he had wouldn't last long, but with a bag of salt he could live indefinitely off the country.

What it would look like to anyone—anyone who knew anything about it, that is—he'd pocketed as much as he could lay his hands on of Ed's money, and made tracks as fast as he could lay foot to the ground.

But nobody knew anything about it except him, and *he* knew that he hadn't done that. And so—?

After a moment he knew he wasn't going back.

The way Ed's treated us all he owes us something. I've got the boat; this money's Caroline's. She ought to have it; after all, he turned her out of her home. At least she'll have something when I leave her over in Dulverton.

Someday, if I can, I'll pay Ed back, and somehow I'll find a way to send word to him to look in the nail keg. But I'll be damned if I'll go back there now.

He got up, took the gun and strode off inland over the scrubby dunes.

The land back from the shore was low and sandy, covered with bushes. Nate hadn't gone a quarter of a mile before he sighted a rabbit loping leisurely in and out among the scrub. It was a long shot with a gun he wasn't used to; he missed the rabbit completely, but he fell in love with the gun. It had a fine, smooth action and was lovely to handle, fitted his hands as if it had been made to order for them. Wonder where Ed got it? He'd started to say, and then hadn't. Anyway, he knew it was my gun.

What times we could have had together, Nate thought, stopping dead in his tracks, if Ed had only come home the same as he was when he went away.

How could it be possible for anyone to change that much, how could a man be two men at once? For Ed was two men. He was the harum-scarum kid who had gone away, quick-tempered, somebody you could count on. Somebody you could defend. At least he had seemed so at first, the night he came home.

God, I was glad to see him.

But now Ed was also a man who could take part in what had gone on aboard Ringgold's ship; he was a man who could kill another man —a boy—and leave his body to drift senselessly, with open, astonished blue eyes, down through the mud and stench of a place like the Flowage.

I wish I hadn't seen it. If only I hadn't seen it.

But the sight was there, right behind his eyes, powerfully proving a point, not soon to be forgotten.

Ed wasn't somebody you could defend now.

How could it happen to a man? Could it happen to me? Say I went through the same things Ed did, how could I know?

No one could know. A man had to take what came and do the best he could. If what came was something that turned him into someone who could stab another man— He thought suddenly, If it could happen to Ed, it could happen to anyone.

The idea hit him like a blow. If you believed that, then you believed a man wasn't really a man, but only a kind of plaything for whatever chance brought to him.

I don't believe that. It's just been proved to me, but I still don't believe it.

Sorely puzzled and bewildered, he stood stock-still, waist-deep in the low bushes and scrub.

This damn gun, he thought. I ought to dig a hole and bury it right here. Every time I touch it, it's going to remind me of Ed. Going to make me think about stuff like this that doesn't make sense. Or maybe makes so much sense that it turns my stomach.

Over on a woody slope, a long distance away, a slight movement caught his eye, and he froze stock-still in his tracks. A small spike-horn buck stood there; the movement Nate had seen out of the corner of his eye had been a slight switching of the buck's tail. He was scared, you could see that, but not very much scared; he was just making up his mind whether what he'd seen or heard was dangerous enough so that a deer ought to run.

Damn fool I am, crashing around in here like a cow. I might have had him. Maybe I can get him yet.

Moving slowly, he hunkered down, praying the buck wouldn't run till he got the load into his gun. Cautiously he thrust the long barrel out through the twigs, took aim and pulled the trigger. The deer leaped into the air and landed on legs that bent under him, the delicate knees slowly giving, even while the legs made motions of running. Then he fell over and lay still.

Nate went leaping through the brush, pulling out his knife as he ran. The deer was still twitching, consciousness slowly going out of its eyes, when he leaned over and bled it.

The gun leaned against the crotch of a bush. He gazed at it while he waited for the deer to bleed into the sand.

That's a gun, he thought. I wish Pa could've seen that shot.

The deer was a young one, small. Last year's fawn. His meat would be tender and good. Venison for supper. Nate's mouth watered at the thought of it.

Chance, luck, whatever it was, the hell with it. A man was his own man, whatever came. All he had to do was be able to handle it. No voice within him, of malice or even of friendly warning, whispered, What about the deer's luck?

Walking back to camp with the gutted carcass slung across his shoulders, carrying the gun in his hand, he felt better, as if he had left behind him in the scrub the unreal ideas which had so shaken him.

I guess I can handle what comes along.

He strode elatedly back to camp, and as he came near, called out, "Hey, Caroline, I got a deer!"

And when she didn't answer at once, he let out a bellow, "Hey, Caroline!"

Caroline came out of the lean-to. At least, after a moment of stupefied shock, he saw that it must be Caroline. She was dressed in his spare suit—the one she'd washed so carefully and dried on the line, supposedly for him, so he'd have dry clothes to put on, say he got wet. They were too big for her, but she'd gathered them in. The jacket hung on her in folds; she'd shortened the pants, tied them around her waist with a belt of rope. She made a queer enough picture over-all, but what shocked Nate to the bottom of his soul was her hair. It was hacked off as short as his own and stood up all over her head in scrubby little curls.

His jaw dropped slowly; he was flabbergasted, it was a moment before he could think of a word to say.

Caroline said composedly, "Oh, good. You got a deer."

"What in the name of—? What d'you think you're doing? You've spoilt my other pants."

She looked down at herself. "Oh, I don't know. For you, maybe. They just about fit *me*."

"I never saw such a sight in my life. You gone crazy? What'd you cut your hair off for? It looks awful."

"It looked awful before. You said so," she pointed out. "It's better this way than it was all dirty and straggled around, seeing I didn't

114

have any other way to keep it clean and decent. Why don't you put that deer down? He looks heavy."

Nate dumped the deer off his shoulders. He flexed his cramped arms, feeling the circulation start to come back in them. The deer'd been heavier than he looked, and Nate had gone farther into the scrub than he'd thought.

He turned on Caroline. "How d'you think I can find a place for you with anybody decent, and you looking like that? There isn't a decent woman anywhere'd take you in now."

"I don't plan on any decent woman taking me in," she said. "When I leave you, I'm going on my own."

"You ought to be ashamed of yourself."

"I ought to be. I'm not."

"You needn't think a trick like that'll make me take you with me, either."

"No. I don't expect so."

"Well, what'd you do it for?" He moved toward her.

Caroline backed away from him, over by the fire. She said, "What I do's none of your business. You land me over to Dulverton, that's all I ask."

"I thought you wanted to go with me."

"I did. I don't now."

"You don't?"

"No. I don't. I wouldn't, not if you was to get down on your knees. That's funny, too, because all my life if anybody'd said to me, 'Go with Nate,' I'd have gone. Anywhere. You were always the one," she said, and her voice shook a little with grief or anger, he couldn't tell which, or it might have been both. "But after the way you've acted, blundering around being mean to show me you don't want me and how much you don't want me, I've had enough. You just put me ashore over to Dulverton."

"What d'you think you'd do over to Dulverton? In a rig like that? Get hooted off the streets, land in jail, don't think you wouldn't."

Caroline's chin came out. "I don't plan to let on to anyone I'm a girl," she said.

He looked her slowly up and down, then began to laugh.

"You'll have to shave yourself off in spots and places, then," he said.

"All right, laugh!" Her eyes began to shoot sparks, the red came up in her cheeks. "I can fix it, with some clothes to fit me. And then I'm going to get a man's job. I'm sick of being bossed around somebody's house, not amounting to anything."

"What kind of a *man's job,* as you call it?"

"I can learn one."

"All right. Go ahead and skin that deer, to start with."

Her eyes went past him to the dead deer, and he saw with satisfaction that the idea made her a little sick.

"I could do it. If I had to. I don't have to."

"You have to. Don't make any mistakes, you have to. Go on. Do it."

She stood, quietly defiant, staring at him, and presently Nate walked over to a bush nearby and cut himself a switch. He came back with it, planted himself in front of her.

"Now, you either skin that deer, or you get out of my duds and back into your own."

"No," she said. "No. I won't, Nate. And don't you dare touch me, I warn you."

"Go ahead and warn," he said between his teeth and reached for her shoulder.

Knowing Caroline, he expected her to fight like a cat and was prepared for it, but there didn't seem to be any fight in her. Only her eyes had turned from blue to black; her face looked white and pinched. He took a cut with the switch, and a blinding cloud of something dry and dusty and prickling flew into his eyes. She had been holding a handful of ashes from the fire, and she had slapped him with it, right across the bridge of the nose.

Nate let out a roar of pain. He clapped both hands to his eyes, sat down on the sand. He couldn't see anything. He felt as if a swarm of bees had hit his eyes. He tried to clear away with his fingers the blinding, stinging burn.

Caroline said in an agonized voice, "Oh, Nate, Nate! Take your hands down," but he couldn't; it seemed as if, if he took the pressure of his fingers off his eyeballs, they would fall out of his head.

Then a waterfall of cold liquid went down over his head—sea water, he realized from the taste of it—washing away some of the pain. Now he could feel the tears streaming out of his blinking eyes, the icy trickle of the salt sea water down his neck.

Caroline said, "Here. Here's a cloth. You can wash a lot of it out," and she put into his hand something soft, guided his hand to the rim of a bucket of cold water. He dabbed and sponged; after a while he abandoned the cloth, scooping up the water with his cupped hands, sloshing it into his eyes.

Presently she brought him hot water, and that was better. After a while he could see, but the light hurt and his lids felt puffed out, half-swollen shut.

He spent the afternoon lying in the subdued light of the lean-to, with cloths wrung out of hot sea water over his eyes. As fast as the cloths cooled, Caroline brought more.

He didn't sleep much that night; he lay awake, wondering, horrified, if he were going blind. The next day he lay around in the tent and slept a good deal. On the third morning, the day the gale went down, his eyes were still sensitive and they watered a good deal, but they were all right—he could see.

But by this time, now that he didn't have to worry about his eyes, he was as stubbornly mad as he had ever been in his life. The silence which came from him, as he strode grimly around the camp, loading the boat, could almost be heard. He didn't say a word when he discovered the deer carcass with the skin haggled off of it—a terrible job, the meat hacked and gritty with sand. He just went off and left it lying where it was.

Caroline herself said nothing. She turned to and worked, helping carry things down to stow aboard the boat. Whenever they met, as they unavoidably did, face to face, from time to time, he ignored her, and she didn't seem to care. She still wore his clothes.

In the same grim silence they sailed past Boston Harbor and up the Massachusetts coast to Dulverton. It was a fine, warm day, with a southwest wind. Soft haze lay in the sky and against the distances, dulling down the edges of things, which for so long had been sharp and bright with northwest weather. The boat sailed well with the following breeze; Nate thought what a fine time he might be having, if only he could have been alone, if only he could have looked ahead, past the sail and the cargo, without having to see the back of Caroline's cropped head or her stubborn, set little profile.

It was hard to believe that she had done such a thing to him, but it was all of a piece, he told himself morosely, with what had gone on between him and his whole family. Nobody you could trust; nobody cared a hang about you.

At Dulverton the whole waterfront was nothing but shipyards, most of them with work on the ways. He put in at a wharf and made fast. As he was tying the stern line, he saw that Caroline, her canvas carrying-bag under her arm, was starting up the wharf ladder. For the first time in two days he spoke to her.

"Where you going?"

She made no reply. She climbed the ladder, a little awkwardly because of the bag, disappeared over the edge of the wharf.

Nate went up after her, saw that she was walking away without looking back. He caught up with her where the wharf spewed out in a mess of lumber piles and boat-builders' gear into the muddy path which did for a street along the Dulverton waterfront.

"I asked you where you're going," he said roughly.

"As far as I can get away from you," Caroline said.

"Well, wait, can't you? I've got no objection to that, but I can't just go off and leave the boat there."

"Wait what for?"

"You've got a little sense left, maybe. You know you can't be turned loose in a strange town in that rig, with no place to go."

"I'm all right. Go tend your precious boat, and I'll tend to my own business."

She didn't raise her voice, just spoke quietly as if she weren't mad, only put upon until things were past a woman's strength to bear. It enraged him more than if she had screamed and yelled at him. All right, he thought, Let her go.

He pulled out his handful of gold pieces.

"Here's some money. Get some decent clothes and go to an inn. Before I go I'll find a good place for you to stay."

"Thank you. I don't need all that. Three or four of those is plenty to tide me over."

He said, "Take it, damn you, Caroline," and dumped the pieces into her outstretched hand.

Caroline held them for a moment, looking from them to him.

"What would you do," she said, "if somebody twice your size started to lick you? Wouldn't you defend yourself the best way you could?"

"I wouldn't play anybody the dirty, underhand trick you played me. I'd fight honest with my fists, no matter how bad I got licked."

Caroline laughed. "Oh, my Lord! What a chance I'd have had fighting you with my fists! You don't see it, do you?"

"No, by God, I don't."

"No, and you never will. You'll go through life just like your ma, seeing your own side of things and nobody else's. As long as people think and feel the same way you do, they're all right. But the minute they set up for themselves, you stand off in judgment. Way high up, like the rooster on a weather vane. I thought I—" She stopped. "I thought I could stand it. But no."

"I didn't ask you to stand it."

"No, you didn't. I don't need all this money. Take some of it back. You may need it."

She picked out four pieces, put them in her pocket—his pocket. Then she held the rest of it out to him. When he didn't take it, she opened her fingers, let the gold pieces slide to the ground.

"Well," she said. "Good-by, Nate. Good luck."

He stood glaring after her slim back as she walked away. She turned the corner of the path that led up from the waterfront into the town, looked back once and vanished from his sight.

Nate picked up the money and put it into his pocket. He went back to the boat.

She certainly deserved all she'd get, and she'd get plenty, a girl dressed up in a man's clothes, running around alone in a strange town. Be lucky if she didn't land in the stocks or the ducking pond.

Serve her right if he just went off and left her. Of course, he couldn't do that. Let her think he was going to though. Let her stew around alone for a day or so. See how she liked it.

He hunted up the boss of the shipyard, who was glad to get hold of a trained hand, if only for a few days. He worked all that day spiking timbers into the frame of a sloop the fellow had on the ways.

Relenting a little, he planned, the first evening, to go up into the town to look for Caroline. But that night he was worn out and his eyes were sore. He turned in aboard the boat and slept like a log till morning.

In the morning Gorham, the boatyard boss, found a couple of hands who could go to work on Nate's boat, so that Nate was busy laying out what he wanted done. He had a new, permanent mast stepped, with a boom which would be way ahead of the old, detachable mast and spritsail. He had a couple of watertight lockers built in for'rad, which would serve for storage space and for bunks. Then, with one rowing thwart removed, the space for'rad of amidship decked-over and a hatch that would close tight, he had as snug a living cabin as a man would want.

The second night he went up into the town, made the rounds of the inns—the respectable ones that is, where a girl like Caroline could stay. There were four of them. She was not at any one of them, and this enraged him all over again. He came back to the boat, thinking, Let her go, to hell with her.

But by the end of the week, when the boat was finished, taut and snug, with tarred seams and new canvas, he had hunted all over town and he still hadn't found Caroline. When she had gone out of sight around the corner that first morning, she seemed to have vanished off the face of the earth.

Nate was ready to go. By that time he had visited all the hostels in Dulverton, respectable or not. No one had seen Caroline.

No one seemed particularly interested either. There was too much excitement everywhere in Dulverton, as in every other town within a day's ride or sail of Boston. The town seethed over the news. Ringgold, the West Indies pirate, had at last been taken. His phenomenal luck would at last run out, tomorrow, on Gallows Hill.

"They're hangin' him and his whole bloody-handed crew," Nate heard a stout sailor say. "What's left of them, that is. And anyone who give them aid and comfort, like the Carnavons."

The sailor was leaning over the bar in a waterfront dive, with his nose deep in a mug of rum, so that his speech was a little muffled. It was the first Nate had heard of the talk; he'd been too absorbed in his search and, by this time, in his worry over what could have happened to Caroline, to do much listening. But he had caught the name "Carnavon" and was interested because Carnavon Brothers was the firm who had taken over his father's warehouse.

"What's happened to Carnavon's?" he asked.

The sailor took a long swig, set the mug down with a satisfied "Haaah." Then he turned around to look at Nate. "The scuts took Ringgold's cargo and sold him a load of shot and powder," he said. "Law and order wants to know why. They're all in it together with Ringgold, Carnavon's is, and have been for years, if you ask me."

"Ringgold?" Nate said. "*Jake* Ringgold?"

"Jake Ringgold, the murderin' devil. Him that killed my uncle and his two boys on the high seas. And who knows how many more poor souls? They're hangin' him in Boston tomorrow, busted noggin and all. And I'll be there to holler 'Hurray!' "

The barkeep said, "They ain't hangin' the Carnavons, I heard. At least not Michael. But Frank Carnavon was seen aboard Ringgold's ship before she sailed. The British is after him, but Frank's took cover and can't be found."

"A man the size of Frank Carnavon won't get far or stay hid long," the sailor said, and a guffaw went up.

Under cover of the laughter, Nate eased himself away from the bar and went out. He supposed he could have heard more, if he'd stayed, but he didn't know that he wanted to. Ringgold had been a pirate on the high seas. Ed had been one of his crew.

He walked down the narrow street to the waterfront, climbed dully down the ladder into his boat.

She was ready to go. Clean and polished, everything secure. Supplies stowed. He even grinned a little, thinking of the two window sashes lashed for'rad under the floor boards. Part of Piper's advice anyway, he'd taken. The way he felt now, stirred up and worried, he guessed if he could have found Caroline, he might have taken the rest of it. It was hard to say what he'd feel like if he found her. But he couldn't find her, and now he didn't know where else to look.

After a little he climbed the ladder again and went along to the snug house on the shore side of the wharf, where Gorham, the shipyard boss, lived with his family. He asked Gorham to keep an eye out for Caroline, left some money with him for her in case she turned up.

Gorham, by now, knew his story. He and his wife were sympathetic; they promised to look out for Caroline if they found her. Nan Gorham gave him a packet of cheese and fresh bread, sweet-smelling from her oven.

He felt warmed and comforted as he went back down the wharf. He'd done what he could, short of staying here, short of going back home, making sure they were all right there. Ma might have walked into trouble in Boston, but if she had she'd walk out again; she hadn't been doing anything unlawful, trying to return the pirate's money to him. As for Ed, he had his own actions to answer for. I don't want to see him ever again.

Nate stopped on the head of the wharf, looked at the sky. It was a fine, clear evening, the stars beginning to come out, a soft, steady wind from the southwest blowing.

He climbed down to the boat, cast off his lines, bow and stern. He shoved away from the wharf with an oar. When he was clear, he hauled up his sail. The canvas went up sweetly, with a rattle of rope in smooth new blocks; it filled with wind. Under the bow he heard the beginning whisper of the water.

He looked behind once at the town of Dulverton, huddled squalid and weather-beaten above its harbor. The sky behind it was pale with faint afterglow from the sunset. A few specks of light were beginning to come out here and there.

Carnavon Brothers was in trouble, no doubt of that. The *West Wind* was impounded, the warehouse was closed until the authorities could discover to their satisfaction just how innocent the firm was in its dealings with Ringgold, the West Indies pirate.

To anyone who knew the Carnavons, the matter was open and shut—simply, no one believed them guilty. Warehouse owners and dealers along the waterfront thanked their lucky stars it hadn't happened to them. For if the so-called Captain Morrison in his apparently innocent West Indies vessel had come to any one of them with a valuable cargo to swap for an outfitting, they would have dealt with him as Carnavon's had, and no questions asked. They were on the Carnavons' side, but only to a degree.

Competition was stiff along the waterfront. With one trading firm less, all the others would benefit. Michael Carnavon was a smart man; in the opinion of some, the ship chandlers particularly, he had been hogging too much business. Thus, while Michael's acquaintances along the waterfront championed him in private, in public they sat back silent, with wary eyes. The town magistrates, some of whom also had waterfront interests, considered this suspicious. The King's men and Lieutenant Niles, of the warship, considered it condemning.

Tension in the town was high. Too many people had lost money and relatives in the West Indies trade. The life of the town was in its shipping. Anyone who had money to spare had it invested in shipping, or in a trading vessel of some kind, and a trading vessel was often a family affair. It went out in high hope, manned by fathers, brothers, uncles, nephews and sons; if it vanished forever, or word filtered back months later, of robbery and murder on the high seas, people could not be blamed for wild and vicious excitement now that the means for revenge was at hand.

The authorities had lost no time. The trial of Ringgold and his crew was short. Lieutenant Niles had not hanged them at sea; with an eye to his own popularity in Boston he had brought them back to make a public spectacle. The only thing that held up the hangings now, was Ringgold's broken head, which had to heal sufficiently for him to make his appearance on the gallows.

Broadsides were written, ballads composed and sung, hawked about the streets for a penny or two, and the town seethed. Lynch mobs formed at the slightest provocation and went howling up and down the streets. The pirates would have been hauled out of jail and executed five times over, if the magistrates and Lieutenant Niles, foreseeing some such demonstration, had not spirited them by night off aboard the warship, where they were kept under close guard by a squad of British marines. Thus lacking victims, the mobs dispersed unappeased. Their emotions backed up. There was considerable talk about town at first, then a growing resentment against Carnavon Brothers, or anyone else who might have known that Captain Morrison was Ringgold the Pirate, lying bold as brass in Boston Harbor.

Hangers-on and loafers remembered the woman with the satchel who had come riding in a wagon up to Carnavon Brothers' warehouse and asked for Ringgold in broad daylight. It was told, losing nothing in the telling, how Frank Carnavon had tried to persuade her that Ringgold wasn't in Boston, how, finally, he had taken her in his skiff and rowed her off aboard Morrison's ship. True, most people found this hard to believe of Frank. But in a time of tension and excitement slowly heading up to a shattering point, who could believe anything? Anybody was capable of dirty deeds. And any lout with a bellyful of rum found he could gain an attentive audience in the tavern, simply by adding to the scandal about the Carnavons.

The woman was Frank's woman; no, she was Ringgold's woman. No, she was the slut kept aboard Ringgold's ship for the easement of the sailors, ashore for a rest and a leave while the ship was in Boston. The Carnavons knew who she was; she had stayed at Mike's house. Mike's cook and housemaid had seen her there, waited on her. There was no end to the scandalous talk; public resentment steadily grew.

Frank Carnavon was nowhere to be found, but Mike had had,

three times, to answer searching questions in magistrates' court. He told a straight enough story. The trouble was, he couldn't prove it. No one seemed to want to believe that he and his brother hadn't known Ringgold from the beginning, hadn't, under cover, been hand in glove with him for years.

Well, Mike could understand that—blast their eyes, the shipping boys would do any kind of underhand business to hamstring Carnavon's. As for the story about Frank and the woman, it was crazy, like most of Frank's escapades; it was innocent, of course, but to believe it so, you had to know Frank.

The woman obviously had known Ringgold. How had she known? Who and where was she? She hadn't mentioned her name.

Corkran and Mike had brought her, with Frank, back to Boston in the *West Wind*, after picking them up miles offshore. It had been a job beating back in the gale. They hadn't got in until morning. Then Frank had got out of his bunk, none the worse for wear apparently, and had told his story. To hear him talk, he had fought a whole pirate's crew singlehanded, rescued the woman, come out of it the hero of all.

The woman had waked up wan and pale and tired, obviously half-sick, shaken by her experience. It would have been cruel to question her, even if Frank had permitted it. He knew all the story, he said; it was something to do with the woman's son, and no sense talking it around until they were all sure how much trouble he was in. Frank was going to see she got home; when he came back was time enough to satisfy idle curiosity.

In the early morning he had taken the woman ashore, harnessed Mike's carriage horses and driven out of town with her. And that was the last anyone had seen of Frank.

There were a good many dead vegetables about this time of year, what with people giving their cellars the spring cleaning. On the way home for the last time from magistrates' court, Mike was hit in the back with a rotten cabbage, and he saw the handwriting on the wall. He hadn't gone out in the street in daylight since, but had begun quietly to put his affairs in order.

This morning he had come down to the warehouse before dawn. Now it was growing dark, and he had been working all day. He was sure now that before long an attempt would be made to arrest, possibly lynch him. He didn't plan for either emergency to happen.

When people all went crazy at once, as sometimes happened, given provocation, and when law and order went along with the mob, no one even remotely concerned with the affair was safe. Mike laid careful plans with Corkran Teague. He was going to leave town. The only thing holding him back now was Frank. He couldn't go off and desert Frank. It was like the silly spalpeen to go off with this woman; she wasn't a bad-looking woman, or wouldn't be, dressed up. He'd done it before with other women, at least so he'd have everyone believe. The thing was, he was holed up somewhere with her, not knowing a thing in the world about what was going on. Some morning he'd come driving back into town, big as a rooster and crowing like one, in Mike's rig, right into the teeth of the cabbages or the mobbing or the lynching—whatever the town boys had worked themselves up to by that time.

Mike didn't plan for that to happen either. But his hands were tied, because he didn't know the least in the world where Frank was.

"There," he said, shoving-to the drawer of his desk from which he had taken everything which might conceivably be of value to him. "That's the end of it, Corkran, me boy. We'll take the loss of the warehouse and the vessel and my house in town. The rest of it's in hard cash we can take with us when we have to go."

Corkran said gloomily, "You seem pretty chipper over it all."

"What's another way to be?" Mike asked.

He knew Cork was sunk in despair over the loss of the *West Wind.* That she was lost, there could be no doubt. She was impounded now, would be confiscated and sold. Things had gone too far for Carnavon's to save anything, except by stealth. Mike couldn't say he was surprised, now he thought things over. For months Carnavon's had had the bulk of waterfront trade, largely due to his and Corkran's astuteness; none of the other firms loved them for it. Under cover of darkness Mike had called on several of his business friends; they had one and all been warmly sympathetic, but Mike knew now where he stood. Another time, somewhere else, he reflected, he would not have to stand the losses of a warehouse, a fine residence and a stout vessel. He would foresee and prevent it with this expensive knowledge of how the world looks upon a successful man.

"Dog eat dog, Corkran," he said briskly.

He buckled the last strap of the valise holding his papers, snapped it to make sure it was taut.

"And where will Michael Carnavon, that great city man and ship chandler, go now?" Corkran asked softly.

"Where he will be big frog in the puddle," Mike said. "This is no proper place for an honest man to conduct his business now, as you know, Corkran. Too many people. Too many taxes. Too much law. In a way this that has happened, cruel and trivial though its beginnings were, is a good thing, for without it I'd no doubt be sitting here on me arse till I was a gaffer old and gray. Come, we'll go north to new country. To Maynard Cantril's country where we'll build the *West Wind* twice over, poor mourning lad!"

"There'll never be a better ship," Corkran said. "Nor the man born who could build her."

"Tush, man! Maynard Cantril could build her with his eyes shut. But I'll not try to comfort you. I know you loved the old pumpkin."

"Pumpkin, begod!" Corkran fired up. "I'd as soon sail one as that thing I bought you over to Dulverton."

"The *Bessie?*" Mike said. "Sure, she's a horse-trough. But she'll serve our purpose, which is to get us and our goods safely away."

"I and my boys could sneak aboard the *West Wind*, sail her out of here before the lobster-backs could grunt in their sleep," Cork said savagely.

"No doubt you could. But the Britisher knows the *West Wind*. Any of his ships can outsail her."

"Christ, you think he can't outsail the *Bessie?*"

"He does not know the *Bessie*. In the *West Wind* we'd be over-hauled and taken before we'd gone a league. And in that case," Mike added thoughtfully, "I'd be in no ways surprised if they hung us all. The *Bessie—*"

"Blast and damn the *Bessie!*"

"Well enough. But no one would think of looking aboard such a hulk for the Carnavons and Corkran Teague."

The compliment smoothed Cork's feathers a little, and it was time something did, for Mike needed him. Almost any small matter could upset his plans now. It was time for cool heads, not hot tempers.

The *Bessie* was a sloop, small but able, which had been used for years as a kind of trading scow, carrying goods and supplies to the settlements on the northeastern coast. She lay now in Dulverton Harbor, ostensibly loading trade goods for her summer's trip north. But also aboard of her, hidden belowdecks, were Mike's wife Sally and

126

his two young sons, guarded by a couple of Corkran's men, and the load she was taking on was not only trade goods, but Mike's household and other possessions. The wives, families and goods of Corkran's boys, the men who had been the crew of the *West Wind,* were being loaded aboard tonight.

The owner of the *Bessie,* an aging man named Bright, had been glad to sell her for such a fat price as he had never dreamed of getting. He was a Scotsman who for years had longed to go home. Part of the price of the *Bessie* had been his fare to Scotland on the first ship, and the ship had sailed. Mike had to admit the one lucky thing about the whole affair—finding the *Bessie* to hand, with an owner who'd cleared out and wouldn't be around to talk when the hue and cry started. A cousin of one of Cork's boys, no one remotely connected with Carnavon's, had done all the dealing with Bright; people were used to seeing the *Bessie* periodically set sail out of Dulverton Harbor loaded with goods. The plan seemed foolproof.

Mike hoped he'd be equally lucky in finding that clown of a Frank before the time came to go.

"Cork," he said. "Where do you suppose the fat bastard's gone?"

"Off on a toot," Corkran said. The one thing that could rouse him out of his gloom was the thought of Frank whom he loved. "Hell only knows. I've got the boys posted around at the taverns and a couple watching the turnpike in case he comes prancing in. But we can't wait too much longer for him, Mike. Things don't look good today."

"They do not," Mike said. "Did you hear the new ballad they're singing in the streets?"

"I did, that. Carnavons weren't mentioned in it at first. We are now."

Mike grinned at him. He hummed a few bars of a tune, presently began to put words to it in a clear, sweet tenor:

> *"Oh, Ringgold the Pirate-O,*
> *Blow wherever the winds blow,*
> *With his bloody Turkey Feather*
> *And his pantaloons of leather,*
> *And his black, black flag in the morning-O."*

Cork said apprehensively, "Shut up, you fool."

"It's a fine song," Mike said. "Shouldn't be surprised if Tiswell Far-

rell made it up. It sounds like him. What does it say about the Carnavons now?"

"Everybody makes it up," Cork said. "A verse a day."

He caught the grin on Mike's face, and slowly his own face relaxed.
"All right, ye devil," he said. "You're half-pirate yourself, no doubt will
be whole-pirate before you're through, and God help all! Here's what
they say," and he himself burst into song.

> *"Mike Carnavon he made a deal*
> *All on a windy night,*
> *To fit the bloody pirate out*
> *And fit him out full right.*
> *With guns and shot and powder*
> *All stowed below the hold,*
> *And Frankie he rowed off aboard,*
> *To take his pay in gold.*

"That's what they're singing in the taverns now. About tonight they'll
get worked up to going out to your house, Michael, me boy. And
when they find it cleaned out and you gone—"

"Then God help all," Mike said. "With or without Frank, Corkran,
you're right, the time's come to go. We'll have to leave word for him
with someone."

"Who can you trust?"

"I can't trust the wheel of the world," Mike said. "But I've got to
leave word for Frank we've gone to Somerset. Old Job Crawford loves
the boy, and he'll be the only one left here."

"Job? You crazy, man? The old rumpot'll bleat it to the first
passer-by!"

"I could leave a letter in a place only Frank would know, and tell
Job to tell Frank to look in that place."

"Write down where we are and where we're going? I'll strangle the
old cock first!"

Mike picked up his valise. "I won't desert Frank, Corkran, without
a word. Let there be an end to it."

He started through the door, Cork at his heels, protesting in a whisper.

The warehouse was dark as a tomb, beginning to smell like one. In
the cellar they found old Job, humped on the pile of sacks in the
corner which were his bed. He was drinking rum by the flickering

light of a candle end and was already well on the way to low tide in his bottle.

"You see?" Cork said. "I warn you, Mike, if you tell the old woods' hog a word, I'll wring his neck before we go."

Cork meant what he said, Mike could see that. He groaned.

"Begod, if I could only find that damn woman," he said.

Job blinked his little red eyes.

"Frank's woman?" he muttered. "She's Joel Ellis' wife, used to own this business here. Dead now, poor Joel."

Mike made a leap and grabbed him by the shoulder. He shook hard and the bottle flew out of Job's grasp onto the floor, where it lay, faintly gurgling.

"Oh, my God, set my bottle up, Corkran, like a Christian man!" Job wriggled in Mike's iron grip, then hung limp, the tears running down his cheeks.

"Talk, man!" Mike said. "I knew Joel Ellis, but where did he live?"

"Down in the swamp," Job blubbered. "Set my bottle up, for the love of God!"

Cork picked up the bottle, held it tilted in his hand so that a few drops ran out. "Say where Joel Ellis lived, or I'll wash the floor with the lot of it."

"He runs a tavern now," Job said. "On the turnpike. Down River-ville way. Only poor Joel's dead. Give me my bottle now, Cork."

"Come on," Cork said. "I know that tavern. People named Ellis run it."

He handed over the bottle, and Mike, letting go of the old man, gave him a pat on top of his tousled white head.

"God love," he said. "Bundle him into the skiff, Cork, with us. He'll die here alone, and he's saved the heart within me, if we find Frank before the bailiffs do."

"Oh, God, you Carnavons!" Cork said.

He looked disgustedly at Job and then back at Mike, and he saw Mike's jaw come out. Another argument was on the way and no time for it.

He picked Job's bottle out of his hand, tapped him smartly with it on the bone back of his ear. He caught the old man's body as it slumped, tossed it over his shoulder like a sack.

"Why, goddamn you, Cork, you've killed him," Mike said furiously.

"Killed him, nothing! He'll be all right when he wakes up, and he won't be making a drunken noise when we sneak past the Britisher."

Cork led the way out of the door.

Mike paused a moment to look back. The candle end, flickering in the draught, showed him the cellar of his fine warehouse, packed to the beams with rich stuff.

In a little while he would be sailing with Cork and old Job around to Dulverton in Frank's skiff, and then to Riverville in the *Bessie* to find Frank, if, please God, Frank should be there. After that, away into the wild parts of the world, never to see this place again.

Thoughtfully Mike prized the candle end off the corner of the packing case where it had been stuck in its own tallow. He set it down, carefully upright, on the pile of bone-dry sacks. Some shavings were nearby in an opened box, and he arranged a great wad of those to hold it upright and to be handy when the candle had burned down a trifle more. Then he followed Corkran down to the landing place to the skiff, where he peeled off his outside coat, wrapping it around old Job's unconscious body.

"What a fine, dark, windy night," he observed cheerfully, helping Cork to set the skiff's sail. "Fine for secret sailing, Corkran, lad. If there should be a fire on the waterfront tonight, with this wind I don't doubt but more than one of them elegant warehouses would go."

"God's blessing on it," Cork grunted. "Give the townspeople something to think about besides hunting down honest men. And now will you shut the teeth of you on your tongue whilst we skin out past the warship?"

The skiff slid silently out into the Harbor, past the sleeping ships, past the man-o'-war whose hulk loomed black and menacing, faded, went out of sight in the thick darkness.

When it was safe to move again, Mike reached down and felt of Job's face. The old man was all right, at least so far. His face was warm.

Mike's own teeth were chattering with chill, and Cork grunted, "Put your coat back on, you fool. That old plug's full of rum, don't know whether he's cold or not and won't, praise God."

"Oh, no, Cork," Mike said softly. "If we find Frank, I owe the old man a great debt."

He glanced back at the faraway, scattered lights of the city of Boston. Low down among the wharves, a hot, orange-red light was beginning to glow.

130

"Let it never be said that Michael Carnavon doesn't pay his debts."

It had been no part of Frank Carnavon's plans to tarry at Mrs. Ellis' tavern, when he had driven her home the morning after the *West Wind* rescued them. She had been then a lady in distress, who needed to get home at once with no means to do so, and Frank, having saved her life twice over was still feeling gallant. That he was interested in her he couldn't deny—not as a woman, God forbid. A man could not live a day within gunshot distance of that tongue. At times he could not help recalling that as a woman she had much to recommend her, as who should know better than he; though a decent man should put that part of it out of his mind, and she defenseless.

All that, he thought regretfully, and a waste for any man unless he cut out the tongue of her.

What fascinated him, he told himself, was the rest of her story. How had she, a poor woman, happened to come in to Boston bringing to the pirate Ringgold four thumping bags of gold? If, as she said, her son had stolen it, then her honesty was a thing to wonder and marvel at. It was not an honesty which Frank himself had ever encountered in man or woman. He would like to see this son, who must have been one of Ringgold's men. It was not at all a new thing for Francis Carnavon to be interested in hearing the end to a good tale. And surely, a man with any heart at all in his bosom would see the poor woman got safely home.

Oh, he gave himself plenty of reasons for taking her.

He went in a hurry and without much ado, because Mike did not care to have his horses and carriage borrowed at any time and would lace into him anyway, for what he would call running off with a woman. Small business it was of Mike's. If he did not have enough to occupy him at the warehouse, then he had little to do nosing into the private business of his brother.

On the way to Mike's house to borrow the carriage, Frank stopped by his own rooms and dressed himself up very fine. He was not, he told himself firmly, doing this to impress the woman. Simply, he could not ride around town in a fine rig like Mike's, dressed in a dirty

131

suit of borrowed workman's clothes. Someone, begod, might think he had stolen the rig, and with reason.

It could not be denied, he thought, driving back to the waterfront in the carriage, that Francis Carnavon was the great lunk of the world, but he cut a better figure in a velvet weskit than he did in a sailor's jacket, and she had implied, if not said outright, that no woman could be interested in him.

They drove out of Boston at a spanking trot behind Mike's good horses. The windy weather had dried up a good deal of mud on the turnpike, except in the worst spots. It was cold but not too cold, exactly the kind of weather in which Frank felt best. He talked freely and merrily, trying to cheer Lizabeth up, but, as he told Mike afterward, it was like talking to a woman of stone.

"I tried everything," he told his brother later. "I even tried insult, lightly, thinking that the edge of that tongue would be better than nothing at all. But at last I gave it up. She was not herself, as I came later to know, and I could kick me arse all over the world for the fool I was."

Lizabeth was far from being herself. Both physically and mentally, she was wretched. She was worn out and draggled, in sodden, shrunken clothes, still damp from yesterday's soaking. It was a great trial to her to be without her stays; she felt undressed and indecent. She knew quite well how and why she had lost them; whatever the necessity had been, she could not forget. She needed rest and a bed, but she could not bring herself, in such a plight, to go to Cousin Annamaria Bussey's. Cousin Annamaria's sharp nose would be into the business up to her eyes. That was a place to go in your good town clothes, driving yourself, not dribbled and drabbled, driven by a stranger. And certainly not without your stays. Cousin Annamaria would never let her forget it as long as she lived. And so Lizabeth permitted Frank to drive her home. The more quickly she got there and sent him forever on his way, the better she'd feel. He was, of course, a stranger, and he had been kind and courageous, but she never wanted to see him again.

Yet when he appeared, driving Mike's fine carriage, in all his glory of velvet and fawn-colored smalls, she was furious with him, she could not have said why. She huddled her small, sea-stained person into the seat beside him and refused to speak, praying only for the ride to be over quickly.

But for this chattering Irishman, riding along cheerfully beside her, dressed up like a popinjay, she would now be aboard that terrible ship, dead or worse than dead. He had saved her from that and she supposed she owed him a great deal. Had the rest of the tale not happened, she could have received her reward in peace—the good woman saved by Providence because she deserved to be saved. But it was no part of the fate of a good woman to be seen naked by a stranger, like a common whore.

From rage she passed into a state of confusion and shame; the shame was worse. The whole thing was part and parcel of the incredible thing that had happened to her, a thing so outrageous that it had shaken her to the depths. She had believed firmly that good was rewarded and evil punished, an automatic process attended to by God. Yet here she was, a good woman who had stood forthrightly up for good, doing her duty as she saw it. And evil had met her more than halfway; it had come over her threshold in the person of her own son; it had caused her to be kidnaped by a gang of filthy, murdering pirates, to be seen naked by a man who had no right to do so. The man had saved her from the pirates. The rest of it was irrevocable, established. Nothing could save her from that now.

When the carriage drew up in the tavern yard, she drew a breath of relief. In a moment he would turn his rig around and go away. She got out at once without waiting for him to help her, though Frank climbed gallantly out of his side of the carriage and came around to help. She said, "I have to thank you very much, Mr. Carnavon," and walked to the inn door without so much as a handshake.

Frank stood stupefied. Was this the way it was going to end? He did not wish this experience to be over. Moreover, for the last mile or so, he had been hungry, and he'd been all puckered up, wondering what she was going to feed him. Surely she wouldn't send him back all that way without a meal? His stomach rose in protest.

"Mrs. Ellis," he said, "you've a tavern here and I'm a starving man."

"I think it would be better if you went on your way," she said.

"Is the milk of humankindness soured in you entirely?" he demanded. "Oh, surely not!"

She shrugged and laid her hand on the inn door.

The door was locked.

Lizabeth shook it, with an expression of astonishment on her face.

Then she pounded it with her fist. She called sharply, "Nate! Caroline! Betsey! What's the matter? Open the door."

But there was no answer, and she turned, bewildered, back toward Frank. "This door's *never* locked."

Frank said later, telling the story of it to Mike:

"I was about to say I would break the door down for her if she wished it, when there was a sound of unbolting, and this touzy wench stuck her head out the door. She says, 'I'm sorry, Ma, but Ed says if you haven't brought back his money, you can't come in.'

"You could see that was a facer for my lass, but it made her mad, which was a good thing under the circumstances. She says, 'Has Ed gone the rest of the way crazy? Get away from the door, Betsey,' and she starts to push. But this Betsey's a stout wench, and Lizabeth no bigger than a cricket. She was beat from the beginning. For a minute it was pull, devil, pull, baker. Then I see Lizabeth losing, so I thought it was time I did a stroke of work for me dinner. And for other things, as I was later to find. 'Tis no use glowering, Mike, the thing came over me like a sack over the head, more than mortal man could fight off had he wished to, which I did not.

"I walked over and gave the door a hell of a kick. It flew inwards and knocked the wench galley-west. I went right in over the doorstool.

" 'Lock your ma out of her house, will ye?' I says. 'Scat and put the dinner on, ye fat bitch, or I'll put the stick to your tail!'

"Betsey scuttles off with a squall, and then I see this Edward. He's standing in the other door of the kitchen, white as a candle and not much thicker. He says, cool as a cucumber, 'Who're you?'

" 'I'm Francis Carnavon,' I says. 'At your service. And you?'

" 'Edward Ellis. I own this tavern. Get out of it.'

" 'So you're the bully boy ran off with Ringgold's pot,' I says. 'I could say I was glad to meet you, if 'twas any kind of pleasure, which, begod, it is not.'

" 'Ed,' his mother says. 'Go back to bed. You mustn't be up. Where's Nate?'

"He says, 'Where's my money?'

"You can see she's worn out by the way she looks at him.

" 'Back aboard Ringgold's ship, where it belongs,' she says.

"He does nothing but give a little shrug, but I tell you, Mike, that little shrug was a nasty sight. It's as if he's calling her a damned liar to her face, and I felt meself begin to burn. 'It is that,' I said. 'I was there

134

and see the little pipestem's face when she give it to him. It is worth a man's life to look *once* on goodness and honesty, me young friend,' but I might as well not have spoken for all the mind he paid to me.

" 'Ma,' he says. 'You either hand that money to me, or you clear out of here and don't come back.'

"She is standing by the door of the room off the kitchen, looking in, with a white face, and she seems not to have heard him at all. She says, 'Ed! Betsey! Nate's clothes are gone. Where is he?'

"Betsey chimes in. An unattractive wench, with a voice that would take the bristles off a pig. You can see she's enjoying the whole thing, and could I have laid hands on her, I'd have let her have a clap on the chops, but she was staying out of me way, as well she might. 'Nate and Caroline have run off together,' she says. 'There's only Ed and me left here now.'

"Lizabeth says, 'What are you talking about, Betsey? And what are you doing anyway? Hustle out to the kitchen and fix Mr. Carnavon some dinner. Of course Nate and Caroline haven't—'

" 'Oh, but they have,' Ed says. 'They stole my boat, the same way you stole my money. Cleaned out your larder, too. Go and look.'

"But she believes him at last, you can see, and it is a body blow. I guess, be jasus, Mike, it was there it began and I knew I was going to be in love with her, seeing her stand there like the last prop she had under her was gone.

"It was an odd thing, surely, to catch a man unaware, without a thing led up to. It hit me in the stomach like the flat of a shovel, and I says to meself, 'Frank, ye fool, ye thribble fool, run!' But me feet stuck to the floor.

"I says gently as I could, 'Who is Nate, Mrs. Ellis?' and Edward, he's watching her, but he swivels his eyes around to me.

" 'He's her other son,' he says. 'Her good son. Both thieves, but they're the good people, make no mistake about that.'

" 'I've made no mistake,' I says. ' 'Tis easy to see what I see.'

" 'Well, now that you've seen, drag your fat belly into your wagon. Take her with you, unless she wants to spend the night in the street. She won't stay here unless I get that money back. Get out of my house, Ma, before I call the bailiffs!'

"The rage was boiling in me like a torrent. 'You'll talk to your mother like the lady she is!' I says. 'And let me hear no more of bailiffs. it's ill talk for one of Ringgold's men.'

135

"He doesn't even look at me. 'You'll hear plenty of talk of bailiffs, Mr. Carnavon, unless you get out of here and mind your business.'

" 'Her business is mine,' I says.

"I don't know what got into me, for the thing came out of itself, I had not thought I was going to say it.

" 'She is doing me the honor of becoming my wife,' I said. 'So you will kindly address your insults to me.'

"Lizabeth goes stiff all over and spins around to look me in the eye. I expect a blast from that tongue of hers. But she only says, 'Oh. That's kind, Mr. Carnavon. Thank you,' and for a minute I was that flabbergasted I nearly fell flat on my face.

"This Edward, the lizard, he smiles.

" 'You're taking my father's wife as you took his warehouse,' he says, smooth and polite as could be. 'And on my money, for I don't doubt that's your reason for it. It's enterprising of you, Mr. Carnavon.'

"I took a step toward him, and then I see he has a knife in his hand.

" 'This would make a mess of that pretty weskit,' he says, and I see straightway that violence wasn't the way to handle him.

" 'Your money's by now in the hands of the British,' I says. 'Where you'll be, me lad, at a word from me, with the rest of Ringgold's men.'

"He didn't turn a hair. 'Are you trying to make me believe Jake Ringgold's been taken?' he asks.

" 'He went out of Boston Harbor last night with the warship on his tail,' I says.

" 'They won't catch him,' he says, and the bastard grins a little. 'One on him though, if they do. You really stirred up the hornets, didn't you, Ma? Betsey, my lass, it looks as if we'd have to be honest innkeepers for a while. Betsey's going to marry me, Ma. We could have a double wedding.'

"I swear, you'd have thought from the friendliness in his voice that by-gones was by-gones, but there was a high flush on those curdy cheeks of his and he was fingering the knife in a way I didn't like. You had to hand it to him for keeping his voice down and his head cool. But there was a stinger there and out it came.

" 'And you and your Irish fancy can live here, Ma, with Betsey and me, if you want to, and take orders from the real master and mistress of the inn.'

"There was a pewter pitcher standing on the shelf by me elbow and me fingers closed on it, but he had the knife at me gut before I could wink.

" 'No?' he says. 'Don't care to?'

"I stood there wondering what I'd better do. It was a sharp knife and a long one. Me guts did a kind of curl backwards from it.

"And then Lizabeth, with her back stiff as a board, walked past us and out through the door. 'Francis,' she says to me, 'if you're ready, we'll go.'

"I couldn't believe me ears, but I was willing to take a chance they hadn't lied. I says, 'Good day to you then, Mr. Ellis, and I wish you joy of your wedding.' And I turned me back on him and his toad stabber and walked out of the inn, expecting to feel the damned thing hit me behind at any moment.

"We went to Gloucester and had the banns published there and got married, because I well knew if I came back to you in Boston, Mike, me lad, you'd have your nose into me business, and it wouldn't have taken much to lose me Lizabeth. Begod, it wouldn't take much now, the state she's in, and no wonder to God she is at all. I let her rest and sleep at the inn in Gloucester and bought her new clothes—the best pair of stays in the colonies, begod! She may never love me at all, but I think she will when the time comes."

"The great lunk of the world," Mike said, wagging his head a little. "It passes me why I was in such a taking when I thought I'd lost you."

Frank smiled. "No doubt because life would be dull had you not my business to mind," he said.

"Where were you for a week? In Gloucester all that time? The talk was all over the coast; how did you miss knowing what happened to Carnavon's?"

"A man on his honeymoon rides a cloud," Frank said. "Though, begod, 'twas nearer a thunderhead at times, poor lass. We stayed quietly at the inn, keeping to ourselves. At the end of the week, in the evening, we put back to Boston, I thinking I'd leave Lizabeth at your house till me own place was fixed for her. And on the turn-pike I met Cork's man, who told me all that had happened to you and me. He told me where to find you, that the *Bessie* would head for Riverville to pick me up, so we turned the horses back the way we came. I was just in time, there on the hill, to see the warehouses on the

Boston waterfront going up in smoke and flame. Me brother Mike is a man of parts. 'Tis proud I am to be a Carnavon. Oh, the fine blaze of it! The damage that was done will not be forgot by the bastards for time to come."

"Blind luck and chance," Mike said. He shrugged, modestly pleased with himself. Then he laid a hand on Frank's arm.

"Jobbick Butler was last aboard the night we sailed," he said. "He was ashore waiting for his wife and child to come back from a visit to the country. We nearly had to leave him, but they got here in the nick of time. He brought news, but there is no need for your wife to know it."

"What news?" Frank asked. "Her son?"

Mike nodded. "Her son. Your friend, Edward. Ringgold's men, what was left of them, put the bailiffs on his trail, no doubt for revenge, because it was through him they all were caught. He has been arrested. I don't doubt he will hang with the best of them."

"No," Frank said. "No need for her to know. Who knows beside Jobbick? Anyone who'll talk it about?"

"No, I asked him to keep it quiet because of Lizabeth."

Frank was silent, thinking of the white face, the thin body, charged with evil, that had been Edward.

" 'Tis a nasty death, hanging," he observed softly. "I almost wish I'd fought him to a finish, him and his toad stabber."

"Why? No doubt he'd have finished *you*," Mike said.

"No doubt. Where do we go now, Mike, me love?"

"North," Mike said. "To Maynard Cantril's place. Away from the laws and the crowding."

"To Somerset? With Maynard Cantril and his Indians? Good," Frank said. "No doubt we can make better laws for ourselves to serve our turn."

"And will," Mike said between his teeth.

The *Bessie* spanked sturdily north, driven by the southwest wind. Corkran Teague, straining her under all the canvas he could crowd on her stubby spars, swore at her and called her a horse-trough. But she was steady as a rock. She was used to carrying, though her cargo now of men, women and children, and household possessions, was not the kind of load she was used to, and it was not light. Under the stars she went up the wild coast and vanished from Boston as completely as if she had sunk into the sea.

Through the first part of the night Nate sat huddled up by the tiller, steering by the stars. There would be no moon until toward morning, but the night was not dark. The southwest weather made the sky milky and the stars dim, but they were there, and off to the west he could make out the line of the shore, black and low-lying, a mile and a half away. The wind blew softly, not much more than a breeze; it would, he thought, die down toward morning. Now it was enough to keep the sail filled and the boat steadily on her way. He had no way of telling how fast she was sailing—slow, compared to the way she straightened out before a stronger wind.

Fast enough, he told himself, so that by morning I'll have left them all behind.

But it didn't seem to work that way.

He had thought that once on his way, the trouble would slough off, leaving him free. Simply to go, to put miles between him and his family, was what he had looked forward to. He hadn't looked beyond. New places and a new Nate, swept clean of all the confusion and heart-searching, his mind peaceful again. It wasn't going to be like that at all. The farther he went, the worse he seemed to feel.

The wake he was leaving behind was like a thread, stringing out long and thin, but as it diminished growing not weak but strong. He glanced behind at the faintly seething stir of bubbles lightly following the boat, vanishing astern in the darkness. That was the way he'd thought it would be with him. Get gone and the rest of it would go, too.

As long as he could keep his anger stoked up, what he was doing had seemed all right. It was the thing to do, if he were ever going to be a man with business of his own, instead of a boy with a trail of family spread out behind him, always between him and anything he undertook. But as the night wore on and the chill of it struck through him to his bones, it was hard to stay mad at anyone. Ma and Ed and Caroline kept going through his mind, like hounds following a trail. It boiled down to one thing: they were all in trouble, and instead of sticking around, he had slid neatly out from under.

He set his teeth to keep them from chattering. Ma, he told himself. She'll get them through it. They don't need me. Caroline can always

139

go home if she wants to. Maybe that's where she went. That was why he couldn't find her in Dulverton.

Of course she had. He convinced himself of it and was temporarily comforted.

The pale shimmer of the moon began to spread out over the east. The moon was on the wane now, coming up about three in the morning. An hour or so until daylight. And would he, he thought, shaking himself inside his clammy jacket, be glad to see the sun!

You wouldn't think, the way you'd longed to sail away alone, having it above everything else in your mind, that it would be such a cold and lonesome business.

What did you expect? he asked himself angrily. There's bound to be cold and lonesome times anywhere, and three o'clock in the morning's a poor time to judge. The sun'll make all the difference. As soon as he could see the shore clearly enough to make a good landing, he'd haul up, cook a hot breakfast and go to sleep.

He tried to put his mind on a hot breakfast and the comfort of the campfire he'd build behind a sheltering ledge somewhere.

At that moment the boat hesitated a little, as if a hand had reached out from somewhere, grabbed her keel and then let go. She grated slightly, not even a bump, just a soft-sliding-over something solid, and then she was on her way again, sailing steadily.

Nate started up with a jerk. He stared overside wildly, but in this light the water was silky-looking, opaque; he couldn't see down into it—only the noncommittal, growing shimmer of the rising moon along the surface. Nonetheless, that was a ledge he'd skated over the surface of; and a crinkle of fear went coldly along his spine.

What am I doing sailing at night, damn fool, not even knowing what it's like here? I don't know these waters north of Boston. For all I know, I may have sailed her into the middle of a mess of rocks.

The half-wafer of the moon, pulling free of the horizon, showed him a great, heaving expanse of milky water to the east; ahead, past the sail, he could see a long, black mass, lying low, a point making out from the coast, or a long reef of rocks, he couldn't tell. For a shocked instant, not believing that he could have been such a fool, he stared at the thing; then convulsively he yanked at the tiller, slacked off the sheet, in his confusion not remembering which he ought to do, which he had done first. Far out where he hoped and prayed he had deep water, he turned his course again into the northeast.

He sat, cramped and cold, holding the tiller between his upper arm and body, while he tried to flail some feeling back into his legs and thighs. It couldn't be long till daylight.

Pa would have said, "It's a good thing the Fool-killer wasn't around tonight," he thought. But, shoot, what if he had gone aground, it wouldn't have killed him. Calm night, no sea on those rocks. Ebb tide, though. The tide would have gone down and left the boat high and dry. Maybe some sea and wind would have come up with the next flood, and then he'd have been a goner.

One thing, the bump on the ledge had jerked his mind out of the half-sick, numb circling-around it had been following for most of the night. He could think now.

Either I've got to stop going ahead blind and crazy, put my mind on what I'm doing, or I've got to turn around and go home. Which?

A slight scrabbling came from his decked-over cabin for'rad, and he pricked his ears toward the sound. Rats? It would have been easy enough to pick up a rat or two while the boat was lying at the wharf in Dulverton; if that was a rat, it would be at his food box.

Ought to have thought of that and turned the boat out before he left. The thought of the dirty mess a rat would make in the small space of his nice, clean cabin made him sick. Damn it, there'd been so many things to think of, all piled on at once. What he'd wanted was to sail away leaving everything behind him, but here was the whole works, responsibility, worry, trailing along; and now he had rats. What was the use? He might as well turn around and go home. Maybe at daylight, he would.

The rat, making again his slight scrabble among Nate's things, grew as large as a hound dog. All Nate's hatred concentrated on it. He looked around for a club.

A small black and white kitten came out of the hatchway, stepped into the moonlight, lifting its feet delicately on the wet boards. It stopped short at the sight of Nate hauled back with uplifted oar handle, spat, then leaped to the top of the cabin and sat down just ahead of the mast.

Nate stood frozen. Then sheepishly he put the oar down. "I'll be darned," he said aloud. "Where'd you come from? You'll never know how near you came to getting the noggin knocked off you."

141

He tried to snap his cold fingers at the cat, but he couldn't even feel his forefinger with his thumb, let alone make a sound with it.

He called, "Kitty, kitty, kitty. Pss-tt. Come on," but the cat sat there, affronted, a small black and white patch on the edge of the sail's shadow.

"All right, I don't blame you," he said. "Take your time. But watch yourself, if I have to come about."

He felt better, even a little warmer, and over in the east was a growing streak of light.

Darned if he'd ever thought he'd be so glad to see something alive. Even a cat.

By daylight he could see the rocks he had almost come to grief on—a great reef, surrounded by black, solitary ledges, awash, making out to sea from a rocky point of land. Ahead of him, inshore, was a small, low-lying island, and he sailed for it, warily edging the boat in, keeping an eye out for shoaling water, until he saw the cove and stretch of shingle he was looking for. He put the boat into the cove and grounded her; she nosed into the pebbles of the beach and came to rest gently as if she, too, were tired out.

The kitten got to its feet, looked down over the bow of the boat and leapt ashore. It made off at once, up the low bank into the brush, without a look behind.

"Hey," Nate called after it. "Don't go off now. No knowing what you'd run into in this wild place."

He jumped ashore with the anchor, carried it up the beach, dropped it in a clump of marsh grass. He put his boot on it to drive the flukes into the tough earth; then he parted the brush and went into it after the kitten.

She hadn't gone far. She was standing galvanized, at the top of the bank, looking anxiously about at the tangle of scrub. Nate scooped her up and tucked her under his chin, feeling the warm silky fur snuggle comfortingly against his neck.

"You don't like it here," he said. "Well, damn. I don't either. We won't stay."

It was a wilderness of uninhabited land, dropped like an afterthought into the ocean, blown over by the wind, palely colored by the soft greens and reds of coming spring. Nothing in it cared whether a human being lived or died. A man could lie down here with no one knowing, and presently, little cold-eyed animals would eat the flesh away from bones which could stay here forever, bleached by sun and rain, uncovered by even a rag or tatter of clothing rotted away. Nothing would give a damn. The flies, the scrub animals would be glad of a meal, that was all.

It was the first time in Nate's life that a wilderness had seemed anything but a fine place uncomplicated by people, where a man with a gun was king of all. He went where he liked, had a good time, took what he wanted; his camp was home, secured from wind and cold, not only by shelter and a fire, but by a warmth within himself. Here there was no warmth within, and it seemed that no campfire he could build would drive away his feeling of icy loneliness.

I better build one though, he thought, and eat something. Maybe I'll feel better. And find this little critter a meal, too.

He began, through a red haze of weariness, to look for driftwood sticks, but there weren't many. The tide had scoured the shingle clean except for a big old dead spruce-tree log, and he'd need the ax for that.

Better shut the cat up in the cabin so she wouldn't wander away and get lost.

He turned back toward the boat and was suddenly aware that down on the beach ahead of him, was a sound of chopping. He stared, unable to believe his eyes. Caroline, in a sailor's garb of pants and leather jacket, was using the ax on a dry log, making the chips fly.

She looked at him and put the ax down, waiting while he came stumbling down the beach toward her. "I see you found Fuf-Fluffy," she said, choking a little. "You seem to like her all right, seeing she stowed away on you."

But Nate said, "Caroline. Oh, my God, Caroline," and he put his arm around her shoulders and held her close, feeling against his cheek the pressure of her sharp, cold little nose, and the warm trickle of her tears.

The *Bessie,* slogging along at a sturdy four knots an hour, made her voyage in a little under five days. She could have done it in three if Corkran Teague had been willing to sail at night after he got into the waters he did not know north of Boston. But long ago, as a boy of fifteen, he had come with his grandfather and a crew of fishermen into these wild, northeastern waters and had spent one bleak, unforgotten winter at a fishing stage on an outlying island. He recalled a sullen and treacherous coast—many islands, thickly wooded, numberless coves and bays studded with rocks washed over by savage tides. Left to his own devices, Cork would have not been caught dead in the *Bessie* in such waters. But if Mike Carnavon wanted to sail off the map, Corkran Teague was the boy who could take him there.

"Not in the dark, Mike, me boy," Cork said. "Not into that hellhole, and me with the only chart of the place I have what I picked from Maynard Cantril's mind. By night I'd as soon take a ship down a cowpatch, and by daylight it's little better."

So in spite of Mike's fuming to get gone away, Cork found anchorage for the *Bessie* each night at dusk, which was in a way a good thing, for Sally Carnavon, Mike's wife, and more than one of the sailors' wives spent every hour the ship was under way being dismally seasick.

Corkran had no high opinion of the expedition. Himself, he would have had no part in it, except for the necessity. After twenty years he remembered too well the place they were going, though he had never been to the town of Somerset. That was to hell-and-gone somewhere up a river, but it would be like the rest of the scratch towns dropped down by a good harbor where trees for lumber were. For some years stout vessels built there had been bringing down to Boston cargoes of lumber or salt fish or sea birds' feathers—whatever the people had to sell. It was no trade, compared to the roaring commerce in and out of Boston. The men were a leathery lot. The only thing the north had to recommend it in Cork's eyes, was Maynard Cantril, who built good ships and who knew how to sail them, or he'd never get down past that rack of rocks and islands and rubble where the devil had tripped his apron string.

The ships were the only thing that consoled Cork. For the rest, he was a city man, banished to a howling wilderness.

"What can we do there?" he asked. "For the love of God, Mike?"

"Business," Mike said succinctly. "Trade."

"Trade? What? Hens' feathers? Tan the hides of the heathen? There's a future in leather, maybe?"

"Lumber. Lumber and ships. I had, you remember, a good deal of talk with Cantril. Fish, if I have to."

Cork eyed with distaste the low-lying distant shore slowly dissolving into a purplish mist with coming darkness. They were lying-to, he guessed, somewhere above the New Hampshire coast; anyway, there were some hellish scraps of islands away to the east'ard there, that no one but the devil would have or want.

Now it begins, he thought.

Tomorrow, if he remembered, low sandy shores; then rocks and islands, ledges awash or out of sight under the ship's keel, anywhere you'd least expect a ledge to be.

"Fish?" Frank said. "Ah, God, the nasty things!"

He was passing along the deck behind them, his wife's cloak over his arm, and he stopped briefly, his hand on Mike's shoulder.

"A dish of pheasant, now that would take away the taste of that dog turd we had for supper," he said.

Cork spun on him. "You'll eat worse than boiled codfish and like it, me boy, before we're through with this fool's journey," he said. "I'll see you with a leaner belly in a month, Frank."

Frank backed away. He was in no mood to talk to a man in a temper, and even Mike, he saw, didn't look too happy.

At least, he thought, my wife has not been seasick.

Let them gravel on each other, he had other business. He said cheerfully, "Ah, I could lose some belly," and went on down the deck to the stern where Lizabeth was standing at the rail.

"You've had a bad day, lass," he said. "Are you warm?" and he laid over her shoulders the cloak he had brought up from below.

She said, "Thank you. I was chilly. The air's better out here."

She was polite to him, remote, as if she were a long way away still, and Frank sighed. Somewhere there was warmth in her, if only he could find it. He couldn't have been that mistaken.

Give her time, he thought, poor lass. She's lost her lifetime, and no rest at all with Sally and the rest puking in the cabin all day long.

He stood beside her wondering if there was anything to say, knowing she wouldn't talk unless he did.

"It's a wild country we're headed for," he ventured at last.

"Yes. It would seem so."

"Different from what we're used to."

"Yes."

"You don't mind too much?"

"No. Not too much."

No telling whether she minded or not, for there was no more feeling in her voice than in the wooden ship's rail she had her hands on.

He said, "If there's anything more I can do—"

"You've done more now than most men would. I'm grateful."

"Oh, Lord," said Frank. "Grateful, oh, Lord."

"What would you have me be?"

He put his big warm hand down over hers where it clenched on the rail and was startled to find it so cold.

Like the claw of a poor bird, he thought. But I will make it up to her until her hands are soft.

"Let it go, lass," he said.

"I've given you all you asked," she said.

What words, to be sure, he thought. I could have had better from a whore, for in that case I should want no more than I got.

And then he thought what had happened to her and felt himself ashamed.

The poor woman has lost her sons, deserted by one, thrown out by the other from the home she spent her life in. What would any woman in such a case see in your fat, selfish hulk, Frank Carnavon? Let it go till time heals it and then be in the right place at the right moment. But do not devil the poor lass now.

He sighed, thinking how pleasant it would be to devil her in bed the night, and in the darkness now falling over the sea and the distant, wild, unfamiliar land, his stomach rumbled dismally.

"Tch!" Frank said. "It seems I'm fated to be a—" He almost said "lonely" but substituted for it in time "a hungry man."

"Hungry?" Lizabeth said. She turned sharply away from the rail. "That cook's a fool. To spoil fish like that when a good meal would've meant so much to a whole boatload of people. I could show him a thing or two."

It was the first spark of interest she had shown in anything, and Frank caught at it eagerly.

"I don't doubt you could," he said. "And I wish to God you had, for me guts is rolling like wheels. But Frank Carnavon's wife is not a cook for a shipload of louts, nor ever will be."

"And that's where you're mistaken," Lizabeth said roundly. "Frank Carnavon's wife has been a cook all her life. She likes to cook. It's well enough to be a lady with soft hands. But do you think I'd let any man make the fool out of me that your brother's wife is? She's in there now, howling because she had to leave a fine carpet in Boston, when she ought to be on her feet comforting her two little boys. Poor little tykes, they cried themselves to sleep, and what could I do, a stranger they were not sure of? And she lolloping around on her bunk, puking and squealing like a parrot!"

That's my girl, Frank thought. That's the tongue of her that would peel an ox, and praise be to God, it's come to life again!

Satisfaction and pride welled up in him. He did not say a word, hoping she would go on, and presently she did.

"She's lucky to have her boys," Lizabeth said.

It came out quietly in a voice that did not reveal the feeling behind it. It was the first time she had mentioned what had happened to her.

"She is surely," Frank said. "As we both know."

He pressed the hand which seemed to have grown colder under his.

"I know as well as you do," she said, "that I'm no kind of a wife for you."

"No," he said. "As things are now, you are not. I would be a liar if I said so. I have been, in my time," he went on soberly, "a great liar to women, but I will not lie to you. I have seen you to be too honest. How could I expect more than I have had? I took you when you were struck down by your losses, with no one to turn to but to me. God forgive me, it was not to be hoped that I should get otherwise than a woman of stone. I have always been the fool of the world, leaping in with great feet when a wiser man would have known better."

He stopped, hoping she would say something, but she did not.

"I am a man of large appetites," he said. "And in my lifetime, I have seen no reason to starve them. A man's life is not long enough to taste the good things of the world, and you might say I have more than tasted. Do you think I am wicked because of it?"

"I don't know," she said. "I might have thought so once."

She sounded bewildered, and Frank said quickly, "Let it go. 'Tis no time to think of such things when you're so knocked and bandied."

"I know you're a kind man," she said stiffly. "I've said some hard things to you which I hope you'll forget."

"We could both forget a good deal to our profit," he said. "And I'll say no more now except this: If in times to come, you wish it, I will let you go. But you must remember I am a man who has had no courtship. What I have done I have had to do in a terrible hurry, which is a sin against God and a good woman. I wish you to know that, in different case, I would have courted you with gentle things, and you should have had gifts and—" he cast about in his mind for a sample of the best he could think of "—and a journey to Bowker's Tavern to eat the pheasant pie."

He paused, remembering.

"Ah, God," he said mournfully. "Pheasant pie!"

Lizabeth started. She moved away from the rail.

"Show me the place where that supper was hasseled up," she said over her shoulder to him.

Frank stood looking joyfully after her a moment before he started along the deck.

Maybe she hadn't taken in all he'd tried to say, but one thing was certain, the look she had given him was not the look of a woman of stone.

"This is the galley," he said, showing her the place. " 'Tis not fit for a lady."

"It is if there's food and a cook-place in it. Is there a light? It's dark as a pocket."

While he fumbled with flint and steel, he was astonished to feel her hand on his arm.

She said, "I won't have you go to bed hungry."

"Frank's in a bad way," Cork said, glancing after the two shadowy figures as they passed along the deck toward the galley.

"He was born in a bad way," Mike grunted. He was standing looking off over the water, lost in thought, only half-listening.

"I always thought when he finally hooked up, it'd be to something a little more blossomy," Cork said. "Meself, I like a woman to take hold of. Thin and little's not to my taste."

"There's more to Frank's wife than meets the eye," Mike said absently. "Shut up, Cork. I'm thinking."

"You better think. Think hard where you're going to end, since you'll consider none of my planning."

"You do agree we had to leave Boston?"

"I do. But—"

"And get out of sight for time to come?"

"Sure. But there are places besides a howling wilderness, Mike. We could've gone south."

148

"To cities where all the land is owned and it's dog eat dog again? I've rubbed the skin off me elbows too long. Push here, shove there, and any place you find to sit is rubbed smooth from the pants of the man who owns it."

Cork's heart sank. He had been hoping to turn Mike back from the north. The town of Portsmouth was not too far away; he knew Portsmouth. It was up and coming, plenty of room there, if only Mike would try. The least Corkran had hoped for was some town along this coast that he'd heard of, where people he knew had been. When Mike did not answer him further, he stamped his feet with frustration.

"Somerset!" he snorted. "What do we know of Somerset?"

"Enough," Mike said. "It is a small town at the head of tidewater on the Crookshank River, where there is a waterfall. Andrew Cantril and his sons built it; the old man is dead now. They have a mill—a sawmill—and a shipyard; the trees grow down to the back door of the mill, so that all is needed is to cut them down and saw them. The venture can be bought, lock, stock and barrel. The Cantrils are sick of it. Sick of it!" Mike took a deep breath. "When the great trees go back into the country no one knows how far!"

"I'll bet no one knows!" Cork exploded. "A howling wilderness, for God's sake, and you with a boatload of women and children!"

"And a poor stick of a ship's captain for whom I am soon going to have to make a sugar-tit," Mike said. His voice was full of scorn, but to himself he was grinning quietly in the darkness. "Have you piddle in your veins instead of blood, Corkran, since we all got rich in Boston? Why, a broody hen hovering you would hatch out a baby chick, fluffy and peeping, and pretty to look at, as we all know, not the Corkran Teague who came with me from Ireland, the boy who had only to blow with his breath to set the world ablaze."

"Shut up, damn you, Mike!"

" 'Tis true a wilderness has no wine and featherbeds. They will come in their time, if thirsty and tired men who have drunk spring water and slept on the bare earth still want them. They will come to the city we will build. Take heart, Corkran. The ships you will sail through the terrible waters which now so frighten you, will bring them from Boston, from England, from the world. It makes a beautiful circle, Corkran, there is no end to it. The wilderness, the

149

men, the city. The featherbeds and wine. And the long crawl into the wilderness again."

"The waters do not frighten me," Corkran said in a choked voice. "I've sailed them before. And if you do not shut up, Michael"—he cocked back his fist—"I'll knock your damned head off!"

Mike put his hand on the angry man's arm.

"We're in it together, Cork, me lad. You know we cannot stay within cable's length of Boston even if we wished to, which I, for one, do not. We cannot even stay Carnavons. I have been thinking what I shall change my name to, when we go ashore at Somerset. I think the name of Frank's wife, which sounds well with Michael. How does it sound to you, Cork—Michael Ellis? Like the renegade Irishman who burned down innocent warehouses, may their ashes rot well?"

Cork swore.

"I'll be Corkran Teague to the end of my days, and be damned to you, Michael Carnavon!"

"No, you will not. You will choose a name not Teague, and you will grow vast and poetic whiskers, so that no one will know you when you take down our cargoes of furs and lumber to Boston. We will build ships, not like the *West Wind*, but like Maynard Cantril's vessels. They are good, Corkran, adapted to these waters."

"What tubs!" Cork said, but he spoke half-heartedly, knowing now he was so far in the wrong as never to haul foot out of it again unless he agreed with Mike, the silky devil.

"No. You know they are not tubs." Mike went on thoughtfully. "We will put other sawmills on the edge of that great forest of trees. Think of it, only one mill now, in that mighty country of forest! There will be room for my skinned elbows. You can sail us to Somerset?"

Cork snorted. It was a question not requiring an answer. He said, "Maynard Cantril in Somerset knows you. He'd recognize Michael Carnavon."

"Maynard is my friend. As for the rest, I, too, have fine stiff whiskers which will grow. Which are growing, from the way the becurst things itch. Have sense, Corkran. What will you call yourself, when we put ashore in Somerset?"

"O'Neill," Corkran said sheepishly. "Me mother's name. But Corkran I'll not change."

"Good enough." Mike slapped him on the shoulder. "We'll be rich as kings someday, and the town we build will be big and rich. In God's sweet name, what is that glory that I smell?"

A rich, savory scent of cooking was blowing along the deck from the galley, and Mike snuffled the night air like a hound.

"That glutton Frank," he said. "He's got his new wife to fixing him dainties. I told you there was more to her than met the eye. Come along, Corkran O'Neill, let us shove him a couple of seats down the trestle."

He went along the deck, stuck his head into the galley.

"God love you, Mrs. Ellis," he said. "Have you some of that for your starving brother and his friend?"

Frank, blinking at him in the wavering light, pulled back his fist. "'Tis Mrs. Carnavon you're speaking to. Take it back or I'll break your jaw."

Mike grabbed the fist and waggled it up and down. "'Tis too tough a jaw," he said. "Or words would have broken it already the night. No, Frank. Mrs. Ellis. And here is how it is, me love."

The town of Somerset at the head of tidewater on the Crookshank River, consisted of eleven houses with adjoining sheds and barns, a sawmill, a shipyard and wharf. The houses, all belonging to the sons, grandsons and assorted relatives of Andrew Cantril, were set down on a shelf of cleared field and pastureland, paralleling the river. Behind them was the forest which ran back nobody knew how far. They were neither log cabins nor shacks, but solidly built, gabled houses, modeled after the houses of England and Massachusetts which Andrew Cantril knew; they were all spacious, with eight, ten, or even fifteen rooms each. For old Andrew had had no lack of building material, and he built to accommodate the size of his family.

In the beginning Andrew Cantril had had a vision. He had been fifty years old, when early in the century, a shipbuilder and carpenter with nine grown sons, he had brought his family and his sawmill up the coast in the vessel he had designed and built himself. He had looked ahead and had seen as many as a hundred vessels of that design sailing out of Somerset loaded with Cantril cargoes. The country was rich in marketable products, chiefly lumber. After his mill was set up and running, and he had sawed lumber for houses and barns, another vessel, the shipyard and the wharf, he set out to create a stockpile to establish his trade.

He had everything at hand pointing toward success—ability, great skill amounting almost to genius, energy and vision, the manpower of his brawny sons, the raw materials for building what he would. But he had one thing pointing toward failure, which in the end outweighed his assets and wrecked his enterprise. He was an egomaniac whose mania was centered in power.

His wife, who died of a broken spirit, long before her family went to Somerset, bequeathed to her sons a docility and weakness which might have become a woman of her time, but was no help to them. They grew up obediently learning skilled trades under their father's dictation. If they minded the old man's overbearing methods, it was easier to take than one of his rages. At sixty he was still able to thrash any one of them, and sometimes did. But not one of the Cantril boys, with the exception of Maynard, could work alone or at all, except under direction; and when the old man went to pieces, his enterprise followed him piece by piece, like an old wagon.

There were forty-seven Cantril grandsons, all with a slice of the old man in them, and they were something else again.

When Andrew came to Somerset, the cleared patch of land along the riverbank was inhabited by a tribe of Indians—owned by them, if such undemanding tenancy could be called ownership, for generations. They were a pastoral not a warlike tribe, living a lazy, uncomplicated life of hunting and fishing; how long they had been there no one could say, but the bank of the river, for rods back from the water, was a shell heap in places ten feet thick.

Andrew Cantril, for some cloth, knives and a few knickknacks, bought a great tract of land from these Indians reaching, according to the deed made out by himself, "westward to the end of the forest, southeastward to the mouth of the river." This covered, so far as he was concerned, everything. He made the chief, Smoking Stick, and all the grown men of the tribe sign the deed with crosses, which he showed them how to make. Then he proceeded to drive the tribe off the land. For it was a part of Andrew Cantril's mania that no man whose name was not Cantril should own land, or even live on his tract by the Crookshank River.

The bewildered Indians—they had not understood the deed, only the "gifts"—went without much protest. They were peaceable and lazy men; they knew of other rivers as comfortable to live beside as the Crookshank.

For the first year or so the Somerset enterprise went well. The Cantrils built some houses, another vessel. The sawmill turned out enough lumber so that Andrew could send a few cargoes down to Boston. But the Cantril boys—young men now—were listless. The virtue was already beginning to go out of them under the old man's continual browbeating; the wilderness life, truly, was horrible to town men, who could see nothing now to look forward to at all. Somerset, too, was a town without women, and old Andrew, believing he could remedy what was wrong, went up the coast in his vessel to the river where Smoking Stick's tribe had newly settled. Again, for some cloth, knives, knickknacks and a little persuading, he made a deal; he bought nine young Indian women and brought them home as wives for his sons.

A practical man, old Andrew.

He might as easily have let his sons go down, one by one, to do their courting in Boston; his vessels made periodical trips with Maynard as captain and four of them as crew, Maynard being the only one he could trust out of his sight. But he swore that if any of them brought back a woman, he would shoot her. He had a great sense of family solidarity; any woman one of his sons might find and marry would be of unknown blood, an unknown quantity. Someone he might not be able to handle, who might corrupt the line, bringing forth who knew what for offspring. He had, too, a certain sentimental feeling about the Indians being the only other true inhabitants of the Crookshank River country besides the Cantrils, and he hated outsiders of any kind. His practical mind solved the problem directly and simply.

His sons needed wives; he could handle his sons and he could handle the Indians. He looked ahead, for he expected to live forever, and saw a great clan of grandsons and daughters, all of this malleable clay, with himself a kind of king. He couldn't have been more mistaken.

The Indian girls were, one and all, daughters of Smoking Stick by the women of his tribe. They had tribal names of which there is now no record, but the surname, if it were one, must have sounded something like "Pie," and Andrew meticulously wrote it down in his Bible.

The names as recorded by him were: Susie, Anna, Lizzie, Ansy, Delie, Feensy and Rebecca Pie. And Rebecca Turtle.

How Rebecca Turtle got in there is not known, unless, as is not likely, Smoking Stick ran out of daughters. It is known, however, that an eighth Pie girl, name unrecorded, died young, so that John, Andrew's second son, had no wife. There may be significance, also, in the fact that Rebecca Pie, who married Maynard, the only one of his sons for whom Andrew had any respect, is given separate listing; though this may have been because Maynard married her legally, taking her down with him for a ceremony in Boston, whereas his brothers' wives were common law.

Old Andrew must have preened himself on having so prettily solved his problem, at least temporarily. Grandchildren began arriving regularly at the rate of seven or eight a year. The Cantril young men straightened their discouraged shoulders and went back to work with some enterprise. The old man might have lived to establish his kingdom if he had been able to handle his grandsons as he always had his sons. But he had failed to consider one thing: that characteristics sometimes skip a generation.

Most of the young boys looked like Andrew—the spit-and-image. And they were wilder than hawks. For Smoking Stick's father had been a warrior and a man of parts from a powerful tribe beyond the mountains now known as the Adirondacks. His fighting blood proved an unknown quantity indeed. Something quite terrible and, in a way, beautiful came from the odd admixture of genes. The Cantril grandsons were hunters and woodsmen from the time they were able to carry a gun, which was almost from the time they were able to walk alone; as they grew up they went streaming out of Somerset into the forest, like a migration of wild birds. How much their mothers were responsible for this, no one can say—the Indian girls, Susie, Anna, Lizzie, Ansy, Delie, Feensy, Rebecca and Rebecca, whose dignified and musical tribal names were so early lost. But their sons went back to their kinsmen, the Indians, and they went armed with the white man's know-how and with his weapons.

The daughters stayed at home and there were a good many of them, until Somerset became almost as much a town of young, unmarried women as it had been in its beginnings a town of young unmarried men. And young Lemuel, the eldest grandson, son of Anna Pie and Joshua Cantril, stayed. Though he made long visits to the tribe, now moved back beyond the mountains, Lemuel stayed because he knew himself to be his grandfather's heir. He looked like old Smoking Stick, and his name among his kind was Smokepole, a corruption of his grandfather's, but he was more Andrew Cantril than he was an Indian.

"No good damned Injun," old Andrew would say whenever he encountered one of his grandsons, and he had a way of spitting at their boots which young Lem didn't care for. When he was twenty-five young Lem one day spat back and made a bull's-eye. In the battle that followed the old man came out second best. He was badly hurt, and after that he was never the same. That was the year he really started to saw lumber, the year he was seventy-seven.

For years, until the day he dropped dead lifting on a big log, old man Cantril sawed lumber. The piles lay stacked along the riverbank, slowly weathering from yellow to brown to gray. Maynard Cantril tried to market some of it, taking an occasional cargo down to Boston. He tried to teach three of his wild nephews to navigate, with the result that three of the Cantril vessels were wrecked and lost. That left one, and Maynard had plans for another, but building a vessel took time and care and manpower. Andrew's sons were growing old; his grandsons were not builders. In the meantime old Andrew went on sawing. He was stubborn as a mule, half-crazy, and he liked to saw lumber. His sons found it expedient to keep him in saw logs, but that was all they could do.

Boards, clapboards, shingles and deals lay in towering piles, sometimes not even stacked, burying the Indian shell heaps deep all along the waterfront, down to high-water mark, and if an extra high tide undermined a pile or so and sent them floating down the river, no one knew nor cared nor missed them. There was plenty more nobody knew what to do with. After the old man's death, Rufus and John, his eldest sons, made out to carry on the business. Someone had to, and Maynard refused to have anything to do with it. He had had enough, he said; now that he didn't have the old man riding his heels, he was going to work on ship models. That was his life work, anyway. He was sixty years old, there was little enough time for what he wanted to do and learn. Seeing he was the only one who could navigate, he agreed to take two cargoes of lumber a year down to Boston, enough to maintain the Cantrils and bring back necessities. Nobody needed much. They all lived off the land.

So Maynard retired into his workshop, a ramshackle building on the head of the wharf, and worked there alone. He built, for the most part, ship models, carefully developing ideas tucked away in his head for years. He had peace for the first time in his life. Occasionally he built a skiff or small sailboat, which he took down on his semi-annual trips to Boston and sold, which was how Frank Carnavon happened to get his Cantril skiff. On each of these trips Maynard was gone a long time. The four old men, his brothers Matthew, Mark, Lemuel and Enoch, who went with him as crew, said he spent days on end visiting shipyards. They spent their days visiting Boston; they came back each time and said to Rufus and John that if only they could sell Somerset, they could go live in Boston.

Occasionally Rufus would say to John that it looked now as if the Cantrils'd never have their hundred vessels, and John would grin his slow, melancholy grin and agree. Two vessels, even old ones, were enough. Why break your back getting more of anything than you needed? The Cantril "boys" had had enough of that when Andrew was alive.

The grandsons scattered to the forest; only the old men, the girls and women remained at home. Susie, Anna, Lizzie, Ansy, Delie, Feensy, Rebecca and Rebecca were all dead. Each time members of the tribe visited Somerset, they took back into the woods with them some of the grown girls, their sisters or cousins, so that no family remained intact. Two of the eleven houses stood empty in the fields. Beyond the waterfront leaned and rotted old man Cantril's enormous heaps of sawn lumber. Forty years after he had founded his city, his people were living in worse squalor than the Indians he displaced; most of them had gone back to the Indians.

Nathan Ellis, sailing his renovated ship's boat into the mouth of the Crookshank River, noticed with interest the amount of refuge lumber which had gone adrift from somewhere and was lodged in quite sizeable heaps along the shore. He had been seeing odd sticks of it for quite some time; he noticed that the character of the shore was changing from rocks and pebbly beaches to muddy, tree-overhung banks. There also was considerable current coming down.

"Hey," he said to Caroline. "We're going up a river. Must be a saw-mill up there. Look at all the drift lumber."

"I don't know that I want to go up a river, do you?" she said. She looked with distaste at the muddy banks. "I like it near the ocean where it's clean."

"So do I," Nate said.

He grinned to himself. She could let on all she wanted to that it was the dirty riverbank she minded, he knew better. A mill meant a settlement, and Caroline, decked out the way she was in sailor's garb, had had a rough time in the settlement they'd stopped at on the way up the coast. They'd put in at Weymouth to see if they could find a minister to marry them, and she'd been hooted at on the street, fol-lowed by a gang of yelling kids, to say nothing of the way the min-ister reacted.

Couldn't blame them. Caroline in pants looked more like a woman than she did in a dress. In a way it served her right. Nate couldn't help telling himself so, though on the trip north he'd had to admit that Caroline's pants were a lot more sensible aboard the boat than a dress would have been. She'd been a help to him, took to sailing like a duck to water, and with a skirt to trip over, she'd have been over-board half a dozen times.

The sailor's garb was all she had. She had had to stow away in a hurry and had left her satchel in Dulverton.

When they finally found a minister, Nate had tried to get a word in edgeways to explain their plight, but the old fellow took one look and began to bawl out a whole sermon on the sin of being unwomanly. He was so mad that his tongue was dry—you could see it every time his mouth opened, which was a good deal; you could, in fact, see a long ways back into his hot, pink throat. Caroline appeared to be fascinated by the sight.

But after a while she spun around and walked away, her back stiff as a stick, and Nate went after her. No use to stay around and listen. From all he could gather out of the froth of spouting texts, the min-ister was refusing to marry them anyway. After they got back aboard the boat, Nate wanted to go ashore again and buy her a dress, but she wouldn't hear of it. All she wanted, she said, was to get away from Weymouth.

"We ought to get married," he said, worried.

"I wouldn't get married here, not by a man like that, if I never got married. I don't care if he is a minister, he doesn't know the difference between right and wrong."

"Of course he does, or he wouldn't be a minister. He's *partly* right, I guess."

"He thinks it's worse for me not to be dressed up like a lady than for us to live in sin," Caroline said. "And that's nasty minded."

Well, it was for a fact, if somewhat puzzling. They were living in sin, all right. Married or not, he wouldn't have it different. When he thought what he'd almost missed, going off alone in a sulk, it turned him cold in his boots. And Caroline in pants, helping him sail the boat, made a lot more sense than Caroline in a long skirt, sitting in the stern with her hands folded.

He put up the sail and came about into the smart southwest breeze, and presently they had left the town of Weymouth a long way behind.

"Look here, Nate." She was sitting on the floor boards with her back against the cabin in the middle to trim the boat, and the halyards made a kind of dancing shadow across her cropped head.

"Look here, I won't be made to live in sin, even by a minister."

He grinned at her. "Well, I don't see what we can do, unless we stop living in sin. I don't know as I want to do that, Caroline."

She said soberly, "I, Caroline, take you, Nathan, for my husband."

He felt a little foolish coming right out and saying a thing like that, but he said it. "I, Nathan, take you, Caroline—"

After he'd said it he felt good, just as married as if there'd been a minister to it; more so, maybe, because it had been private between him and Caroline, which was the way a wedding ought to be.

They had a good trip up the coast, southwest wind all the way. It was lucky, that spell of southwest weather. Because as they went farther north, they could see how dangerous this coast was. Everywhere were islands, large and small, some with high and some with low shores, all rocky. Ledges, half-awash or sunken, poked up in channels where the signs were all for deep water. They ran solidly aground on a hidden bar one forenoon on an ebbing tide, and had to wait until after dark for the flood tide to float them off.

The boat lay there, canted, high and dry, with a waste of clam flats all around her; Nate, making an estimate, judged there must be a big rise and fall of tide in these parts—twelve feet at least, on this one, from eight to sixteen over a period of times of the moon, according to the tide marks. That was considerably different from the tides he was used to. He stowed this fact into his mind where he was filing away the information he was getting day by day.

A man, to make a living—to live—on this rocky coast, with that great stretch of ocean away there to the east and these big tides pouring in and out over unknown nests of ledges, would have to know a lot more than Nate did. Luckily the boat wasn't hurt any by her plunk onto the bar, but with a little more wind, say, and a ledge instead of a mussel bar, he could have ripped the bottom right out of her. He thanked the Lord for the southwest wind. This place in an easterly would be a hell-hole.

Now in the mouth of the Crookshank River, Nate was figuring he had come about as far north as he wanted to. All morning he had been looking for a place to camp for a while, until he could look the country over, decide where to settle down. There had been plenty of places that looked good to him, none of them exactly what he'd had in mind. As long as the fair weather lasted, he kept telling himself, he thought he'd like to see what lay around the next point of land.

He said now, "What say we cut across this river mouth and see what's out around that point? Ebb tide, anyway. Current's too strong to go up the river."

Caroline appeared to be thinking.

"Nate, does that lumber belong to anyone?"

"I wouldn't say so, gone adrift like that," he answered.

He had been wondering the same thing himself. If he'd wanted to settle down here in the mouth of this river, which he didn't—after the Flowage he'd had enough fresh water and mud to last him, he guessed—he could have scavenged enough waste lumber here to build a house.

It was a thing to remember, in case they did find a place within sailing distance of this river. Get the wind and tide right, they might, with luck, be able to float a raft of lumber quite a ways.

They went on past the mouth of the river, past the next point of land. The islands grew more numerous, thickly wooded, with heavy green trees and undergrowth coming down to the water. The channel wound deviously between them; there seemed to be plenty of water in the middle of it, but Nate wasn't taking any chances. He had learned his lesson. He reefed down until the boat barely made way, and kept his eyes peeled for any possible change in the color of the water that might mean ledges.

159

Caroline, without being told to now, got up on the bow to keep lookout, in case the water shoaled quickly.

"You suppose it's *all* like this up in here?" she asked dubiously. She hadn't liked going aground on the mussel bar, and while she hadn't cut up any, the way most womenfolks would, Nate could see she was against its happening again.

"I don't know," he said. "These islands couldn't get much thicker without joining onto each other somewhere, could they? Maybe we better go back down the coast a ways. I remember seeing some good places back there."

He didn't want to go back though, and he hoped she didn't. He liked the islands. They had a clean, secret look of never having been handled or squabbled over, a you-be-damned, take-it-or-leave-it look.

"A man'd have a crazy time sailing around here in an onshore wind," he went on. "You take these tides, it wouldn't surprise me if the whole works ran right out of this channel twice a day. I never saw such a hole."

Caroline said, "You want to go back? I don't."

"You want to spend the rest of your life hearing me growl about the tide?"

"Wouldn't mind it."

The kitten had climbed up beside her, and she scrubbed her hand the wrong way through its fur. "Wouldn't be the tide, it'd be something else," she said. "Look, there's a mountain up ahead there."

"So there is. More than one, looks like. Channel's opening out, too," Nate said.

Past a low point of rocks the channel led into a bay about five miles wide, sheltered on the east by a long, wooded hook of land. To the north lay what looked to be a fairly sizeable range of mountains.

"That's awful pretty," Caroline said. "I never saw any real mountains close to, did you, Nate?"

He said, "No," absently, wondering if this would be the place. That wooded point, shutting off the easterlies which sooner or later would come roaring in off the open ocean; that was certainly the kind of thing he'd been looking for. And those mountains to the north there made one of the prettiest sights he'd ever seen. If there turned out to be a good harbor anywhere inside that point of land—

"Come on down and steer while I shake out the reef points," he said. "I guess we can take a chance on making a little better time."

160

Out of the lee of the islands the wind was blowing across the open bay, making a sweep of whitecaps to the land. The boat tore down across it at a great rate before the wind, sailing faster than Nate had dared to sail at any time during the whole trip north.

He thought, Maybe I'm a fool to let her go like this. But it must be deep water. If there's a ledge anywhere near enough the surface to plunk her on, in this wind it'll be breaking and I can see it.

Anyway, he wasn't going to reef down again. Up there right ahead, looked like the end of the journey, and he wanted it to end. It had been a fine thing to look forward to, and it would be still better to remember. But right now there wasn't any part of it he'd want to do over. Every minute had been a strain, keeping his eyes open for ledges or shoals, never any time when he could loaf along the way he liked to, letting the boat sail herself. He realized suddenly how tired he was.

There were times when a man needed to come home and rest.

He could see now that there was a harbor. It opened out ahead of him, sheltered on the west by another point of land.

It might be home. He couldn't tell yet.

Ledges over there to port, he thought, his mind registering the white rollers and the black fangs thrusting out of them. Deep here at the entrance. I won't need to reef down.

The boat went past the ledges into calm and sheltered water. The brisk wind made, in here, little more than a riffle. The harbor seemed to go back for a long way into the land, narrowing as it went. It could be a river mouth, but it didn't look like one, more like a tidal inlet. At the north end of it, about ten miles away, was a big blue-shouldered mountain, with a cap of snow.

Nate looked over at Caroline, his eyes blurred with weariness. "I guess we could stop here," he said. "If you like it."

The *Bessie,* anchored in the Crookshank River next to one of the Cantril vessels, looked like a hen roosting beside an albatross. As Corkran unloaded her and supervised the ferrying of goods ashore, he was heard to say that the best thing to be done with her was to set her adrift and let her go to hell-and-gone down the river. He was astonished when Frank said no, he would like to have the *Bessie* himself.

To Maynard Cantril, Michael Carnavon—whom he now agreed to know as Mike Ellis—with his pocketful of money was like a messenger from heaven. This was what Maynard had prayed for—new blood, new energies, above all new hands to build the ships he had designs for. The other Cantrils could sell out, go where they liked. Maynard was going to stay and work. Not like his brothers.

The elder Cantrils, Rufus and John, were tired men, bewildered by a business which they had no taste for; they had lived their lives, since their father's death, in a growing petulance, considering that their youth and young manhood were buried under old Andrew's tottering piles of lumber. They looked on the Somerset country as gutted and worn out like themselves. Why, it was impossible now to cut a tree at the back door of the mill, falling it to best advantage so that it could be rolled a few feet and slid in through the door. The old man had cut down all the best forest. If you wanted logs now, you had to haul them a quarter of a mile. And with what? The horses were all old.

The arrival of the tall Irishmen, with their beginning beards, was at first like a gale of fresh wind blowing over the dying town. Mike's beard was coming in black, and so was Corkran's. In time to come the difference would be that Mike's wife kept his clipped and hand-some, while Cork's grew as it would into a glossy flow of which he was to be tremendously proud. Poor Frank had no luck with his. His coloration was red, his growth irregular, so that he produced, in all directions, a wild, auburn stubble. He looked, now, very ferocious; nevertheless, it was to him that the eyes of old Rufus and old John turned most often, as the five men sat in what had been Andrew's room at the mill.

They had sold out lock, stock and barrel to Michael and Francis Ellis. Houses, land, mill, wharf and shipyard, the lumbering rights along the Crookshank—everything. Even the Cantril vessel, which was to take the remaining members of the family away. Maynard was to sail them all, with their things, down to Boston and leave them there. Then he was coming back, and for most of them that would be the last of Somerset.

But now that the deed was signed and Maynard gone—he was out superintending the loading of the vessel—Rufus and John were scared. From outside came the sounds of a great stir and bustle as the Cantrils loaded their possessions. Four of the Cantril grandsons, hearing the news by some sort of forest grapevine, had come in, thrown aside their weapons; they were going with the ship. They were noisily helping with the ferrying; their yells of jubilation, like gulls' cries, came muffled through the thick walls of the old mill. Rufus and John lingered. Their dim eyes darted here and there; their hands fingered this and that, while in bewilderment they tried to realize the breaking of a habit of forty years.

The two tall black men, the Irishmen, were here, there and everywhere, poking, prying, asking questions. All business. Rufus was getting mad. After all, this mill was the Cantrils' business. There'd never been anybody here but Cantrils.

Who was this upstart to be told how much money the ventures to Boston had made for years back? How much lumber the mill could turn out, working at capacity? Things that had always been Pap's business, things that only he had known. Rufus burned within himself with a slow anger as he heard John, fumblingly, not accurately answering questions.

Was there always this much current over the falls of the river? What was there in August when the river fell? Could the mill operate the year around?

The questions beat in his mind as he remembered. He and Pap and the boys had answered them years ago. Any fool would know that this was spring water, this head coming down, covered with slashes of foam and hunks of drift. This was the time of year when the mill worked hardest. Now it was silent. What was wrong?

Pap—Pap—the mill's stopped.

He heard Pap say, as if Pap had been in the room with him, "Well, ye worthless, goddam son of a cook, go and start the mill."

"Well," Mike said briskly. "I guess that's all you gentlemen can tell me."

He waited for them to go, and when they sat still, not moving, he said impatiently, "That's all, me friends. I'll get the rest from Maynard."

The anger burned in Rufus.

"And what more do you want? What more can you get from Maynard that you can't get from me?"

"Faith, the specifications for the Cantril vessels," Mike began, and old Rufus leaped to his feet with a shout.

"No, by God, you bastard! No one gits them vessels but Cantrils. No one's ever got 'em, nor ever will!"

He stuck his face into Mike's. His eyes were rheumy and his breath was bad. Mike recoiled.

"Hell, man, we've got them," he said reasonably. "You and your brothers sold them. They're here. Here in the deed."

Rufus looked at the paper as if for the first time. Oh, yes. But that was yesterday. Yesterday he had wanted to sell. Had spring fever or something. Didn't mean a thing. Today he felt better, didn't want to sell.

"I'll just take that paper back," he said. "We've decided we don't choose to sell."

Mike carefully removed the deed from the reach of Rufus's fumbling hands. He said, "You've sold, man. It's too late."

Rufus opened his mouth to splutter. Anger with him had never been an effective thing, and it was not now.

He said vaguely, "Don't belong to us to sell anyhow. Belongs to young Smokepole. He ain't going to like finding you here, is he, John?"

Mike's eyes narrowed. "Who might he be? Is he one who might have legal title here?"

Old John said, "Shut up, Rufus, you're crazy. The prop'ty belongs to us all right, Mr. Ellis. But young Smokepole, he allus figgered he was the heir to it. Something Pap said once. Never signed no paper."

"Cork, you better go find Maynard," Mike said. "I don't like the sound of this."

Rufus swelled up as if in anger, but it was more grief than anger. "We're the ones!" he shrilled. "John and me. Maynie ain't got no say."

The red Irishman, the one with the crazy stubble on his chin, got up, slipped his hand under Rufus's elbow.

" 'Tis a sad thing," he said, "to be leaving the home of a lifetime, Mr. Cantril, and needs more thought, perhaps, than you and your brothers have given it."

"That's jest it," Rufus mourned. "All of a heap, without thinking. It's only the young ones wants to git away. We'll be lucky if Pap don't hant us, John and me."

"You and your brother come with me," Frank said. "We will walk over the property and discuss like decent men, and if you decide you do not wish to sell, then Michael will give you back your paper. Shut up, Mike. You cannot make the old man sell if he does not wish to."

He led the two old men out of the mill and along the rutted road, past the piles of rotting sawdust and piled lumber to the riverbank. Out in the river the *Mary Cantril* lay swinging to her cable. Rowboats were ferrying back and forth, loaded with goods.

Rufus and John hung back a little, talking in low voices, for there was the *Mary C.* out there loading in the river, with the kids yowling like the savages they were, for joy; and John was saying to Rufus what a mess it would be now if they did not sell, and Rufus was thinking that now he did not have to sell, maybe after all, it was the thing to do.

Frank waited till they caught up with him.

"'Tis a sightly place and all," he said. "If I owned it, Mr. Cantril, the devil himself would not make me sell. But then I have not spent my life here, seeing nothing of the world."

"That's it, that's it!" John said excitedly. "Rufus and me, we ain't been down the river sence we come up it, forty years ago."

"And that's a shame," Frank said heartily. "The world is too lovely a place for a man to grow old and never see it. Boston, now, is a great city, to which all the world comes. With money, and you will have a great price for your land, there is nothing you cannot have in Boston. Wine, women—"

Frank smacked his lips. John looked at Rufus and Rufus looked at John, and each became a little brisker, a little younger in his mind.

"Yaas," John said. "I've heard about them Boston women."

"And you've heard no lies," Frank said.

From somewhere in the forest back of the town a musket cracked, and he heard the whine of the bullet passing above his head. It thwacked into the lumber pile beyond him, splintering the edge of a board. Frank ducked. He jumped for shelter to the nearest pile of lumber and stood behind it. The two old men followed him, leisurely talking with each other.

"Where'd you go?" John said. "Oh, yaas. Well, Rufus says he'll sell."

And Rufus chimed in, "Yes, I guess we'll really sell."

Frank eyed them quizzically, his head on one side.

"In that case 'tis a joyful occasion, Mr. Cantril," he said, "calling for some slight celebration." He pulled out of his pocket the flask he carried, offering it to Rufus. "And who might it be who is careless with a musket or a damned poor shot?" he asked.

Rufus took the flask, upended it in his mouth and let it gurgle awhile before he handed it to John.

"That's liable to be Smokepole," he said. "But if he'd wanted to hit you, he would of."

"Well, it was accommodating of him," Frank said. "Is it a habit of his then?"

"Not to call a habit," John said. He eyed the flask and remarked petulantly, "Don't be such a hog, Rufus."

After an interval, when the flask was empty, Frank linked arms with the two old men and led them down to a rowboat on the river, where a couple of young Cantrils were about to shove off for the ship.

"The grandfathers need to be put carefully aboard the vessel," he remarked politely.

The tall young half-breeds looked at each other with dead-pan faces. "Drunker'n hogs," one of them observed.

"No," Frank said. "They have only been transacting business as decent men should, with a draught or two of poteen."

He watched the boys help Rufus and John aboard the boat.

God forgive me, he thought, but 'tis time they left this savage place, poor old men.

"Who is this Smokepole they've been telling me about?" he asked meditatively.

"Cousin," one of the young men said.

"Where is he now?"

"He's hunting."

They pushed off the boat, the current took it out into the river. The two old men sat stiff and glassy-eyed. The two young men rowed, their faces expressionless.

One of them shouted, "You'll know Smokepole when you see him. He'll make himself known."

Of the Cantrils, thirty-seven went away from Somerset in the *Mary C.*; Joshua stayed, and Maynard was to stay also, returning with the vessel after the trip to Boston. These two were the only ones among the Cantril "boys" who had never entirely knuckled under to old Andrew, but for very different reasons. Josh was the dull one, not much more than a natural; he could not work because he could not think. He had only one distinction; he was the father of Smokepole. And Maynard was the bright one.

Maynard had learned from his father how to build ships. For forty years, ever since as a boy of fifteen he had started to pick Andrew's brains, he had slowly and patiently added to his knowledge. While his eight brothers spent their lives in boredom and petulance and inevitable slow rot, Maynard grew, because his brilliant and gifted mind was absorbed in shipbuilding and vessels were his life.

His pencil was a piece of charcoal, or a three-cornered section of soft, terra-cotta brick; sometimes a nail, if he were in a hurry and nothing else was handy. His eraser was his jackplane so that the files and records of his drawings were in thin, delicately marked shavings that fell to the floor, were trampled, swept up, in time burned. There was no need to keep the drawings; they were only Maynard's sketches. Those which looked good to him were quickly transferred, in scale, to a loft floor, to molds, to plank and timber and hackmatack-knee. In the time that Maynard Cantril used it, he set down on his table top a great record of ancestral memory—memory, that is, for his own place and time. The memory went back to a burned-out, hollow log with a mat of leaves for a sail, to a Phoenician galley or an Indian canoe; it came from wherever men had had to figure out problems of displacement and sheer and wind resistance, from wherever they had had a river or a sea to cross. It had traveled a long way and for many years in time to get to Maynard Cantril, not that he knew or thought about that.

Old Andrew took the credit for the Cantril vessels; it was not his. It was Maynard's. For Maynard took the old man's original design and added a thing here and straightened out a quirk there and overlaid the whole with a blueprint of his own, so that in the end the Cantril vessels were very little like the stubby sloop which Andrew had designed and in which he had sailed his family up the coast so long ago. It was immaterial to Maynard who got the credit so long as he was left alone to work.

He had other designs in his head now, besides the Cantril vessels. The vessels were his baby, his first love, but they were finished. He didn't see how he could improve them, though doubtless, he told himself modestly, they could be improved. This was lumber country, but it was fishing country and river country as well. Cargo vessels were the first need. Well, they had a cargo vessel. Maynard, dreaming over and above the sound of his father's yawp, kept in mind the time when the country would open up. Men coming into it would need small, capable fishing boats and shallow-draught barges which could float loaded down a river, claw themselves back again against the current. For the country would open up, Maynard was sure of it. One man, even Andrew Cantril, couldn't stop it. The old man might drive the settlers off the Crookshank, but it was a big country, and, Maynard told himself, looking around at his father and brothers in his silent, meditative way, it needed something besides Cantrils. He did not mourn when his father died and Somerset fell to pieces. The half-crazed old creature was not cold in his casket before Maynard, working alone, began some experimental models of small boats.

What he set down on his table top were the lines of the Chebacco boat from Essex, and his own modified version of it which, in years to come, men would develop into a useful fishing boat, the pinky; and he set down plans for a cargo carrier, the river barge which other men were to modify later on and call a "gundalow." It could not be said that he "invented" these designs, any more than he invented the pea-pod design which he worked on; he was one of many, out of his time, studying and adapting the ideas of other men, so that the hulls and rigging of the boats he built would be practical and useful in the particular waters on which they were to sail.

Mike Ellis, hunting for him to give him a few last instructions on the day the *Mary Cantril* was to sail, found him at last off aboard the *Bessie,* thoughtfully poking around down in her hold to see how she was built.

Not a man to waste words, he listened silently while Mike talked.

"Workmen," Mike said. " 'Tis skilled hands we need, and many of them. Charley Tansley will take care of getting supplies and equipment. But you know the shipyards. I would have you loot them of every shipwright and carpenter you can persuade to come, if you have to kidnap some of them."

Charley Tansley had been the mate of the *West Wind;* he and some of his crew were to go along to help sail the *Mary C.* back again. Mike would rather have sent Cork, but Cork was too well known around the Boston waterfront; besides, Charley was a good enough man. With Maynard as his skipper, he would do.

Maynard said reflectively, "You'll have to let me keep my house.

I guess Rufus sold it along with everything else. A family the size of mine, I've got to have a roof over their heads."

"Good Lord, man," Mike said. "You'll have a deed to the house and land tomorrow. And a partnership in the enterprise here, if you'll keep on building your ships."

Maynard nodded. He had it in mind that with skilled workmen, he could build the Cantril vessels with one hand and his new models with the other.

"How big is your family, man?" Mike asked. He liked this quiet man, who seemed to have nothing in common with the rest of the tribe —a worthless lot, if Mike ever saw one.

"Four boys," Maynard said. "Seven girls."

Mike looked at him with awe.

"Is your wife living, then?"

Maynard shook his head.

"God bless you, then. Are your boys grown? If they are like their father, I'd be proud to have them work for us."

He thought it possible that Maynard's sons might be different from the other Cantrils, seeing Maynard was. But Maynard's eyes clouded and he looked away.

"My boys ain't home," he said. "Only my girls now."

His sons were among the hunting and wandering Cantrils, and Maynard did not even know where they were.

"But Josh wants to stay," he went on. "He's a carpenter. He helps me."

He did not say Josh was a good carpenter, or how much his help was worth, or that the only reason Josh wanted to stay was because Smokepole was hunting in the back country somewhere. He did not say he felt responsible for Josh, because Josh was seventy and a fool.

Mike said, "Good enough. You find a place for Josh, put him on the payroll. You'll have the say in the shipyard, Mr. Cantril, I hope you know that."

Pay? Maynard thought. Pay for old Josh? Who of the Cantrils had ever had any pay in their lives?

The idea tickled him, and for the first time he smiled.

"'Bout the workmen," he said modestly. "I won't have to kidnap none."

"No? It's a wilderness to ask people to come to, Mr. Cantril."

Maynard straightened his shoulders a little. "There's many men all along the coast," he said, "would be pleased to work with me."

Mike stuck out his hand. "A good voyage then, Mr. Cantril, and a fair wind home."

He climbed briskly down over the *Bessie's* side and into the skiff to go ashore.

Maynard went back below. He was tickled to death to have a chance to look over the *Bessie*. Her builder had made mistakes, but she had a little something. He'd seen her before many times, never close to like this. Old Bright, her former owner, always stopped at Somerset with his trade goods once a year; from the beginning, he'd never allow anyone but Rufus aboard of him. When the *Bessie* dropped anchor at Somerset, old Bright would load up a musket. He would draw a bead on every skiff that left the landing, yelling at the top of his lungs, "You keep off from here, ye light-fingered bastards!"

He had good reason. The young Cantrils were used to taking what they wanted. None of them ever saw the color of money.

Pay? Maynard mused. That's a good one.

Maybe with a little money he could buy something to keep the girls contented. They were all mad with him now because he wouldn't let them go with the others on the *Mary C.* He couldn't blame them. There was nothing here for a passel of growing girls, not even marrying, unless they married their cousins the way most Cantril girls did, went into the woods with the Injuns. Maynard be damned if he was going to have them do that. He'd had enough fight already over it. Them cousins, they warn't going to git his girls. The rest of the folks were going, he'd be glad to see the last of them. Relations or no relations, becusst to the whole works. There were fifteen new menfolks come in off the *Bessie,* some of them unmarried, looked like nice boys, too. If Maynard's four marrying-age girls didn't get suited out of that lot, it would be their own fault, first time they'd ever had a pick.

Contentedly he poked around down in the *Bessie's* forepeak. That difference, it was in her stem. And that there, that was hackmatack. Old, but solid as the day it was built.

In his office at the mill, which had been old Andrew's room, Michael Ellis set down the rolls of his new town. He used a leather-bound ledger which he had brought with him, which already was a quarter-part filled with the business records of the Boston firm of Carnavon Brothers.

The names read as follows:

Michael Ellis, wife and two sons
Francis Ellis, wife
Capt. Corkran O'Neill
Charles Tansley, mate, wife and child
Frederick Smith, ship's carpenter
Jobbick Butler, boatswain, wife and two sons
Ansel Miles, able seaman, wife and child
William Tansley, able seaman
Matt Williams, able seaman
Robert Welch, able seaman, wife
James O'Brady, able seaman, wife and three children
Pierre Gordeaux, able seaman
Charles Ushant, able seaman
Nicholas Goddard, ship's boy
Maynard Cantril, shipwright, seven daughters
Joshua Cantril

When Maynard Cantril and Charley Tansley got back from their trip down the coast, Mike was able to add the names of twenty workmen and their families to his rolls.

Tansley reported that the British were making Boston uninhabitable with their regulations; a towse over this and a law over that, everything taxed, until a good many men were disgusted, ready to go elsewhere. He could have brought back twice twenty workmen, if it hadn't been for Maynard Cantril, who put his foot down. He wasn't going to bring back just anybody. He was going to pick and choose his workmen. After the stores were loaded, Maynard sailed the coast, visiting shipyards. He brought back men of his own acquaintance from Gloucester and Salem; he brought back Jim Gorham of Dulverton, and recruits from Portsmouth and Weymouth. Twenty families —no more. It would be a squeak, Maynard said, providing living quarters for even that many before the snow flew.

Lumber would sell anywhere, like hot cakes, said Charley. He had an order from a yard in Gloucester for a whole shipload. In Charley's opinion they had a gold mine.

Mike agreed. He'd never imagined such a gold mine in his life. He watched the new workmen being ferried ashore from the *Mary C.*—sober, horny-handed men, with chests and bags of tools on their shoulders. Then he rolled up his sleeves.

He sent Corkran off to Gloucester with the *Mary C.* piled high with lumber, with orders to come back loaded with more stores and equipment. He set the new workmen to building houses for themselves and their families.

All summer long the hammers rang on the banks of the Crookshank, through the long hot days and the August drought, when the river ran low and the water over the falls dwindled to a lacy trickle; in the breathless nights, by lantern light, when sweat ran down and tool handles grew slippery with it, for the great forest behind the town cut off the prevailing southwest wind, and so far up a river there was little cooling from the sea.

The men worked in shifts, willingly. They were not building a town for Michael Ellis, but for themselves. Each man was given land, free run of the lumber piles and time to build his house and barn. In return for this he signed an agreement with Ellis Brothers that he would stay and work. He was to be given time, by agreement, to plow and plant vegetables and grain crops, to cut firewood and to harvest.

Mike worked it out carefully on paper, put the paper away in the drawer that served him for an office safe. He had had men work for him for most of his life; he had learned that when the greatest number were contented, working hard and accomplishing something for themselves, then an employer could expect miracles. It was simple. Mike had great faith in the hands of men. Working as hard as anyone, he yet found time to stand back and see the new town grow.

By September the new houses and barns were up along the river. Vegetables and grain were ripening for harvest. Hay was in. The *Mary C.* went like a shuttle all summer, carrying lumber down the coast, bringing back cargoes of meal and salt pork, molasses and other staples: window sashes, scrap iron, wagon wheels, horses, cattle, pigs and oxen. A new smithy was in operation down by the mill, turning out, for a beginning, sled runners.

Mike drew a deep breath. The profits of the enterprise, if all went well, were going to be considerable.

In August Sally Carnavon—she had never been willing to call herself Mrs. Michael Ellis—caught a fever and died, or rather, puled her life away without any desire to get well. She had never got over the loss of her fine establishment in the city, her carpets, her silver, her clothes. Her summer had been spent indoors in the big, comfortless house which had been Andrew Cantril's, hating it, hating Mike, being shrewish to her two small sons.

Mike supposed he grieved for her and missed her as a decent man should miss his wife; actually, her death freed him of a carping, uncomfortable relationship which had seemed alien to a place in which the winds of his accomplishment blew free. The little boys, Shawn and Colin, missed her hardly at all. They had seen little of her all summer—she couldn't stand noise. All summer they ran like little Indians, growing brown and stringy and wild, for there seemed to be something about the town of Somerset which bred wildness in the young.

So Mike buried Sally in the thorny, overgrown Cantril cemetery on the hill at the edge of the forest in back of the town. He was sorry, but in time he forgot her as if she had never been. It was the second death of the summer, for old Job had not lived long in the new land.

A few days after the funeral he remembered to enter Sally's death in the town rolls, but even then it seemed of less importance than the news, heard that morning, which had caused him to take his leather-bound ledger off its shelf. Doubtless the time to make full record of the new item would be later on, but his mind was full of it now, and it did seem that of such a thing certain note should be made. After all, the little creature may have existed three months ago when he first set down his list of names, and such a list should be complete.

Frank, the spalpeen! After nearly half a lifetime! Maybe now he'd come ashore off that hulk of a *Bessie,* live in a house and do some work like a human.

With a half smile, Mike wrote into his town rolls after "Francis Ellis, wife," the words "unborn child."

All summer Lizabeth had been readjusting her life. The machinery of readjustment in her moved stiffly, for she was forty-two; habits, opinions, prejudices, set hard in her young womanhood, were deeply grooved by half a lifetime of use. It took a stunning blow to change her; this blow Lizabeth had received.

At first, when she realized that Nate and Caroline had deserted her, and Edward and Betsey had thrown her out of her home, she had been in a fury of hurt and angry pride. A lifetime of slaving for these children, loving, tending, raising them to be decent and good, and this was the way they treated her!

After all I've done for them, she thought, with her head high. It was only later that she felt the crushing grief and sense of loss.

She might have stayed and fought Edward, if she had not already been numbed and bewildered by her experiences of the day before. But too much had happened to her; a whole nest of old values had been tumbled down and ripped apart. She needed time to rest and think before another crisis had to be met, and no time was given her.

It was in a kind of blind numbness, almost a state of shock, that she took the only way out offered to her, which was to marry Frank.

The possibility that the "children" could get along without her never entered her head. *She* was the indispensable center around which her household moved. Without her the whole structure would fall to pieces, the spokes of a wheel when the hub is taken away. Nor did it occur to her that her constant interference in the lives and affairs of her young people had made her a burden to them.

As the *Bessie* moved irrevocably northwards, the numbness wore away. The wound would heal sometime, but it was a slow, inflamed healing. She felt as if she had been torn in two, left with raw places bleeding. She stood at the rail looking at the wilderness behind the rocky coast, and felt it no greater than the wilderness within herself.

Her mind went over and over the details of home—the routines, the work left undone, which now nobody would do right. The grease and lye ready for the soap-making, the washing—you had to watch Betsey, she never scrubbed the colored clothes clean. The sheds. The taproom floor needing sand. And the "children."

She told herself miserably that in one thing she would harden like a rock—she would never want to see one of them again.

If Frank had been a different kind of man, she might have made no change but have gone on slipping into middle and old age, a grim, sharp-edged and embittered woman. But time and rest were what she needed, and he gave her those. He was courteous and considerate; his big, gentle body gave off relaxation and a gaiety such as Lizabeth had never known. She had never in her life been exposed to gaiety, the good Joel having been a serious-minded man.

Beyond her misery she became increasingly aware of Frank. He was always there with warmth to match her chill. It seemed to her she was forever cold. For as the *Bessie* sailed north she left the spring behind. In Massachusetts the leaves were already greening on the trees, but in this country their buds were closed and sealed, as if there were never to be so soft a thing as spring.

Lizabeth's honesty, her respect for a bargain, stood her in good stead now. If she had stayed idle, mulling over her misery, she would have been finished. But she had married, given a man her word to be his wife, and be his wife she would. Frank wasn't one to force a woman, though he needed one often. His needs were transparent as glass. When his laughter stopped and he began following her wistfully about, "underfoot," she called it, she could tell, and she went to him of her own accord.

Aboard the *Bessie* she made him more comfortable than he had ever been in his life. For after Mike had started to assign living quarters ashore, it could be seen from the beginning that there were not enough to go around. Frank was all for staying aboard the *Bessie*; it was too crowded ashore, he said, he wanted his life to himself for a while. So Frank and Lizabeth settled down in the *Bessie's* cabin, in the anchorage in the Crookshank River.

Lizabeth had no objections; while she couldn't see how a woman could keep decent house aboard a boat, she told herself she didn't care. She didn't think she'd ever be interested in keeping a house again. For a time she had nothing; then almost imperceptibly, something stirred in her which was more and better than anything she had ever had.

She had discovered, not without a certain sense of shock, that Frank would not take her unless she wished it, that unless she came willingly to meet him, the sexual act meant less than nothing to him. At first she could not understand, Joel's needs had been simple.

She said one night, "Go on. You've a right to."

And Frank said curtly, "No, lass. I have no wish to turn my wife into a whore."

He let her think about it a little before he touched her again.

"Oh, Lizabeth," he said gently. "The harm that has been done you!

In time it will go better, have no fear. But I could wish for us that we had met each other long ago."

The *Bessie* swung lazily to the river current; the April sun shone; presently the spring came. With bewilderment, Lizabeth found that she was not only a woman but a dear companion, welcomed into, not pushed out of, a man's affairs. At first Frank took little part in the enterprise ashore, being content to stay quietly aboard the sloop. Thinking, he told her. He was not sure yet whether he wanted to be a part of Mike's project. So far in his lifetime, he had always gone into things with Mike, and the way it generally turned out, Mike after a while found no proper place for him, so that Frank lost interest.

"Because Mike's the sharper and the cleverer man," he said. "He has no patience with my fumbling."

"H'm," Lizabeth sniffed. "It sounds to me as though he pushes you out. I haven't found you a fumbler."

Frank grinned. "It doesn't take the push of the world," he said. "At least, it has not so far. But it has been a great jump for me, as for all of us, coming here from the city. I can see how a man's work could lie in this place; already I have come to like it. But for the time, I do not see my place in it."

He, too, was making adjustments.

With Joel she would have poked and pried, given him the edge of her tongue, because she could never abide an idle man. And Joel eventually, maddened, would have gone ashore and taken up the first work at hand merely to be rid of her.

But she found it pleasant to go with Frank ashore, while he hunted deer and partridge in the forest, or to take the skiff and drop down the river fishing. He was not like Joel and her boys, always pushing her away; Frank always wanted her to go. She found she did not care for the shooting, herself, but it was fun to dangle a line over the skiff's side and pull up flounder or cod, knowing as she did what a dish she could make for Frank's supper.

In the first week of August, while the summer's drought hung on and the water in the river dwindled, Sally Carnavon died. Lizabeth nursed her as best she could, but there had been no hope from the beginning. She felt no grief for the whining creature, as she could see no one did; only a fool would say that a woman who eked out life as Sally did would be better off living. She had died alone, though her husband was beside her, cursing him with her last breath for bringing her to this hateful place to die. After the burial in the Cantril cemetery, her vain and shallow life was as if it had never been, except that a vague and foreboding melancholy hung over the town and voices were quieter.

It was the loneliness of the death that shook Lizabeth.

To bear a man children and yet hate him so, she thought. In spite of herself, her mind went back to the scene of another deathbed less than a year ago. Joel's.

But I grieved for him, she thought. He was a great loss to me, and she found, with a sense of stiff astonishment, that she could not recall Joel's face.

After the funeral she and Frank went back aboard the *Bessie*. Flats stretched out from the shore now, even on the flood when the tide came up the river from the sea, the river water was so low, and Frank had to carry her out to the skiff, staggering through mud to his ankles. Aboard the boat she laid out dry clothes for him, cleaned the mud off his boots, cooked the evening meal. They ate on deck in the cool, not saying much, both quietened by the grim day just passed.

A slight gurgle of water ran past the *Bessie's* keel, the slow river letting back the salt tide which had replenished it. The air off the land smelled dead and piny from the resin cooked out all day by the sun in the great forest, a dry, exhausted smell, mingled with dead grass and mud flats and weed. The sun was setting red behind the forest. Great, spiky shadows of trees fell on the raw, new lumber-yellow buildings of the town.

Frank said, "You're tired, lass. It's good it's over for her, the poor thing."

"Yes," she said. "It is."

She looked at him thoughtfully and down at her fingers, turning over and over a pewter spoon.

"Frank," she said. "It's time we made plans, I think."

"I think so, too," he said. "God bless you, lass, for that 'we.'"

He leaned back against the *Bessie's* rail, puffing on his pipe. "I'm ready to come out of my idleness. But it's been good here on this little boat, a thing we both had need of. I wanted to make no change until you were ready, too."

"I'm ready," Lizabeth said briefly.

She gestured over her shoulder at the town. "There's too much to

177

be done there for us to sit out here alone, like a pair of nesting ducks in the river. Did you see those little Cantril girls? No decent clothes even at a funeral, and burrs in their hair. I swear that little one had on a meal bag."

Maynard Cantril kept a tight rein on his girls when he was there to do it, but his work kept him often from home. His eldest girl, Rachel, kept his house for him.

"And acting like little heathen savages, as if a funeral were a sight to see," Lizabeth went on. "Their sister looks like a slut."

"I'm afraid she is that," Frank said.

He admired Maynard Cantril, but everyone in Somerset knew well enough how his girls were acting, running after Corkran's sailors.

"I could help out some there," Lizabeth said. "Your brother's little boys, too."

Frank glanced at her with a smile.

"Do you not be making plans to take care of the whole town," he said. "You have your hands full with me."

"Yes, I do," she said. "But we ought to take part in the town, Frank."

He nodded. "I'll have to push Mike over a little," he said.

"From all I can see he needs help. You won't have to push hard."

"H'm, perhaps not. Have you thought where you would like a house?"

"Have you?"

She did not even think how she had changed. If it had been Joel asking that question, she would have had an answer ready—the house located, planned, half-built in her mind.

"There's a place just above the falls," Frank said. "Not away from the town, but not in the middle of it. When the river is high again, it would be the sound of the waterfall outside the window."

She nodded. "Then we'd better begin to build," she said.

She thought a moment, but could think of no words to tell him what she had to tell. In her girlhood she had had plenty of words, easily spoken with warmth and generosity; speech, now, had been for many years too sharp a thing. But even as she sat thinking, the un-spoken words said in her mind, If something happened to him as it happened to Joel, I would not be able to live, and she said aloud, "I'm going to have a child."

To her it sounded abrupt and coarse, but not to Frank. His jaw dropped with astonishment and the part of his face that could be seen above his beard turned bright crimson.

"Begod," he said in a whisper. "What a world's wonder."

She misunderstood him.

"Well, I'm forty-two," she said. "But I don't s'pose I'm past my use."

He did not even hear her, but sat slowly wagging his head. She began to feel put out with him; it wasn't after all something she'd done alone.

"I had to say so sometime," she said.

"Frank Carnavon of all," he said groggily. "Father of a son! Or of a daughter, 'tis no great difference. That great lunk of the world, a father!"

"Stop it!" Lizabeth said, biting off the words. "Don't you dare to run yourself down! No finer man ever lived, nor a better father!"

"Why, lass!" Frank said. "Why, lass!"

He reached out both hands and took hers blindly, and for once, her hands were warm and his were cold. She saw to her astonishment that tears were running down his cheeks.

"Well, now," she said. "Well, now, Frank."

For the life of her she couldn't think of any more to say.

But he could, now that he was over his first shock.

"The treasures you give to me the day," he said, marveling. "With no more fuss and feathers than you would hand a man the tea to his supper!"

His eyes began to twinkle as he looked at her sitting primly across from him. He sat puffed out with pride and merriment behind his terrible witches' bush of whiskers, and then, seeing in her face a beginning answer to his grin, he burst out laughing with a great bawl of joy.

Young Lem Cantril, called Smokepole, in early April had gone into the woods to find the tribe. The newcomers were too many for one man, even Smokepole, to handle alone. He gave no sign of his rage, of the violence contained within him, beyond the one musket shot which had so startled Frank; after that Smokepole vanished into the forest.

He was raging because Uncle Rufus and Uncle John had sold Somerset; Somerset and the forest around it belonged to him. All the Cantrils knew how old Andrew had left it. True, there was no paper; it was not a country of paper, it was a country of words. And Smokepole being part Indian considered a man's word more binding. He based his claim on Andrew's word, uttered a long time ago, when young Lem Cantril had not yet grown big enough to break his grandfather's head.

"You ain't no good, God damn ye," the old man said. "But you're my eldest grandson and you'll have Somerset. I'll learn ye to saw lumber, or I'll break every bone in your body!"

Smokepole was thirty-five now. He had not done a lick of honest work since the memorable occasion of his fight with his grandfather. It was not a part of his plan ever to do any again. Hell, he didn't have to; he owned Somerset. It was all right with him if Uncle Rufus and Uncle John and Uncle Maynard ran it, picked what fat they could out of the Cantril mill. Life in the woods was pleasant; Smokepole wasn't ready to settle down. When he was, he figured he could handle them three old boobies all right. They all had one leg in the grave anyway.

Smokepole had grown up seeing how it was possible for one strong man, if he were big enough and made enough noise, to own and boss a lot of lesser men. From his boyhood up Lem had watched his grandfather. He had nothing but contempt for the rest of the Cantrils, running around like sheep, scatting when the old man said, "Scat." All they were good for was to wait on the big one, do what he said. It looked pretty simple.

What you did, you got a whole lot of fools around you, the more the better; you scared them good, then you set them to work, while you sat back and did the bossing. According to Smokepole his grandfather had made one mistake, he'd spent his life working. You get enough fools, there'd be plenty of them to do the slaving.

He could not believe his ears when old Josh his father came back into the woods where Smokepole had a camp with four of his cousins, bringing the news that the old men were selling Somerset. He lit out for town, boiling, and his first setback came when the four cousins, two of whom had been to Boston a couple of times with Maynard, deserted him to go on the ship with the Cantrils.

Smokepole took a good look at the newcomers and decided against trying anything alone. He fired one shot to record his intentions, though; then he went off to get help from the tribe.

The trouble was, he couldn't find the tribe. They didn't seem to be down along the coast in any of the places where they usually were in the summer, eating shellfish and hunting, and that was funny. He walked a long way back into the country, he judged about sixty miles, to their winter quarters near the mountains. They weren't there either. Smokepole was puzzled. He spent part of every summer with the tribe, and they'd never been hard to find before.

The explanation, if he had known it, was simple, though not one he could have brought himself to believe. The tribe was avoiding him.

They, too, had had the news from Somerset, and Charley Cantril, the chief, had called a council. The young men agreed that Smokepole would probably be along sooner or later, expecting them to do something; so far as they were concerned, Somerset could sink in the river —they'd had a bellyful of it. Let whoever wanted it have it, but Smokepole would want a war.

The tribe wasn't against a war when there was a necessity for one, but they needed a good reason, and Somerset wasn't; not, anyway, to keep it for Smokepole. They were about fed up with him anyway, coming into camp whenever he felt like it, throwing his weight around and raising the devil with the squaws, yawping that he was worth any five dog-Indians and them part Cantril, and ought to have his say and his pick. So far they'd put up with him because he was the best shot in the country—they were practical men, and a supply of meat outweighed, always, a little discomfort, but Smokepole was too much like Andrew Cantril for any of them to feel quite easy with him.

He made no bones of saying that when he took over Somerset the tribe would have to move out of the woods and work for him, and while they laughed at that behind his back, the fact remained that Smokepole could outshoot, outrun, outfight and, just possibly, outthink any two of them. And they all remembered Andrew Cantril.

Thus, to avoid present trouble until the council could decide what was best to be done, Charley loaded the tribe into the canoes, and they moved for the summer to an island some nine miles offshore. It was a fine, big island—not one the tribe was accustomed to summering on because it was so far out, but it abounded in shellfish, the fishing was good; the tribe settled down peacefully, to await developments.

It was the middle of September before Smokepole gave up hunting for his people in the forest and came back to the coast. His last cast had been far to the south, so that when he made the coast, it was not at Somerset, but at the mouth of the river five miles below the town. It had been a long trip and he was tired. He was also beginning to realize that if the tribe had wanted him to catch up with it, he would have. Smokepole was no fool. The only place he hadn't looked was off on the islands. No use to go wild-goose chasing off there, there were hundreds of islands and the tribe might be holed up on any one of them. But Charley'd have to bring them ashore before the fall gales set in; when he did, Smokepole would meet him on the shore and there'd be a reckoning. He'd about decided that the time had come for him to take over Somerset. If Charley and the boys didn't want to help him, then he'd take them over, too.

Well, there was the damned old Crookshank River. He was glad to see it, if only to spit in it. He hated it, but, hell, he owned it, or he'd know the reason why. It was all damn foolishness for a man like him to live like a dog with a lot of flea-bitten Injuns, while some slobbering fools got fat off of the Cantril mill. In a little while, after he got rested, he'd walk along to Somerset, see what the situation was.

He sat down on a mat of dry leaves and grass under an oak tree, leaned his back against the trunk. In front of him the mouth of the Crookshank, where it widened to meet the sea, was banked with color, the red and orange leaves of the hardwoods flaring so bright against the blue that it hurt his eyes. He was used to shade in the woods. Leaves that bright this time in September meant only one thing to Smokepole—that it had been a dry summer down here on the coast. If he'd known that, he'd have waited for a rain. Drought in Somerset meant that all the wells would be low, which also meant that anyone who didn't want the summer complaint would have to lug his drinking water from the boiling spring in the pasture. Smokepole grinned faintly. Not him. He wouldn't be the one lugging no water.

A sound of voices coming from along the riverbank made him start, sit up and listen. Somebody up there a ways. Now who could that be? If 'twas any of them fellers thought they'd bought up the town, he'd have himself some fun.

He picked up his gun and slid into the underbrush, circling, coming out again on the riverbank a couple of hundred yards upstream, where he could peek through the bushes unseen.

A boat piled high with drift lumber floated at the edge of the water. Two fellows he'd never seen before, one of them big and husky, the other one slight, were busy loading on more. They were barefooted, wading in the shallow water.

Smokepole's eyes narrowed. His throat worked with righteous anger.

Why, the thieving sons of bitches. Stealing Cantril lumber! Even if it was drift, it still belonged to the Cantrils.

He hitched himself to his feet and slouched noiselessly down the low bank, his eyes slitted and cold above his rifle barrel.

This was the fourth time Nate and Caroline had crossed the bay to this place after lumber; Nate was figuring that one more trip and he'd have enough to snug them in for winter. They had got enough, so far, almost to finish their small cabin, but he wanted now to put up a lean-to for stores. With luck he could get it done before the snow flew.

Caroline saw Smokepole first; Nate was back-to, lashing the deckload. She gripped his arm with a little cluck of terror, for Smokepole coming down the bank wasn't a pretty sight. He had on a round cap made out of rabbit skin. The fur was worn off, showing patches of dirty hide. This was pulled down to his eyebrows. His whiskers grew up nearly to meet it, so that what she saw seemed to be a face of hair with two dark slits of eyes. He was barefoot and his clothes hung in rags, showing more of him than was decent. His travels through the woods had been hard on his clothes. She thought for a split-second that he was some kind of animal, like a bear walking on his hind legs, but there was nothing unhuman about the rifle.

Nate spun around. He gulped a little at what he saw.

Smokepole said, "What in hell you think you're up to, stealing my lumber?"

Nate backed away a little before he could stop himself. From ten feet away he could smell the woods' reek, like a fox's, that the fellow gave off.

Nate said, "I thought it was driftwood, didn't see how it could belong to anyone."

"Well, it does. It b'longs to the Cantrils. To me."

"All right," Nate said reasonably. He was feeling plenty scared, the way the man's eyes looked at him from in back of the rifle barrel. "Don't look like you want it, leaving it to rot on the shore. Some of

183

it's been here for years. But I'll be glad to pay you what you think it's worth."

Smokepole shifted the rifle. He spat a straight stream, so that Nate had to move his foot.

"If the Cantrils," Smokepole said, "wants to leave their lumber on the shore to rot, it ain't none of your damn business."

"All right. Then what d'you want me to do?"

"Unload it."

"Oh, hell!" Nate burst out. It had been a terrible job hunting the sound lumber, wrestling it out of the jackstraw piles and getting it secure aboard the boat. "It's waste lumber, for Godsake!"

"It ain't the lumber. Us Cantrils has got lumber to patch hell a mile. It's you, snooping around here, causing damage on Cantril prop'ty. Ain't nobody 'lowed along the Crookshank but Cantrils. You're lucky I ain't blowed your head to hell off you, and maybe I will yet."

Caroline said roundly, "I never heard of anything so stinking mean! If you've got so much lumber you can afford to let it go adrift, what do you care if someone picks up some to use? We'll pay you for it."

Smokepole started a little and stared at her. After a second or so he began to grin. "Well, dog my cats!" he said in a high falsetto. "Look what we got here!"

Caroline flushed. She drew back behind Nate.

Smokepole's grin broadened. "Tell you what," he said to Nate. "I'll trade you the lumber for ten minutes up in the woods with her."

Nate balled up his fists. "You put that gun down, give me a fair chance, I'll knock your teeth down your throat," he said.

"Oh, no." Smokepole patted the gun stock. "I don't fight tit-babies."

Caroline, standing in the water by the boat just behind Nate, suddenly screamed. It was high and bloodcurdling, pure terror, and both men, startled, spun toward her. She doubled up, still yelling, and then scrabbled into the boat all anyhow, with a big, purple-backed crab hanging onto the toe of one bare foot. The crab was all of four inches across its back and its business claw was a crusher. Nate swore and made a grab for it, but Caroline was kicking so furiously that he missed.

"Hold your foot still!" he yelled at her. "Dammit, hold still!"

He caught her flailing ankle and twisted at the crab, parting it from its claw, which still stayed shut-to on Caroline's toe. He figured she could tend to the rest of it herself. The fellow holding the gun appeared to think it was a laughing matter; he was doubled up, howling. The gun muzzle was wobbling some. Nate hauled back his arm and let go the crab with all his strength. The way he'd been swinging an ax, among other things, all summer, had limbered up his arm muscles; being red-hot mad helped some, too. The big crab hit Smokepole squarely between the eyes with a dull, punky crack.

Smokepole let out a yowl and his gun went off, the blind shot plunking into the water half the boat's length away. Nate got the gun by the barrel and twisted it away from him. He whirled it around his head and let it go out into the river, where it landed with a splash and sank. He turned back just in time to see Smokepole charging at him with a knife, and to jump to one side. The jump, being automatic, was fast; it was also nicely timed. Smokepole had charged headfirst and high, an old fighting trick of his which didn't often fail. If his shoulder caught the other fellow just right, it would topple him and knock the wind out of him. This time, however, it didn't catch anything, and Smokepole, with nothing to stop the impetus of his flying leap, landed on his face in the water. It was the kind of thing that kids, diving off the riverbank, would have called a belly-smacker.

Nate didn't wait to watch him flounder to his feet. He grabbed up his anchor, dropped it into the bow of the boat on top of the tangled anchor rode, gave the boat a good, running shove out into the current. With a hundred feet of water between him and the shore, he looked back. The man was standing on the shore shaking both fists and swearing a stream of blue filth that made his ears burn.

Nate hadn't had time to realize how mad he was; he did now. There was something about the squalling, filthy words—and in front of Caroline, too—that finished him. He picked up his gun, which lay in the stern sheets beside him, primed it and drew a bead on the flailing figure on shore.

Caroline had been sitting with her back up against the cabin, nursing her toe. She let out a gasp and an "Oh, Nate! Don't!" and made a grab for his arm.

Smokepole, seeing, turned around and started to scrabble up the bank. Nate's bullet smacked into the dirt not two inches from his leg as he ducked into cover. The bushes shook a little behind him, showing where he had gone; then they were still, and there was nobody on the riverbank. The smoke from the shot floated quietly upwards against the background of flaming leaves.

Nate put down the gun. He hauled up his sail, teetering the heavily loaded boat precariously as he moved about the cockpit.

Caroline didn't move; she just sat huddled up rubbing her toe, and he saw she was crying to herself, turning her face away so he wouldn't see. He let the sail flap, the sheet dangling for a moment, while he knelt down beside her.

The toe was swollen, turning black and blue, but it could wiggle. It wasn't broken.

Nate took the small, cold foot between his hands.

"It's all right, honey. Wasn't anything but a crazy old woods' bum, anyway."

"Crazy old woods' bum nothing!" she burst out. "He tried to kill you."

"Well," he said. "We're even. For I sure as shooting tried to kill him. You hadn't joggled me, I guess I'd have plowed him."

He reached down into the cabin, hauled out her heavy, threadbare old winter coat and his own jacket. He wrapped her as warmly as he could in the coat and was about to tuck his jacket over her feet, when Caroline, seeing, came to a little.

"No, you put your jacket on," she said. "I'm all right now, and you must be cold, too."

He wasn't, he realized. He felt fine—warm and tingling all over, and about twice his natural size, as if everything inside him had stretched. He grinned at her, wrapped her feet in his jacket. "If I'm cold, I'll holler for it," he said. "You get good and warm."

"Put on your bub-boots," she said with a hiccup.

He stuck his feet into his boots and stamped them on, thinking it was a good thing he was warm anyway. The boots were damp; they leaked, and he needed new ones. The hard summer's work had raised the dickens with his clothes and with Caroline's too. She mended where she could, but she hadn't any material to use for patches, and now they were out of thread. Another difficulty, they'd both grown some. Caroline was taller, and he was both taller and wider; he was over six-foot-one now, and his muscles were busting his shirt out at the seams.

They'd have to go somewhere pretty soon, he thought, and lay in the stuff for winter.

186

He'd had it in mind to make a trip upriver to this town where the lumber came from; there were a lot of supplies to lay in before the cold weather came. He sat thinking about it while the heavily laden boat wallowed tranquilly across the bay toward home.

If all the Cantrils were like this one he'd just met, he guessed he'd better plan to go somewhere else. There must be other settlements within sailing distance. Only, of course, he didn't know the waters very well. With winter supplies they'd have a loaded boat, and if they ran into weather down amongst those shoals and ledges—

Cantril, he thought suddenly. I wonder if that's where Maynard Cantril hangs out? If that's the kind of a rig he runs, I don't know that I'd ever want to hunt him up and work for him.

But he remembered the big, quiet, slow-spoken man who had come in to Mo Brown's shipyard in his fine vessel.

I don't believe he's like that; that fellow's just some crank gone woods' crazy. Be foolish to let him scare me into making a wild-goose chase down the coast before I found out about this town. If I run into him again, well, I've outsmarted him once. Hell, wasn't my fault I didn't outsmart him for keeps.

He wondered how he'd have felt if he'd killed the man and found it was impossible to say.

I don't know as the son of a gun deserved to be killed, but he needed something to slow him down, and he sure did his best to kill me.

It was something he'd wondered a lot about, and he still didn't know. But if it had been Ed instead of Nate—

He thought of the difference between himself and Ed—Ed, who went off like a charge of powder, thinking afterwards; himself, slower—but when the explosion came, it seemed to be just as violent. Ed would have jumped that hairy devil and fought him till one of them was laid out cold. He wouldn't have pushed off the boat and then taken a shot at him, when he was back-to going up the bank.

Nate shrugged. Whichever way, it didn't seem to matter too much. He had got out of it with a whole skin; Caroline was kind of rucked up, but she was safe. The thing with Ed seemed far away and long ago, dimmed out; only, he realized, he didn't blame Ed as much as he had in the beginning.

I ought to have got his side of the story out of him, he thought. But it's too late now.

He beached the boat at their home cove and stepped overboard into the shallow water; she was too heavily loaded to nose up on to the dry shingle. He lifted Caroline out so she wouldn't have to get her feet wet.

"You go on up to the house," he said. "I'll be up and start a fire as soon as I tie the boat. Guess I won't unload tonight, I'm too tired. She'll be all right here till morning."

Caroline wasn't saying much, but he could see she felt better. She wasn't even limping badly, only walking with a certain tender care for her left foot, and when he went up to the cabin she had the banked-up coals raked out and supper cooking—venison steaks frying with a little plant she'd found in the woods that tasted like onion. There wasn't anything else. Even the salt was low, and the cornmeal was long gone.

Nate ran his hand over the short, silky mass of curls on the back of her head. Her hair was still short; it was the only way she could keep it clean and decent, with what she had to do with. Nate himself had whetted up his knife a couple of times and trimmed it for her, and he found he liked her hair that way.

"Lord, Caroline," he said, "that smells good."

"Even deer meat again?" she asked.

"What's wrong with deer meat? Looks fine to me."

She was being pretty quiet for her; he judged she was still getting over her scare. It was too bad a thing like that had had to happen. He hoped it wouldn't leave her nervous. So far she'd been fine in this lonesome place, not that they'd had much of anything to scare them. No one ever came here; at least no one had in the past three months. There were bears and bobcats in the woods, might even be a panther or two, but all the animals seemed to be more afraid of humans than humans needed to be of them. The bears came up around the cabin at night only if you left foodstuff where they could get at it, which he and Caroline had learned early not to do.

She never seemed to mind being left alone at the cabin; he didn't leave her often, but there'd been a few times when he'd gone out fishing and exploring the big bay and had been gone all day. He'd always found, when he got back, that she and Fluffy, the kitten, had made out fine. That was before he'd known there was any such critter in the country as that blasted woods' bum. Of course, though, he was over on the other side of the bay.

They took their supper over to the bunk to eat it, the bunk being the only comfortable place in the cabin to sit. Nate had brought in two sawed sections of log for chairs, but they'd been in the way in the small room, no good to sit on anyway, and he'd rolled them out again. The bunk was a good one though, he'd taken time to make it comfortable—high off the floor to be out of the draughts, thick layers of dry marsh grass spread with their blankets. For plates they had pine chips, smoothed, hollowed out on one side, and their spoons were whittled out of flat sticks. To cut their meat they handed his knife back and forth.

"You all right?" he asked.

He saw she wasn't eating much.

She nodded. "Just tired," she said.

"Well, you go to bed. I'll clean up."

"Oh, no, I'm all right."

"You done eating?"

"Yes."

He got up, picked the rejected plate out of her lap, scraped the venison into the cat's dish. Then he took the greasy wooden chips to the door, hers and his own, and scaled them down over the bank into the cove. He heard them splash in the water, shut the door and came back dusting his hands.

"There," he said. "All cleaned up. Now you go to bed."

"You'll have to eat off the floor tomorrow," she said. "You've chucked out all the dishes."

"More where those came from," he said. "Your toe hurt you any?"

It didn't, or if it did, she wouldn't say so. She got into bed and lay there quietly while Nate finished up the rest of the chores. When he got in beside her, she was so still that he thought she'd gone to sleep.

He lay stretched out with his arms behind his head, feeling tired out but, for some reason, wide-awake. His head buzzed with the events of the day; he guessed, now he stopped to think of it, that he was more scared right now, thinking what might have happened to him and to Caroline, than he'd been while the thing was going on. No use to have it over though, and get the horrors. If he were going to lie awake, he'd better use the time to make plans. There was so little time to plan, so much to do. Still work to be done on the cabin, endless supplies to be laid in for winter.

Their clothes were finished. His boots and Caroline's shoes were worn right through the soles. They couldn't start a winter here without warm clothes and footgear, it was out of the question. Salt and meal, needles and thread, spoons, plates, cooking pots. Now that the cabin was nearly done though, he thanked the Lord he'd taken Ev Piper's advice about those window sash.

They lay silently, he and Caroline, while the fire cast a warm glow on the rough walls made out of salvaged Cantril boards, with studs of three-inch spruce trunks hewed half-around.

Nate had built the cabin back against the woods with windbreaks of trees and undergrowth on three sides, the fourth side facing the harbor. He still lacked shakes for the roof. Once this dry spell was over and the fall rains began, the roof would leak like a colander. He'd be lucky, too, if the chimney didn't melt down, though he was pretty proud of that chimney.

He'd had fun building it, had had to figure carefully the stresses and strains of the flat rocks fitted on to each other against a keystone long enough to keep the whole structure from tumbling into the fire-place. It worked, too; had a good draught in any kind of windy weather, except, of course, a southerly. Why that was he couldn't say, but he'd worry it out sometime. He had an idea it was because the trees back of the house were taller than the chimney, made a down-draught. In time he'd get that fixed, too. But blue clay wasn't any kind of a substitute for good lime mortar. It hardened all right, filled up the crevices, but it was likely to crumble. He could see a couple of cracks already, and the Lord knew what rain would do to it.

Have to buy some lime over in the town. And some shakes or shingles.

He thought suddenly about how much he was counting on going over to the town. This summer had been the most fun, the best time he had ever had in his life, settling down here in the cove with Caroline, building the cabin, exploring the back country and the bay, finding the big waterfall up the tidal inlet by the foot of the mountain. All summer he'd wished the days were thirty-six hours long and that he had six pairs of hands. He still couldn't see up over the work that had to be done before winter set in. But now he wanted to see some people.

Living away by yourself was fine for a while, when you needed to; he was beginning to realize a man could have too big a dose of it. Of course, he'd had it in mind to go up to the town all summer, when he got time. Once or twice, days when he'd been out fishing or exploring the bay, he'd seen the sails of vessels over on the horizon to the west, heading down through the islands toward the river-mouth. It had made him feel kind of good, knowing other men were as near as twenty or thirty miles away. After this afternoon he felt as if the pins had been knocked out from under him with regard to the town, because maybe this fellow Cantril was a sample of what lived over there. Maybe the farther away Nate stayed, the better. Anyway, he wouldn't dare to take Caroline into a mess like that, at least until he'd been once himself and found out what it was like.

Beside him she stirred a little and Nate said, "You awake?"

She said, "M-mmm?" in a sleepy voice, and he didn't say any more. Let her sleep. They could talk in the morning.

Caroline wasn't asleep, or even sleepy. Every time she closed her eyes, she saw that horrible hairy face coming at her out of the dark. But she'd made up her mind, coming up here with Nate, that she wouldn't make a fuss over things, be a weight hanging onto him, the way he'd said, in the beginning, any woman would do. So far this summer, when she'd been scared or upset by something, she'd managed to keep it to herself. She guessed she could manage this; it was only a question of waiting until the picture of that awful man went out of her mind.

Caroline had had a good time all summer, too, not as good a time as Nate had had, but she had what she wanted. If there had been certain drawbacks to living with him, she'd learned to put up with him. She couldn't remember a time when she hadn't loved him.

If he had gone off and left her in Dulverton, the way he'd meant to, she thought likely she would have died. When she had thrown the ashes into his eyes, it seemed to her her heart was broken, seeing him so hurt. And when she had walked away from the wharf at Dulverton, she'd known she was finished forever, unless, somehow, she could make out to go with him. She had hidden at first among the lumber piles on the Dulverton wharf, sneaking down aboard the boat the first night and stealing food out of the sack when Nate was asleep. The kitten, Fluffy, was all she'd had for company. Then she'd met Mrs. Gorham, the shipyard boss's wife, and Mrs. Gorham and Jim had taken her in. She'd stayed with them until the evening Nate came up to the Gorhams and told them he was ready to sail; when he went back aboard the boat, she had gone down the wharf ladder just ahead of him, with Fluffy in the front of her jacket. He hadn't come below that night, so he hadn't known she was there, shivering and crying in one of the bunks.

Now, lying beside him, she knew he loved her; she had only to put out her hand to him.

It's worth it. You can't have everything your own way. If he's like his mother—and his father, too, she thought, remembering Joel Ellis —it's the way he's been brought up, and he can't help it.

It had seemed to her that settling down on this wild coast and making a home was an enterprise that belonged to them both, that her part in it would be as great as his. She worked as hard as he did; she could see that even in the outdoor things which he considered wholly his own, she'd been a big help to him. Of course there were certain things that only he could do. That was all right, she wanted no part of them. But in the planning—like the laying-out of the cabin—they both would have benefited, if he'd only been willing to talk things over before he went ahead. Instead of pushing her right back into being his little idiot sister, which was the way he'd always treated her at home and which now was hard to take.

As a result the cooking hearth was too low and so was the kitchen sink; they were both back breakers to work at. But when, during the building, she'd pointed it out to him, he'd just acted as if she were making a criticism of *him*, and then he'd gone right ahead and finished the work the way he'd started it. He was so proud of it when it was done that she hadn't said any more. But she wondered how long it would be, if he'd had to work over that hearth and that sink, before he'd have ripped them out and fixed them so they wouldn't make his back ache.

It was the same way with the work out of doors. He wouldn't listen to a single idea she had. The only effect she seemed to have on him, she noticed that sometimes, maybe a couple of weeks after she'd suggested something, he'd come out with the idea, big as life, as if it were his own. Proud as could be because he'd thought of it all by himself.

She supposed it was a kind of backhanded compliment. No one wanted to be praised all the time. Only sometimes, she thought, sometimes it would be nice.

She could have stood it better, too, if he'd keep out of her part of the work, seeing he wouldn't have her around his. But when he was in the house, he was into it up to his nose, coming out all the time with suggestions about the kitchen things—how she could have done this better, or why didn't she do that? or hang the kitchen pots over yonder. Sometimes his suggestions were good ones and she used them. The one about the pots hadn't been, but it had come after a tiresome day and had made her put out. So she had hung the pots where he said; and the first time he'd walked near them he had whanged his forehead on the big copper kettle, just as she'd known he'd do, and had sworn at it something outrageous.

When you're alone with someone, like this, she thought rebelliously, it seems as though you both ought to be people. Not one grown-up, the only one who knows anything, acting as if the other's nothing but a baby. It makes such a fool of you.

For a moment she thought what it might be like to live with Nate if she didn't love him, and she saw a picture in her mind of a grim and awful boredom. The picture scared her, almost worse than the woods' bum had today, and she pulled herself up short.

I guess I better remember that Ma Ellis brought me up, too, she told herself sternly. Because if anyone's sitting in judgment, I am, right now. I'm lucky to have any kitchen at all, seeing the hard work it was. I ought to be thinking about the way he got us out of that mess today. Most men would have knuckled right under, but Nate didn't.

The fact remained, however, that that, too, had been a cooperative venture. The memory of it struck her suddenly as funny. All at once she felt a lot better, and she began to giggle.

Nate stirred. "What's so funny? I thought you were asleep."

"I was thinking about that crab latching onto my toe—" For a minute she couldn't speak. The laughter shook her so that the dry marsh grass rustled under them.

Nate put out his arm and hauled her comfortably over against his side. He thanked the Lord she was feeling better.

"That was lucky, you know it?" he said. "Old crab was in the right place at the right time. Learn you to be careful though, walking around in the water barefooted."

"Well, I'd been walking around him for quite a while," she said. "He'd been out and in, under the edge of the boat all morning. I thought maybe if I had a good reason to yell, that man would look at me instead of you, and then you could do something. So I just gave the crab a poke with my toe."

There was a short silence. Nate said in a horrified tone, "You poked that thing with your bare *toe? On purpose?*"

"Mm-hm."

The giggles began again. She said through a mouthful of laughter, "And then you let him have it right in the head, made a noise like a punkin. That was a trick you learned from me, you know it?" She didn't know what had got into her, bringing that sad old business up now, but she couldn't help herself. "Fellow got the drop on you, let him have a faceful."

Nate put his other arm around her, his mouth over hers.

"Lord, honey," he said after a while. "What a damned fool I was!"

She didn't know that she wanted to answer that, but he was waiting for her to say something. So she said, "Which time?"

Nate chuckled. "The time I tried to sail off here alone, without you. Oh, Lord, Caroline, what if I had!"

For a long time there was a silence in the cabin.

Caroline woke up in the early morning before the sky had even begun to lighten. Living here in the cabin this summer, so far away from other people, she had developed a kind of sixth sense about necessities. She woke up with the feeling that she'd forgotten something. It was pitch-dark in the cabin, cold—oh, yes. Neither one of them had remembered to bank the fire. If she got up now, she might be able to salvage a coal or two, kindle it fresh, but by daylight it would be out. And she hated to cook over a new-made fire, all that smoky blaze, when coals were so handy.

Nate was sleeping heavily, the breath whistling a little through his nose. No sense waking him, he was tired out after yesterday, and he'd need to be rested if they went over to the town today. Knowing Nate, she thought it likely that he'd tend to getting the stores right away; now that they might have to make a long trip, say they couldn't get what they needed over where the Cantrils lived, it was the next thing to be done.

She found the coals she'd hoped for deep down among the ashes, and kindled them carefully with shavings. As she crouched over the growing fire feeding it with small sticks, she realized that she felt wide awake and rested, not a bit like going back to bed. She felt rested inside, too, as if something which had been anxious and straining and tired for a long time had quieted down, happy, as if something wonderful had happened. Oh, yes. Nate had come right out and said, last night, that he wasn't sorry he'd brought her with him.

She supposed she'd known it really, but he hadn't ever said. She'd wondered sometimes, if he weren't making the best of a bad job, because here she was and he was stuck with her. He'd tried hard to get away from her, too. But now she was sure; Nate didn't say things he didn't mean.

She didn't want to go back to bed; it seemed such a waste to sleep away a minute of this feeling of happiness, which wasn't like anything she'd ever felt before. She'd never in her life been sure anyone had wanted her; she remembered way back, when Pa Ellis had brought her and Betsey home, how put out and flabbergasted Ma had been. Through all those years, even though they were nice to her and Betsey, she never could feel that she'd really belonged to them. Nate was the only one of them she had ever loved. And now she did feel sure that she belonged to him.

It seemed as if the end had come to a long, unhappy time. This summer had been fun, but always in the back somewhere was a shadow on it—Nate hadn't really wanted her to come. There'd been times when she'd felt so lonesome she didn't know what to do. She'd wondered while they were getting the cabin built, if the warm weather would ever come. The snow stayed on the mountain back up the inlet, into May. Nights it seemed as if the cold blew down on their canvas shelter right from that snow. She remembered the cold hands and the chilblains. She'd thought she'd never again see a fire burning, except through the spread fingers of her own cracked, red hands. This fire, though, this one was nice.

If she weren't going back to bed, she might as well think over the list of things they needed in town. They needed so many things. They'd never be able to remember that great long list of supplies. She'd spent a lot of time when she was by herself, learning it by heart. *Salt. Molasses. Boots. Thread. Cornmeal,* was the way it started. She was sure she could say it all, but suppose she forgot something, and they got back here and found they didn't have, say, thread.

Out by the cabin door, she remembered, was a smooth board end which Nate had sawed off a planed board when he built the bunk. She slipped quietly out to find it, closing the door behind her so as not to lose the little heat the fire had made in the cabin.

It was cold outside and dark, all the darker for her having come out of the fire-lighted room. It was cloudy, not a star showing, and windless. She could sense rather than see the great black sweep of water to the west, lying motionless under the cloud-muffled sky. As her eyes got used to the dark, she could make out the ragged sprawl of tree branches against the clouds, the big trees, three to four feet thick through their trunks, in the woods behind the cabin.

A little light was beginning to come into the sky over there. Must be almost morning. You couldn't tell, the trees always hid the sunrise.

She found the board end and went back with it into the cabin. With the point of a sharp nail from Nate's tool box, she began scratching into the smooth surface of the board the long list of things they'd need to take them through the winter.

Salt. Molasses. Thread. Boots. Cornmeal . . .

The list went on and on. It covered the smooth side and ran over on to the rough side of the board where the surface was splintery, and she had to bear down hard with the nail.

There. That was all. She couldn't think of another thing. She checked it over to make sure nothing had been forgotten.

Now it was getting light. She'd better make breakfast and wake Nate up so they could get started, say he wanted to go today and the weather was willing.

Nate got up and dressed and went out to look at the weather. When he came in, the first thing he said was, "Caroline, I'm going to take a sail over and have a look at that town today. I've decided I'll be better off alone. Say I run into a fight, I won't have you to think about."

It flattened her right out. It hadn't entered her head that he wouldn't take her with him.

She thought, What if he gets hurt or killed over there, on the same side of the bay as that awful man?

"I'd rather take a chance on a fight," he said, "than bring the boat back from Weymouth, loaded deep through the shoals. Might run into an easterly, too, this time of year."

He'd thought it all out last night before he went to sleep, carefully balancing one chance against the other. Now, looking at Caroline's face, he wondered if he'd chosen the right course. He said, "You'll be all right. I'll start right away so's to be back before dark."

It took her a minute or two. She had to push down how much she wanted to go to a town, see some people, walk into a store, if there was one, and pick out the cloth for a dress. She had to push down the worry about what might happen to Nate over there. But she said, "Fluffy and me'll make out. It's a good thing I woke up early and scratched down the list on a board. One of us alone'd never be able to remember it all."

Nate went off at daylight with the board end tucked under one arm, his gun under the other. He offered to leave Caroline the gun, but she said no.

He had taught her to shoot the gun, and she could if she had to, but she hated it. Besides, nothing had bothered her here so far, she didn't think it was likely anything would today. He was likely to need the gun more than she did.

The early morning clouds had cleared off, the sun coming up clear, with a westerly breeze which wasn't much more than a puff or so now, but which might be brisk toward afternoon. He would have to beat across the bay, but coming home he could probably count on a fair wind.

Caroline watched the boat go out of the cove, the pale-gray sail dwindling down to a dot as it went farther away across the bay. It was bad luck to watch a boat out of sight, and she wasn't going to; so when the sail got so small she could barely see it, she went into the cabin and shut the door.

She spent the forenoon pleasantly enough, doing chores around the cabin. That was the way to make time pass—work hard. She laid out plans to fill up the whole day, and more. This afternoon she'd walk out along the shore, spot and mark flat rocks for Nate to get for the foundation of the shed. She didn't worry at all, until around one o'clock when the wind began to blow.

It was the beginning of the autumn changes, if she had known it, the end of the summer. It began with slowly increasing gusts of wind from the southwest, blowing the full length of the long, open bay, kicking up a white-capped chop. Caroline had cleaned the cabin and hung the blankets out to air. She had scrubbed the floor and was down in one corner finishing it off, when a gust of wind baffled down the chimney, picked up a cloud of ashes and blew the feathery stuff all over the room.

Caroline said, "Oh, blast!" She scrambled to her feet, surveying the nice clean damp floor to which most of the fireplace ashes were sticking. Then she realized that the chimney, for all its drawbacks, had never done that before.

The cabin was sheltered on three sides; she'd been so busy she hadn't noticed the weather. Now she looked out the window. The bay beyond the cove was covered with nasty-looking, low, green rollers, crested with white. Even in the cove itself, down in the lee of its hook of land, there was a surge and ruffle of water.

She looked out at it, thunderstruck, and fought down a rising panic. Nate couldn't possibly bring back a loaded boat in this.

She put on her things and went out. Behind and above the cabin, the tree tops were tossing; the wind was going through them with a queer, thundering sigh. Along the beach, past the cove, she could hear the rollers. The whole land- and seascape was moving in a way she hadn't seen it do before.

She thought, How'll I ever stand it here alone, if he doesn't get back tonight? What if he tries to come and doesn't make it?

She felt her stomach clench, cold and stiff, inside her; for a minute it was hard to breathe.

"Oh, God," she said aloud. "Please God, don't let him start back in this."

The kitten came around the corner of the cabin chasing a dead leaf. Fluffy was more than a kitten now; she was three-quarters grown, but she still kept her flighty ways. She went across the clearing, following exactly the motions of the leaf, as if she herself were as light, as erratically blown by the wind. Caroline watched her out of sight in the undergrowth. She began sturdily to pull herself together.

Of course Nate would have the sense not to come back in bad weather. He knew what his boat would do. If it was sensible to stay over on the other side of the bay, he would. So far as being alone a night in the cabin was concerned, she guessed if the bears and panthers didn't bother when Nate was home, they wouldn't pick out a night to come around the cabin when he was away. There were Indians in the woods; they had never come here.

If Nate did come home, he wouldn't want to find the cabin full of ashes.

She went back into the cabin. She found if she hung her coat part way over the fireplace opening, it stopped the draught down so the ashes wouldn't blow. The fire was very low, only coals. She'd better get herself a good hot meal and then let the fire go out, because if the wind got much worse and the coat didn't work, some coals might blow out onto the floor.

She cooked venison and greens, making the job last as long as possible. She forced herself not to look out of the window at the gray-green, smoky-looking sea.

The greens were goose grass, which she'd found growing down in the rock crevices along the shore. They had a sour-y, sharp taste, not very good without a piece of salt pork to boil in with them, but their liquid made a hot drink to go with a meal, when you didn't have tea. The first mouthfuls went down hard past the lump in her throat; she couldn't taste anything. She found she felt better though after the hot food.

By the time she had cleaned up the dishes, the fire was out black. She spread the canvas tarp over the fireplace opening, propping and anchoring it with sticks. Then she washed the floor again.

At dark the wind was blowing a full gale. Caroline went to bed with the sound of it thundering in her ears, the deep-throated whistle and howl through the trees above the cabin, beneath it the water-washing sound of rollers on the beach. There was no rain. Clouds scudded across the sky, with here and there a dim star showing. She put Fluffy into Nate's place, huddling around the warm, furry ball for comfort.

"You're nice," she told the cat. "But you're a poor substitute, you know it?"

After what seemed a very long time, she went to sleep.

She woke in the night with a start, wondering what had waked her, and groped around Nate's empty place in bewilderment for a moment, before she realized he wasn't there. Fluffy wasn't there either; she was sitting on the sill of the western window, her round outline silhouetted against a queer red light in the sky.

Must be morning. I've slept all night, she thought, with a feeling of thankfulness because so much time had passed. But that's a funny-colored sunrise. That's awful funny.

She got out of bed and went to look. The wind had gone down some, at least it didn't sound so loud, and the tarp over the fireplace had stopped billowing in and out.

The western sky was smoky orange-red low down near the horizon, and it was all in one spot, she realized, not spread out over the sky like a reflection of the sunrise.

199

It wasn't a sunrise. The night was still dark, nowhere near morning. That was a fire over there, a big one.

Oh, dear. I hope it isn't in the town where Nate is.

She huddled, shivering, by the window, her face pressed to the glass, watching the ruddy glow, which grew brighter as she watched, against the low, angry western clouds.

By and by she grew so cold that she had to get back into the bed again; she couldn't seem to get warm and she couldn't get to sleep. She lay waiting for morning. It seemed a year, a lifetime, a generation, before the light began to come; and in the western sky, the great, ruddy, hot glow grew and grew.

As soon as it got light enough to see, she dressed and went down to the shore of the cove. Beyond the islands a great, thick pillar of purply-gray smoke was rising, lined out northeastwards with the wind against the bright morning sky. She could smell it—the hot, acrid, hair-raising smell of a forest burning. The wind was still high, but it had gone down a lot; there were whitecaps on the bay, not flattened-down, smoky crests. Nate could come home today.

And then, bearing in between the points of rock that made the harbor, she saw the sail. For a moment it seemed as if the heart flew right up out of her throat on wings and went out to meet it.

Boat isn't loaded, she thought. He must've left the load for later. But I don't care, just so he's home.

She stood happily, waiting for him to come close enough so she could call to him. And then she saw it wasn't Nate. It was Nate's boat; that man aboard of her wasn't Nate.

She stood frozen, her heart pounding, for a moment; then she fled in blind terror up the path past the cabin and into the woods.

Smokepole, on the day before, had had to walk the ten miles up the river to Somerset, a thing he hadn't planned on having to do. When he first saw that fellow and his girl stealing lumber, he'd figured at once on sailing home in comfort. He was going to knock them around some, pay them off for their thieving, then take their boat. Serve them right if they were left stranded, the damn robbers. It hadn't worked out that way.

Smokepole walked. The lump on his forehead swelled up to the size of an egg, pained him with a good solid ache. The water from his ducking in the river ran out through the holes in his pants. His gun was gone; he'd just as soon be without his right arm. He'd never been in the woods without a gun before. Starting out on his walk, he got furious at his wet, uncomfortable pants and took them off. His idea was to wring them out, but he was pretty mad—the pants came in two pieces with the first twist or so. He gave them a fling into the bushes and went on into town in his shirt.

His hunting shirt was of deerskin—it was good for another season —but the pants had been some kind of no-account stuff Uncle Maynard had brought up from Boston, worn out anyway. He'd have to be careful going down into town, not to run into Uncle Maynard. The fringe on the shirt barely covered him, and Uncle Maynard was as careful of them girls of his as if they were somebody, not just a job-lot of Cantrils. Anybody else Smokepole didn't care a hoot about, but just as well any time not to run edge-on into Uncle Maynard. Not that Smokepole was scared of him, but sooner or later he and Uncle Maynard were going to have to bang together. There wasn't any doubt in Smokepole's mind as to which one would bounce, but he wanted to choose his time and place, and he wanted to have his pants on.

He trotted out of the woods at the edge of town. He was damp and uncomfortable; his legs were scratched where he'd come through some blackberry thickets, and he was still so raging mad and full of grievances that he was passing the first houses before he noticed that this town he was coming into wasn't Somerset at all. Or if it was, it was changed in three months' time out of all recognition.

He came to a dead stop. His jaw dropped with astonishment, wagging a little. He glared wildly from side to side. New houses. New building down by the river. The beginnings of a good gravel road laid out, right slap through the middle of town. It was Somerset, there was gramp's mill down there. With most of the lumber gone. Looked like more than one gang'd been stealing lumber around here. There were his uncles' old houses, his father's house.

But these new houses scattered around here, they weren't Cantril houses. Them men down by the shore, they were that new gang, not Cantrils—no, they wouldn't be, the Cantrils was gone. Only Cantrils left around here was him and Pap and Uncle Maynard's folks. And them woods' dogs hid out somewhere with the tribe, cuss 'em—wait till he got his hands on 'em!

His father's house was a big old fifteen-roomer, third one down on the road into town, and Smokepole went confidently up the back steps and in at the door.

A strange woman standing by the sink in the kitchen, turned around, opened a round, pink mouth and screamed. A man came bounding through the woodshed door yelling, "Get out of here and get covered up, ye varmint! They's womenfolks here!" He made a dive for the musket hanging on deer's horns over the fireplace.

Smokepole backed away out the door. The men he'd seen down by the shore, they were coming up the road on the run. They had guns, too. He ducked into the big, leafy lilac bush at the corner of the house and stood stealthily peering out, figuring what was the best way to run.

The man came out of the house, hot-eyed, with his gun cuddled under one arm and a pair of old pants over the other. He strode over to the lilac bush.

"I see ye go in there, damn ye!" he said. "I ought t' blow the light through ye. I will, if I see ye move in there."

He balled the pants up, gave them a fling into the bush.

"You put them pants on, and then you hout outa there!"

Smokepole hauled on the pants.

"Damn, dod-blasted redskin!" the man said.

"Ain't no redskin," Smokepole said. He came out of the bush and stood facing the man, eying him coldly over the muzzle of the gun. "I'm Lem Cantril."

"Smokepole, eh? We heard about you. Kinda been expectin' you to show up. You better hyper back to the Injuns. Nothin' for you here, now."

"That so?"

The man, who was Jim Gorham, shifted the gun muzzle a little. "Yeh, that's so."

The other men were getting closer. Smokepole could hear them coming up behind him. He stopped edging his knife out of the sleeve of his shirt.

"Looking for my father," he said. "Thought he still lived here. Where is he, you know?"

One of the men behind him said, "Old Josh lives over in the ice-house now."

"Turned the old man out of his house, eh?" Smokepole said.

"Sold his house. Got the money for it. Ask him," Gorham said. "Now you put foot. You come around here scaring my womenfolks again, I'll blow a hole in ya drive a hoss through."

Smokepole turned his back and walked out of the yard. He went past the group of men silently, his face expressionless, kept on up the road by which he had come into town and vanished in the woods.

Womenfolks, hanh? Well, the Cantril womenfolks was used to seeing men with their pants off. They damn well better be. If these shove-ins, whoever they were, didn't like the way the Cantrils done things, they could go back where they come from. They could start packing just as soon as Lem Cantril could get his hands on a good gun.

The men stood gazing after him. Gorham said thoughtfully, "There's a troublemaker, if I ever saw one."

"Sure looks like one," somebody else said. "You see his eyes? Goddam Injun. Ought to plugged him, when we had the chance to."

Andrew Cantril's old icehouse was a small, one-roomed shack on the shore of a pond, a hundred feet or so back in the woods. Josh Cantril lived in it alone now, happier and more at peace than he had ever been in his life. He was the product of the life he had lived. A dull boy to begin with, he had had slammed out of him early, his few brains and his small dignity. He had learned simple carpentry, could drive a nail and plane a board, but think he could not, and now he had no necessity to think. Maynard wanted him to come down and help in the shipyard; Josh could see no reason to. He lived by hunting, had some money from the sale of his house to buy supplies with; the icehouse roof was tight. He did not regret his big house, his wife, long dead, his sons gone from Somerset. His only dread was that Andrew might not stay dead, or that Lemuel would come home. He had had a crawful of human beings of all kinds. Old and slovenly, in the icehouse he was without doubt the most contented man in Somerset.

He was comfortably dressing a deer on the floor in front of his kitchen fire, when Lemuel appeared at the door.

Josh said vaguely, "Is 't you, Lemuel? Kind of dolled-up, ain't you? Be you white man today, or be you Injun?"

Lemuel didn't say. He stood in the door.

Josh got up, stepped across the body of the deer, so as to have something between him and Lem.

"You hungry?" he invited. "Nice little buck there. I shot him right out the back door early this mornin'. He ain't quite skun out, but you can easy cut you off some steak."

His voice died out as he saw how tore out Lem was. He began to dither a little.

"Awful, awful, awful. Told your Uncle Rufe 't wan't right, 'twas your prop'ty. He said nothin' legal to prove it, only your grampa's say-so, and he dead. No paper. His, he said, his'n John's, b'longed to them. So they sold out'n gone. Took the money."

Lem still said nothing. He went over to the corner of the icehouse, picked up Josh's gun which stood there.

"Now, Lemuel, where's your own gun? You can't have mine. It's all the gun I got."

Worried, Josh laid hands to the gun. But Lem gave him a hard push in the face, banged his head against the wall. He began loading the gun out of his own powder flask, and when the charge was rammed down, he made for the door.

"You empt' out that tub, Pa," he said over his shoulder. "It's liable to stink, and I want to sleep here tonight."

"Why, it won't neither!" Josh said indignantly.

Damn sprig, hitting his father, making his head ache. He felt of his tooth, but it wasn't any looser than might be.

Now where was Lem going with that gun? Somehow or other Josh had to manage to get that gun back. He went out of the icehouse and along the path to the edge of the woods, peering after Lem.

He saw Lem marching down the gravel road, looking neither to left nor right. He stopped at a house on the way, was out of sight briefly; then he appeared again, heading for the mill. He went into the mill. For a minute or so nothing happened. Then there started up a terrible row, a rattling and a banging around inside the mill. From all over them men, them black Irishmen, if so be they were, were running to the fight, carrying their tools, hammers and such things. Josh stuck his neck out like a turtle.

Oh, Lemuel, he said to himself. You hev stuck your head into a hornet's nest.

At that moment Lemuel came sailing out of the mill door. He ran a few staggering steps, bent over, and then sprawled flat, plowing a ways before he came to a stop.

Booted him. Must of.

Josh's jaw worked, opening and closing his mouth very fast.

Behind Lemuel came that big fat Irishman, the one with the red whiskers.

Now, him, no knowing what *he'll* do.

But the rest of the men, them Irishmen, they got there. There was a great hassle of flying arms and legs. Then Lemuel broke away, crawled out from under the pile like. He took off up through town with the whole lot of them after him.

Josh suddenly got scared. "Don't bring 'em here!" he bawled, jumping up and down. "Don't bring 'em here!"

But Lemuel wasn't seeing fit to stop anywhere. He went on past Josh, legs flying, turned into the log road and ducked out of sight into the woods.

Josh waited till the chase went by. Then he went back into the icehouse, shut the door. He was hungry; he hadn't been this hungry since Pa died. He cut off a thick steak from the deer's haunch, sat down to broil it over the coals, cackling and marveling to himself.

Booted him and run him out of town. By the goldarn! Never thought I'd live to see Lem git his can-uckance.

In his pleasure he forgot about his gun.

Hope he never comes back. Ain't fit to live with. Sore as a pig's eye all the time. Hit his old father, loosen up his tooth. Fuss and towse over a little tub of deer's guts that anybody'd know wouldn't stink to bother anyone for a couple of days yet.

After a while the pursuit, in groups of two and three, began to straggle back past the icehouse. They didn't have Lemuel, so Josh judged he'd got away.

Frank had at last, and to his own great relief, cut off his whiskers. In the fight with Lem Cantril, on yesterday, he had got a knife cut

—not a serious one, though without the great, hairy bush on his chin, it might have been. He and Mike had been in the mill office when Cantril came through the door, waving a gun and ordering everybody out of the mill. Frank had let go the first thing at hand, which happened to be Mike's inkstand, not much of a weapon because it was small. But it had made Smokepole dodge, and while he was dodging, Frank had jumped and got hold of his gun barrel. Lem got in one jab at Frank's face with his knife before Mike booted him. He might as well have stabbed a mattress. The keen blade sheared off a dollop of red hair and the point made a half-inch cut, not very deep, in Frank's chin.

It was enough. All summer he'd been waiting for an excuse. Disguise or no disguise, the donkey's winter coat on his face itched him cruelly. There was no one anyway, not here, who cared whether Frank Ellis was Francis Carnavon.

He lolled on the deck of the *Bessie,* waiting for dinner, enjoying his nice clean face. It was cool today; the southwest wind was coming up, beginning to blow, but the anchorage was sheltered from it. The *Bessie* felt only the river current. Now and then the wind brought along the deck the savory fragrance of Lizabeth's cooking.

'Tis heaven here, Frank thought.

He had thought to be cold and unfed in this place, coming here from the city he loved, nothing a man could eat in this black wilderness; and here he was warmed for life by a good and an interesting woman who could make a tasty dish out of the brown stones of the sea. He sniffed with appreciation, ran his fingers over his face. Francis Carnavon—Frank Ellis, that is. Shaved, about to be fed, someday to be a father.

Was never a man so blest.

One thing marred his contentment these days. He did not yet see how he could take creative part in Mike's doings ashore. Mike expected him to, he knew; Lizabeth did, too. Frank thought so himself. No man should sit idle, a parasite, while tremendous things were going on. A town was being born, a wilderness opened up to make room for the homes of men. He had no lack of interest in that; he was fascinated by it. The thing had great scope, a kind of poetry. He had watched the houses go up, the naked frames raw and yellow against the trees of the forest. There were times when the thing brought tears to his eyes.

Some of the houses were no longer raw and yellow; they were being painted brick-red now, since one of the Gorhams had found the red ocher in the field. Paint for houses from a bare field pit—there was no end to the bounty of God.

No, it was no lack of interest. It was simply that the project was Mike's. Frank was deeply proud of Mike, knowing that behind all was his brother's energy and genius of planning. Ashore, Mike moved implacably as the great saw blade moved through the logs in the mill.

But to work with Mike was not comfortable; he wished to tell a man what to do, when, where, and how fast he must do it. Then, like as not, if you became interested in the work, watching it grow under your hands, into it would thrust the nose of Mike; before you knew it, the hands of Mike would push yours away and the work be finished *crick-crack,* and you left with the frustration.

I am not, God knows, a builder of empires, and it is they who are needed here, Frank thought, squinting his eyes against the glare on the river. But in a small way I might build a village, or even me own house, given time to savor the work and watch it grow.

But his own house up above the falls, Mike's men were building, egged on by Mike, lest cold weather come and find Frank and Lizabeth still living on the *Bessie.* In the meantime Frank worked about the mill, or he kept books and tally sheets in the office. A useless thing surely, because each evening Mike himself went over the books.

He did not criticize Mike, a fine, warm-hearted man, a good brother, made for great accomplishments. The fault, if there were one, lay in Frank's own methods which were leisurely. Yet Frank did not lack self-respect. There should be room anywhere for both him and Mike.

For the world surely would be a sad place, if no man ever stopped to look around and see God's grass grow. If so be it grew under his feet, then grass itself was a miracle, too, one of the beautiful mysteries of the world.

A small boat was coming up the river, and Frank squinted, trying to make out whether it was one of the town men or a stranger. From the shape of the sail, it was a stranger.

I hope 'tis no more of the Cantrils come home to claim a birthright, he thought. I have had a bellyful of them.

A queer lot to be sure, the Cantrils. The life they must have led here appalled him. He had heard about some of it from Maynard, of whom he had made a friend; even Maynard, he could see, had a standoffishness amounting almost to hatred for strangers.

Frank fingered the sore spot on his chin. He glanced down at the loaded gun on the deck beside him. He had brought out the gun because ducks were beginning to fly on the river; though the fine way he felt, he didn't really think he wanted to hurt anything. It occurred to him that for a man of peace, he had been forced by circumstances into some odd positions.

He watched the boat draw closer. The young fellow steering hadn't any look of the Cantrils, for all he was in rags and tatters. He was coming in warily though, eying the *Bessie,* eying Frank, keeping a sharp watch of the movements on shore.

Frank got up and went over to the rail to watch him go by. The boat—it was a decked-over ship's boat—would have to pass close to the *Bessie* to miss the mud shoal making out far from the shore, now the river was low. But the fellow didn't appear to know about the shoal. He was headed right for it.

Frank called out to him. "Hi, friend, sheer off, you're into the mudbank, there."

The young man sheered off, headed upstream a little and came about. Frank watched while he downed sail and let his boat drift back with the current, so as to fetch in alongside of the *Bessie.* It was a smart piece of judgment which Frank admired. He said so, looking down at the fellow and wondering where on earth he had seen him before. Seeing the boat was drifting down by, he tossed down a rope's end.

The fellow caught the rope's end, stood looking up at Frank.

"Be darned if I ever thought I'd be glad to see one of the Carnavons," he said. "I was looking to be welcomed by the Cantrils."

"Carnavon!" Frank said, taken aback. " 'Tis Frank Ellis I am, unrecognizable because I shaved me whiskers off the night."

The young man grinned.

"You must be blood kin to me, then," he said. "I'm Nathan Ellis. I saw you a couple of times at the warehouse in Boston, when I was in there with Pa. You remember Joel Ellis? I'm his son."

"Begod!" Frank said under his breath.

He darted a glance back over his shoulder at the galley, but Lizabeth either hadn't heard anything, or she was somewhere else. This, without doubt, was Nate, her other son—the one Frank hadn't seen,

208

come tailing up the coast in search of his mother. Frank heaved a sigh. If this one were anything like his brother, the man of peace was in for another battle. Frank was tempted to give the rope's end a good jerk, dump the fellow in the river and be done with it.

Nathan Ellis, however, didn't act as if he wanted a fight.

"I'm sure relieved to find someone like you here, Mr. Carnavon," he said. "I was looking for a warm reception, seeing I had a fight downriver yesterday with one of the Cantrils. But I had to find some kind of a town. My wife and I live over on the other side of the bay, plan to winter it out there, and we're up against it for supplies. You think I could buy what I need ashore here?"

"I don't doubt you could," Frank said.

"Well, I hope so, it'll save me a trip down to Weymouth. Thought I'd try it up here first, take my chances on a fight."

Nate realized he was saying more than he needed to, seeing Mr. Carnavon didn't look any too interested in him and his problems, but it was so darned good to talk to someone. He went on babbling, it seemed to him, like a fool.

"I wasn't doing anything but pick up refuge lumber down at the river-mouth," he said happily. "Didn't look to me as if anyone wanted it. But this Cantril fellow, he got mad, said I was stealing it."

"What did you want it for?" Frank asked interested. He himself had noticed the old drift lumber downriver. "Couldn't be of much worth to anyone, rotten as it is."

"We built our cabin out of it." Lord, it was wonderful, just talking. "There's sound stuff there, only you have to hunt for it. I took four boatloads. I thought I'd offer to pay that fellow for it, if I could find him and he was cooled off enough to let me talk to him."

"Pay for driftwood left to rot?"

"Well, they own it. It was worth something to me, might be to them. I got a good cabin out of it. It's only right to offer to pay."

Frank looked down at him thoughtfully. This Nathan of Lizabeth's, you couldn't help seeing that he was her son. For in spite of his rags and his wild appearance, there were her looks and her forthright honesty.

What should I do? Frank thought. In God's name, was ever a man so tried! She has been a long time getting over these sons of hers, she is still not over them, but I have seen her change and begin to be happy with me. Will this boy turn her back to her old sharp, nagging self, destroy my peace of mind and hers, reminding her of unhappy times that are over and best forgotten? And she with a child coming?

"The Cantrils," he said aloud, "as their Uncle Josh keeps telling us, 'took out and gone.' The last one of them who wished to make trouble left us yesterday. I don't doubt he was the same who fought with you over the driftwood." Frank fingered the patch on his chin. "I had a fight with that one, meself."

In spite of his problems, the humor of the situation struck Frank. He grinned. "It would seem, Mr. Ellis, that we have some things in common."

"Well, a fight, anyway," Nate agreed.

He was puzzled about what else there could be, thinking, Maybe he means the warehouse which was Pa's and might have been mine, if Carnavon's hadn't bought it; and oh, yes, the name, for some reason he's calling himself Ellis now. That was queer. And what was he doing anyhow, the last person you'd expect to see here on this old sloop, up a godforsaken river at the end of nowhere? Maybe Carnavon's got into the same kind of trouble Pa did and had to get out of Boston. Whatever it was, this one was a nice fellow, someone to talk to.

I must look like a fool though, standing here with my mouth open, everything running out of it.

He stood beaming up at Frank, and his mouth *was* open, good will and friendliness sticking out all over him.

Frank sighed. "Come aboard, Mr. Ellis," he said. "Me wife's getting dinner."

"Thanks," Nate said. Lord, how he'd like to! "I wish I could, Mr. Carnavon. But my wife's alone, and I've got to get my stuff loaded so I can catch the first of the ebb downriver. Besides, it looks as though it's coming on to blow. I'll be over again though."

"Good luck to ye, then," Frank said. He wasn't going to push his luck. He would tell Lizabeth, let her be the one to say whether she wanted to see her son. "Me brother Mike bought out the Cantrils," he went on. "If you'll go ashore, he or Maynard'll open up the storeroom for you."

"Maynard?" Nate said. "Would that be Maynard Cantril?"

Frank nodded. "Maynard runs the shipyard here," he said.

Nate coiled his end of the rope, tossed it up to Frank. He said, "Thanks, then. I'll see you again, Mr. Carnavon."

The light current tugged at the boat and started to drift her down by the *Bessie*. He was busy for a moment; then he got the sail up and stood in for shore, waving his arm, and Frank lifted a hand in farewell. He stood looking after the boat for a moment and then went slowly below.

The table was set in the *Bessie's* cabin. The kettles were off the fire. Lizabeth sat waiting, stiff as a ramrod, on one of the built-in benches. Her cheeks were flushed. There was a look about her Frank didn't like, and he began uneasily.

"I've kept you waiting, lass. I'm sorry."

"Never mind if your dinner spoils," she said. "Just so you can have a good chew with someone."

Frank stared at her. It had been a long time since he had heard that particular note in her voice; he'd hoped never to hear it again—the nagging, petulant grate on the nerves that the world over meant an unhappy woman.

He went straight to her.

"You heard, Lizabeth."

It was stupid of him to think she would not have heard, the *Bessie* being so small. Only his great hope that she would not hear had stood between her and the sound of her son's voice.

"Did you not wish to see him? You had only to come on deck."

"No," Lizabeth said harshly. "I don't want to see him."

She looked at Frank standing unhappily beside her, and put both palms to her cheeks, pressing hard.

"They went off and left me when I needed them most," she said. "I don't want anything to do with them."

He knelt and put both arms around her unyielding body.

"Oh, Lizabeth, my dear love. Let them go, then."

She did not move. "Leave me alone, Frank. I'll get over it." She shrugged him away, and he rose to his feet, rebuffed and hurt.

"But no need to be angry with me," he said. "Will you give me my dinner now?"

"Whatever happens, a man has to think of his stomach, I guess." She got up with a flounce, but he stopped her, a hard, unyielding arm barring her way.

"No. 'Tis the sour stomach of the world I'd have, if you fed me, and you with this anger."

"Oh, don't be foolish. Of course you'll eat your dinner."

"No. I'll not, then."

"Frank," she said, "you'll just have to—"

She was going to say, "take me as I am," but the look in his eye was something she had never seen there before and she stopped.

"They are only the young setting up for themselves," he said quietly. "They do not love you less, only themselves more."

"Selfish and ungrateful, after all I did for them—"

"And who is not? What is gratitude? A belittling thing, Lizabeth!"

"Nonsense. Children ought to be grateful. And look at mine! I worked my fingers to the bone and what did I get for it!"

Frank looked at her curiously.

"And when you were working your fingers to the bone," he asked, "did you do it only because you thought you might get something for it?"

"Don't talk foolish. I thought I might at least expect help when I needed it."

"Or did you do it somewhat for the joy and satisfaction you had in your love for your children? 'Tis a great joy to protect the helpless, but 'tis not selfless, Lizabeth. Look how you are, angry and bitter because what they are doing is being a man and a woman, not two children! Be glad of it that they no longer need you!"

"Don't tell me he doesn't need me!" she burst out furiously.

She had not been able to resist, after she got over the first shock of Nate's voice, going out on deck to peer unseen past the deckhouse. She had thought at first that of course he had come north looking for her; when she found he had not, she told herself that the sight of him, the wreck of his clothes had appalled her. "I brought that Caroline up to keep a man's clothes clean and mended, and look at him! What's she thinking of, the lazy—"

"You are only jealous," Frank said. "Your children have been setting up their home in a wilderness. You yourself should know what the lack of a thing like a needle might mean in this place."

"Jealous! Maybe I am—" She realized what he had said and she spun toward him, the angry telltale red rising on her cheekbones.

"Jealous! And what right have you got to talk so, what do you know about my young ones and me? I had them, I had my whole life before I ever heard of you, and it was—they were—"

She pulled up short, at the sight of his face. Never in her life had she permitted herself such an outburst; feelings should be put sternly down, handled alone and in silence. But these feelings had been put down so long, they came tearing out with almost a sound of tearing. She could not stop, even though something said to her, This is Frank.

She said, "If anyone's jealous, it's you yourself, Frank Carnavon!"

"I am that, lass," he said, his deep, sorrowful voice cutting in over her shrill one. "I am jealous beyond anything I have ever known. The joy it would have given me to toss your bright young son into the river, to wish he had never come here! But is jealousy to turn a man into a savage, or a child, thirteen years old only? Oh, Lizabeth, what a souring of the good, kind mother's milk, that you cannot see how a grown man does not need his mother! It is his wife he needs. I need my wife," Frank said bleakly. "And she has gone away."

She stood staring at him, her face twisted and crumpled, so that for a moment he thought she was going to cry.

"Oh, Lizabeth, Lizabeth," he said. " 'Tis we should be grateful to children for being so dear. When we have had them and they are grown, should there be left an ugly thing like a debt to pay? Why, a child repays us a thousand times over by being a child. I say this, a lonely man, who has been warming cold fingers over the great fire lit by his small son—or daughter, 'tis no matter. I am thinking the time will come when I must let my son go to be a man, and I do not know how I will feel. But should I put myself in his way, my great hulk for him to stumble over, when the young have so hard a time, and 'tis no easy thing to learn to be a man? 'Tis the fool of the world I am"—he put out his arms to her—"and he not born yet!"

"Oh, Frank," Lizabeth said.

She went to him, leaning her head wearily against him inside the circle of his arms.

He stood softly stroking her hair.

"There, lass, 'tis out of you and gone. Let it go. Your son Nathan makes a sound like a man. At least to me. He is married, responsible, taking care of his wife, in such a hurry not to leave her lonely in the woods the night that he would not eat his dinner."

At the word "dinner" the empty stomach inside Frank rumbled dolefully and long.

"I'm sorry, lass. 'Tis me inner man as always, tumbling me dignity, reminding me that Frank Carnavon is a great lunk, the fool of the world."

There was a silence.

"Begod," Lizabeth said, her voice, muffled against his shirt, mimicking his Irish speech. "Begod, your inner man is less of a fool than you are."

Frank started as if she had bitten him. A ghost of a twinkle came back into his eyes. "Praise be to the angels, here's"—his voice choked a little—"here's my wife come home again."

"Let me go," Lizabeth said.

She put both arms up around his neck and kissed him on the lips. "I'll dish your dinner for you, great lunk, your stomach's all you think about. I only hope it isn't spoilt, that dinner's a good one. But mind you, Frank, when we've eaten, you can row me ashore. I've got to see Nate and help him pile up Caroline's kitchen things. I may not be much good to him, but I won't have him go back there, wherever he's going, forgetting half the things they need."

Frank burst out laughing.

"I'd need that meself," he said. "Any man would, God love you, you stubborn witch!"

Nathan tied up his boat at the wharf and went up the ladder. There didn't seem to be anyone around on the wharf; he wondered where he ought to go to find Mike Carnavon and his storeroom.

Well, it was dinnertime, people were probably home eating. He could eat himself, but he'd better not take the time to. He'd have to hustle anyway, to take advantage of the tide, and from the looks of the sky, it was sure coming on to blow. Maybe the thing to do, now he'd found out there were decent people here in the town, was to go right home now without his load, come over tomorrow or the next day, and bring Caroline.

There was a new shed on the head of the wharf, with a couple of windows facing his way and a closed door. Might be someone in there'd know about the storeroom. He walked along, took a look in at one of the windows. Under the window was a big rectangular shelf or table top, and on it, sketched on the smooth planed wood, the model of a boat.

He leaned closer to the glass. The drawing drew him like a magnet, and after a moment or so, he went along to the door, opened it and went in. There was no one there, and he crossed the room, stood by the table, studying the drawing.

The shed on the wharf was Maynard Cantril's new workshop, partitioned off for him to use, a snug place where a fire could be built on the hearth when cold weather came—not that Maynard ever knew when he was working, whether he was cold or not. The room had no furniture, except a shelf for tools, knocked against one wall, and the great, rough work table set where the light from two windows could fall on it without reflection.

Maynard himself had built the table out of two planks of clear pine set solidly on four sections of pine logs. He hadn't bothered to take the bark off the logs; all he asked of the underpinning of his table was that it be solid. It was a table built to last for more than one man's lifetime. The planks he had dovetailed cunningly, working with plane and scraper until the soft, butter-colored punkin pine shone like satin, and there could be seen neither the marks of his joining nor his tools. It was his work surface, and on the gleaming wood he drew pictures of the boat models he had carried in his mind most of his life.

Nathan Ellis stooped a little over the table, seeing for the first time the work in which he had been interested for so long, and whistled through his teeth with admiration. He tapped with a ragged fingernail a section of the sharply drawn, beautifully complete design.

Now *that*, he said to himself. Now *that* is something I've always wondered about—how it was done.

He stayed in the shop for quite a time. At last, hearing steps on the wharf outside, he came out of his absorption, started for the door and then stood frozen in slack-jawed amazement. The woman standing there was his mother.

She said, "You've grown, Nate. Stocked up some. I believe you're taller."

And she stepped forward and laid her hands on his arms, aware of the hard, tough, leathery young muscles under the ragged sleeves.

If Maynard Cantril had come into his workshop and found a stranger there, he would have given him the rough side of his tongue, because now that he had some privacy for the first time in his life, Maynard was jealous of it. But he did not come. He was up in the woods hunting for Smokepole.

After the fight at the mill on yesterday, Maynard had taken his gun and unobtrusively slipped away along the woods' roads and trails of the forest, hunting like a hound in widening circles, coming back, now and again, to Josh's hut. But Josh was no help. He neither knew nor cared where his son was.

Maynard had known his nephew for a long time. He had, on occasion in the past, been able to talk Lem out of his rages; he thought he might do so now. Of all the Cantrils, Maynard was the only one who had any understanding of the curious, split-up way Lem's mind worked.

So long as he was Lemuel Cantril, with his half-baked, selfish notion of being king of Somerset, he was not dangerous. Andrew Cantril's ego combined with Josh's inertia canceled out: the one assured Lem that he was the best man, of the best blood in the world, the man most suited to be a king; the other that he had no need to do anything about it. But there had been times, and Maynard remembered them, when someone or something had punctured the stone wall of Lemuel's pride, and then he became Smokepole, the Indian, whose mother, Anna Pie, had been Red Flower—Fire. The word was the same for both, in Indian talk. Whose grandfather had been Smoking Stick, and whose great-grandfather, Fire-Driven-Before-The-Wind, among his own people *had* been a king. Smokepole, the Indian, had ritual and religion behind him; he had a terrible pride which could not stand insult.

The tribe, when Smokepole went on one of his tears, either removed itself or held him down by main force until he got over it, if they had to. It was always less complicated to go somewhere else; and Charley Cantril, the chief, shrewdly guessing ahead, had taken the tribe to the offshore island shortly after Somerset was sold. Maynard knew where the tribe was; two of the boys, Fryer and Dod, had been in to town during the summer, quietly scrounging supplies. They had come in by night, going to Maynard's house and waking him; and Maynard, knowing it was better to let them have what the tribe needed than to have the storeroom broken into, had got up and gone down with them to the wharf, and had helped them load their canoes out of town stores.

So it was foolish to count on the tribe; they couldn't be reached in a hurry. On the second afternoon, when the southwest wind came up and blew a gale, Maynard knew they couldn't be reached at all. What was done he would have to do himself. He spent the whole of that day in the woods, not even going home to eat. He did not find Smokepole.

The first day Smokepole was holed up in a thicket, sleeping. On the second day he was resting, letting his bruises heal—he had taken a bad beating in the fight at the mill—and making his plans. For the two days he did not eat. He lay almost motionless on his back in the thicket, all the second morning staring up into the thickly twined branches close to his face. At noon he moved, sliding stealthily out of the thicket, to a place in the forest he knew.

There he cut the hair off his face with his hunting knife, a painful operation which he endured silently, and he dug up some strong, flexible cordlike roots of a spruce tree. He performed a ceremony of great dignity and seriousness, a ritual taught him by his mother, Red Flower, whom the Cantrils had called Anna Pie; so that that afternoon when the gale began to blow, he was not surprised, only thankful that certain gods approved.

At dusk Smokepole went out of the woods, moving like a shadow from tree to tree. Overhead the gale boomed in the pine tops; stopping at the edge of the forest to peer out over the darkening fields, Smokepole leaned his hand against a tree trunk, and he felt the great column, three feet thick, shudder in the wind, while under his feet the earth stirred with the heave and vibration of roots.

This field was the one where the red ocher deposit was, the traditional paint pit of his people. He wormed his way out through the tall, dry grass to the paint holes. They were deeper than he remembered them, seeing the new people in Somerset had been digging there for red ocher for their house paint. With certain ingredients from his pouch, he mixed his paint; then Smokepole, descendant of chiefs, took off his white man's clothes and painted his face and body with the designs which meant war.

Maynard Cantril, a little later, coming into the field for a look at the

217

paint pit on the off-chance that he might find some Indian sign there, saw the bundle of clothes carefully rolled and bound with flexible tree root, and he felt the hackles rise on his neck.

He ought to have warned the town before, instead of thinking he might be able to calm Lem down alone. He whirled and stared at the forest blackening down now with night shadow. There was no movement except the wind, no sound but its thunder and crackle among the lashing branches of the trees. What was needed now was someone from the tribe, someone who could read Indian sign. Any one of the boys without doubt could tell him where Lem had gone. But Maynard Cantril was no woodsman. He walked to the edge of the field, stood peering here and there into the woods.

And then he saw among the shadows, the curl of orange flame leap up, the sudden spurt of smoke. And he saw Smokepole.

Smokepole came bounding out of the forest in great jumps, his tall, naked figure, curiously painted, lit up from behind by a flaming bundle of dry grass drawn at the end of a thong tied around his waist. He shot out into the field, the bundle disintegrating as he went, and it seemed to Maynard that the grass of the field behind him exploded.

Maynard readied his gun and fired a shot; in that light it was like aiming at a dancing knife blade. The shot missed. He saw Smokepole balance briefly on the edge of the paint hole with the bundle of clothes in his hand, then plunge across the field and out of sight in the undergrowth on the other side.

And then Maynard himself ran down the woods' road and into the town, yelling at the top of his lungs the shout that for centuries has struck terror to the hearts of any people living in a wooded country:

"Fire! Fire! The woods is afire and burning!"

It is doubtful if Smokepole, in his exaltation, even heard Maynard's shot. There was enough of the white man left in him to realize that in a boat on the water tonight, where he planned to go, he would need his clothes; to return to the pit for them had been part of his carefully laid plan. For the rest, he was what his father would have called "all Injun." Naked as he was born he ran the full length of the town to the waterfront, his clothes in one hand, his knife in the other. He jumped into the first boat he saw, which happened to be Nathan Ellis' lying at the head of the wharf, cut loose the rope which tied her and put out into the dark, wind-murmuring river.

Men saw him go, but the passage of the screaming, painted apparition had been too quick and too paralyzing. By the time they had collected their scattered wits, closed their astonished mouths, Smokepole had vanished in the darkness on the water. There was no pursuit, because in very little time the men of Somerset had more on their hands than they could manage.

The fire came pouring like water across the fields and pastures, tinder-dry. The roaring gale drove it quickly into the town. In twenty minutes the houses nearest the woods were burning. Three months of bone-dry weather had cooked the moisture out of everything; the old Cantril houses went up like paper torches. The resinous new ones, some built out of greener lumber took a little longer. For three hours the town of Somerset stood up against the black night sky in high, rippled-orange sheets of flame. The fire wiped over the old Cantril rabbit warrens, their filthy outhouses, their old vegetable cellars where last year's rotten cabbages and potatoes lay in moldy barrels, which the new owners had not yet had time to clear away; smoke and gases carried away into the high windy sky the last grimy vestiges of Andrew Cantril's dream.

The dry topsoil in the fields burned down to bedrock; in the woods the great pines burst with sounds like musketry. The town's stock— the precious horses, cattle and pigs—perished with the barns, except for two cows, left out overnight in open pasture, who managed to make it safely to the river. No one could think of stock when there was barely time to get the women and children away.

The people of Somerset spent the night on a small island in the river a little below the center of the fire, so that the smoke, while bad enough, could be borne; to which they were ferried by a miracle of small-boat handling in wind and flying water. It was nip and tuck— the last boatload left the shore just as the buildings on the wharf and the mill burst into flame. They saved nothing; a few bundles of clothes and bedding which the women were able to scrabble together—that was all. And Maynard Cantril saved his worktable. After he had given the alarm, it was the first thing he thought of—the design sketched on it was new, an experiment not yet built. He up-ended his table, over and over, out through the door of his workshop to the head of the wharf, tied a length of rope and a boat's anchor to one leg of it and dropped it into the river.

For the rest, the town was gone, and four people dead. No one thought to warn Josh Cantril; the fire overtook him on the way to the river. Jobbick Butler's family, in their panic, thought they had left behind a child; they had not, he was only in another boatload and safely on the island, but Jobbick went running back to see. In the night a puny baby died on the island from heart failure caused by cold and terror. And Michael Carnavon, not believing his own eyes— that a fire could travel as fast as this one did—and thinking he had time to fetch his cash box and records, lay dead under the smoking ashes of his mill.

No man has ever devised a way to stop a forest fire. It is surprising to think that the mind of man, which has invented curious and intricate mechanisms for flying the sky, for investigating the blood circulation of a mouse, for destroying small islands so that their very rocks melt and trickle down into the sea, is powerless before so simple a thing as fire running through dry woods on a windy night.

He can do only one thing—stand away, while the horror destroys the sweet, familiar face of the land he knows; only afterwards can he go back to the blackened, stinking hole in the ground, which was once his home.

Yet it seemed in the morning, there would never be any use in going back to Somerset. The pits of coals which had been barns and dwelling places glowed hotly; the fields were sheets of gray ash, seeping smoke, where underneath the dry topsoil was burning, and over them the heat waves danced. Even the surface of the new gravel road was blackened. The wind had gone down somewhat, but it still blew briskly from the southwest. The fire was eating back against it into the great stand of trees.

"And there," said one of the mill sawyers, looking at it with gritty, red-rimmed eyes, "there goes your lumber."

The people of Somerset were stunned, deathly tired and grief-stricken; they were not licked, though for a time they thought they were. Food had to be found, shelter for the night. There was no time to sit around and wonder how anyone felt.

Mike was dead; to Frank's astonishment, people turned naturally to him, not as leader, but as someone to whom they could come for assurance. Had Mike been there, he would have been a leader—here, there and everywhere, organizing, putting in order, saying what to do. Since he was not, the men gathered at daylight in a close-huddled knot on the shore by the boats, to take account of assets and decide for themselves what to do. Frank could not believe Mike was dead; whenever he thought of it, he felt only a queer numbness. Like everyone else, he had no time to think of it, and for that he was grateful.

"Faith," he said, "I think the first thing to do is load into the boats and drop down the river, get the women and kids out of the smoke."

He was a little surprised when the men of the group stopped talking among themselves to listen to him. They seemed to expect him to go on, so he did.

"Some should stay here with boats, to see what later may be salvaged over yonder," he said, sweeping his hand toward what had been Somerset. "Though I doubt it will be much. I have fishing lines and a flounder spear and my gun aboard the *Bessie*. Did anyone save his gun and powder?"

It appeared that five men had saved their guns and a small amount of ammunition. Nearly everyone had a fishline or two, since these were kept, for convenience, aboard the small boats, and one man produced a clam-hoe.

"Why, 'tis riches!" Frank said. "We'll not live like kings, begod, but we'll live. Now, Corkran left three days ago, and he will be back in ten, and the *Mary C.* as you know is bringing winter stores this time. So 'tis a matter of ten days only till the vessel comes. The *Bessie* will shelter the women and small children, but not here choking in this smoke, unless there is a change of wind. Maynard, friend, you know the country. Where should we go? 'Tis good fishing at the mouth of the river. There's clams and mussels, and should be game in the woods."

"There's game there now, all right," Maynard said in his slow voice. "This fire's chased all the game there is down there, probably. But this time year, you can't tell what the wind'll do. If so be it hauled around nor'west, the fire'd be down to the mouth of the river before we was."

"The other side of the river, then?"

Someone said, "No, that's all swampland over there."

"I think we better get right away from here," Maynard said. "Un-

221

less there's rain, that fire'll twizzle around in there for weeks. Dry's it is, there's probably places where it'll burn all winter, unless there's an uncommon lot of snow. I'd say go clean over to the other side of the bay, be out of the way of it."

"I think so, too," Frank said. "Nathan, is your harbor over there deep enough to float the *Bessie?*"

"Plenty," Nathan said briefly. "Good hunting and fishing, too."

He had been standing there, nervously shifting from foot to foot, wondering what to do. His boat was gone, with his gun in it, too, and it looked as if these people needed all their boats. But he was worried out of his life about Caroline. Not that she wouldn't be all right, but she'd been all night alone, and she must by now have seen the smoke and flames on the other side of the bay.

"Then we'll go there," Frank said. "I think right away, because of the tide. Maynard?"

"Yeah," Maynard said.

"Well, if we're all going there," Nate said anxiously, "could I borrow a boat and start out now? My wife's over there alone."

Maynard turned quickly to look at him. "Over there alone?" he said. "For godsake, son."

He reached for his gun, which was laid carefully across the stern of the beached skiff beside him.

"I'm going to take my skimmer and go out amongst the islands to see the tribe," he said. "They'll have some stuff laid up for winter, and they'll help us, if we'll help them later on, say we eat up their stores. Some of the boys'll come in and hunt and fish for us, too, till the vessel gets back. Come on, son. On the way I'll drop you over on your side of the bay."

He seemed to think there was a hurry; nonetheless, after the other men had helped him launch the small sloop he called his skimmer, he sailed her across the river into the stink and smoke that still hung over the burned wharf, and fished his table out of the river.

Nate helped him haul the unwieldy, dripping thing in over the side, stow it in the cockpit upside down, where it took up almost more room than there was.

He thought, in his worry, his anxiety to get started, My God, the Cantrils are *all* crazy.

But he saw, when the sloop came about and headed down the river, that this Cantril wasn't so crazy he didn't know how to sail a boat.

Nate had never seen a boat sail the way Maynard Cantril's "skimmer" did.

He thought, watching the old man at the tiller, I guess I never really saw a boat handled before.

They had to beat downriver against the wind; the flood tide had made, and though it was not yet running strongly, it was a current against them. Yet the boat, on short tacks, tooled along without any fuss; Nate watched the big hands on the tiller with awe and admiration.

The wind was still high at seven o'clock when they came out of the mouth of the river. The flood tide was flowing strongly up from the east against the southwest wind. The bay, out from under the lee of the land, was mostly curling cross-chop, crested white. Maynard put the boat into it, and she went tearing. She seemed to be all sail—a tremendous spread of canvas for so small a hull; and as the spray began to fly, Nate thought uneasily, that if he were sailing her he'd reef down some. But Maynard didn't. He seemed to take no notice of the flying water. Presently, Nate, spotting a bailing bucket under the thwart, hooked it out with his foot and began to bail.

Maynard said something.

"What?" Nate hollered back. If the old boy'd ordered him to do something, say reef down the sail, he didn't want to miss it.

"I said, goddamned skimmer!" Maynard yelled.

"Who—me?" Nate said blankly.

"This blarsted boat. Ain't no good. Never was."

"My soul, Mr. Cantril," Nate said, staring at him. "I never saw a boat like her."

"No, and never will again. I built her, but she's the first and last, by God. Go, go, go, that's all she *will* do. If I sailed her the way I ought to be able to, she'd go to bottom. Now *that* one, that one drawed out on the table there, I *think* I've worked all of the cranks out of." He gave the sheet a yank, and the boat plunged, the water flew. Maynard began to swear. "There! See? Sink, damn ye, sink! It's all you're good for."

Nate, seeing the need for it, began again hastily to bail. He judged he had never made the trip across the bay so fast in his life, perhaps never would again. In spite of his anxiety about Caroline, he couldn't help enjoying himself, though he bailed most of the way until the boat shot into the shelter of the home cove, and he saw, to his relief, Caroline sitting quietly on the beach by the landing place.

She got up and came down the shore toward him. Nate saw she looked white and hollow-eyed, pinched around the mouth. He said, "You all right, honey?" and held out his arms. She walked into them for a moment stood rigidly against him, pressing her face into his spray-wet jacket.

"I guess you had a night of it," he said, holding her tightly. "I couldn't get back before. The town burnt up, over there, and someone stole the boat."

"I know," she said. "He was here. Oh, Nate, I thought it was you coming home, and it wasn't, it was him—that man you had the fight with."

Her voice stopped with a kind of breathy tremble, and she closed her mouth, biting hard, he saw, to keep her chin from shaking.

Nate went cold all over. A dry, brassy taste came into his mouth. It was a minute before he could say anything, and when he did, his own voice shook. "Oh, my God, honey," he said. "Did he—he didn't hurt you?"

"He didn't catch me," Caroline said. "I ran into the woods and hid. I climbed a tree."

Nate tightened his arms around her, and within their shelter she felt a relief so intense that if he had let her go, she would have fallen down. It was almost worse than having been so scared, because her knees hadn't felt limp then. They did now. She had never fainted in her life and didn't know what it felt like, but for a moment things seemed to swim a little and go away. Then they came back, sharp and clear. She felt better. Nate's cheek, rough and whiskery, was against hers, and he was mad. She could tell; it seemed to her she could feel the rage coming right through his shirt.

She said, "Don't be mad, Nate. I'm all right. I don't think he even hunted for me. If he had, he wouldn't have had any trouble finding me. Fuf-Fluffy, the pest, was right under the tree where I was, yowling her head off. But he didn't come into the woods. He went into the cabin and ate a lot of venison. I guess he was hungry. Then he went off in the boat again."

A deep voice behind Nate said, "Did you see him go, Mis' Ellis? Which way he headed?"

She'd forgotten, in her relief, that Nate had had somebody with him. And here she stood, hugging Nate, right in front of a stranger! She stepped back a little to look at the big, stooped man, who stood there leaning on his gun.

"He went out by the point there," she said, pointing. "Out of sight around it. I saw him from the top of the tree. I guess if I hadn't, I'd still be up there."

"H'm," Maynard said. He stood looking thoughtfully away, past the point, to the wooded islands in the east. "Well, no need to be scairt no more. He won't be back here. That's where the tribe is, over amongst them islands. It's quite a ways off."

He thought, Wonder how he found out. Maybe saw campfire smoke or something, or ran into one of the boys. Well, after a blow like he had, he's liable to sleep for a week. 'Twon't take me a week to ketch up with him.

He turned away from his contemplation of the islands.

"He eat all the deer meat you had?" he asked. "Because if he didn't, I expect this feller of yours and me, we could use some."

"Oh," Caroline said.

For a minute it seemed to her she couldn't go back up to the cabin, cook venison over the remains of the fire that awful creature had used. The smell of cooked meat, when she had finally dared to come back to the cabin, the greasy scraps dropped down on her clean floor and walked on, had made her sick to her stomach, while she cleaned up the mess. Her hands were scratched and sore, her arms lame from clinging so long to the top of the tree. It had seemed hours, days. And Fluffy miaowing at the foot of the very tree where she was . . .

Oh, Lord, she thought, what I'd like to do is just to stick my head back into Nate's jacket and stay there for a week.

And she pulled herself together.

"We've got lots of deer meat," she said. "He ate a lot, but we had nearly a whole deer. You come right up. It won't take me a minute to fix some."

She turned and went up toward the cabin, and neither of the men could have told by anything that showed, that she wasn't as serene as she sounded.

"Women beat all," Maynard Cantril said. "By God, they do!"

"Yes," Nate answered. "*She* does, anyway." He was still so mad that his voice shook. "You're going out there, Mr. Cantril? To the islands, I mean."

"I plan to."

"I want to go with you. I've got to try to get my boat back. And—" He was about to say he had a score to settle but stopped, remembering that after all Lem Cantril was Maynard's relative.

"You're welcome. Be glad to have you," Maynard said.

It was the first time in Maynard's life that he had ever welcomed the companionship of any man, much less told him so. He was surprised at himself, but the fact remained, he'd kind of taken a shine to the young man. Couldn't say why. He guessed it was because Nate hadn't turned a hair, coming across the bay in that becusst crank of a skimmer—acted as if he'd enjoyed it. Most of men would have been scairt to death. And they'd have had reason to be.

Nate, unaware that anything out of the ordinary had taken place, went on. "I hate to leave her alone again so soon. Maybe we could hold off leaving till the folks in the *Bessie* get here. You think?"

"Yeah," Maynard grunted. "Go this afternoon. Have the ebb tide with us. Breeze's going down, but that dod-damn skimmer she'll sail if a man breaks wind, 's what she was built for. Ain't no good in heavy weather. Damn thing!"

At noon the *Bessie*, heavily laden, with her trail of heavily laden small boats, headed out of the river-mouth, past the autumn-colored capes and islands, into the bay. The wind had gone down to a smart breeze. The bay was quiet. Behind, the great pillar of smoke from the burning forest no longer lined out raggedly northeastwards, but stood straighter against the blue and tranquil sky. Against it the flotilla of small sail looked courageous but lonely.

The tribe's summer island, nine miles at sea, lay peacefully dreaming in the afternoon. Five miles long, it was heavily wooded with spruce, against which the pale-yellow leaves of an occasional birch tree stood out like candlelight. The shores were tumbled piles of red granite, weathered grayish-pink, with here and there a beach of polished, round stones.

Maynard's skimmer, very ladylike now in the mild afternoon breeze, almost a calm, slid along the northeastern shore, her sails drawing nicely, though Nate himself could scarcely feel the wind.

She was, Maynard said, a peaceful goer on a good day. Sail in a barrel down cellar with the cover on.

Long shadows of trees lay across the rocks. The trees themselves had a dark and secret look, neither welcoming nor hostile.

A man could take that or leave it, Nate thought, watching the noncommittal shore slip by. But take it or not, it's there when he lands and will be after he's gone.

From here the island did not look as if any man had ever landed there. But Nate caught, now and again, a faint whiff of campfire smoke; and when the boat rounded the island's high, east headland, he saw let back into the rocks, a sheltered sand cove, its flats drained by the ebb tide, some skiffs leaning on their keels, high and dry, and canoes drawn up on the beach.

"Well," Maynard said. "There's the tribe."

"My boat's here," Nate said. He pointed. "That one hauled up over there."

"Lem's here, then."

Maynard drew a long breath and let it out slowly, as if he were disgusted or weary or both. He headed up into the cove in the shoaling water; then, thirty feet from the flats, when Nate thought he was about to let the boat go aground, he came about, slacked off the sheet and dropped over a light anchor. Nate let go the halyards and downed sail, wondering if Maynard planned to swim the rest of the way. Seeing his boat up there, Nate almost wanted to himself. But she was at high-water mark, a hundred feet of flats between her and the water. Either he'd have to wait for the tide, or the tribe would have to help him haul her down. He looked questioningly at Maynard, but Maynard said nothing. He pulled out his pipe, sat comfortably filling it and gazing at the shore.

"Set down, son," he said at last. "Some of them'll be off, when they get around to it."

There was no movement, no sign of life on shore, except for some dogs drowsing in the sun and a few gulls wrangling over a pile of offal on the flats. Three or four fires smoldered, great heaps of ash sending off drifts of smoke, pale in the sun. Clam and mussel shells lay bleaching in sheets and piles; smooth paths through them were beaten down hard and black. The shelters were rough lean-tos of several kinds and shapes, made of brush and poles. Some had deer hide hung for windbreaks; some had grass.

Maynard sat smoking, contemplating this latest stronghold of the Cantrils. His face was expressionless.

Presently a tall young man crawled out of one of the shelters. He was naked except for a breechclout; his body was a deep, almost chocolate, brown, smooth, except for a tangled mat of hair on his chest. He came leisurely down over the flats, his big, brown feet sucking through the mud. At the water's edge he stopped. His face was neither welcoming nor hostile.

He said, "Hi, Pa."

"Well, Zeke," Maynard said. "You here? I thought you was up-country this summer."

"No. Been here awhile. Maynie's here, too. What you want, Pa?"

Maynard jerked his head toward Nate. "This's Nathan Ellis. Lem stole his boat and his gun. He wants them back."

The young man stood. He did not look at Nate. He did not look at his father. He said, "Charley don't feel too good about folks that sets the woods afire, Pa. That's a good stout boat. Charley figgers he'll keep it, and Lem needs a gun."

Maynard said, "You go get Charley, Zeke."

"Lem had a hard deal from them Irishmen," Zeke said. "You know yourself, Pa, that's a hell of a thing to do, set the woods afire just to smoke a feller out of 'em."

"That's Lem's story," Maynard said. So far he hadn't taken his pipe out of his mouth. Now he did. "You go up and tell Charley to come down here. I want him to hear mine."

Zeke shrugged. He turned and went back across the flats, ducked out of sight into one of the lean-tos.

The skimmer swung a little with the tide; the campfires smoked. On the flats the gulls tore greedily at fish heads and fiercely at each other. One of the dogs lifted his head and stared languidly at something, dropped it back to his paws again.

Zeke backed out of the lean-to. Another young man, who might have been his twin except, as he came closer, it could be seen that he

228

was older, walked down across the flats. This one did not stop at the water's edge. He stepped calmly in, swam the few strokes out to the boat, hauled himself smoothly over the side. He shook like a dog, and the water drops flew.

He said, "What's the matter, Uncle Maynard?"

Maynard knocked out his pipe on the gunnel. The dottle fell into the water with a slight hissing sound.

"Charley, Lem's here."

"Yeah, he is."

"Where is he?"

"He's sleeping."

Maynard eyed him, tucking his pipe away in his pocket.

"How's he sleeping, Charley?"

Charley said nothing. His expression did not change, except for his eyes which seemed to narrow a little. He glanced, once, up at the camp, then back to Maynard.

"He's sleeping off one of them Smokepole tears of his," Maynard said. "Ain't he?"

Charley shook his head. "Said he'd been on a drunk. Said he only lifted some of the Irishmen's whisky, Uncle Maynard. They hunted him like a dog. Set the woods afire."

"And you boys are all pretty sore at the Somerset folks for burning up the woods," Maynard said softly. He waved his arm toward the west, where the sun was dropping down toward the reddish-gray pall. "Smell it, Charley. Taste it, in everything you eat. You will, when the tribe comes ashore. For a long time, till it rains. There won't any one of you boys live long enough to see them woods grow fit to live in again."

Charley's eyes had followed Maynard's gesture. They turned back to Maynard as Maynard paused, and they looked sick.

"I ain't rubbing it in," Maynard said. "Lem done it—Smokepole."

A small, clear puddle of water had formed on the floor boards by Charley's foot. He put a long, brown finger down, trailed it gently through the water.

"He said them Irishmen'd blame it on him. What do you know for sure, Uncle Maynard?"

Maynard sighed patiently.

"Lem come into town," he said. "Tried to drive the men out of the mill. That I saw myself. They said he shot at one of them. I heard the shot. They said he tried to knife another one. That I didn't see. I saw them run him out of town."

"He said he had a fight."

"I saw Smokepole at the paint hole," Maynard went on. "I saw him towing a bundle of grass afire around through the woods and fields. I was up there trying to find him, stop him before he did something crazy. Now, Charley. Somerset's gone. Four people's dead, one of them Josh. And the woods are gone."

Charley said, "That's so."

He did not raise his voice and he did not move.

"Them folks in there's adrift with their women and young ones," Maynard said. "They need help. I want you boys to go in and help hunt, take in some stores."

"Can't spare much, winter coming on."

"I know that. But the *Mary C.*'s due back in ten days. I'll guarantee you'll get back more stores and powder'n you'll lay out, Charley. You remember I let Fryer and Dod have a couple of canoe-loads for nothing."

"All right."

"Good, then. Now, this feller needs his gun and boat back."

"All right." Charley got up. "The boys'll bring out the gun. We'll need the boat to take the stores ashore." He stood a moment, back-to, poised on the gunnel. "What's your say, Uncle Maynard?"

"Well, I don't feel we any of us got a call to put up with Lem any longer, Charley."

Charley slid into the water like an otter. His sleek head gleamed as he stroked ashore. He went back over the mud flats to the camp, and the camp, as if it had been watching and waiting for him, came to life. One moment the beach was deserted, sleeping in the sun; the next, it was swarming with people. Women, children and dogs were everywhere; every shelter seemed to sprout at least half a dozen brawny young men. They were big and brown, broad-shouldered, slim in the hips; they shone in the sunlight. Andrew Cantril's grandsons and great-grandsons, in their native habitat, were quite a sight to see.

"It's a big tribe," Maynard said. "About as neat-run a place as you'd find on earth. Charley, he's the chief of it. He's Rufus' boy. Them four fellers up by the fire, they're the ones to watch. There's Charley, and the one next to him, he's full-blooded Injun, old Chief Smoking Stick's own grandson. He'd head up the tribe, if Charley hadn't outrun and outhunted him. Them other two, them's my boys, Maynard and Zeke."

He spoke with no pride nor lack of pride, only casually, as one giving information.

"Look, they're having a council," he said. "I don't think it'll take 'em long."

The young men were gathering in a closed-up group around the fire. The women and children were hustling out of sight into the huts. The black heads clustered in, bent down, attentive. The council, as Maynard said, did not take long.

Someone yelled, not loudly. The group broke up, scattering. Ten or fifteen youngsters started for the canoes; they began lifting them, carrying them down across the flats to the water. The big fellows stayed together, milling around one of the huts. Four of them, one after the other, ducked into it.

Inside the hut a rumpus started, yells and curses, the sound of blows. The hut rocked. One side of it bulged outward and fell flat; a big, brown body rolled across it in a backward somersault, gathered together and dived back in again. The roof and remaining walls collapsed. Mixed debris of grass, spruce boughs and deer hides heaved up and down, fell apart. Charley's black head and his wide shoulders appeared through the opening, followed by other heads and shoulders, and the four young men hauled out of the ruins a fifth man, who struggled and twisted, yelling curses.

Nate, watching tensely, his hands clenched on the gunnel, was not aware of the canoe coming alongside, until the bow of it bumped lightly almost under his fingers. A slim youngster with you-be-damned black eyes and an impassive face, handed him up his gun.

"Fryer," Maynard said. "You tell Charley to shoot him, and get it over with."

The boy made no reply. His black eyes gleamed; he flashed Maynard a look. Then he dug in his paddle and streaked for shore.

Maynard shook his head. He got up quietly, began to haul the anchor.

"H'ist sail, son," he said. "We better start back," and then, seeing Nate's white face, his eyes staring in bewilderment, he paused, his big hands motionless on the anchor rode.

"I wouldn't have had it happen quite this way, but there ain't a God's thing I can do," he said. "These folks is Injuns, and about the

231

worst crime there is to them is to burn up woods. The woods is their life. You kill the woods and you kill the Injuns. What you saw there was a trial and a judgment, and what's going on now is just as legal as a hanging'd be in some other parts of the world. I said my say when I told Charley my vote was to get rid of him. I can't do nothing now."

His hands moved again; he boated the dripping anchor and stowed it in the bow.

"My God!" Nate said under his breath. Fascinated, feeling cold all over, he could not take his eyes off the spectacle on shore.

The tribe was streaming down across the flats, hauling along the still fiercely struggling man. The brown backs of the men holding him heaved and buckled; it appeared that Lemuel Cantril was not an easy man to kill. The boys on ahead had stakes and axes; at the water's edge they were driving the stakes deep down into the mud. Around the straining group the tribe closed in, a dark, confused flurry of backs, flying arms and black bobbing heads.

Behind him Nate heard the rattle of the blocks as Maynard hauled up the sail. The skimmer was beginning to move.

On the beach the racket quieted. The clotted group split apart. The young men straightened up their bent backs and walked away in twos and threes, leaving Lem Cantril spread-eagled, tied to the stakes to wait for the flooding tide.

The snow-capped mountain which Nate and Caroline first saw when they sailed into their harbor, they named Winter Mountain because snow came early to it and stayed late. It was small, as mountains go, a thousand feet high, wooded with heavy spruce growth. Its summit was smooth granite, rounded and bulgy like a cluster of big stone bowls thrown down bottom-up, whose surfaces glistened in the sun after rain and on the first day of November, were white again with snow.

It had rained a little the day before, a short-lived, sluggish downpour, turning cold. In the night a cold front passed, with a screaming north wind which cleared the weather; but it left the mountain summit gleaming white, and halfway down its sides the powdered spruces looked gray and furry, like an old bear's pelt.

"Shows what's coming," Nate said. "Well, let 'er come." He didn't care much. He felt snugged-in and rich, the new, tight shed full of stores, the warm clothes—all the things which had come up the coast in the *Mary C.* And they had neighbors now, he and Caroline. There were ten tight cabins built among the trees by the harbor; in the spring when the rest of the folks came back from Weymouth, there would be more.

In the first ten days after the fire the men of Somerset, helped by the men of Charley Cantril's tribe, built rough shelters for their women and children out of any material which came to hand. With the Cantrils they hunted the woods and fished the bay, and nobody starved. Across the bay the fire in the forest burned fiercely, for the wind boxed the compass and there was as yet no rain. In the night the hot, sour smell of it blew over the water, waking the women, causing the children to turn restlessly in their sleep. On the tenth day Corkran O'Neill, met at the mouth of the Crookshank River by men posted there for that purpose, brought the *Mary C.* into the harbor.

Cork came ashore, tight-lipped and grim. He mentioned only once the terrible, stunning grief for his friend and cousin, whom he had loved more dearly than a brother. He said, gripping Frank by the hand, "My heart is dead." Then he drove quickly and efficiently into the job of unloading needed supplies.

Most of the women and children were sent down to Weymouth for the winter. The people of Somerset were not giving up; in a meeting held around their campfire, within the semicircle of bough and grass huts, the community voted to stick together. But it was a question of supplies and of how many cabins could be built before the snow. So the women went, with ten men to look out for them through the winter. The rest stayed; it was a plentiful country, and they had their stubborn teeth in it. Some women stayed. Caroline stayed, and Lizabeth would not leave Frank, though he did his best to make her go.

"I've always had my children easy," she told him. "And I've talked with Nan Gorham. She knows all anyone needs to know. I won't go, Frank. I won't leave you."

The last vessel-load of lumber to come out of Somerset Corkran had sold at a high price. He had bought supplies, but he still had some money left. On the trip home after he had left the people at Weymouth, Corkran brought back into the lumber country, a load of

233

lumber. The *Bessie,* leading a flotilla of small boats like a fat hen with a trail of chicks, crossed the bay again. Working within a stone's throw of the burned, reeking forest, the men salvaged drift lumber from the old piles along the shores by the river-mouth. Some of it was burned; a good deal was not. They took anything that would hold together. They found a bonanza on the east side of the river, where the fire had not come. They went up to Somerset and picked the ruins clean. Not that they found much—two small heaps of old deals lying by the shore, which the fire had erratically left unburned, odds and ends rooted out of the cooling ashes, every scrap of old iron from the mill.

They found and buried the dead, though there was little to be put decently into the ground. Of Josh Cantril they found not a sign, for the heat of the great fire had dissolved his brittle bones to ash. Frank, standing heartsick beside the raw earth which covered the poor remains of his brother, stayed awhile after the other men had gone away.

The old Cantril cemetery had been burned over, exposing the narrow sunken mounds. The wooden markers were all gone from the graves of the Indian girls, so that now no one could have told which was Susie, Anna, Lizzie, Ansy, Delie, Feensy, Rebecca or Rebecca. Andrew Cantril's grave his sons had marked with a granite boulder; the mound was just discernible, the impersonal stone half-hidden by a drift of ashes. In front of Frank stretched the gutted town, the blue river running tranquilly past its blackened bank; behind him was the ruined forest, like a vast, rolling plain of ugly, giant toothpicks, through which rose delicately, the veils of smoke.

" 'Tis a terrible place to leave you," he said softly. "Oh, Michael, my dear, 'twas a great country you found to come to and bitter to me that only now do I see my way in it."

He knelt by the grave and let his tears run, and after a time, went slowly down to join the others.

He thought, as he walked, that it was bitter, also, that under a great stone fallen from the chimney of the mill, he had found intact, Mike's leather-covered ledger in which he had entered his first records of his town.

The tribe stayed until the first heavy rain, which started in the middle of November. The rain came from the northeast, a great roaring storm which howled over the bay for the better part of a week. Water fell in clouds, streams, torrents; it flooded the countryside, filled the dry wells and stream beds, so that in the still nights which followed, the sound could be heard of the waterfall up the inlet; and it put out at last the great fire of Somerset. Charley Cantril was anxious to be gone; the tribe needed to snug into its own winter quarters; it was only a question of days, hours, perhaps, before the snow.

The young Cantrils had fished and hunted, bringing in to the camp an abundance of fresh food; they had helped build the cabins. And they had done something else, for the Cantril Indians were a happy people; they had filled the place from morning to night with their gaiety. Now they were going, loaded down with their equal share of the available supplies and powder to see them through the winter.

The Somerset men called a meeting; Frank Ellis, as the chosen head of the community, spoke its formal thanks to the tribe and wrung Charley Cantril's hand.

"'Tis sorry to see you go we are," he said. "And glad to have you stay here, if you will."

Charley said nothing. His brown face, as usual, was noncommittal, but his glance indicated the forest. Already the tribe was on the move, the brown forms melting away through the dark columns of the trees, the shouts of jubilation dwindling down to echo. Charley spoke at last. He picked up his gun, shifted his heavy pack a little to ride more easily. He said, "I can't hold the boys here any longer." And then he trotted after them, vanishing from sight almost at once among the trees.

"If you need anything, you have only to come to us," Frank shouted after him. It was Frank's opinion, formed in the past two months, that Charley could have held the boys anywhere, for as long as he wanted to.

As Maynard Cantril said, it was a neat-run tribe.

After the meeting, which settled down to a sober discussion of winter plans, Frank followed Nathan down to the shore. He found him beside his boat which was moored to the beach; she had been aground, but was beginning to float with the incoming tide. Nate was bent over, looking at a deep, fresh gouge in her planking.

"You found a rock, I see," Frank said, leaning to look.

"I've found a lot of rocks," Nate said gloomily. "I've had her on about every ledge in the bay this summer. She's taken a beating."

"But you know where the ledges are now."

"Well," Nate said. "No." He ran his fingers over the furry wood. "Not all of them. But I know where they ain't."

Frank chuckled. He sat down on the beach, and Nathan stretched out, relaxed, beside him.

"You don't need to laugh at that old chestnut," he said. "The first man said that who ever crossed a channel straddle of a tree."

He liked Frank and admired him, as everyone did. People looked to him; he seemed, in his quiet way, to be able to say what to do in most matters; without commanding anyone, only by answering what he thought best, Frank ran the community. More than anything, Nate marveled at the change in his mother.

He said so, gruffly, now, thinking perhaps Frank might like to know how he felt about it.

Frank nodded. "We have a great thing between us, she and I," he said. "She is happy."

"Well, I don't know what to make of her keeping her nose out of my business," Nate said, grinning. "She never did, before."

He felt he could say about anything to Frank, who would know what he meant—would know now that he was, in a way, saying thank you, not voicing any disloyalty to his mother.

"She knows if she puts her nose into your affairs, I will beat her," Frank said, stretching lazily. "The Carnavons have always been great beaters of wives. What do you think of Corkran's talk about the sawmill, Nathan?"

"Well," Nate said, "we've got to have one, and the waterfall's there. The stuff to build it's another matter."

"Corkran is put out with me," Frank said. "Because I made him spend the little cash he had left on the winter stores for Charley's people. So now we have no money to equip the sawmill. We had the great battle, Cork and I, but 'twas an obligation to be kept, Nathan. You agree?"

"We all do," Nate said. "Cork does, too, you know."

Frank nodded. "He and me brother Michael met the world dog eat dog for many years," he said thoughtfully. " 'Tis true, that is most practical, if you look ahead only until tomorrow. But I could not help but think what Charley had done, and what we promised, and 'tis not outside man's thought that such help might, in time to come, be needed again. So now we have no money to buy the sawmill which we sadly need. Was ever a man so tried!"

Nate sat listening with half his mind; with the other half he was thinking.

"With all the money Carnavon's had!" Frank said. "And now there is not enough to build one little mill! I would give a hundred pounds off my bones for one small pile of gold pieces, Nathan!"

Nate started. "I know where there's some," he said slowly, turning to look at Frank. "In a nail keg on a shelf in a shed, doing no good to anyone. Only, it belongs to my brother."

Beside him there was a silence.

Then Frank said, "Your brother Edward?"

Nate nodded.

" 'Tis part of Ringgold's loot, no doubt?"

"Yes. I—"

Something in Frank's face stopped him.

"You know about Ed?" Nate said at last.

"Yes. He is dead, Nathan."

Frank put out a hand and laid it on his shoulder, rocking him slightly.

" 'Tis sorry I am to be the one to tell you, for I can see that you do not know," he said. "Edward was caught and hanged in Boston, with the rest of Ringgold's men. We heard it, and then I had Charley Tansley check the facts, the first trip the vessel made, the summer. Because of my—because of your mother, I wished to know, to protect her when she heard. She does not know. I thought it best not to tell her, at least until our child was born. I am sorry for it all, Nathan."

Nate sat, his knees drawn up under his chin, his arms clasped around them. He looked off over the blue water of the bay, not seeing it. Within him he felt the old, knotted, almost physical pain coiling itself together again, and he realized he had never, since he had seen Ed last, been wholly without it. Then he put his head down on his knees and cried, feeling, after a time, the pain dissolve and go away, and he knew at last he had parted with Ed forever.

In the moonlight Cowrie Cove was a silver coin, strung at the end of a silver necklace of varied waterways stretching away into the swamps. The tide was full. A small ghost of a wind was enough to slide Maynard Cantril's skimmer across the cove into the mouth of the Flowage. The three men aboard of her were silent, the boat herself made scarcely a ripple in the water.

Maynard waited with the boat, while Nate and Frank walked along the shore on the path to the inn. It seemed strange to Nathan that nothing had changed at all—Piper's house, the sand, the bleak hillside tufted with low growth but powdered now with snow. The windows of Piper's house were blank with moonlight; nobody moved there. Nate thought, with a wry grin, For once I've gone by here in the night without Piper's knowing.

They had reason for going quietly, he and Frank.

The inn was deserted, the windows broken. The door swung by a hinge. Nate forced himself not to look at it. The wagon shed was there; it too was open to the weather, and kids had looted it of everything that looked to be worth a penny. But who would bother with a nail keg, bound with rusty iron hoops, half full of rusty iron? No one, it would seem.

He picked the nail keg off the shelf where he had left it, lifted it to his shoulder, and he and Frank went back down the hill.

At Piper's house, Piper was standing in the yard.

"I see ye go up by," he said. "Thought first was strangers. How be ye, Nate?"

"Fine. How're you and Jenny?"

"We keep. You take the window sashes with ya, Nate?"

"Uh-huh."

"How 'bout the woman?"

"Her, too, thank God and you, Piper."

Piper grinned. He spat thoughtfully, peering up at Nate from under his bushy eyebrows, which the moonlight made delicately silver. "Never regretted nothing?"

"No. Don't rub it in, Piper."

"Wasn't."

Piper craned his neck curiously at the nail keg on Nate's shoulder. "Never found much left, up there to the inn, did you?"

"No. Not much."

" 'Tain't no wonder, the way that Betsey done. No use to rake it up. Less said the better."

"That's right," Nate said.

He hesitated. All the way down the coast from Somerset he had been dreading Betsey. Not that he wanted to see her, if he could help it, but he felt an obligation to find out where she was, see she was taken care of if she needed to be. He had thought he might find her at the inn, but the empty house with its black, gaping windows, looked as if no one had lived there for a long time.

He said, "Where is Betsey, you know, Piper?"

"She run quite a rig up there for a while," Piper said.

It was all very well for him to say he wasn't going to rake it up; he couldn't help gossiping.

"She had a lot of company. Company you 'n I wouldn't care for. Then I guess she got sick of it, for one day she and this feller she had— don't know who he was, stranger to me—they cleaned out the inn. Sold two-three wagonloads of your ma's stuff, lugged off the rest. Some said they went west. They ain't around here now. Stealing, warn't it, Nate?"

"I guess so," Nate said. "Don't much matter, Piper. Ma and I won't come back. Betsey might as well have the stuff as for it to lie there and rot."

Piper drew himself up. You could see he didn't approve of that. "Some might feel that way about their pa's place being stove up," he said. "Some might not."

He thinks I ought to feel worse about it, Nate thought. Maybe I ought to, I don't know.

He glanced around him at the familiar landscape on which the moonlight poured down, seeing it now as a place already half-forgotten. The ties that had held him to it—mainly the responsibility for Betsey and the inn—were gone, and over that he felt nothing but relief. The only things worth keeping—about Pa, about the good times with Ed— they were going back to the new place with him. There was nothing left here in this place too full of memories.

"We've got to go, Piper," he said. "Got to catch the tide down the bights."

He held out his hand, shifting the keg a little, and Piper's curiosity at last got the better of him.

"What's in that kag anyway? What you got there, luggin'?" he asked, and Nate tilted the keg so he could see into it.

"Your pa's old scrap iron, ain't it? My God, Nate, iron must be skurce up where you be."

"It is," Nate said. "And a man can always use it, Piper."

Back at the shore they eased the boat out of the shallow water at the brook-mouth, and Maynard set the sail. The skimmer ghosted down through the bights to the sea, where the *Mary Cantril* waited for her, her spars sharp and black against the moonlight and the white sky. While Maynard and the crew unshipped the skimmer's mast and hoisted her light hull to the deck of the vessel, Frank and Nate examined the keg.

Under Joel's rusty trove of iron, Ed's treasure was as Nate had left it, and in the morning, in Boston, Charley Tansley bought the equipment for the mill.

The people of Somerset had learned a great thing from Charley Cantril's tribe—not merely how to build snug cabins and live off a countryside, for many of them were already old hands at that. True, Charley's boys had skills and tricks which were valuable to know; they were all hunters and fishermen. But the great thing, the main thing, had been unspoken and untaught when, at the edge of winter, the tribe had made off into the leafless forest with joy and anticipation; and the Somerset people saw that unless men were desperate or frightened, cold weather need not be a time of hardship.

In the months to come they did not find it so. They had tight roofs, plenty of firewood and enough to eat. The *Bessie* was hauled up on shore for the winter, but the *Mary C.* swung to her cable in the anchorage. Though they had to chop ice from her hull on cold mornings, she did not freeze in; the swift rise and fall of tide broke up the ice in the harbor and drifted it away. The *Mary C.* was their lifeline.

Corkran made two trips in her down to Weymouth during the

winter, with varied cargoes, saw logs, salt fish, skins and sea birds' feathers. The Somerset men missed nothing which might be gathered up and traded for stores. It was surprising how many items there were—even feathers for featherbeds brought a good price. Best of all, lonely men had something to look forward to. When the *Mary C.* went down to Weymouth, they could go too, and visit their wives and children. The winter was cold and long; it brought deep snow, ice, iron ground; but there were days on end when a man could work outdoors—mild days, when spring seemed not far off, frosty days not too cold for a man, when the blue sky and the sun on the snow lifted his heart, and his work and his hope warmed him. When they could spare the time they worked on new cabins. On Corkran's second trip certain women and children came back on the *Mary C.*, and families lived together again. There was no sense in being afraid of winter.

Stone by stone, before the cold weather shut in, the men had transported the foundations of Andrew Cantril's mill across the bay, and boated them to the waterfall on the stream above the new town. It had been a backbreaking job, but cut stone was cut stone, hard come by anywhere. Before the snow the foundations were laid, and now they were working in the woods by the waterfall hewing beams and baulks. The waterfall was frozen hard; only a little current dripped down, forming great rippled daggers of ice which broke off with a clatter when the sun warmed them at midday. The tote-road from town was open, and around the new mill an open work space shoveled away; from these small works, to east and west, the forest spread mile on mile of mighty trees, muffled and drowned in snow.

It was here by the waterfall, on the second of February, that Frank was working when word came up from the town, by team and sled, that his wife needed him.

Frank laid down his ax. His ruddy face turned pale and he started off down the road at a run. Nate, who was driving the team, turned the sled around and caught up with him; even so, he had to hurry the horses. And then, for all Frank's hustle and worry, when they got back to town, Nan Gorham and the others wouldn't let him into his cabin.

He was all for hanging around the doorstep, but the day was lowery and cold, making ready to snow again—no kind of weather to be out in, unless a man were working, keeping warm. Nate finally persuaded him to come over to his own cabin, where Caroline comforted him as best she could. She herself was having a lively day, for Shawn and Colin, Mike's boys, who lived with Frank and Lizabeth now, had, like Frank, been turned out of their home, and they were underfoot waiting for dinner. They tiny cabin was jammed, but jammed cabins full of hungry people were nothing new to Caroline. She hushed the boys and talked consolingly to Frank while she got dinner—a good one too; though Frank, when he sat down to it, found for the first time in his life that he couldn't eat a mouthful. It was midafternoon before Nat Gorham sent for him.

The baby was a lusty, red-faced boy, already cleaned up and lying in his cradle. Nan was there, doing something at the sink. But Frank walked past both of them without a glance. He leaned over Lizabeth's bed, looking down at her, and she opened her eyes and smiled at him.

"You're all right, lass," he said shakily.

Lizabeth nodded. She was not badly off, only tired. The baby had come easily, as she had been sure it would.

"Did you see him, Frank?" she asked. " 'Tis a son, not a daughter, as the case might be."

He understood the gentle mimicry of himself and was touched by it, and Lizabeth, knowing him so well now, was not surprised to see his tears.

"There now, great lunk," she said. "No need to puddle up. I'm well enough. Go look at your son. He looks like you."

For a moment he made no move, except to cover her hand with his own. "God love you, lass," he said huskily.

Then he bent down to look at his son.

There was a long, amazed silence, in which Lizabeth, in her weariness, thought she must have dozed for a wink or two. Frank's voice roused her.

"—the likes of you!" he was saying. "Me grandfather himself, had you only a beard now, not me son! I wonder if the name of you might not be Michael?"

"Of course, if you want it to be," Lizabeth said.

She smiled drowsily at him. "What day is it, Frank? I want to be sure about his birthday. I've lost track a little. Is it the first or the second?"

"The second," he said. He let go the corner of blanket which he had been holding in his big fist. " 'Tis Candlemas Day, my dear. The day the Blessed Mary took her Son to the Temple. A day for mothers

242

and little sons. And a fine day too, for the sun's not shone a minute of it, meaning the winter'll soon be gone. Me old grandfather, the image of yon small man"—he jerked his head toward the cradle—"would say:

> 'If Candlemas Day be dry and fair,
> The half o' winter's come and mair;
> If Candlemas Day be wet and foul,
> The half o' winter was gone at Youl.' "

Nan Gorham, a woman of tact, who had stayed back-to at the sink, said quietly, "She ought to sleep now, Frank."

"I know," he said in a contrite whisper. "I talk too much. 'Tis hard not to, the way I feel in my heart, the day. I'm going, and me thanks to you for your helping us."

He tiptoed to the door, closed it after him.

Outside, the winter afternoon was falling toward darkness—a snowy darkness, from the look of the sky and the gun-metal sea. A cold east wind was baffling the treetops, but the row of cabins did not feel the gusts, sheltered by mighty trunks and overhanging boughs. The women had built up supper fires. The men were home from the woods and the village snugged in for the night.

'Tis not much to look at now, Frank thought, looking down from his doorstep at the ragged row of cabins. Like my son, a small beginning.

He thought of the tiny, wrinkled, old-man face, and his heart swelled with pride.

But 'tis not too much to hope that we will make something great of it. Ourselves and our waterfall and our sons.

He went down the step and along the road to the storehouse to make sure that someone had remembered to pick up the ax he had left by the waterfall—the ax that in this wild country was more precious than jewels.